"Where is she?" she asked in a low, throaty voice.

I held out my hand. "Hello, Mackenzie. I presume it's Mia you've come to see. You can't blame me for thinking it a bit odd, considering the last time I saw you with her, you were tearing each other's hair out."

She shrugged. "That's why I've come here. To make up!"

"Mia is sleeping and she desperately needs her sleep. She's had a terrible shock. Rest is the best cure. After... after..."

"Your mother totals herself?" she helpfully filled in.

I raised my eyebrows. "Well...yes..."

"Even when your mother was Superbitch?"

"That's a horrible thing to say, and quite untrue...."

Mackenzie collapsed onto a sofa. She was wearing the softest kid boots I'd ever seen. "I didn't know her that well," she said. "I had to see Mia. Soon as I heard. I feel so bad about everything. I wanna make it up to her. I hate being bad friends. Mia and I go back a long way, you know."

"She's told me..."

Mackenzie pulled a face: "Told you what a jerk I am? Well, I never gave her much reason *not* to think it. I've been trouble for her ever since we met—two little green kids from New York. She was the poor little rich girl and I was the crazy hippie. She's been trouble for me, too."

"Do you mean David?" I slipped in.

"Do you know where he is?" she asked. "Just how much *do* you know?"

It was the moment I'd waited for. "Just about everything...." I said.

Her eyes glittered with tears. "You know everything— huh?"

Nothing could have thrilled me more. It was finally acknowledged by the Queen of Fashion herself that I, Colin Beaumont, was indeed confidant to the entire fashion world. I *did* know everything. And I can now start at the beginning, not inventing a word, merely remembering what I observed, what I heard while listening quietly at the end of a telephone... to all the events that led up to today and my two guests.

It all began one day in Paris at the Spring, 1962, collections. . . .

Labels

Harold Carlton

BANTAM BOOKS

TORONTO • NEW YORK • LONDON • SYDNEY • AUCKLAND

LABELS

A Bantam Book / April 1988

ISBN 0-553-26990-9

Published simultaneously in the United States and Canada

Bantam Books are published by Bantam Books, a division of Bantam Doubleday Dell Publishing Group, Inc. Its trademark, consisting of the words "Bantam Books" and the portrayal of a rooster, is Registered in U.S. Patent and Trademark Office and in other countries. Marca Registrada. Bantam Books, 666 Fifth Avenue, New York, New York 10103.

PRINTED IN THE UNITED STATES OF AMERICA

KR 0 9 8 7 6 5 4 3 2

Prologue One

MIA
SCARSDALE, 1951

She awoke on Sunday mornings to the sound of her mother's laughter. To a child of seven, the laughter sounded happy, like someone being tickled. As she lay there, drowsy, she could hear the laughter turn to giggles, then to cries. Mia usually smiled and went back to sleep. Mommy and Daddy were just playing.

One Sunday morning, however, suddenly curious, Mia tiptoed along the hallway to her parents' room. She kept well out of sight, smiling to herself at the funny trick she was playing. They would be so surprised when she ran into their room to tell them she'd been watching! As they now fell silent, she peered around their doorframe.

Daddy was *kissing* Mommy! She wanted to shout out and race into the room, but something cautioned her to remain silent. Daddy was wearing only his pajama bottoms, and when he knelt on the bed, something hard pushed against the front of them. He reached inside his pants and freed this... thing. She knew little boys had these and that they were not to be shown to anyone. They were strictly for going to the bathroom, her teacher had told her. Why wasn't Mommy angry at Daddy? Mia's smile turned into a puzzled, slightly sour grin. But Mommy, instead of being mad, took hold of the thing and held it! Daddy's head went back, he closed his eyes and said "Aaaaahhh!" as he did when Mommy scratched his back for him. Strangely, he seemed to be enjoying this....

Mommy slipped out of her nightgown and lay beside

1

Daddy. Her flat breasts had dark brown circles on them
and Mia watched Daddy kiss these circles and lick them,
making Mommy giggle and moan. Mia was confused; she
didn't understand this game. Daddy rolled onto his back
and tugged off his pajamas. Then he rolled over onto
Mommy. Without kissing her, he lay on top of her. How
heavy he must be! How that thing between his legs must
press into her! Yet Mommy didn't seem to mind. She was
breathing heavily, and in a strange, hurried voice, she
said, "Put it in!"

Daddy reached down and pushed Mommy's legs apart,
and Mia could see by the way his bottom went up and
down, that he was pushing that thing *into* Mommy, dig-
ging it into her! And still Mommy didn't complain, she
just let him! Her parents moved faster, her mother pushing against her father, clutching his shoulders, her long
red nails sticking into his flesh. Daddy began to groan,
and her mother gasped as if she were thirsty. Daddy now
panted hoarsely. The sounds were frightening: Had they
both gone crazy? As much as she wanted to run away,
Mia remained rooted to the spot.

Her parents moved against each other for a long time as
she stood watching, frightened and fascinated. Suddenly
her mother cried, "Pull out! Pull out!" and Daddy sat up
quickly, kneeling, holding onto his thing and pulling at it,
his eyes tightly closed, his face twisted. Stuff shot into the
air from him and he gave a great shout, then collapsed
over Mommy, breathing in noisy gasps.

Now Mia wanted to be alone to think about what she
had seen. As she tiptoed away, she heard her father ask,
"Any good?" and her mother reply with annoyance, "As
usual, you were much too quick." Too quick? It was one of
the longest games Mia had ever seen grown-ups play!

So that's what made Mommy giggle on Sunday mornings, she thought. It was nightmarish and horrible, and
somehow she knew she could not ask anyone about it.
Feeling sick, she ran to the bathroom and threw up.
Afterward, she carefully swished water around the sink,
brushed her teeth, found her favorite book, and climbed
back into bed. As she lay there, she made herself a
solemn promise: She would *never* let a man do that to her.
Never!

Prologue Two

MACKENZIE
THE BRONX, 1957

"You are *not* my mother!" the little girl screamed at her astonished mother. It was four-thirty, and Esther Goldstein had been waiting with the other mothers at the school gates. Now, her eleven-year-old Marsha was disowning her.

"Don't be silly, honey. . ." Her good-natured face looked puzzled. "Of course I'm your mother."

"You're *not*! You're *not*!" Marsha screamed, hot tears running down her cheeks.

The other mothers regarded Esther sympathetically, shaking their heads. Each day brought another hysterical fit from the child: The girl was not normal. Only last week she had refused to answer to her name, insisting she was now to be called Mackenzie.

"Will you come home if I call you Mackenzie?" her mother tried. Through her tears, but with some satisfaction, the girl nodded.

Another mother said, "Excuse me, Mrs. Goldstein, but you're too soft with her. She needs a smacked bottom."

"We tried that," Esther Goldstein said wearily. They had tried just about everything with Marsha, but this child was impossible. Where had she come by this devil, this craziness?

For most of her short life, Marsha Goldstein had held the conviction that she must be the abandoned daughter of a rich heiress who had left her with a Jewish family in the Bronx until the time she could be reclaimed. On that

3

happy day, it would be emblazoned on front pages across
the nation that Mackenzie Vanderbilt or Whitney or
Rockefeller had for some reason been brought up as
Marsha Goldstein on the Grand Concourse. She would
then be launched into the world of fashion and high
society.

But Marsha was starting to lose faith in this fair, tale.
As her features filled out and her body became distinctly
plump, any imagined resemblance to Gloria Vanderbilt
demanded a lot of imagination. Recently there had been
hysterical tirades with her family, endless teasing from her
two brothers. At only eleven years, a full-fledged snob
was living on the Grand Concourse, hoarding her small
allowance to spend on fashion magazines. She was probably *Vogue*'s youngest reader.

Abe Goldstein made all his children attend Hebrew
classes weekly and temple on Saturdays. Marsha had
always hated the religion. She argued with the rabbi about
how there could have been an Adam and Eve if man were
descended from apes. When he could not convince her,
she pronounced the Jewish religion "dumb." She began
eating Friday's dinner before her mother blessed the Sab-
bath candles, and escaped temple on Saturdays by leaving
soon after her brothers brought her to the ladies' section,
then running off to movies with her non-Jewish girlfriends.

Now, Marsha stopped at the entrance to the gray apartment building.

"What's with you now?" her mother asked.

"I'm not going in unless you promise to make everyone—
Daddy and the boys—call me Mackenzie from now on.
Promise?"

"Yes! Yes! I promise! I'll sign an affidavit! I'll get a legal
witness—what do you want from me already?"

Mackenzie entered the apartment building triumphantly.
It was the first of a series of demands she would make on
her family. She had started to re-create herself.

Prologue Three

COLIN
PROVENCE, FRANCE, 1968

These are the early traumas of my two main characters. Will they overcome them? I think anyone's story is the story of whether they overcome their childhood or not.

I introduce Mia and Mackenzie to you without apologies or the usual pretense that "any resemblance between these characters and living persons is coincidental." In my story it is no coincidence: My characters *are* living people. And as I write these words, Mia and Mackenzie are actually beneath my roof, living out the climaxes of their sagas. Providing me with the conclusion to *Labels*, my tale of the fashion world.

At six o'clock this morning the dogs started barking, the cats wailing, and the doves cooing. Surprising, because in this sleepy little corner of Provence, the animals have been well trained to remain silent until eight. My Provençal treasure, Françoise, usually arrives at seven-thirty, so I awake to the comforting sounds and scents of coffee being brewed, croissants heated. But today at six, in addition to the din of the menagerie, there was also the distinct hum of a motor. Françoise has no car.

I peered through my bedroom curtains. It was the local taxi. Standing by it was an extremely elegant woman with a fistful of franc notes. The first Queen of Fashion had tracked me down. I pulled on my robe and ran downstairs to open the front door.

"Mia! Welcome!"

"Colin, darling!"

She threw herself into my arms and began to sob, to the great interest of Monsieur Robert. Beret rammed to one side, he carefully eased his taxi down the short drive, one eye on us. I gave him a wave as I hugged Mia. I had rehearsed this scene, but now that it was upon me, I groped for words. I am especially embarrassed by bereavement, and this beautiful creature was mourning a mother she had always hated. I was not sure how to console her. "You'll meet again in the next world" may have sounded like more of a threat than a comfort.

Since her mother had not only been my best friend but also the woman I loved, the situation was doubly charged.

"I am so terribly sorry," I said lamely.

Mia took a deep breath, leaned back and looked at me. "I'm glad you called. I came the moment the inquest ended . . . I needed to see you so much. Just to talk—to get away from all the people, all the reporters and vultures. They destroyed her, and now they want to offer sympathy. I suddenly realized that out of all the people in New York, you were the only one, the only one who—" She broke off, crying.

"Who loved her?" I finished for her, and she nodded silently. She took another deep breath and managed to compose herself. Glancing at her watch, she said, "I have no idea what time it is here. Did I wake you, Colin?"

"Heavens, no! I wear pajamas at all hours of the day. . . ." We studied each other closely, she to decide whether I was joking, I to see whether her grief was genuine or assumed for my sake.

Even tear-streaked she was beautiful. Especially in crisp black linen, a color she rarely wore. Of course, Mia would look beautiful in rags. She dabbed a handkerchief to her cheeks, her full head of blond, gently waved hair falling against her face. She had intense blue eyes, a peaches and cream complexion, white teeth, long legs. Great beauty always brings out an absurd jealousy in me. Perhaps one of the curses of being unattractive myself is that I have always envied and wanted beauty, settling for it in my home, my garden, my friends and pets. I believe, however, that beauty is at its best in the human, female form.

"Why did you summon me here?" she asked as we moved up the creaking old staircase to my best guest room.

"I thought I could help you in your grief. . . ."

"It's not even really grief," she confessed. "I'm crying, but the tears are of frustration, anger! Why didn't she love me? Why didn't I help her when she begged for my help? Now there's such an unfinished feeling—I'll never be able to confront her, I'll never *know*!"

"Oh, you might find out more than you imagined there was to know," I said mysteriously.

"Yes . . ." She stopped at the top of the stairs and looked around the tiny hallway. "How pretty you've made it, Colin!" She held out her hands to me and I clasped them. "You knew her so well. You'll tell me everything?"

"Everything," I promised. I threw open the door to her room. No woman who saw the *broderie-anglais*-draped bed could ever resist its inviting embrace.

She sat on the bed and gently kicked off her shoes. "So much has happened to me over the last two weeks, you won't believe it, Colin. I'm a woman now."

"Yes . . ." I narrowed my eyes at her. "There is something . . . different about you. You're in love, aren't you?"

She nodded, closing her eyes, lifting her legs onto the white bedspread. The next moment, her head on the pillow, she was fast asleep.

I closed the door gently. We had a lot to talk about, and there were many gaps in my story I wished to fill in. While I had her, I was damned if I would not take full advantage of her presence.

I tiptoed downstairs to the kitchen, opening a packet of French biscottes, which are such a poor substitute for bread, then making coffee before Françoise arrived. I was lifting the cup to my mouth when I heard a new motor's purr. I never get two visitors on the same day or even in the same month, so I ignored it. A figment of my imagination, I told myself. But then a definite cry of "Fuck *you*!" in an unmistakably Bronx accent shattered the peace of Provence. I hurried to the living room window and looked out to see the other Queen of Fashion.

"This I *really* don't believe!" I said aloud. What the hell, I asked myself, was this one doing here? Obviously, I answered myself, in hot pursuit of the first one. The two cornerstones of American fashion were about to collide under my roof! I opened the front door.

The woman who stalked up my walkway was dark, elegant, plump, and quite startling-looking. She was the Red Queen of Fashion, as opposed to the White one. Her hair, artfully cut to stick out in tufts, looked as if she had pulled out half with her own fists one manic-depressive evening. Doubtless she had paid some manic-depressive hairstylist a small fortune to do it. There were touches of violet and fuchsia in it. She, too, was dressed entirely in black, with the difference that she was born to wear black. Her loose, oversized clothes were like men's pajamas made from crushed heavy silk. A knitted black coat curved to her body, showing her Rubenesque shape. Her eyes met mine. Magnificent, flashing eyes: dark, heavily lashed, clever, a little decadent. Her red mouth was sulky. She had an air of very determined, expensive chic. The kind that is self-achieved, not innate. I know the difference. An aura of L'Air du Temps perfume liberally splashed on neck and body and to hell with how much gets lost on the floor, surrounded her. An enormous Italian leather sack, big as a suitcase, hung from one shoulder. Several long silk scarves in different shades of purple, plum, and violet trailed from around her neck. Chunky silver, gold, and ivory bangles, rings, necklaces, and belts clinked at her wrists and waist. The entire effect was mesmerizing. I wanted to sketch her, paint her, photograph her.

"Where is she?" she asked in a low, throaty, almost rasping voice.

I held out my hand. "Hello, Mackenzie. And what brings *you* here?"

She twisted her mouth into a wry smile. "Some welcome!" she said. We shook hands coldly.

"I presume it's Mia you've come to see, so you can't blame me for thinking it a bit odd, considering the last time I saw you, you were rolling around on the floor with her, tearing each other's hair out."

She shrugged. "That's why I've come here. To make up!" She turned her attention to my garden. "*Gorgeous!*" she stated. Then, a little shyly, "I always loved your drawings, Colin. When I was just starting they kinda, like, inspired me, y'know?"

I smiled. The shyness, after the display of aggression, was amusing. I ushered her into the living room.

"Won't you sit down? Mia is sleeping, and she desperately needs to sleep. You probably do too?"

She shrugged. "I don't know *what* I need! I'm still not even sure where I *am*!'"

"Mia's had a terrible shock," I said. "Rest is the best cure. After... after..."

"Your mother totals herself?" she helpfully filled in.

I raised my eyebrows. "Well, yes...."

"Even when your mother was Superbitch?"

"That's a horrible thing to say," I told her, sounding terribly English to my own ears. "And quite untrue."

Mackenzie looked at me for a moment, and suddenly collapsed onto a sofa. She was wearing the softest kid boots I'd ever seen. They were rumpled, glove-quality leather, and drooped around her ankles. I caught a glimpse of purple stockings.

"I didn't know her that well," she said. "I only know what Mia told me about her."

"Well, *I* know her—knew her—*very* well," I said. "She was one of the kindest people. She was a genius, and one has to make allowances for genius...."

"Maybe one has to make allowances for mothers?" she said flatly. There was a long silence.

"A drink?" I suggested.

"You got Perrier?"

I opened a cabinet, selecting a bottle. "Ice?"

"It doesn't matter."

I handed her the glass and she greedily slurped up the water like a child. I pretended not to hear. Then she tucked in her chin and belched loudly. I must have looked horrorstruck because she noticed, gave a little giggle and said, "That's nothing! Wait'll you hear me fart!"

I frowned, as if such things were unheard of in my genteel cottage. She fascinated me. The contrast of behavior coming from such a deliberately styled exterior made me wonder what she would do next.

She gasped, "Must've been dehydrated!" and set down her empty glass. "They showed such lousy movies on that plane, and then that taxi! He gave me a goddamn tourist ride around the whole fuckin' district!"

"Monsieur Robert would never do that—especially to one of my visitors," I remonstrated.

"Wanna bet?" she rasped. "Anyway, I'm here now." She

spread herself heavily on the sofa. "I had to see Mia. Soon as I heard. I feel so bad about everything. I wanna make it up to her. I hate being bad friends. Mia and I go back a long way, you know."

"She's told me."

Mackenzie pulled a face. "Told you what a shit I am?"

"She certainly never said that!"

"She has too much class, but it's what she thinks. I never gave her much reason *not* to think it. But I *love* her, for Christ's sake! I always did! I've just been trouble for her ever since we met—two green kids from New York. She was the poor little rich girl, and I was the crazy hippie. She's been trouble for me too. Funny..." She fiddled in her giant purse and came up with a stick of gum, cramming it into her mouth.

"Do you mean about David?" I asked.

Her eyes glinted. "Don't tell me he's here too?"

I gave a noncommittal shrug.

"Do you know where he is?" she asked. "Just how much *do* you know?"

It was the moment I'd waited for. I sat down, sipping from my coffee cup. "Just about everything," I said.

Mackenzie seemed lost in thought. Finally, she raised her majestic head, with its mane of ruffled, tufted hair, and looked straight at me, her eyes glittering with tears.

"You know everything, huh?" she asked.

Nothing could have thrilled me more. It was finally acknowledged by the Queen of Fashion herself that I, Colin Beaumont, was indeed confidant to the entire fashion world. I patted her hand. "Want to tell me all about it?"

She stared at me for a moment, then suddenly reared back like a hissing snake. "Why should I?" she cried, glaring at me. "You're a weird little man, you know that? You think because you're a midget you can get everyone to tell you their secrets—you think that gives you a right to—" She broke off, her fist in her mouth like a naughty child, horrified at her own outburst. "I'm sorry," she gasped. "I didn't mean to call you a midget."

"That's all right." I waved a generous, forgiving hand. "As it happens, I'm an inch taller than the official midget height."

She stared at me. "You *are*?" She shook her head. "Why, that's *won*derful!" she said, holding up her empty glass as if to toast me. She slumped back against the sofa.

"Yeah—I'll tell you everything," she said wearily. "I just wanted too much, Colin. It was like I could never get enough! I like men too much. I *need* admiration! Love! Success! In abnormal quantities! That's what my life is all about. And now..." She groped in her huge purse as her eyes filled with tears. "Now I think I've lost the only man I've ever really loved, because of my sheer pigheadedness! Oh...Colin!"

I held out my arms to her as the tears overflowed, and for the second time that morning a Queen of Fashion laid her head on my shoulder and wept. Royal tears or not, my shoulder was in great danger of becoming rheumatic.

I *did* know everything. For the simple reason that I'm one of those people that others seem to confide in. They did more than confide: They revealed their innermost selves, told me their most intimate secrets. Since I'm truly interested in other people's lives, I suppose I provided a quality of listening which was in short supply. People came to me and I heard their problems, absorbed them. A lot of this is perhaps due to my appearance, which I'll describe shortly. For the moment, you may believe that I bear a close resemblance to Cary Grant.

You see, when I retired a year ago from the world of fashion, I had to do something. Too active to tend solely to my garden, the accumulated secrets clamored to be let out. I started to write a gossipy book about the world I had left behind. And what fun would that sort of story be if I did not base it on the famous fashion people I knew so well?

All of you are involved, if even in the smallest way, with my characters and my story. Few of you do not own a sweater, a pillowcase, an eyeliner, a bar of soap or pair of underwear that does not sport the name *Gold* or *Anais du Pasquier,* or *David Winters* somewhere on it. Your purchases have made my friends millionaires. For all the good that's done them.

Failure in love is even more bitter when you have everything else. It's so much harder to understand. My Queens of Fashion have dedicated their lives to fashion, sometimes forgetting the very reason for fashion's existence. Which is, surely, to make you look wonderful? Desirable? To attract a mate? Mia Stanton and Mackenzie

Gold often overlooked this. For, you see, being at the top
of the fashion tree today means revenues from sheets and
towels, makeups and colognes, underwear and luggage—
it is a very different world than the old fashion greats ever
dreamed of. Chanel was more than happy with just
Number Five. Christian Dior was satisfied with a couple
of perfumes and the odd silk scarf. Today, the sky's the
limit and being a fashion designer means being a business
person, a media figure, a *star*!

For me, fashion was a livelihood. As I look back on the
years in which I worked, I find it sad that today my career
is almost nonexistent. I was the last of a line of fashion
artists. I wielded pencil, charcoal, and brush, adding the
fantasy, the exaggeration, the interpretation of a new look.
If Dior made waists small, I drew six-inch waists. If
Audrey Hepburn made eyes the focal point, I made them
larger than the body. I loved fashion, lived for it, dreamed
it. And twice a year, when Paris made fashion a world
talking point, I was there when they unveiled the collections amidst such secrecy that they were not even allowed
to be photographed. They were, however, allowed to be
sketched, and that was where I came in. My sketches
were splashed over pages and pages of Paris reports. The
fashion artist, in the fifties and sixties, had a certain
power.

For the record, I *am* an inch short of officially being
classified as a midget. An inch too tall, that is. If I were
five feet nine inches instead of four feet nine inches, my
whole life would have been different. Possibly this is
merely a delusion, because as well as being tiny, I am also
not particularly attractive. My face is far from classic and
my eyes, sometimes called "kindly," are hidden behind
glasses. In an industry where appearance is everything, I
could only survive through my talent and luckily I had it:
in my fingers, my hands, even my nose—I could sniff out
fashion. As I guided fashion editors toward the best
outfits of a collection, I became a respected artist.

My working life was spent entirely in the fashion industry, but when I retired to this house in Provence, I told
myself I never wanted to hear a word about fashion again.
I canceled my subscriptions to *Vogue, Bazaar, Divine*, and
ordered gardening books. But it isn't that easy to kick a
lifelong habit. Fashion is my lifeblood, and before long I

had reordered all the magazines. When I lay down to sleep in this quiet countryside, fashion continued to jump about in my brain. Tell! it cried. Tell *all*!

As I began my novel, I found out what thousands of authors already know: Characters are only believable when based on real people one has known. So now I start at the beginning, not inventing a word, merely remembering what I observed, what was said to me while I listened quietly to all the fashion greats who confided in me, and witnessed many of the events that led up to today.

It all began one day in Paris at the Spring, 1962, collections. . . .

Labels

Book One

One

The loudspeakers at Pierre Balmain hummed with a Piaf medley—it was corny even for Paris. The band of fashion artists, always treated as second-class citizens at the showings, had been banished to a cramped row of gilt chairs at the foot of a stairway. Colin Beaumont was in a center seat. The first Paris collection for Spring, 1962 was about to be presented. But because Balmain had not exactly blazed a fashion trail for some time, the occasion was more social than professional. American buyers and press waved to each other across the crowded salon; it was too soon to pretend they had scooped each other—this was the collection presentation at which they could still be friendly.

The animated face of the directrice, Ginette Spanier, greeted the more celebrated fashion-magazine editors. Kisses were pecked into the perfumed air. A German journalist pretended to faint, hoping for a better seat. Four Japanese buyers were politely escorted out, giggling, their impersonation as "press" seen through immediately by Madame Spanier's sharp eyes. Suddenly everyone was hushed, like an audience at a children's school play.

A woman's voice over the address system said, "Welcome to the Pierre Balmain Spring, 1962 'Jolie Madame' Collection. May we remind you that shoes in today's collection are by Pierre Balmain. Stockings and panty hose by Balmain. Wigs by Balmain. Parfum de Balmain. Jewelry and furs by Pierre Balmain. And makeup by—"

As a grotesquely over-madeup model stalked down the runway, an American artist called out, "Makeup by Walt Disney!" The artists all laughed while continuing to sketch every buttonhole, seam, and pocket that the Pierre Balmain team had come up with. It was, after all, what they were

19

paid to do, and there were many more collections to attend. Balmain was usually the first to show in a crowded Paris week where the big stars showed at the very end, like proud beauties making a late entrance to a party, knowing everyone awaited them.

Colin's neighbor, an American who, judging from his features, was half Chinese, said "These little gilt chairs give me a little gilt ass!"

Colin nodded, shifting. The armchairs of honor, called *fauteuilles*, went to influential American fashion editors, encouraging them to stay awake. Top editors lapped up this special treatment, including Maynard Cowles, "grand old lady of American fashion," and her fashion editor, Coral Stanton. Both ruled *Divine*, the ultraglossy monthly that made *Vogue* and *Bazaar* look like supermarket checkout magazines. *Divine* was always at least one season ahead: *Women's Wear Daily* dubbed it the "fashion intellectual's magazine." It was the book in which a designer most craved to be featured, where an artist or photographer or model dreamed of appearing. Its reputation was now wholly due to the amazing fashion antennae of Coral Stanton, "Her Fashionness" as *WWD* called her. She obviously operated in spite of her boss Maynard Cowles, privately known as "Her Boringness."

Relishing her reputation, Coral opened the *New York Herald Tribune* to read Hebe Dorsay's column, blocking the view of several people behind her. The Balmain models paraded by to her supreme indifference. Balmain advertised its perfume in *Divine*'s expensive pages, so this was a protocol visit. *Divine* would feature one photograph of a Balmain creation, just to keep them happy.

A tiny cup of espresso was sent down the row to Maynard Cowles, who was drowsing. Important editors received these little shots of caffeine toward the end of the showing to revive them from the perfumed stuffiness and prompt their memories of the clothes they wished to photograph. At the finale—a bridal gown by tradition—they would ask to see certain models again, perhaps for sketching by their artist. This was to the intense fury of the *vendeuses*—elegant, older sales ladies in black, who had smuggled private clients into the press showing and were pawing the ground in their impatience to take orders. The *vendeuses* believed the press to be a waste of time. Private clients were where the money was, they believed, upfront where you could see it. A ballgown, worn with family jewels, photographed at the Opéra, paid for with a check drawn on some old family bank: That's what haute couture meant to the *vendueses*, and God help anyone who interrupted its smooth passage.

"*Cette Americaine!*" a *vendeuse* spat, as Maynard Cowles suddenly reached out to feel the fabric of a satin-tulle concoction sailing past. There was no love lost between the French and the Americans, that was for sure. It allowed for all sorts of subtle digs and snubs, including that of ill-mannered New York buyers demanding to see dresses modeled again after the collection, as they snacked on canapés and champagne in full view of starving, half-fainting models. It didn't matter; the French needed the dollars, and the Americans needed the chic; this very resentful exchange kept the French couture going.

There was a burst of applause as the bride sailed to the end of the runway, and a flurry of movement as journalists got ready to race across Paris to the next showing. Colin Beaumont closed his sketchbook with a flourish.

"Fuck Jolie Madame!" he muttered, and his neighbor automatically replied, "She should be so lucky."

The next showing was at Patou, near the Place de la Concorde. Colin would share a taxi with someone, but for the moment he remained seated, gazing around at the passing parade of people. He watched Catherine Deneuve, a young actress he had recently sketched for French *Vogue*. Near her, a British *Vogue* girl glistened in Vaseline—her reaction to the makeup look. She looks like a buttered, boiled potato, Colin thought. He watched as a dowdy group of British journalists followed Ginette Spanier to the press office, where she distributed handouts, black-and-white glossies which could be used in their columns. In the main salon a press assistant fanned Maynard Cowles with handouts while Coral Stanton impatiently fingered the peplum of a black dress, the best thing in the collection. The model, pale and tired, was doing her best to smile at the important American editor.

Suddenly Coral noticed Colin watching her and waved. His heart skipped a beat as he glanced behind him to see whom she was waving to. She signaled to him again, mouthing "I want to see you!" Glancing at the groups of clients, buyers, and *vendeuses* between them, she shrugged, scribbled something on a pad, tore off the leaf and gave it to a young salon assistant, with a nod toward Colin. He watched as the girl carried the scrap of paper around the room; a little angel bringing him a message that would forever change his life. . . .

"The chic bitch left for Paris this morning," Mia Stanton wrote in her diary that night. She had invented this new name for her mother—the chic bitch—and enjoyed using it as often as possible. "Last night the chic bitch and Daddy called me into the living room. They said they had an important announcement. Then they totally ruined my life. I blame the chic bitch entirely for this. . . ."

Mia was seventeen, and the announcement was that her parents had decided to live apart.

"Your father's had a very good job offer," her mother told her. "His company wants to build up investment opportunities out in California, and he'd be a fool not to grab it. *I* have no intention of living out there—"

"Why not?" Mia had asked her. "You're his wife."

"My work is in New York," Coral answered quickly. "I haven't worked this long and hard to throw it all up and become a Californian housewife. Your father and I haven't got on for some while, Mia. You're not a child—you must have noticed. Rather than continue to make three people unhappy, we have this wonderful chance to change our lives *now*! It's bound to be for the better!"

"Not for me!" Mia cried. She stared unbelievingly at her father. Surely he would tell her this was all a joke? He looked away, his face flushed. He was a handsome blond man with a rugged, outdoors complexion and a thick moustache. He cleared his throat and glanced up at Mia with regretful eyes.

"Your mother's right," he finally said. There was an awkward silence. Mia willed him to invite her to leave with him. But he said nothing.

Finally, she blurted, "Can't I go with you?" She knew, from the expressions on both their faces, that it had been the wrong question. He had no intention of taking her, and now her mother would know—as if she didn't already—that she did not relish the idea of living alone with her.

"Mia, honey—" He moved to put his arm around her,

but she shook it off. She wanted that arm around her so much, but it would have reduced her to tears, and it was very important at this critical moment in her young life that she keep some semblance of pride.

"I don't want you to think I don't love you very, very much!" her father said gruffly. "But—"

"Oh, *please!*" Mia cut him off, starting to sob in spite of herself. She stared from one to the other, helplessly. "You *married* each other! You married each other for better or worse! It's your *duty* to—" She broke off, unable to continue.

"Mia, for God's sake, don't turn this into a soap opera!" Coral snapped. She reached for her purse and withdrew a wallet. "I'm going to Paris tomorrow, and I really don't have time for a lecture on marriage. We'll survive, you and I. You'll keep in touch with Daddy, maybe spend vacations with him." Her father nodded. "Don't attempt to make me feel guilty. We kept this home together for you. Here's some money for while I'm away. I'll call you from Paris. I'll be at the Crillon, as usual—the number is by the phone if you need me." Coral continued to talk of practical matters. Of forwarding various pieces of furniture to Los Angeles. Of insurance policies. Of lawyers.

Mia confided to her diary: "It was as if I didn't matter, didn't exist. I don't know how I'll cope without Daddy. He never says or does much, but at least he was *there*, between the bitch and me."

That night, trying to sleep, she thought about her childhood.

"Why doesn't Mommy love me?" she remembered once asking her father.

"We have to remember Mommy has very important work to do," her father had explained.

Throughout her childhood she had always been told to "be quiet for Mommy, she's been working hard. Don't talk too long on the phone, Mommy's expecting an important call. Walk on tippy-toe, Mommy's sleeping. She's had a terrible day. Mommy has a big day tomorrow." The magazine was what it was all about, of course. The magazine was surely why her mother couldn't really be a wife to her father, couldn't really be a mother like the other mothers. The dummy issues and proof copies lying about the house were a constant reminder of what ruled their lives. Flung in despair against a wall if Coral was unhappy with it, cradled like a baby in her arms if it pleased her, the source of laughter, tears, treats, or punishments; *Divine* was the ruler of the mood at home.

"I've never felt close to the chic bitch," Mia wrote. "The only time we ever got together was in her precious closet. If only she had lavished *half* the love and attention she gave her clothes on *me*."

As a child she had spent afternoons in the immaculate confines of Coral's closets. Touching the clothes, inhaling the perfume that clung to them, she came nearer to her mother's essence. She loved the Dior brocade opera coat, the Gres draped white jersey, light as a feather. The Chanel cardigan suit with chains sewn around its edges. She would finger the fabrics, looking inside at the silk linings and labels. Once a year the has-beens were weeded out and sold, or banished to the "museum" in the attic. The names themselves were fascinating to Mia—Mainbocher, Dior, Bill Blass, Norman Norell—some of them people she had met at Coral's annual cocktail party in the offices of *Divine*. For these parties Mia's hair was done by a famous stylist and she wore her best dress, handing around canapés, enjoying the stylish crowd fussing over her.

After looking at Coral's clothes, she would move to the shoes. Sometimes her mother had found her in the closet and smiled her approval. "Look at them, *feel* them...." she urged. "See these? Made for me by a Paris magician, Roger Vivier. He invented this little square heel." Mia would stare at the shoes, perfect satin almonds in their stiff wire trees, the luxury, the perfection, filling her head with wonder. Other kids had toys to play with; she had her mother's shoes.

"They cost over a hundred dollars," Coral had whispered. "Don't tell Daddy—he wouldn't understand." It was an unbelievable amount of money! How highly her mother must rate herself to shod her feet so expensively.

"How much do these dresses cost, Mommy?" Mia would whisper. Coral laughed deep in her throat. "More than a thousand dollars, darling! But Mommy gets a special price from her designer friends. They sometimes give her these clothes for nothing so Mommy will wear them and everyone will see and admire them. If Mommy wears something, everyone else wants to wear it too."

Later in life her mother's great style would be a source of embarrassment to Mia. But while she was still a child it added to the glamour and wonder of her mother, spinning a fairy-tale aura around her, placing her out of reach. That mixture of wonderment and disappointment, of yearning, craving, and resentment at not being cherished, would numb this beautiful child's feelings, confuse her, make life difficult. But as a child all she knew was that her mother did not have the time to play with her. Stacks of papers and photographs prevented access to her lap, and little affection or warmth came from her.

What warmth there had been in childhood had come from her father or from Wayland Garrity, her mother's best friend, who was a sort of honorary uncle. He had held her on his lap, taken her for outings and walks, played games with her. He had a gentle way with her, and she loved him even though she'd once heard her father tell her mother, "He's not a real man!" That had puzzled her, but from an early age she had been assured by Wayland that they would only tell the truth to each other, and she trusted him. "No bullshit," he had promised, the first time an adult had used an adult word to her; and she had respected him for it. Her father and Wayland had always been there to explain things to her, to explain her mother to her. Coral, on the other hand, treated her as if she were one of her readers, to be lectured on clothes and style.

"When you buy clothes, buy just a few but make sure they're the best!" Coral would advise. "Buy *one* wonderful dress, *one* superb suit! You'll always look great in it, and you'll always love wearing it."

"But I want *lots* of clothes, Mommy," Mia had said, and Coral laughed her throaty laugh, closing the closet, locking up the treasures.

Fashion fascinated Mia—it was the key to her mother, to her attention, to her interest. She loved her visits to the magazine's offices where crazy, colorful people wearing fantastic clothes and painted faces, laughed, kissed, cried, and made a comic opera out of life. *Divine* was a world of fantasy, unlike any other world because it created dreams.

"We're years ahead of our rivals!" Coral would crow,

leafing through a new issue of *Vogue* or *Bazaar*. "Years ahead!" These were magic words for a child. Mia drank it in, picturing her mother living in some future age, ahead of ordinary mortals. When Coral arrived home at night, Mia imagined her speeding back through time to the present, stepping off a time machine to land in Scarsdale; "the last place in the universe I wanted to live!" Coral often said. But Harry Stanton had put his foot down, insisting his daughter live in a safe, secure neighborhood, and not in the Manhattan that Coral longed for.

The morning after the divorce announcement, Coral came to her room, perfectly madeup, ready to step into the limousine that *Divine* had sent to whisk her to the airport.

"Bye, darling. See you in a week. Be good!"

"Have a safe trip, Mother," Mia said sleepily. *I hope her plane crashes*, she thought, unable to accept the idea of living alone with her. She envisioned herself as a motherless teenager, knowing her father would then be forced to send for her. *Nobody* wants me—that's the truth, she thought. She turned over in the warm bed and fell into an unhappy sleep.

Colin Beaumont met Coral Stanton in her suite at the Crillon the day after the Balmain showing. The woman who had the power to make careers happen overnight wanted to see *him*! He wore his starving-in-a-garret outfit, not so far from the truth: blue jeans and black turtleneck.

"Colin!" Coral hailed him as he was ushered into the crowded suite, smiling across the photographer and his helpers, the models, stylists, hairdressers, and makeup artists. She was using her own suite as background to the Paris coverage. *Brilliant*, Colin thought. He recognized the photographer—Helmut Newton—who was gaining a reputation for erotic photography which made fashion sexy for the first time in magazine history.

The magazines were in deadly combat at Collections time to see who could be the most original. *Bazaar* had rented a circus tent and performers, their models balancing precariously on elephants and on tightropes. Avedon had models running along the Pont Neuf at dead of night while spotlights flashed summer lightning. Couture clothes were only allowed out of the showrooms at night—they

were needed in the daytime for the continuous showings
to store buyers and clients.

In Coral's suite models applied lipstick, leaned against
rococo gilt mirrors, posed against the art deco bathroom
walls, or lolled on unmade beds which stylists kept rum-
pling artistically. A tall, glorious creature dipped a croissant into a cup of chocolate as Helmut Newton clicked
away, murmuring encouragement, and stylists tossed fresh
red roses and copies of *Le Figaro* and the *Herald Tribune*
onto the bed.

"Isn't it a madhouse?" Coral called out happily.

Colin had sat in an unobtrusive chair, but Coral beckoned
"Over here!" and he had to get to his feet and walk across
the room in front of everyone. He would never get over
feeling freakish. He held his head high and thought of
Toulouse-Lautrec.

Coral was already in conversation with a hairstylist by
the time he reached her. She was pencil slim. Rather a
mean little face, he decided, but she certainly made the
most of what she had: white skin, an uptilted nose,
and intelligent, almost cunning, blue eyes. Hair that was
tinted red and cut intricately high and tousled. Throwaway chic, Colin thought. Her scarlet lips were a little
ungenerous. He'd heard she was getting divorced.

Coral looked across at the model who had been posed
with her skirt pulled up to the thigh.

"The news of that skirt is in the fullness, Helmut," she
told the photographer. "I'm all for the risqué, but let's see
the clothes, darling." She pulled the skirt down to calf
level. "*Now!*" she led Colin into a small dressing room,
clipboard in hand.

"You're an angel to have come at such short notice,"
she told him.

He smiled. As if she didn't know full well that anyone
in the business wouldn't drop whatever they were doing
to rush to her side—the opportunity to be published in
Divine overcame all obstacles.

"I love what you did for French *Vogue*," she said as they
sat down opposite each other. "The portraits of Deneuve
were exquisite. *I* would have bled them across two pages.
I don't know whether you'll appreciate my suggestions,
but I happen to think a rougher style could add a whole
lot more pizzazz."

"Rougher?" He had heard she was a creative meddler.

She leaned toward him. "Balenciaga and Givenchy don't show to the press until a month after the other houses. They don't *need* press. They *are* fashion, and their clientele knows it."

"I agree."

"This time Hubert has agreed to show me some unfinished outfits. They're only tacked, so I'd like them sketched. But in a rough, unfinished way, as if they were pages torn from a sketchbook."

"How many pages will this run?"

"How many outfits can you charm out of him?"

"I don't know. Maybe he'll be sorry for this little runt of an artist and throw me a few more crumbs from the fashion table?"

"*Colin!*" Coral sat bolt upright. "I don't want to *ever* hear you refer to yourself in that way again, but *never*! Do you hear?"

He smiled, touched. They stared at each other, feeling a moment of closeness. An assistant poked her head into the room. "Mrs. Stanton? Dorothy doesn't like the Patou!"

"Doesn't she indeed!" Coral jumped to her feet. "Call Monsieur de Givenchy tomorrow, Colin. I'll need the sketches to take to New York with me on Friday. Good luck!"

As he left the suite, he heard her commanding voice: "Now, what is this, Dorothy? Would you prefer to run up and down the Paris boulevards the way *Bazaar* makes their models work? Or will you put on the goddamned Patou and lie on the bed?"

He walked through the streets to the metro station, dazzled by Coral. Am I in love with her? he wondered. But why would she ever notice *me*? A midget-sized runt of a fashion artist. Don't do that, he lectured himself. *Use* your height—make it an asset, not a liability. Coral would notice him only if he became the best artist or the best friend she had ever had. He vowed to be both those things.

The next day he sketched eight outfits at Givenchy. Coral's name had opened all doors. Hubert de Givenchy himself came out to meet him, wearing a tailor's smock, behaving with the perfect politeness one expected of a count. Colin's drawings were ultimately splashed over four pages of the magazine's Paris issue, and together Colin and Coral began a new direction in *Divine*'s layout.

Colin understood the direction, the quintessence, of fashion. He sometimes saw much more in an outfit than the designer intended. In his own way he would influence the sixties as much as a Quant or a Courreges. When the issue of *Divine* launched his career in America, calls came from advertising agencies and publications. Coral wanted more drawings too. Colin packed up his few belongings and left Paris with a one-way ticket to New York. Coral had changed his life; one day he would change hers.

Two

"I'm having a massive clear-out!" Coral called from what used to be her husband's closet. "I'm banishing *anything* without a designer label!" She had arrived back from Paris the day after Harry Stanton had moved out, and was losing no time in claiming the extra closet space.

Mia watched her from the door. Coral wore trim black velvet pants, a huge white silk blouse, and, as a gesture to housework, a bright red bandana around her head. She looked like a dancer in some modern dance company, perfect for a photo in *Divine* which could be wittily captioned: "Clothes for cleaning out after a departed husband."

"Did Daddy ever ask if he could have custody of me?" Mia suddenly asked.

"Custody?" Coral echoed. "Of *you*?" She sat back on her heels and burst into laughter. Her eyes narrowed as she stopped laughing. "Mia, you have just seen a forty-eight-year-old man leave all his responsibilities and go off to the land of year-round suntans. What on earth do you imagine he'd want with an eighteen-year-old daughter?"

Mia looked down. "Maybe I could take care of him?"

"He's probably dating some girl as young as you! Think how embarrassed you'd be about *that*, knowing what a prude you are!"

Mia's eyes overflowed, but she kept them resolutely on her mother's cool blue stare. Coral shook her head and went back to cutting shelf paper.

"We're here now, Mia, without your precious daddy. We may as well make the best of the situation."

"How?" Mia's mouth turned down as she finally gave

in to her tears. She was furious with herself for being so weak. "You're always being so mean!"

"It's not exactly flattering to see you whining and pining for your dear lost father," Coral snapped.

"If you'd spent more time with him instead of with your stupid magazine . . ."

Coral smiled grimly. "My stupid magazine pays the bills. Your father wasn't the greatest provider. Listen, Mia, *every* girl adores her father and resents her mother. It's such a cliché. Let's try to be a little more original, shall we?"

Mia turned and ran to her room. Coral bit her lip as she pressed a thumbtack home. Mia had already cost her an early promotion at the magazine. Way back, when she was pregnant and working at *Divine*, her boss Maynard Cowles was fighting a bout of alcoholism. Lloyd Brooks, the president and publisher, had called Coral into his office. He'd always flirted with her, and she hadn't discouraged him. But after one look at her enlarged stomach, he had muttered, "Forget it!" She knew, she absolutely knew, that if she hadn't been carrying Mia, she would have become the youngest editor-in-chief in *Divine*'s history.

Maynard had undergone short, expensive rehabilitation at a discreet spa, and the fashion staff had covered for her. *I'd be editor-in-chief, and Maynard would have been out on her well-dressed rear,* Coral thought bitterly. She could never look at Mia without being reminded of what she had been denied.

Mother and daughter formed an uneasy truce in the following weeks. They tried to be polite with each other. It seemed to be working, until Mia returned from school one afternoon to find Coral home early, the drapes closed, a glass of scotch in her hand. It was so unusual that a chill of fear struck Mia.

"Something's happened to Daddy!" she guessed.

"Sit down, darling," Coral said flatly.

Mia obeyed automatically, staring. Coral was drunk.

"Your father was killed in a car crash this morning," Coral stated. Mia continued to stare at her. For once her mother's eyes were unfocused, the bright blue shattered into shards.

"Well, he was never the world's greatest driver!" Coral

suddenly said. She swallowed more scotch. "Those fucking freeways!"

The shock of the word distracted Mia. She watched as Coral drank steadily from the highball glass. The weekly phone calls she had eagerly awaited were over. No daddy was waiting for her in California, wreathed in sunshine. Her plan to visit him that summer evaporated like a Beverly Hills cloud. She would not be visiting him; would never see him again.

Coral held out her arms drunkenly. "*We're* our only family now, darling. We should be very precious to each other. Let's work at it. The key words for the sixties are *relationships* and *love*. Let's work at ours? Somewhere inside me that love is all locked up. Help me find it, Mia."

Mia stared, disbelievingly. "It's too late," she wanted to say, holding her mother while she wept. Way too late. She said nothing, but one part of her held her mother to blame for this loss and always would.

I don't care, I don't care, I don't care.... Mackenzie Goldstein mentally repeated the words as Norman Gershon, an overweight seventeen-year-old, hovered over her, sweat dripping from his neck, jabbing at the lower half of her body with his lower half. It was 1962, and Mackenzie was losing her virginity. She was sixteen, and she wanted a black leather jacket badly....

"Hurry up, Norm!" a boy shouted through the boiler-room door.

"*Shaddup!*" Norm yelled back, right in her ear. She rolled her eyes, but clothes mattered so much—what was an hour of discomfort and boredom? At the end of it she'd have the jacket, and that's all that mattered. She had told her brother she'd do anything for it, even work at their father's store, when he had come up with this idea.

"Twelve-fifty each," Reggie told four eager boys as they assembled in the dark boiler room beneath the apartments. "Okay, Mack?"

Mackenzie shrugged. "I'm not takin' my clothes off. It's gotta be in the dark, and everyone has to wear a Trojan."

"That okay, guys?" Reggie asked, and they mumbled their assent.

The boiler room was floored with hard concrete, and Reggie brought down two blankets and asked all the guys for their jackets. Even so, her back hurt as Norman labored.

"Whatsa matter, Norm?" someone asked, laughing. "Not used to the real thing?"

"I'm comin'!" Norman grunted in her ear.

"So come already!" Mackenzie urged. It was a violation. Breaking and entering, she thought grimly. Something girls have to suffer to get what they want.

"Oooh—" Norman jerked. "Ahhh!" He collapsed on her, and she pushed him off. "There's Kleenex behind you. Don't fall asleep on me, you big lug! Gimme the money, and remember—if you tell this to anyone, I swear Reggie'll kill you!"

"Yeah . . . yeah . . ." Norman wiped himself and zipped his pants, grinning. She shifted uncomfortably on the makeshift bed, waiting for her fourth visitor. She thought of the leather jacket she had tried on three times. It looked fantastic. And it was so soft.

There was only a silhouette of the fourth boy, hesitating before her. She did not know who he was.

"Hurry up," she urged. "Did you put a rubber on?"

"Yeah." He pulled down his pants and crouched over her. She could smell English Leather as she guided him in.

These awkward, stocky Bronx boys were her first taste of sex: So far it had not made her crave more. Sex was little more than being patient. Waiting, while a guy huffed and puffed. One had tried to feel her breasts, but she pushed his hands away. Nobody had dared to kiss her. The condoms had been carefully inspected. "I do not intend getting pregnant one minute before the age of thirty," Mackenzie swore. Maybe not even then; having children wasn't chic. Unless you had loads of money.

She noticed that the guy atop her now felt different. Although she just lay there as she had with the others, he was holding her in a different way, his arms around her body. He did not jab at her, either, but moved slowly, with a little finesse. She felt herself getting excited and wet down there. After a few more silent minutes of his determined movement, he speeded up and she felt an orgasm sweep her. She clutched his shoulders but kept her mouth shut, saying nothing. After his climax, she asked him his name.

"Eddie," he said quietly, pulling up his pants. "Your brother's a pimp, did you know that?"

"Well, you enjoyed it, what are you complaining about?"

"So did you."

She got to her feet and pushed him toward the door. "Here's your jacket. If you say one thing to anyone, I'll get my brother to kill you, okay?"

He left with the others, and she gathered up the blankets. She hurried back to their apartment and took a long bath. In her bedroom Mackenzie counted the dollars greedily. Now for the creative part of the problem: how to explain to her mother where she had found the money.

At eighteen Mia was beautiful. She had her father's blond, all-American looks. She was tall, and never wore her hair shorter than shoulder length. Her friend Karen said it was because she wanted to be the exact opposite of her mother, who practically shaved her skull. Coral thought that very short hair was the look of the truly modern woman. Mia squirmed at the rare appearances Coral made at school events, dreading the remarks she'd hear later.

"Is your mother an actress or something?"

"No, she's a fashion editor."

"Wow! She really looks different!"

Coral dressed dramatically. The hard-edged, shorn head was exaggerated by voluminous capes and coats, shawls, scarves, or throws. She wanted Mia to dress like her, but was violently resisted. Whenever Coral bought her something, Mia would change its look, add a frilled blouse, a fringed shawl, something to soften the edges.

"Wrong, wrong, *wrong*!" Coral would sigh when she saw Mia's version. "You make it look like something out of *Little Women*!"

Late-night sittings and business dinners kept Coral out most evenings. When the latest issue went to bed, she invited Wayland for dinner. Wayland Garrity had recently been made director of New York's most fashionable store, Headquarters, known in the trade as *HQ*. Mia loved it when he visited; she ran to greet her friend. They had not seen each other for months.

"You've become very beautiful, pet," he said. He took her chin in his hand, squinting professionally at her while

Coral mixed drinks. "You've inherited the very best features from each parent."

Mia beamed, basking in the attention. Coral, holding martinis, was at their side instantly.

"What are *my* best features, Wayland?" she asked, handing him his drink.

He laughed. "Anyone who makes up as carefully as *you* do knows every millimeter of her face, Coral dear."

Coral handed Mia a cocktail. "Mia, I want you to join us in this toast. Wayland? This is the last time you'll dine in this house—"

"Just because I said Mia was beautiful?"

"*No!* I'm bursting to tell! We're moving to Manhattan!"

"*What?*" Mia cried, and Wayland said, "You *are*?"

"I've found a divine apartment just a few blocks along Fifty-seventh from yours!" Coral announced. She sat down, crossing her legs carefully. She always dressed up for Wayland, and tonight she wore a black Dior pants suit. "It's nearly opposite Carnegie Hall. Wonderfully proportioned rooms! It'll be heaven to return to apartment-house living." She sipped her drink.

"But... what about *this* house?" Mia asked.

"On the market since this morning!" Coral crowed. "Keep your room tidy!"

"I..." Mia stammered, "you didn't even ask me what *I* thought."

Coral laughed her silvery laugh. "What *you* thought? Do you believe kids today, Wayland?"

Wayland glanced at Mia sympathetically. "This *is* the only home Mia's ever known, Coral. It's her roots—"

"Well, I'm transplanting her." Coral refilled his glass. "It'll be no hardship, believe me. Wait until you see our views of the city. The place calls for big drinks parties, *mobs* of people! Tinkling pianist, sparkling lights—and Wayland, I'll need your advice on that. You're such a genius at lighting."

Mia ran out of the room.

"What am I going to do with that girl?" Coral asked Wayland, swallowing her drink.

Wayland made a *tsk* noise. "You did fling the news a little brutally at her."

"Oh, *really*! Harry Stanton buried me out here for seventeen years, and I stuck it out for Mia. Now I'm moving to where I belong. I'll have parties, fun, *men*! Yes, *men*, don't look so shocked! I've neglected my personal life shamefully."

"Why not work at making your relationship with Mia a little better?" Wayland suggested.

"I'm *bored* with trying to get on with her!" Coral sighed, pouring them each a fresh drink. "In *her* eyes I'm a murderess. She thinks *I* killed her precious father. Look, darling, I never really wanted a child!"

Wayland stared at her as she lit a cigarette.

"Don't look at me like that. I wish I could love her. She was such a divine baby—those big blue eyes! But as she grew up, she adored her father and always sided with him. Those two did their best to make me feel so god-damn guilty about not being the perfect suburban house-wife. Well, anyone could see I wasn't that."

"Why did you ever marry him?" Wayland asked.

"I was naive." Coral laughed. "I wanted to get away from my parents. Mia was an accident. First my parents tried to cramp my style, then my husband, now my daughter! Well, this time no one's going to stop me from doing *exactly* what I want to do."

In her room Mia called her friend Karen.

"Mom's selling this place!" she blurted into the phone. "We're going to live in the city! Oh, Karen, I could kill myself!"

"Don't be silly! I'll come visit and stay weekends. We can hit some really neat places. Are you telling Bob Wilkes?"

"He won't even notice I've moved."

"Are you kidding? I'm gonna run right up to him tomorrow and say, 'Isn't it awful about Mia Stanton mov-ing to Manhattan?'"

"Don't . . ."

That night she lay in bed staring out her window, thinking. Her last date with Bobby had been a disaster. He had driven her home from a movie and tried to touch her breasts. She had panicked and run out of the car without even saying good night. That had been the last she'd seen of Bobby, a tall, quiet boy with a nonchalant way of scoring home runs. School hero or not, she did not see why one date gave him any right to paw her. She had thought she would enjoy kissing him, but he had been too clumsy, too impatient, too fast. She had felt panicky, nauseated, when he had started to touch her. She told herself that if a man were to kiss or touch her, he would have to be very gentle. She cried in bed that night. Life ahead seemed very grim.

Moving house was as melodramatic as Coral could make it. All the furniture went to auction; Coral believed in wiping the canvas clean. This was her chance to re-create, to reinvent herself. She could arise anew in Manhattan. A young, avant-garde decorator stripped the apartment and scattered light, custom-designed seating throughout. Hidden closets secreted possessions, leaving rooms empty, bare. A stark, lacquered coffee table supported piles of new books. A gleaming stainless-steel kitchen defied anyone to stain it with food. The stage was set for Coral, a glossy, self-created high-tech lady. She was forty-five and at her professional peak, with only one rung left to climb: the rung upon which Maynard Cowles, editor-in-chief, precariously stood.

Three

"It's like a high-tech loony-bin," Mia wrote in her diary. The apartment did not feel like home. She had enrolled in NYU for a year of general studies. Coral believed she'd go on to college, but she had other ideas.

Wayland lived three blocks away and was with them so much, it was almost like having parents again. It was mutually beneficial for Coral and Wayland to stay close. *HQ*, the most fashion-conscious store, worked hand-in-glove with *Divine* on promotions. When *Divine* trumpeted "Navy Blue," you could bet that most windows of the Fifth Avenue store would display no other color. They discussed these promotions and everything else under the fashion sun at one of their apartments or over dinner at the latest "in" restaurant.

What did people think of their odd little trio? Mia wondered. Coral in turban and dramatic cape. Wayland dressed like a refugee from the 1920s in his impeccably cut suit, tie and tie-pin, and shining, almost bald head. He had coached Mia in his particular passion, and she knew most of Bette Davis's famous lines and how to twirl a make-believe cigarette as she said them.

Wayland was the first person to whom she confided her ambitions a few weeks after moving to New York. Following one of their Sunday walks in Central Park, they had ended up in Rumpelmayer's ice cream parlor, and she told him, "I'm going to be the next Chanel!" She held the tiny square ice-cream spoon against her lips, relishing its coldness.

"Oh, pet!" He took her hand. "How marvelous! Coral must be delirious!"

"She doesn't know. You're the first person in the world

38

to know. Fashion's in my blood, I guess, but I want to do it *my* way, not my mother's. Promise you won't tell her!"

"But everyone will recognize your name," Wayland protested. "And if you expect to go to art school—and you should—Coral knows all the deans. She could help you. . . ."

Mia shrugged. "I know. I'll have to tell her, but I won't let her take over."

"You'll go to MacMillans, of course," Wayland said. MacMillans was the fashion school that most successful designers had passed through.

When Mia got home, she found Coral sitting in the spotless kitchen with her French masseuse. Coral wore a white toweling robe and turban.

"You want Chantal to give you a quickie?" she asked Mia. "She just made me feel like a million dollars."

Mia smiled at Chantal. "No, no thanks. I feel great after my walk." When she heard Chantal leave, she found Coral in the white-tiled corridor.

"Why didn't you let her give you a massage? She wouldn't have charged—"

"I don't like being touched like that."

Coral turned away, wearily. "You'd better lick that phobia or you won't make a very good wife."

"So?" Mia stared at her. "Maybe I won't marry!"

Coral spun around and broke into tinkly laughter. She linked Mia's arm. "I guess that's not the wickedest idea in the world!"

She let her mother walk her to her room, and sat on a corner of the bed watching Coral cream her face. A Rigaud candle flickered, sending out its bittersweet cypress smell.

"I've decided to be a fashion designer!" Mia blurted.

Coral paused in her creaming, her cheeks glistening. "Wonderful! I'll call Millicent tomorrow and have her put you down for MacMillans. She owes me a favor or three."

"No, don't call her," Mia said. "I want to submit my work to them like everyone else. I want them to tell me if I qualify for the program."

"You'll qualify if *I* say you're going." Coral's eyes flashed over white-creamed cheeks. "Why make things difficult? When she finds out who you are, *I'll* look bad because I didn't introduce you. She can give me a break on fees, too. MacMillans isn't cheap."

"Didn't Daddy leave anything toward my keep?"

Coral laughed her maddening, mocking laugh. "What he left doesn't keep you in handkerchiefs!"

Mia returned to her room, feeling small and unimportant—her usual reaction after trying to talk to Coral. She would take control of her own life, send drawings to MacMillans and see what they said.

By the time she was seventeen and a senior in high school, Mackenzie had managed to improve her life. She was inseparable from her leather jacket—she wore it every day—and her family all called her by her new name. Her father thought she was going to step from school into his business and carry on the illustrious name of Goldstein Modes. Boy, did he have another think coming! Mackenzie still wanted everything, and she tried to make her mother feel guilty at not providing it.

"I don't have anything to wear!" she cried every Saturday.

"Then *make* it!" Esther Goldstein would yell.

And one day Mackenzie did. She whipped up dresses for herself, using the machine at the back of the main store. Abe Goldstein was in the *schmatta* trade, although Mackenzie told people he was "in the fashion industry." His chain of Goldstein Modes, consisting of two stores, had each opened with a "Closing Down Sale." They were situated mid-Bronx, catering for "the fuller figure," which was the norm in that neighborhood. The top price of a garment was $19.95, which made Mackenzie shudder in disapproval. Abe did not understand quality fabrics and stocked hardly a solid-color dress; they were all lurid prints.

When she tried discussing styles with him, he said, "You're talking fashion and good taste? I'm talking turn-over!" She would put on a disgusted look and Abe would turn to his wife, saying, "See that face? She's ashamed of her own father! And what have I done? Am I a crook? Do I drink? Do I starve my children?"

Esther tried to soothe the tension. "Every kid has a *mishegas* at her age, Abe. She reads a magazine, she imagines she's a Vanderbilt! Try to understand a young girl's mind, darling. Life is so dull for her here."

Abe snorted. "I wish *my* young life had been so dull. I

had to *work*! My boys will come into their father's business with good hearts. *They* won't be ashamed of their father."

When she became a teenager, Abe insisted Mackenzie work weekends in his store. "You learn to sell some clothes, you'll learn a little about life. You'll see what your precious 'fashion' is really about."

But if this was fashion, if this was life, she didn't want to know about it. Grim reality was overweight matrons struggling into cheap dresses, imagining they looked beautiful. She stared at them in dismay. Could she possibly be doomed to remain Marsha Goldstein of Goldstein Modes? *No!* she swore to herself, buying the latest *Vogue* and *Bazaar* and *Divine* with her first commission check, poring over them in her bedroom, eating them up. *I'll get out of here: I know I have talent! I'll get into MacMillans somehow.*

MacMillans would be the gateway to Manhattan and to fame—to Mackenzie Gold—a force in the fashion industry once she had shortened her name. Tweezing her eyebrows to look like Sophia Loren's on the *Bazaar* cover, which was propped up against her mirror, she tingled with energy and ambition.

She wrote so many letters and received so many evasive replies, wishing her luck. She began to write to fashion editors, and to MacMillans' dean for advice, guidance, hope. She wrote to *Seventeen, Mademoiselle,* then *Vogue* and *Divine,* asking anything, any question to which they would have to reply, just so she could treasure the letter, the envelope; to touch something that came from the address on the masthead of the magazine. And she waited at the mailbox each morning, her lifeline to the world outside.

Pages from *Vogue* and *Divine* lined her bedroom walls. She had been born with something, some quality that had never before existed in her family. Not from what she could see in the faded sepia portraits of plain-looking people in dowdy clothes. Her parents were second-generation immigrants who had grown up on the Lower East Side, then moved to the Bronx. If only they'd stayed downtown, she could have pretended she was living in the Village. The Village sounded so much better than the Bronx. Pretend, pretend! When could she stop pretending? When was it going to come true?

Now she opened her morning's mail. Most of it was junk or subscription reminders, but one was from *Divine*—

the glossiest magazine of them all. She used her best letter opener.

"Dear Miss Goldstein..." She shuddered, she would change her name to Gold the moment she left home!

Congratulations on your submission to our Talent '64 Contest. You answered all the fashion-quiz questions correctly and submitted a most original essay. We are therefore pleased to inform you that you have been shortlisted with nine other contestants. The winner will be awarded a full scholarship to MacMillans' three-year fashion course. Your entry forms for the final part of the contest are enclosed, and meanwhile you and the other nine finalists have been awarded a one-year subscription to *Divine*. We look forward to your entry.

Yours truly,
Maynard Cowles
Editor-in-chief

Mackenzie stared at the letter. The first thing in her life that had come true. Her body felt as if it were being iced, then scalded. She opened her mouth wide and screamed, "*Ma!*"

"In my room!" a voice called back.

She raced to her parents' bedroom, where her mother sat on the bed, pulling on reinforced stockings. From the sublime to the ridiculous, Mackenzie thought, thrusting the letter under her mother's nose. "I got into the finals! *Divine*'s talent contest! *Look!*"

Her mother took the letter, fumbling for her glasses. She read slowly, her lips forming the words, beaming at the end.

"*Mazeltov!* Let me kiss you!"

Mackenzie leaned down automatically, her eyes staring straight ahead.

"You're going to win this," her mother said. "I feel it in my heart!"

"So do I." Mackenzie stood, staring out of the window at the gray buildings outside. She could smell the aroma of burnt toast from the surrounding apartments, but now it wasn't depressing anymore, because she knew she was going to get out of this place. She would live in a clean, sculptural, bright building like the ones they showed in the Living pages of *Vogue*.

"I know I'm going to win," she repeated. "I'll grab a doughnut on the way to school."

She ran out of the room, and Esther Goldstein sighed and reached for her other stocking.

It took only a year for Colin Beaumont to become the most successful fashion artist in America. He drew like no one else. His flair for splashing a drawing across a page in flamboyant, exciting lines worked perfectly with the grainy black-and-white photographs of Jean Shrimpton, Twiggy, and Penelope Tree that were taking over the pages of the glossy magazines. *The New York Times* Style pages hired him to enliven their pages. Blown up for store window displays, the drawings looked even better.

"You'd better grab him before Bloomingdale's does," Coral advised Wayland on the phone one morning.

"Does he understand the Youthquake?" Wayland asked.

"He understands *everything*!" Coral enthused, sitting behind her desk at the magazine office. "He *is* from London, you know! He's been teaching me all the latest London expressions, like 'grotty' and 'switched-on.' Oh, you'll adore him, Wayland."

The truth was, she had been jealously keeping them apart, not wanting to waste two escorts in one evening. But it was now the in thing to have Colin Beaumont at your dinner, your party, your tête-à-tête at a fashionable restaurant.

"Nobody gives a tête-à-tête like Colin," Coral crowed, pleased with herself because Colin was *her* discovery. He *was* almost a midget, people agreed. Some even used the word dwarf, but that only seemed to add to his appeal. Although inviting Colin for dinner had started off as a charity effort, his new friends actually got more out of it than Colin did. His views on fashion were eagerly listened to, especially as Britain looked like a looming force in the industry. But more than anything it was his degree of concentration, his lack of ego, his quality of listening, that impressed his new acquaintances and turned them into friends. He was one of those people who effortlessly absorbed the tensions and worries of others. In crude terms, some said that talking to an almost-midget who

had built up a successful career made one feel as if life
was really pretty easy for the fully grown. He was, everyone agreed, better (and cheaper) than any shrink, with
the added advantage of being qualified to discuss every
aspect of their world. A fashion artist was admitted
everywhere—to designers' studios, magazine offices, advertising agencies—and thus had access to all the gossip,
all the news. Colin was supremely discreet, yet he recounted
wonderful stories.

"I can't *wait* to meet him!" Wayland decided.

By the time Wayland proudly walked his new store
artist around HQ's block on Thirty-fourth Street, viewing
the twelve windows for which Colin had sketched life-
sized drawings, they had known each other for a month.
Their walk continued to take in drinks, then dinner,
Wayland choosing a suitably trendy restaurant where
fashion groupies went to be seen. It was not easy for
Wayland, with his own complexes about the way he
looked, to accompany this tiny, odd-looking individual.
But as Coral had promised, there was something about
Colin that made it worthwhile. He was wonderfully witty
in a slightly wicked way; he commiserated about Wayland's
problem of being "terminally single" and helped Wayland
feel better about himself.

"I'm so glad we're friends," Wayland said at the end of
the evening. "We'll probably wind up as two old spinsters
in some quaint New England village."

Colin flinched. He had not referred to his sex life—he
never did. This was, he knew, Wayland's clumsy way of
drawing him out.

"We fashion boys have our own unofficial club, you
know," Wayland chattered on as they walked up Lexington
Avenue. "Every other Thursday night—you can't afford to
miss it—one picks up news that's too hot for *Women's
Wear*. I can't wait to take you. You may even meet some
dish and start a *mad* affair!"

Colin found his key and turned to face Wayland. They
had reached the doorway to his walk-up apartment. Wayland
did not expect to be invited up: The place had already
achieved the status of a small myth. A myth*lette*, Wayland
thought, probably too shabby to show off.

"Wayland, I'm not homosexual," Colin said quietly.

"Oh, dear!" Wayland flustered, sticking his hands into

his pockets. "I thought, I mean—you didn't—and now I feel such a fool, telling you all about *my* ghastly love affairs—"

"Love is love," Colin smiled. "I never judge my friends' love-lives. And since you've told me so much, I may as well tell you *I'm* in love with someone we both know very well. For all the good it will do me..."

"But *who*?" Wayland's eyes protruded with curiosity. "Do *I* know him? I mean, *her*?"

Colin hesitated. "It's Coral, of course," he said, finally. "Since the day I met her."

"Oh, my God!" Wayland gasped. "But, I mean, she *adores* you! She never stops singing your praises. She—"

"As an artist, and as a friend," Colin reminded him. "Not as a man. Wayland, *look* at me! What possible chance does a runt like me have with—"

"Don't say that!" Wayland snapped. "It's cruel. I don't— well, I don't know what to say, really...."

Colin pressed his hand warmly. "Don't say anything. And don't feel sorry for me. I'm very lucky to have all this." He gestured, and his wave took in Manhattan. "And I'm grateful for her friendship. That and her wonderful company keeps me going."

Wayland looked nervously up and down the avenue. "Well—I'd better let you get your beauty sleep," he chattered. "You'll still come to the club, won't you? We'll keep quiet about your secret. No one needs to know *what* you are."

From then on Colin moved in both worlds. It added to his mystery, and made him the best-informed person in the business. He never abused his privileges, and soon *WWD* was calling him "the Fashion Oracle" and quoting him.

"Not bad for a little cockney boy," Colin wrote to his London friends. "I think I like New York. I'm settling in for a long stay...."

Mackenzie was writing her contest-entry for the eleventh time.

"*Again?*" her mother asked, looking in on her typing.

"I'm polishing it," she said.

"What is it—a diamond?" Esther laughed.

For her fashion project, Mackenzie listed the designers, photographer, and models she would use for a four-page fashion spread. She chose the setting of a deserted TV studio, complete with arc lamps, discarded cue cards, cameras, and fake painted backdrops. She sketched the Six Outfits for a European Trip in felt-tip pen, adding tiny fabric samples. But in the section called "About Myself," she gave only the briefest outline of her life.

"List ten things you believe in," was the final exercise. Mackenzie wrote: "Style. Quality. Love. Energy. Health. Uniqueness. Guts. Freedom. Myself. The immortality of fashion. (Not necessarily in that order.)" Let them figure it out, she thought. The judges might find her a little pretentious, she worried, but no one could deny that her entry had *chutzpah*, that Jewish quality of daring which her father always told her she had too much of. She mailed in her entry after kissing the envelope three times and getting her mother to kiss it, too. Now it was up to Fate.

She smiled mysteriously at school when her friends asked her why she seemed so remote and happy. Let me win, she prayed. Let me be out of here by this time next year. Such urgent prayers could not go unanswered.

"Here! You judge them!" Coral Stanton tossed a pile of papers into Mia's lap as she made for the door.

Mia looked down at the pile of papers. "What is this?"

"The contest," Coral announced crisply, ruffling her hair, glancing into the mirror. "The one we run every year. We choose the girl we think shows the most fashion savvy, and she wins a scholarship to MacMillans. It's an old tradition of the magazine—Maynard's very gung-ho on it."

"What do *I* have to do with it? I'm not allowed to enter."

"I just don't have time to go through them all again. I'm too busy with this Americana issue, but I've highlighted a few entries. Everyone appears to be about fifteen; you'll be a far better judge than I could ever be."

"Why can't we do it together when you get back?" Mia asked.

"I'll be dead after dinner with Maynard, you know how she drains me—" The doorbell rang; the car was waiting.

"Good night, darling!" Coral pecked Mia's cheek, gathering her cape around her.

Mia closed the door after her mother swept out, Coral's fragrance still filling the air. She sat down on her bed, her head buried in the entries. If only she'd been allowed to enter!

"You have to remember how shy Christian Dior was, Coral," Maynard Cowles was saying. "I was probably the first member of the American press he dared speak to. I was certainly the first to get an armchair in his salon! After he showed that breakthrough collection, he approached me and said, 'Madame! There is the American press, and there is Maynard Cowles.' He knelt on the carpet and kissed my hand! His collection that season had so much genius that I dedicated an entire Paris issue to it. I said, 'This season, Paris *is* Dior!' Chanel *never* forgave me."

Coral glanced secretly at her watch, hoping the enormous yawn she was holding in did not distort her face.

"The haute couture in those days had an elegance to it," Maynard said, launching into her favorite subject. Coral sighed and took another sip of her black coffee. Perhaps it would keep her awake a little longer. One of the drawbacks of wanting to be the future editor-in-chief of *Divine* was the difficulty of keeping on very good terms with the current, seventy-three-year-old, editor-in-chief. This included weekly dinners at her sumptuous Fifth Avenue residence.

Maynard Cowles was one of the old guard: An American debutante, she had worked as social editor at *Vogue* in the thirties, then left when she married a rich businessman who had died after twelve years. They had no children, and so when Maynard went to work for *Divine*, it became her baby. She knew the magazine business well and had not relinquished the reins for nineteen years. No one put a book to bed better than Maynard. She was never late on deadlines, got the contributors to hand in their material on time, charmed advertisers into increasing their billing. But she was beginning to Lose Touch, Coral thought as Maynard began yet another anecdote. She would never attract new young readers. Her birdlike, white-coiffed figure remained pencil-slim and still had a certain nineteen-fifties' chic. She exuded elegance and fine

living, but—Coral drummed her fingers on her knees under
the damask. Dinners with Maynard tended toward long
reminiscences of Dior, Molyneux, Schiaparelli, and other
famous figures long since dead.

Coral's eyes flashed. "Are you really happy with our
Christmas issue?" she suddenly asked.

Maynard glared at her, struggling to return to the present. "You hate our nativity pages, don't you?" the older
woman asked. "Are you *so* opposed to tradition?"

Coral's eyes opened wide. "Not at all! But imagine a
cover featuring Twiggy or Jane Fonda surrounded by a
'now' group like the Dave Clark Five or the Beatles. They
could all be dressed as Santa Claus, and Twiggy could
wear some darling Jane and Jane dress from Carnaby
Street—something that was available here, of course. Very
switched-on, very *with-it!*" She loved to use the latest
British expressions to bewilder Maynard.

"Rock and Roll, I suppose?" Maynard hazarded a guess.
"Didn't you just photograph some extraordinary girl sing-
er this month? Wearing the oddest clothes?"

"Janis Joplin," Coral said, nodding enthusiastically. "She'll
be a *terrific* fashion influence! All those fringes! Electrifying!" Coral sipped more coffee. She always wore her most
outlandish clothes to dine with her editor-in-chief, hoping
to shock her into realizing how out of touch she was, but
she doubted whether Maynard even understood the importance of the leather pants she was wearing.

"You don't see *Divine* simply featuring beautiful clothes
anymore, do you, Coral dear?" Maynard rang for the girl
to clear the table. "You think we should do films, enter-
tainment, rock and roll?"

"Well, it *is* all fashion influence, these days," Coral said.
"The haute couture, lovely though it is, is becoming an
anachronism."

"*Really?* An anachronism?" Maynard raised her eyebrows.

Coral pounced. "Let's you and I get this quite clear,
Maynard. Fashion is now coming up from the streets."

"The *streets*?" Maynard looked aghast. "I'm very glad to
say I shall *never* be an expert on the streets."

Coral watched as Maynard struggled to take it in. Soon,
she could mutter her usual excuse about having to be up
at dawn for a shoot. This weekly dinner had become a
penance, a punishment, worse—a *bore*! She reached across

the table to squeeze Maynard's hand in a last effort to communicate.

"The times—they are a-changing," she crooned, to her blank-faced hostess. "Like the Dylan song, *we* have to change too. Our clothes and our attitudes change! Pizzazz!"

She left an hour later, exhausted. There had still been no hint from Maynard about retirement, even though she was so obviously out of the fashion mainstream. Coral was losing patience. She would have to go directly to the top, to Lloyd Brooks, and mount some kind of coup. If Maynard couldn't take a hint, well—she almost deserved what was going to happen.

Mia lay on her bed rereading the competition entries. One really stood out. It was from a girl named Mackenzie Goldstein who gave her address as the Bronx, although nothing about her writing suggested the Bronx. She sounded sophisticated, experienced, with the sensibilities of a young, hip girl. Mia read the entry again. Since relatives of *Divine* staff were, of course, barred from entering the contest, she would go ahead. She felt a terrifying sense of inadequacy about her plan to submit a folio of designs to MacMillans. The written application would be as important as the drawings. What if dozens of brilliant young girls wrote like Mackenzie Goldstein? Mia believed in her drawings and designs, but her writing was poor. Could she ever write about fashion in this sparkling way? She stared for a long time at Mackenzie's phone number, an idea forming, and then she dialed the number.

The voice was suspicious. "Is this the time you usually call people?"

"I'm not really supposed to be doing this," Mia said quickly. "I'm doing it as a favor to you because I liked your entry. I'm no one official, but I can influence who wins. Trust me, I'm your age. I want to meet you, talk to you—"

"Do you work for *Divine*? How did you see my entry?"

"I'll explain when we meet. You can trust me, I swear!"

"Trust you? And you can't even tell me your name?"

"It's Mia."

"Well, Mia, whoever you are, I'll just call the magazine tomorrow and ask what this is all about."

"No. No, don't do that! Please! Just meet me tonight."

"Where are you calling from? Manhattan?"

"Take a cab—I'll refund you. There's a coffee shop at West Fifty-seventh and Sixth. I'll meet you there. I'll give you cab fare home too. You could be here in an hour."

It was too weird to turn down. Mackenzie agreed to go. She put on the bat-lady dress she'd made from a complete circle of black silk and crept past her parents' room.

Out on the deserted streets she found a cab, authoritatively telling the driver, "Sixth and Fifty-seventh," as if she had the money. On the backseat she retouched mascara and lipstick, her heart beating quickly.

A tall, blond girl stood outside the coffee shop. "Mackenzie?" she asked.

Mackenzie stared, nodding dumbly. She clambered out of the cab. This girl was very pretty, with an aura of elegance. From a very different world, Mackenzie thought. *Très* Wasp!

Mia strode forward. "How much is that?" she asked the driver.

"Five eighty-five."

Mia handed him seven dollars, then turned and offered her hand to Mackenzie. "Hi!"

Mackenzie shook her hand cautiously. Mia tried not to stare. She had expected someone small, slim, and shy. This girl was overweight, brash, and more than a little freakish in appearance.

"I love your dress!" Mia said, and Mackenzie held out her arms and twirled around on the sidewalk, giggling, the hem rising to her plump thighs.

"I loved your entry," Mia said, ushering her into the coffee shop.

Mackenzie giggled. "I guess you just love everything about me?"

They ordered coffee and doughnuts and sat back, studying each other. "Okay, who *are* you?" Mackenzie asked. "What's this all about? If I'm discovered missing from my room—my parents think we live in Fort Knox after eight o'clock—I'll be in a lot of trouble." She studied Mia's clothes as she spoke. *Not* chic, she decided. Like the back-to-school issue of *Seventeen*.

A tired waitress poured them coffee.

"I was going to give you a lot of bullshit, but—" Mia stopped.

"Did *you* enter the contest?" Mackenzie asked.

Mia shook her head. "My mother's the fashion editor."

Mackenzie gasped. "Coral Stanton's your mother?"

"She asked me to judge the shortlisted entries. Yours stood out over the others. Your writing, your ideas are terrific. I want to get into MacMillans too—"

"What's stopping you?"

Their doughnuts arrived, and Mackenzie took a big bite of hers. Mia grasped her coffee cup with both hands. "I just thought maybe if I helped you win this contest, you could do me a favor in return."

"What kind of favor?"

"Write something for me. An essay to hand in with my folio. I know they won't notice me without a good piece of writing."

"Couldn't your mother get you in?" Mackenzie suggested.

"I don't want *her* help!" Mia blurted. "I *hate* her!"

Mackenzie leaned forward, interested. "That's just how I feel about my dad!"

Mia relaxed in her seat. She hadn't intended to say that, but now that she had, she felt better. "My mother's always made me feel like I was a nuisance to her," she confided. "I have to get into MacMillans, and I'd do it by any means possible, but *not* with her help!"

"My dad thinks I'm a slut, an idiot, and a snob!" Mackenzie chattered. "He's right about the snob part—I *do* think I'm better than those boring Bronx people. My brothers suck up to him—he thinks they're great because they'll go into his business and do what they're told."

"What is his business?"

Mackenzie's eyes flickered. "He's in the fashion industry," she said airily. "A chain of stores. Very successful and all that, but I still can't wait to leave home. I mean, I have to wear miniskirts under my regular clothes just to get out of the house, because my parents would, like, *die* if they saw them! Are you really going to say I should win this contest?"

"If we reach an agreement. . . ."

"Do you draw or design well?"

"*I* think I do. But a good essay would clinch it."

Mackenzie shook her head. "You're *insane*, you know that? I could go straight to your mother tomorrow and tell her everything!"

Mia shrugged. "But your name would get dragged into this, and Mom's publisher hates controversy."

Mackenzie made a face. "So much for truth, justice, etcetera."

Mia reached out and grasped her hand. "*Please!* Just help me and I'll help you."

"Pretty used to getting your own way, huh?"

"No!" Mia cried. "I've *never* had my own way! This was just an idea that came to me tonight. It won't harm anyone. Here—" She pushed a ten-dollar bill at Mackenzie. "Your cab fare home. Just write me something good and you're the winner."

"I don't *feel* like a winner," Mackenzie muttered. "I guess I don't really have a choice. I just hate cheating. I always get found out."

"This isn't really cheating," Mia said. "I liked what you wrote and I think you *should* win." Mackenzie looked dubious as Mia went to pay the check. Mia came back and placed fifty cents on the table. She held out her hand and they shook solemnly. "It was really nice to meet you," she said. "See you at MacMillans. You can send the essay to me at this address." She dropped a card in front of Mackenzie. "Good-bye."

She left, and Mackenzie smoothed out the ten-dollar bill. She had already decided to take the subway home and keep the money toward a new silk scarf. She pocketed one of the quarters Mia had left for the waitress: That poor little rich girl had too much money for her own good. She left the coffee shop and walked to the Broadway subway. Manhattan's sidewalks seemed to sparkle—they were so much more glamorous than those in the Bronx. She'd write the essay—what did she have to lose? What a weird way for her prayers to be answered!

Four

"Awake?" Coral asked Wayland over the phone. "It *is* seven-thirty. . . ."

"I guess I'm awake," Wayland groaned.

Coral spoke crisply. "I did my weekly penance at Maynard's last night, and we are definitely on different wavelengths regarding her retirement. I'll have to see Lloyd Brooks; I can't take much more of her. Wayland— what's your entire annual advertising budget at HQ?"

"What? God, *I* don't know! Two hundred, three hundred thousand? I'm not the accountant; I just create—"

"Well, I want to suggest something *very* creative. I want to suggest that HQ devote seventy-five percent of its annual advertising budget to *us*, for one *incredible* fifty-page advertisement in an important issue."

"Do you have a hangover?"

"But imagine the *impact*! Fifty straight pages in *Divine*! No one's ever come near it. It would win me the editor-in-chief slot overnight if you came through, Wayland. Photographed by someone like Penn or Avedon—"

"We couldn't even afford a *pass*port photo from them!" Wayland wailed.

"Okay, so you use one of the new British boys—they'll do it for a hot meal. It could even be black-and-white, if you want to get really chintzy!"

"Chintzy? And you're talking about a quarter of a million?"

"And a *very* cozy relationship with America's top fashion book! I'd favor you all along the line. I'll instigate a *Divine* Fashion Award and upstage the Cotys! We'll have the award ceremony at *your* store! Wayland, will you at least *think* about it?"

"I'll think of nothing else," he said wearily.

They hung up, and Coral suddenly felt tremendously hungry. She would allow herself a cheese Danish with breakfast. Like some greedy garment manufacturer, she thought, and laughed to herself.

Mackenzie forced herself to go about her usual routine: school, home, helping at the store, but she was bursting with impatience and tension. Should she have gone straight to the publishers of *Divine*? Called the police? There was no one to confide in. Nobody in the Bronx understood the workings of the Manhattan fashion world. Her mother least of all. So she wrote the essay for Mia and mailed it to Mia's address. It was a good one—better than her own. Now she would have to sit it out to see if she had done the right thing. If anything went wrong, if the poor little rich girl screwed her in any way, she would get her revenge somehow, that was for sure!

At La Grenouille, as the lesser folk were shown politely but firmly to Siberia, Coral and Lloyd Brooks got one of the best tables. She smiled, sinking onto the banquette. Gilles, her makeup artist, had performed magnificently; she looked rosy, positively cherubic. Exactly the right, healthy look in which to bury an outdated fashion editor!

She let her gray cape slide off her shoulders, leaning forward to concentrate all her attention on Lloyd's pudgy face. They ate three courses without discussing business— food was important to Lloyd. But Coral whispered to him in a dramatic way, throwing back her head and laughing gaily at his monosyllables. Let those watching think they were holding *some* kind of meeting. At dessert she allowed herself "the merest shaving" of La Grenouille's chocolate gâteau, while Lloyd took a fat wedge, pressing his knees into hers. For once she did not move away completely. She could only wonder, as usual, how such a man had become head of a publishing empire, and once again conclude that Lloyd Brooks II owed everything to Lloyd Brooks I.

"Okay," Lloyd grunted, finishing the cake. "What's on your mind? Why did you want to have lunch?"

"I'm terribly unhappy with the book," she said. She took a tiny sip of champagne, watching him. His slightly bulging eyes and very bulging neck repulsed her. "I've

started to hate everything about *Divine*," she said, warming
to her subject, "the title, the size, the features—"

Lloyd fanned himself with his hand in relief. "You're a
pro, Coral; *all* pros are dissatisfied with their work."

"Maynard stifles me!" Coral cried. "She drains my
energy. She doesn't understand *today*! I've argued all
month with her about a two-page spread on Mick Jagger's
lips. He's going to be next year's fashion influence, but
she doesn't see it!"

Lloyd frowned. "But the woman's a damn robot," he
said. "She never misses a deadline—"

"Fuck the deadlines, Lloyd." She clutched his plump
hand to her knee. "There's a lot *more* to a fashion book! I
have a vision of the book *Divine could* be, and it's *killing*
me! We have to go after the young readers. Young kids
today won't *want* old ladies choosing their fashions—and
advertisers don't think a seventy-three-year-old is a viable
proposition..."

"Is that what you have against her? Her age?" He lit her
cigarette as she kept her cool fingers on his fist.

She inhaled slowly. "I wouldn't care if she were ninety-
nine, Lloyd. *If* she was switched-on, clued-in, with-it!"

Lloyd stared at her. "What *are* these new expressions?
You make her sound like an electrical outlet—"

She laughed. "Come down to my office one afternoon—
you need a crash-course in the new terminology."

"You come to *my* office," he suggested. "There's a
choice of couches. *And* a rug. With you, it would have to
be on a rug! I have a feeling you're a tigress when you
want to be..."

She gave him a knowing look. Likes talking about it,
she thought.

"To get back to the subject," she tapped him, "give her
some Consulting Editor title. Redecorate her office. She
doesn't even need to *know* she's being phased out. Oh,
Lloyd, it's my *turn*!" She had spoken too loudly and a few
heads turned to stare. She gave a peal of laughter to
cover it, moving closer. "And if I mention fifty extra
pages of advertising?"

"From whom?"

"From someone who *believes* in me and is willing to
show it. A quarter of a million bucks in one generous,

dramatic gesture! Fifty consecutive pages in a March or September book!"

Lloyd gave a low whistle. "Is that what her job's worth to you?"

"You won't regret this, Lloyd. You're an astute businessman and you know I'm right."

He grunted, pressed her knee and said, "Only *you* would call me an astute businessman, Coral. To everyone else, I'm a playboy." He squeezed her thigh gently. "How do you do it all without a man? Don't you need one?"

"All the nice ones are married, Lloyd. *You* should know that."

"But some of the nicest have very understanding wives . . ."

She stubbed out her cigarette, thinking of Mrs. Lloyd Brooks II and her fabulous jewels, her charity-committee work, and her separate bedroom.

"We're entering a very exciting era, Lloyd," she told him. "I'll enjoy every second of it, and I want our readers to also."

"And those fifty pages?"

She nodded. "They'll break publishing records, Lloyd."

"I like breaking records." He grunted, signing the check as Coral gathered her voluminous cape around her, running a hand through her hair. God, she was *dead*! The adrenaline from this triumph—for it must be one!—had yet to reach her brain.

Back in her office she nearly tripped in her rush to get behind her desk to call Wayland.

"I just got back from lunch," she whispered. "My thighs are black and blue from Lloyd's attentions. You don't know how close to this I am, Wayland. He was very impressed by the sound of fifty pages."

"The Queen is dead, long live the Queen!" Wayland cheered.

"Not *dead*, darling!" she corrected. "Promoted! We'll pretend it's not quite the same thing."

April came and went and there was no sign. Mackenzie was convinced something had gone wrong. She took a subway into Manhattan and stalked Mia's apartment building, hoping she'd appear, but the doorman only stared suspiciously at her. She was unable to sleep and began to look sick.

"What's wrong, darling?" her mother asked one Friday night. Mackenzie took one look at her mother's concerned face, broke down and told her parents everything. Then she cried as if her heart were broken, her face on her folded arms on the table. Her brothers exchanged glances and bolted from the room.

Esther placed her hand on her daughter's heaving shoulders. "Darling! Why did you do such a thing? The girl is obviously a delinquent!"

"She promised me I'd win the contest!" Mackenzie lifted her face to wail, rivulets of mascara running down each cheek.

"This girl should be ashamed!" Esther said, looking at Abe. "This girl is in for a lot of trouble."

"*I* could be too!" Mackenzie cried. "Everything was going so well...why did this have to happen?"

Abe Goldstein gave an aggravated grunt. They sat for a moment, Mackenzie's sniffs punctuating the silence. The aroma of their meatball dinner lingered in the air. Now I'll never get out of this place, she thought.

"Well," she sniffed, dabbing her eyes. "I blew it, that's all. I'll just have to wait and see what happens...."

"Wait and see, nothin'!" Abe scowled. "I'll see the kid's mother tomorrow. Write her name down for me and give me the address of the magazine."

"Oh, Dad." Mackenzie giggled. "She's the top fashion editor in the country—you think she's that easy to see?"

Abe smiled. "You forget we're in the same business! Maybe old Abe Goldstein can do *her* some good? Like not getting her kid thrown into jail for this."

Mackenzie moaned. "You wouldn't do that to me. One look at you and—" she stopped herself.

"Yeah?" Abe asked. "One look at me and what? Still ashamed of your dad? Like to pretend you're not my daughter? Well, let me tell you something! Your dad— your loud-mouthed dad who you're so ashamed of—is going to save your butt for you tomorrow. I'm gonna stand up for your rights. Who else is gonna do that for you?"

"Oh, Dad!" Mackenzie got to her feet and threw her

arms around his neck. "I'm sorry. I know you mean well. You'll just never get in to see her. It's not that easy!"

Abe disentangled himself from his daughter's arms, his face flushed with pleasure. "We'll see," he grunted.

The next morning he presented himself at Mackenzie's door. He had squeezed into his best, slightly shiny, navy pinstripe suit, his cheeks red from an extra-close shave, his thinning hair combed back with plenty of pomade.

Mackenzie scrutinized him sorrowfully. "You look great. But she'll never see you."

She waved as he left, and went to pray in her room. "Dear God, don't let him louse it up for me...."

Abe Goldstein stood in the center of Coral Stanton's office looking from Coral, to her secretary Virginia, to a long-haired fashion photographer.

"Miss Stanton?" he asked each of them in turn.

"How did you get in here?" Coral quickly stood, her melba toast dropped in surprise next to her black coffee. They had been viewing color slides on a light box.

"Do you have an appointment with Mrs. Stanton?" Virginia stood, too, taking Abe's arm and trying to lead him from the room.

"Your kid's Mia, right?" Abe stood his ground. "Tall, blond girl. Lives on Fifty-seventh Street?"

"*Why?*" Coral barked. "Has there been an accident?"

Abe shook his head. "No, but your kid could be in trouble, Mrs. Stanton. That's why I've come to see you. My kid is crying, and I don't like to see my kid crying...."

Coral stared at him. "And who, may I ask, is your kid? Your child? You're not the father of one of our models, are you?"

Abe reared himself up importantly. "I'm the father of the talent contest winner," he announced.

"But we haven't named the winner—" Coral stopped short. "What did you say your name was?"

"Abe Goldstein." He stuck out his large hand and pumped Coral's warmly. "And you can relax—we're in the same industry! Ever hear of Goldstein Modes?" Coral raised her eyebrows at Virginia, who shook her head. The photographer looked incredulous, and still miffed at being asked whether he was Miss Stanton.

"Is it a store?" Coral asked.

"A chain!" Abe said proudly. "Listen—my daughter thinks the world of you, Coral. She thinks the sun rises and sets on your magazine. Your daughter called her a couple of months ago. About that contest—"

Coral interrupted quickly. "Will you have some coffee, Mr. Goldstein? I believe there's a Danish around somewhere. Please sit down." Abe collapsed with a sigh and a smile onto a black leather couch. Virginia served some coffee. "Scott? Go kibbitz in the art room," Coral told the photographer as Virginia closed the door on them.

Abe stirred his coffee. "I like a lot of cream and sugar," he confided to Coral, pouring some. Coral took a long breath, watching him interestedly.

"What's this all about?" she finally asked. "How is my daughter involved?"

Abe took a swallow of coffee. "Your daughter told Mackenzie she'd help her win this contest if my daughter wrote something for her. She said she needed it to get into the same school."

"MacMillans?" Coral said faintly. "This is very serious indeed."

Abe took a bite of Danish. "Serious, shmerious," he said. "That's your problem, Coral, honey. What we want to know is—is Mackenzie the winner or not?"

"As it happens, she is. But she was unanimously chosen. Mia only read the final entries to give me her opinion. I can't believe—"

"Wonderful! Marvelous!" Abe cleaved the air with delighted gestures. "That's all I wanted to know. She'll be tickled pink. It means everything in the world to her!"

"Well, she's a very talented girl. But this news upsets me very much. To think Mia violated my trust..."

Abe finished his coffee in a long swallow. "Listen, I won't waste any more of your time. I just didn't want to see my kid get done out of something that was rightfully hers. She has talent, you say?"

"She's quite the most brilliant entrant to our contest," Coral said tonelessly. "But the prouder you feel of her, the worse I feel about Mia. I just can't fathom—" Suddenly she began to cry.

Abe sprang up nimbly from the couch and leaned concernedly over her, proffering an enormous white handkerchief. "Now, don't let it get to you!" he told her, patting her shoulder. "You're a pro! I knew you would be. You're a lovely girl." He eyed her critically as she dabbed her eyes. "You got a lot of class, darling," he told her, "but put on a few pounds—your husband will like it better." Coral smiled, handing him back his handkerchief. "I'm a widow, Mr. Goldstein."

"Never mind." He patted her arm. "You'll soon get married again."

She shook her head. "I'll confront Mia tonight—"

"Don't be too hard on her—these girls are at a difficult age," Abe advised. "Mackenzie's always been trouble. I named her Marsha after my dear mother, may she rest in peace, but Marsha wasn't good enough for my daughter. She had to change it to Mackenzie. She probably read the name in *your* magazine. I tell you, Coral, these kids can drive you crazy."

"But you came here to defend her interests," Coral said. She sat back, watching him. "You're a supportive father."

Abe shrugged. "Who else is gonna support her? I guess you have to be mother *and* father to your kid now?"

Coral groped for another cigarette and lit it wearily. "I'm afraid I'm neither. I'm not a very motherly person, Mr. Goldstein." She took a long drag, then sat up straight. "I must make this up to you," she said. "Do you advertise in any fashion publication?"

"Ever hear of the Bronx *Jewish Gazette*? It's only a giveaway, but it has a woman's page. I sometimes advertise my sales in it. *You* know: 'Crazy Prices owing to Sale of Lease!'"

Coral laughed. "And your lease has another twenty-five years to run?"

"Thirty years!" Abe said.

She shook her head, looking at him. "You're the Zorba the Greek of fashion!" she declared. "An irrepressible life-force! What energy! I'll get our advertising department to give you a sixteenth of a page for all the trouble you've been caused. And tell Mackenzie we'll be in touch officially next week."

She saw him to the door. "I suppose when she finishes at MacMillans, you'll snap her up for Goldstein Modes?" she asked.

Abe shook his head sadly, taking her hand and kissing

it. "It won't be good enough for her," he said. "Your magazine has turned her head. She wants to be in high society. She won't be happy until she gets there."

Coral watched his burly figure making its way down the corridor toward the advertising department.

Mia got home from school to find Coral's cape flung over a chair in the entry hall.

"Mia? In my bedroom, please!" her mother called.

She walked into her mother's room, seeing her dress hung up carefully, shoes neatly beneath it. Coral, in a white slip, lay flat out on her bed, a white towel around her head, witch-hazel-soaked pads sunk into the sockets of her eyes. The tart smell was ominous. Mia sat gingerly on the bed's edge.

"Why are you home so early?" she asked.

Coral sat up slowly, like an awakening mummy. As the eye pads fell off her face, her eyes blinked open: Their relentless blue gaze bore into Mia. "I had an unexpected visitor today, Mia. One Abe Goldstein. Fearless avenger from the Bronx of his daughter's honor."

Mia's heart jumped. "The girl I said should win the contest?"

"The very one," Coral agreed. "They are decent Jewish folk. In the rag trade, as it happens, although I'm positive any resemblance between the clothes he sells and fashion is purely coincidental. I couldn't help liking him. I liked the way his daughter meant so much to him. He has *guts*! I was as cordial as I could be—even gave him a tiny free ad for his frightful stores. I thought it the least we could do. You see, I like families that work together. What I want to know is: *Why can't my family be loyal to me?*" The last question was screamed as loud as she could scream. Mia stared at her, terrified.

Coral grabbed Mia's arm and shook her. "How could my own daughter do something that might jeopardize my career? If Lloyd Brooks got a whiff of this, he'd be quite justified in firing me. Mia—I offered my help!"

"I thought I could get in on my own," Mia mumbled. "When I read her entry, I panicked. I was scared I'd get turned down on my writing. . . ."

"I'm ashamed of you," Coral said. "I don't know what to think, but I *do* know I want you out of here! I won't share my home with a criminal. Start thinking of a place to live, Mia."

"Where? What do you mean?" Mia stammered.

"*I* don't care where! You'd better go to your room. But I warn you, it's your room for only one more week."

Mia picked up her coat and ran, blinded by tears, out of the apartment.

"It's the best thing that could have happened to you, pet," Wayland called from his kitchen.

Mia sat in his living room, twirling a tiny sherry glass in her fingers, sipping the comforting liquid. Wayland fussed in the kitchen, pouring peanuts and chips into bowls.

She glanced around. She had thought her mother relentlessly chic, sacrificing all for style, but Wayland had gone much further. Instead of gray carpeting, he had stainless steel everywhere. He allowed his apartment to be used as a preview for room settings at HQ, retaining the most novel, bizarre features of their displays. Today the place was colder than an operating theater.

"A drink, a smoke, a chat..." Wayland murmured, setting down a tray before her on the Perspex coffee table. He was flattered Mia had called on him. So very few people needed his help. Oh, there had been a whole army of advice-seeking students, a slew of Seventh Avenue designers, but Mia had come to him as if he were family.

"You're my family," he told Mia, holding out a dish of nuts.

She took one, saying, "That doesn't mean I can be had for the price of a cocktail like a salted peanut!"

"Bette! *All About Eve,*" Wayland said approvingly, settling onto the couch. "Now tell *all!*"

"I wanted to get into MacMillans so *much,*" she said lamely at the end, realizing it made her sound pretty shabby. "I know it was a really dumb thing to do, but I just couldn't ask her for help."

"Why didn't you ask me? I told you last summer I would help."

She shook her head. "I didn't think. I just had the feeling this girl would help me—it seemed easier, quicker. Now I feel like such an idiot." She started to cry.

"Now, now," Wayland soothed, pouring her some more sherry.

She sipped at her drink. "Do you really think she means to throw me out?"

He sipped from his enormous vodkatini. "You'll move in here," he said. "Keep me company. Cook a little—you *can* cook?"

"If you like tuna, I know a dozen different ways with it." She giggled.

"You can do a little housework for your keep if it'll make you feel better. How's *that* sound?"

She jumped up. "Oh, Wayland!" she said, hugging him. "It's so generous and dear and—"

"Oh, shut up!" he said. "Finish that sherry. You'll have to learn to hold your drink if you live here. This is a tough kind of place, and we drink a helluva lot!"

He mixed another batch of cocktails, walked to his bedroom, picked up the phone and dialed Coral. "Mia's here," he told her. "Have you really kicked the kid out?"

"*Yes!*"

"What about your maternal feelings?"

"Oh, *please!*" He heard her light a cigarette and take a drag. "I could have used my maternal feelings to get her into MacMillans, but she didn't want my help—"

"We all make dumb mistakes," Wayland said. "She's a good kid. You're too hard on her. I've told her she can stay here if she wants."

"That could be the perfect solution. I'm so tired of this personality clash. You've always had a soft spot for Mia—*you* be mother for a while."

When Mia went home later that night, she was relieved to see Coral's room was dark. The next morning, after her mother had left for work, she dragged two suitcases, a carton of books and record albums, and two shopping bags of possessions down to the lobby and took a taxi to Wayland's apartment, three and a half blocks away.

He had given her keys and she let herself in, dragging her stuff to the end of the marbled hallway and opening the door to the spare room. It was a small oblong with a window looking onto the side of the next building. No view, just a sliver of blue sky. She sat down wearily on the bed. She had escaped her mother. Now the chic bitch could stew in her own juice!

Five

Coral stared down at the note on her desk, a lurch of excitement stirring her stomach. It was on Maynard's embossed notepaper and had *Urgent* underlined in red. "See me—at once!" it read.

She had just returned from a preview of a hot new designer, Bettina Chiu, who had based a whole collection on the kimono. She had decided during the taxi ride back to the office to get Bert Stern to photograph some outfits on Verushka. There was a fabulous art deco mens' turkish bath in the Bronx that Wayland had told her about. What if they filled it with dry ice and shot through steam and vapor? she wondered, imagining the layout.

She crumpled the note impatiently and walked down the corridor toward Maynard's office, stopping at the door reading EDITOR-IN-CHIEF. Only for about five more minutes, she reminded herself.

No one was in the secretary's office. Coral strode through and knocked on Maynard's private door. There was a muffled answer, and Coral walked in. Maynard was on the floor in a corner of the room.

"*Darling!*" Coral cried. "*Congratulations!*" She ran around the desk. Maynard was weeping into a lace handkerchief. Coral dropped to one knee to crouch protectively over her. The thrill of victory mixed with sympathy for the crying older woman.

"What *is* this!" Coral cried. "I thought you'd be *celebrating!*"

"*You!*" Maynard glared at her, her hazel eyes rimmed red, melting mascara outlining them clownishly. "Don't pretend concern. *Exult! Crow! Laugh!* That's what you really want to do!"

Coral stepped back and sat in Maynard's chair. "This is an odd way to react to a well-deserved promotion!"

Maynard blew her nose in quick, dainty gusts. "*Promotion!*" she jeered. "That's a word to make you and Lloyd feel better. I could see from his face he didn't believe it any more than *I* did! As if I'd work under *you*!"

"What's so terrible about that?" Coral asked. "Didn't I work under you for years?"

Maynard's eyes glittered. "I made you fashion editor. Wasn't that enough?"

Coral shrugged. "I can't believe you're taking this so personally, Maynard. Promotions, retirements—they're part of life. Did you imagine you'd stay editor-in-chief forever?"

"While I could do the job, yes."

"You've had marvelous innings, Maynard. Step up to the next rung—move up a notch on the masthead."

Maynard shot a look at Coral. "A friend saw you and Lloyd lunching together at La Grenouille last week. She saw him pawing you under the table. Naturally, there's no way I can compete with that! Thank God!"

Coral burst out laughing, and Maynard abruptly scrambled to her feet like a cat. "I've never really liked you, Coral, and I've often wondered why," she told the younger woman. "I think it's because although you've done a good job of overcoming humble origins, you'll never be a lady."

Coral's smile vanished and she looked directly into Maynard's eyes. "*You're* a lady, Maynard," she spat. "And you're out of fashion! No one wants to look like a lady anymore—haven't you heard?"

"That explains your success," Maynard replied, taking a step nearer. Coral moved her chair back. "You use this job as some kind of substitute for any real meaning in your life. I had a wonderful husband, marvelous friends. You've had a failed marriage, a daughter you don't even speak to, and you're only comfortable around homosexuals. In my book, that's not much to crow about. . . ."

Coral smiled a deadly smile. "Why not start clearing out your desk, darling?" she said quietly. "Or would you prefer that I emptied out each drawer in the corridor?"

Maynard shook her head. There was a stillness in the room as both women breathed hard. Coral scented victory; she was about to be ceded to, she felt sure.

"I'd rather *die* than work under you!" Maynard told her.

"Oh, really, darling," Coral said, "now you're being melodramatic. We can easily work out a—"

But what happened next came so quickly that Coral, however many times she would describe it, could not comprehend the speed. Maynard flew past her and wrenched open a window Coral had not even known could open. There was just one accusatory stare, a rush of air, a scream, an echoing scream from Coral—and Maynard had hurled herself into the rush-hour traffic.

Coral screamed again, horror scraping her throat raw, her eyes popping wide open, unbelieving. She fell against a wall and slid to the floor. From down below, horns sounded, traffic swerved with sickening, screeching brakes. In shock she realized she was the new editor-in-chief. The Queen is dead, long live the Queen! Who had said that? The Queen will not be *dead*, she remembered saying. She's simply being promoted! Oh *sure*! she could hear Wayland sneer—to Fashion *Heaven*? Oblivion moved in like a black cloud. As she passed out, her eyes rolling up in her head, she made a mental note: Get Avedon to reshoot the April cover.

"Go to your mother's apartment! Take a cab! Something awful has happened!" Wayland's voice cracked with emotion.

"Is she sick?" Mia glanced wildly around the dean's office where she had been summoned to an emergency call.

"She's all right, but Maynard Cowles is dead! As of this moment the police suspect your mother of pushing her out a twenty-fifth floor window."

"Oh, *God*! Oh, Wayland! Do you think she could have—"

"No, of *course* she couldn't. I know I always said Coral would kill for the editorship, but I didn't mean it literally! I'm a thousand percent sure it was a suicide leap. But your mother's pretty shaky. I think it would be a very good thing if you were there when she got home."

The doorman let Mia into the apartment with his pass-key. She felt sick to her stomach. She stood in the cold hallway for a minute, then she heard a key in the lock. Her stomach jumped as she turned to face the door.

Virginia, her mother's secretary, pushed the door open, Coral leaning heavily on her.

"A cup of tea," Virginia was saying in her clipped British accent. "That's what you need, Mrs. Stanton. It's a proven remedy for shock." They looked up and found Mia watching them.

"I—I—thought I should be here," Mia stammered. "Wayland called me at school. . . ."

Coral stared at her for a second, surprised. Then she broke into a smile. "You see, Virginia? My daughter thought of me! Darling. . ." She held out her arms to Mia. "How sweet of you to come. Under the circumstances, I mean. I really appreciate it."

Mia hugged her mother. She had never seen Coral looking so frail, so vulnerable. It was a revelation. So was the way she felt—needed, able to help.

"Tea," Virginia suggested, "very sweet tea."

"I'll make it!" Mia offered.

"And I'm putting you straight to bed," Virginia informed Coral.

"Don't be ridiculous, Virginia, I'm fine!" Coral protested. "I have a million phone calls to make. Remember, you're my secretary, not my nurse!"

Nevertheless, she allowed Virginia to lead her into the bedroom, and consented to lie on her bed covered by a quilt.

Mia brought the tea and watched as Virginia earnestly spooned sugar into it.

"Now, drink up, Mrs. Stanton!" she urged. Grimacing, Coral swallowed some. She dismissed Virginia. "Mia will look after me," she assured her. Mia saw Virginia out.

Coral lay back against the two plump Porthault floral-printed pillows. She had lit a Rigaud candle, and its familiar, slightly cloying essence floated through the room.

"So!" She held out her hand as Mia came to perch on the end of the bed. "We're a family again! That's the only good thing about tragedies: They bring families together—even tiny families like ours." Mia pressed her mother's hand, still not quite believing this new aspect of Coral. Maybe she was in shock, she thought. "I was so proud to see you standing there when Virginia opened the door," Coral continued. "Rallying around me like that. I'm going to need all the support I can find, now. This incident isn't exactly going to improve my popularity ratings. *Women's Wear* will have a field day tomorrow, you can be sure."

"Was it awful?" Mia asked. "Poor Maynard—how could she do such a thing?"

Coral's eyes turned steely for a moment as she regarded her daughter. "Her career meant more to her than her *life*! *Imagine*! We must never let that happen to *us*, darling!" The phone rang, startling them.

Coral pushed the receiver toward her daughter. "Say I'm resting, darling." It was a newspaper columnist and Mia got rid of him.

"Should I fix you something to eat? A sandwich? Soup?"

Coral considered, "Mmmm, perhaps a wafer-thin sandwich, darling? English style? I think there's a cucumber in the refrigerator. And take Virginia's goddamn sweet tea away, will you? Trade it for a triple brandy. I'll take a little nap."

Mia closed her mother's bedroom door and tiptoed to the kitchen. She toasted some bread and sliced a cucumber into the thin slices Coral preferred, and she wondered if Coral would invite her back to live there again. Brewing some fresh coffee for herself, she kept an eye on the kitchen wall phone so she could catch it during the first ring, before it woke Coral. Suddenly the red extension light on it flashed on. Mia walked softly to the bedroom door and pressed her ear to it.

"Duck-egg blue!" Coral was saying crisply. "Or deep glossy black! I always hated those bland beiges she used. I want a totally different look, and I'm not just talking about office furniture, Lloyd. I mean a different look for the pages, for the layouts, for the whole shebang! I'm throwing out everything she was working on. I want April to have my signature on it from the very first page—from the *cover*! Oh, Lloyd, by the time this issue appears on the newsstands, no one will have the slightest idea who Maynard Cowles *was*!"

Mia hurried back to the kitchen. When she took the food in to Coral, her mother was sitting up in bed, shuffling contact sheets and papers.

"I had to call Lloyd about my new cover," she told Mia brightly. "I got this fabulous idea for painting Verushka's face with a pattern to match her Pucci dress! Maynard never took Pucci seriously!"

Mia set down the tray carefully. "It's such a horrible way for you to get Maynard's job," she said slowly.

"I know," Coral said, and nodded understandingly, making a wry face. "There's an enormous emptiness inside me too." She picked up a cucumber sandwich and looked at it, then set it down. "I've *completely* lost my appetite. I guess it won't hurt to lose a pound or two."

Mia sat on the edge of the bed. "I couldn't help over-hearing some of what you were saying: redecorating her office and throwing out all she was doing on the current issue. Poor Maynard hasn't even been buried yet...."

Coral stared at her coldly. "She's being cremated," she said.

"Don't you think you should wait until that's over, at least?"

Coral's eyes narrowed. "Is that why you came here? To snoop? And I actually thought you were concerned about *me!*"

"I *was*, Mother—"

"I knew this was too good to be true, Mia. A little family of two again! What a joke. You have the roles confused. A child has no right to criticize her parent. And I don't want you leeching off Wayland. I'll have to arrange some kind of an allowance for you. Now you'd better go. I've a lot of work to get through, and I'd prefer not to have you eavesdropping on my phone calls."

Tears stung Mia's eyes as she closed the bedroom door and left. Why did she come? she wondered. She walked along Fifty-seventh Street to Wayland's apartment, furious with herself for allowing pity for Coral to cloud her mind.

"She's a monster, Wayland," she cried as he hugged her. "For a moment I thought Mother and I were going to walk off into the sunset together. She looked so frail and lost—I should have known it was just an act to impress her secretary."

"I'm *glad* she didn't win you back," Wayland confessed. He mixed a big pitcher of vodkatinis and poured them each one. He handed her the drink. "It's *much* healthier for you to be here; *I'll* teach you everything you need to know about the fashion industry and were afraid to ask!"

The next day *The New York Times* ran Maynard Cowles's obituary, and their news story quoted the police as saying they were satisfied there had been no foul play. Coral attended the inquest between shootings. A blaze of flash-bulbs exploded in her face as she slipped out of the limousine that Lloyd provided, wearing a Givenchy black cape and dark glasses. The photograph ran in the *Daily News* and *WWD*.

"All that's left now is for the Thursday night crowd to chew up the news and spit it out," Wayland said as he peered into his bathroom mirror when he got home from work, arranging his sparse hair. "And I'm taking *you*, pet! We'll meet Colin Beaumont there."

"What sort of club is it?" Mia asked, leaning against the bathroom door.

"Gay!" he beamed, "and strictly for the fashion industry!"

In the cab he explained. "We take over the hotel bar every other Thursday. We are the inner circle, the *core*! There's no way we don't know what's happening in this industry. There are stylists, window dressers, studio assis-tants, photographers, models, buyers, even salespeople! It's pretty democratic! Learn to get on with the boys, Mia, you'll get a lot more mileage out of your career if they're on your side, pet. We *are* kinda special: What other minori-ty group do you know that bases its entire philosophy on Stephen Sondheim lyrics?"

Wayland ushered her into a hotel lobby then led the way down a marble and black wrought-iron staircase.

He sat Mia on a blue velvet banquette in the bar, placed a wine spritzer in her hand, and watched with her as the others began to arrive.

They drifted in singly, in twos, threes, sometimes in laughing cliques. They were of all types. She realized that Wayland, the stereotype of the homosexual man, was already out of date. The young, wild hairstylists in jeans or black leather, the bland-looking Ivy League men in three-piece suits, the long-haired photographers' assis-tants who looked like rock stars, were mostly masculine. Mia recognized a TV newscaster, a Broadway actor, a sports commentator, and several fashion people who had drifted through Coral's cocktail parties. A few women did appear, one of them a well-known model on the arm of an equally famous male model. The two looked every inch the all-American couple.

"Both gay," Wayland hissed in her ear. "But they fell in

love! We're all on the edge of our seats to see what happens next! She may just be a cover girl."

"What's a cover girl?"

"When a man doesn't want anyone to know he's gay, he'll get some girl to cover him."

Mia stared at the attractive couple.

"Who's *this*, Wayland?" a good-looking blond boy asked. "Your daughter?"

"Yes," Wayland said drily, without a blink. "From my first marriage to Charlton Heston." The boy glanced at Mia, and she noticed his blond lashes were dusted with mascara.

"She's practically family," Wayland assured him. "Isn't she lovely? Mia, meet Paul-Emile, makeup artist *extraordinaire!*"

"Pretty!" Paul-Emile narrowed his eyes at her. "But crying out for a bit more blusher at the very top of the cheekbone."

"Do it for her," Wayland prodded him. "Transform her!"

Paul-Emile dragged Mia to the powder room, sitting her on the edge of the sink unit. A few deft strokes transformed her into a *Vogue* cover girl.

"I don't believe it," she said, staring into the mirror as he ran a hand through her hair. Could dark pencil, blusher, and eye shadow actually change the expression in your eyes?

When they returned to Wayland, he fell back, amazed. "Do *you* know your stuff!" he complimented Paul-Emile. He peered at Mia, saying, "You could be a model, d'you know that?"

"That's the last thing I'd care to be," she replied.

The bar was almost full. The murmuring had turned into excited chatter. The scent of Aramis and Eau Sauvage, the favorites that season, was so strong that the air was almost ignitable. The suicide was the main topic. Everyone spoke loud enough to be overheard, and seemed to be competing for who could make the cruelest, wittiest comment on Maynard Cowles's death.

"Trust darling Maynard to die in Dior. . . ."

"The chicest corpse *those* cops have ever scraped up."

"You think Dragon Lady pushed her?"

"No, but you *can* hold back a person, you know! You don't *have* to just stand there and wave 'Good-byeeee!' "

Wayland was chatting with someone, but he heard the comment and Mia's gasp. He quickly called for more drinks. They were hoisted aloft on silver platters by young waiters. Most people requested vodkatinis, perhaps because they liked saying the name.

Suddenly, a leading fashion photographer, Mark Wrexler, stood and hushed the room. "It would be wrong not to say something tonight about Maynard Cowles' tragic death" he said. "She was our friend. She was a real lady and a very decent human being. There are many in this room who owe their first break to her. Our world will be a lot poorer without Maynard in it."

There was a long moment of silence, and then applause. Then Wayland stood.

"And may *I* add something?" he said. "I want to scotch any libelous and untrue rumors going around about Coral Stanton. I am here to tell you that she's absolutely devastated at losing a great friend and a mentor. She will be deeply mourned."

There was a stunned silence, then a smattering of applause and a whoop or two. There was also a hiss from somewhere.

"It's true!" Wayland admonished, looking about him sternly. The room fell silent, then slowly the others returned to their conversations. Mia stared up at Wayland, amazed. She had never seen him like this before. He sat down and kissed her. "That had to be said, just for the record."

"Well *done*, Wayland!" a tiny man said, appearing from nowhere. "It's time someone defended our darling Coral."

"Colin! We've been waiting for you." Wayland leaned over to shake their visitor's hand. "You know Mia, of course, *fille de* Coral?"

"How are you, my dear?" He took her hand. "And how is your mother? I haven't dared call—I imagine she's pretty overcome."

"She's coping wonderfully, I hear," Wayland said. "Mia's living *chez moi* now, Colin," he said proudly. "I'm running the most exclusive orphanage! We have exactly two beds!"

Mia was telling the men about her NYU classes when a sudden break in the intense noise of the bar made them look up. Everyone seemed to have turned toward the bar's entrance, where there was a small stir. Some men moved, and in the sudden space, Coral stood, in the blackest of coats, her shorn head bare, her mouth dramatically red in the pale, powdered face. She glanced around her, her presence filling the entire room. She caught various eyes. It was obvious she knew most of them.

"I just got here!" she said very crisply. "And yet I could write the script of what most of you have been saying." There was a quick murmur of reaction from around the bar. Coral flashed a dazzling smile. "I don't blame any of you; I'd probably say the same things myself." She removed the cape, and there was a gasp at the perfectly fitting black sheath beneath it. Coral epitomized chic, and tonight they knew it. "I'm not obliged to defend myself here—this isn't a courtroom! But I want to say I'd give anything—repeat, *any*thing—to have Maynard alive and well here this evening with us. To tell us some of her marvelous fashion anecdotes, to continue being the incredible fashion legend that she was—" Coral appeared to choke up, and dramatically wiped away one glittering tear from an eye. There was a loud burst of applause. She had won the sympathy of the entire room.

Wayland whispered to Colin, so Mia couldn't overhear, "Anything but give up being editor-in-chief."

As Coral moved down the bar, boys and men admiringly parted like the Red Sea to let her through. Now and then someone kissed her on both pale powdered cheeks. Coral was nearing them, and Mia's stomach turned. She ducked down as Wayland stood to greet her.

"Wayland! Hello, darling! *Colin*, thank God I've found you. We need a portrait of Maynard for an appreciation we can just squeeze into March. I want you to do something in soft black crayon, but I need it right *now!*"

"How about ten tomorrow? I'll work through tonight."

"Angel!" She bent to kiss his forehead, handing him a folder. "Here are some photographs you can work from! *Mia!*" She suddenly noticed her daughter and her eyes opened wide. "What on earth are *you* doing here?"

"She's with me, Coral," Wayland said.

Coral looked around the bar disapprovingly. "Surely an all-male preserve should be off-limits for a teenage girl?"

Wayland stood to face Coral. "There's nowhere I go that Mia isn't welcome!" he said.

Coral laughed contemptuously. "I hope that doesn't include the Village leather bars, darling?"

"I seem to remember *you* finding them pretty interesting!" Wayland hissed.

Colin caught both their wrists and tugged. "This is not the place for a tiff, my friends. Too many people have free tickets."

Mia listened, speechless. She had just started to feel adult and sophisticated. Now her mother had arrived and ruined everything, making her feel like a child.

"I have a driver outside," Coral said briskly. "I'll drop you all off."

"We're not quite ready to leave yet, Coral," Wayland said.

"Colin has a drawing to do," Coral explained. "And I really think Mia should be home."

With a sick feeling, Mia watched Wayland glance at his wrist.

"It *is* getting a little late, pet," he said, and gave her a weak glance.

Coral turned to lead the way, and they all trooped behind her like dutiful schoolchildren. In the car they sat silently as Coral gave the driver Wayland's address.

"Who made you up tonight, Mia?" Coral asked from the front seat, "Paul-Émile?"

"Yes, how did you know?"

"He's always overgenerous with the blusher. I've had to stop using him because he made all the models look like clowns."

When they reached Wayland's building, she said, "Merchandising working lunch on Friday, Wayland. One o'clock—don't be late."

He led Mia into the lobby, pressing the elevator button. "I know what you're thinking, pet," he said, taking her chin between his hands, making her look up. "And you're quite right, I'm scared of her. We're so damned involved with the magazine."

Mia leaned back against the elevator wall wearily. "I know she's an irresistible force, Wayland. But I'm going to avoid places where she's likely to be."

When he let them in, she ran to her room and buried her face in her pillow, crying with frustration.

* * *

The decorators were paid triple-time to work through a weekend, repainting Maynard Cowles's office a glossy black. Now Coral could hardly wait to get to the office each morning, taking a taxi, making it wait as she picked up a container of black coffee from her favorite espresso bar on Madison Avenue. She adored *reigning* from her new suite of rooms, the black shiny walls a glamorous, unexpected setting. Her white, powdered skin and blood-red lips startled visitors, frightening some of them. *WWD* did a two-page feature on her "working environment," noting the fresh white flowers filling a giant floor vase, the large desk chair shrouded in real zebra, the intriguing scent of the Rigaud candles, the shuttered windows allowing her to view color slides on the light box. The outfits, pinned to black hangers, waiting to be inspected, hung perfectly ironed on the chrome rail running the length of the room. She breakfasted on melba toast and her coffee, the *Times* open to the Style page, *WWD* nearby.

A spate of new advertisers had enquired about *Divine*'s page-rate. Coral was the electricity that attracted the fashion moths. She sat in her desk chair, glancing with satisfaction around her domain. Her glance took in the willow baskets spilling with bracelets, pins, gloves and scarves. Coral had been known to plan an entire feature around a bangle she loved, throwing in scarves, shoes, gloves, stockings, and—almost as an afterthought—the dress or suit, creating a whole new look. Other times, she would be so enthusiastic about an outfit that she could not bear anything to diminish its impact: It would be photographed on a naked model, hatless, without even an earring to distract the eye.

Her taste veered from near-classic to the most exaggerated, wild fashion America had ever seen. It was, everyone agreed, the way she put clothes together that made fashion. She could make the dullest clothes seem newsworthy by her clever styling and sometimes she was obliged to do this. Like any magazine, *Divine* had to repay advertisers who took expensive color pages. By featuring clothes which were often ghastly, they kept their clients happy.

"The Queen is where she belongs," *WWD* pronounced approvingly, and on the whole, Seventh Avenue, if they could get their minds off making a buck, tended to agree.

Mia became Wayland's project, his pet, his protégé. She was dined at the best restaurants in town, heard all the latest gossip, accompanied Wayland to parties. For a while it was a novelty for him. Then she began to cramp his style.

"My sex life is suffering," he complained to Colin on the phone from his office. "I mean if I spot anyone exciting at a party, there's nothing much I can do about it."

For the first few weeks Wayland remained on his best behavior. He drank less and didn't use his "naughty little black book," which usually supplemented his often barren love-life. But it couldn't last, and one drunken night she heard sounds coming from Wayland's bedroom. She wanted to press her ear against the door, but something warned her not to do that. She heard the front door slam in the morning, and Wayland avoided her eyes at the breakfast she made for him.

"For God's sake, don't turn her into a fag-hag, Wayland," Colin warned.

"Oh, she's several stages past *that*!" Wayland said. "I've coached the kid in Bette Davis's lines since she could talk!"

But when the acceptance letter from MacMillans arrived, the tension in their shared home evaporated. They celebrated with a special dinner out.

Not long afterward, Mackenzie Goldstein was announced as the Talent '64 winner in *Divine*, alongside a small photograph of her.

Wayland peered at it over Mia's shoulder. "She'll be in your year, pet. You'll probably become bosom pals for the rest of your lives."

Mia groaned. "Oh, God, I hope not."

Six

On this sunny fall morning the smell in the air promised that the day would be hot; a sultry, sidewalk, sweaty smell that only Manhattan can produce. At eight-thirty a street-cleaning truck whooshed by the entrance to Mac-Millans School of Art and Design on upper Broadway, spurting water over sidewalk and curb.

By nine a bunch of new students were thronging the entrance, waiting for the doors to open. The excited girls and boys in their late teens had no particular look or style about them; ambition was the only thing they had in common. They were determined to break into a tough business.

A tall blond boy with broad shoulders stood across the street from the school, leaning against a wall, watching as the large wooden doors were hooked back to the walls by a superintendent. Something stopped David Winters from walking through those doors. This was the climax to years of work, and now that the moment had come, physically entering the school took an effort that, for the moment, he was unable to summon. The school accepted few scholarship students—they had to be very gifted and very poor. David had qualified on both counts. Why did fashion mean so much to him? Certainly anyone looking at him would have thought he was a front-line football player, not a dress designer. He closed his eyes for a moment in the morning sun. So this was where it all led? Three years of having his grades scrutinized, his family's income-tax returns photocopied and mailed to the admissions committee, and attending numerous interviews. And finally, the letter that told him he would commence in September!

He had wakened that morning in his tiny studio in the

East Village realizing that life began today. He would be
working on the stuff he had been obliged to hide until
now, for what football teammate would ever have understood his desire to design womens' clothes? He did not
even understand it himself; he just knew it was all he
wanted to do, and now that MacMillans had declared him
extremely gifted, he knew he'd been right.

David had lived in New York since July, staying at a
transients' hotel near Columbus Circle, living on meals at
Horn & Hardart. Going through the *New York Times* ads,
he had come across the big black figure of sixty-five
dollars which turned out to be his monthly rent. He had
not heard of the East Village before. When he found it, he
understood why the rent was so low. He scrubbed the
long narrow room with Clorox, then whitewashed it, but
it still boasted a whole zoo of bugs, many of them new to
a Syracuse boy.

He did not know a soul, but New York in the summer is
not a lonely place. He had his work cut out trying to form
his new persona; after all, in New York he could be
anyone, anything he liked. There were important decisions to be made: Should he dress up in the frilly mod stuff
coming from London, or should he stick to what he felt
comfortable in—jeans with madras shirts—and risk being
thought square? Should he really let himself go with those
hippie clothes the Village was selling? Just be yourself, he
thought, watching his new classmates enter the school.
He moved away from the warm wall and forced himself to
walk across the road and into the school.

A faded blond woman hunched over a register, sipping
coffee from a container, directing students to their lockers,
to the bathroom, to other parts of the school. Now and
then she straightened to look out into the mob, and her
mind could almost be read. Another year's load of egos to
contend with, nontalents to be tactfully discouraged, and
now and then a rare talent who could actually rethink
clothes and create fashion.

Several characters from this new class of '67 were already defining themselves. There were the exhibitionists
and the show-offs, girls who had lost admission cards and
were throwing mild hysterics; one or two outrageously
effeminate boys with long hair and mod clothes; a couple
of elegant Oriental girls; and a character in veiled hat and

long black skirt, dressed as if for a costume party. Mia peered at this girl, and, realizing it was Mackenzie Goldstein, quickly turned away.

As the chaotic line filed past the harassed organizer, Mia gave her name and was directed to room A-2. She soon got caught up in the milling students who almost carried her toward the stairwell and a maze of rooms.

A tall boy touched her arm gently. "Lost?" he asked.

She remembered seeing him in the street, watching the school. She smiled up at his concerned face.

"I'm David Winters," he said, and held out his hand.

"Mia Stanton." They shook. "I was told room A-2."

"Me too." He guided her down the corridor, saying, "In for the three-year course?"

"I may condense it to two. What about you?"

"I'm going to stick with it for the full three years—if the money lasts. I'm on a scholarship, but I still have to find the money for rent and food."

"Do your parents help?"

"Mom tries. My dad is dead. He would never have agreed to this. You know the type—'No son of mine is going to be some goddamn fashion designer!'"

"Most of the greatest designers have been men," Mia said.

He pushed open the door of A-2 and Mia felt a twinge of pride at walking into the classroom with him. No sooner had they checked in with the teacher, than they were told to take stools, and with drawing boards in their laps, were assigned five minute poses. The model was an ordinary-looking girl wearing a Japanese robe.

"Get the feel of the silk, the drape of the robe," the teacher suggested. During the next pose, the door of the studio burst open and Mackenzie Goldstein made her entrance. The veiled cocktail hat and long skirt looked ridiculous, but Mackenzie carried it with a certain air. Everyone looked up and stared at her except Mia, who concentrated on her drawing. After finding a stool, Mackenzie set to work.

At the eleven-thirty break David leaned over toward Mia. "Want to check out the canteen?" he asked.

"I'll wait for lunch, thanks anyway."

He left, and she flipped through the eight drawings she had done.

"Surprise!" Mackenzie struck a mad pose, grinning. Mia stared at her. "You do remember me, don't you? Mackenzie Goldstein? Christ, you *should;* you got me into enough trouble."

Mia shook her head. "You got me into more trouble."

"Really?" Mackenzie placed her hands on her hips. "It was your idea to call me, remember?"

Mia felt her cheeks flame red-hot.

"Listen, if I can be friends with *you,* the least you can do is be friends with *me,* right?" Mackenzie held out her hand. "My friends call me Mack." Mia took her hand gingerly.

"Okay!" Mackenzie smiled broadly, shaking it. "Now, as your friend, my first duty is to advise you not to fall in love with fags. It will only lead to heartbreak."

Mia curbed a desire to go for Mackenzie's throat. "Look, will you just mind your own business? He isn't a fag, and I'm not in love with him. I just met him."

Mackenzie shook her head, taking out a fistful of charcoal pencils from her purse. "Boy, you're green," she said, starting to sharpen them. When she had finished, she withdrew an enormous antique hat pin, then removed her absurd hat. She had a round face with almost Oriental eyes, slanting and mischievous. She had cut her hair shorter, and it stuck up in brown spikes.

"I guess this hat was a mistake," she said, and gave Mia a sidelong glance. "But at least I didn't look like everyone else."

"Is that so important to you?"

"Well, sure it is!" Mackenzie cried. "That's what fashion *is!*" Some girls left the room, giggling together. Mackenzie glanced after them, then turned back to Mia. "Did you know your mother took me for lunch to some swish restaurant when they announced I'd won? It was, like, part of the prize. I admire your mother so much! She's the most elegant woman I've ever met—"

"Look, don't tell anyone here she's my mother, Mackenzie," Mia interrupted. "Okay?"

"Hmmm... why? Nothing to be ashamed of, is it?"

"She threw me out because of what I did with you."

"No kidding? So where are you staying? The Plaza?"

"At a friend's."

"Are you his mistress?"

"Of course not. He's like my uncle. He's one of my oldest friends."

Mackenzie rolled her eyes. "Sounds like a lotta fun." She fished in her purse for a cigarette and lit it wearily, inhaling a long drag. "I hope you two'll be very happy."

When David returned to the classroom and sat down opposite them, Mia found it difficult to continue. Each time their eyes met, she smiled at him.

Later, when the school day ended, he walked her down Broadway. Mia watched him disappear into the subway, then hailed a taxi. She wondered what he would be doing that night, and daydreamed taking a cab downtown, ringing his doorbell, and seeing his shy smile. She could cook dinner for him, sitting cradled in his arms later, watching an old movie on TV. He had already made MacMillans more exciting. . . .

They began their first year at MacMillans by trying to digest an avalanche of information and training. Everything connected with fashion was thrown at them. At an orientation lecture their enthusiastic dean, Millicent Dutton, broke down the fashion industry into four categories: designing and pattern cutting, buying and merchandising, fashion journalism and illustration, and advertising.

"You'll discover for yourselves what you're best at," she advised them. "If anyone isn't sure, you'll find you'll slot naturally into place as the year goes on. To be a designer does not mean you have to draw well. Some of the top designers have their rough sketches redrawn by staff artists. Those of you who do draw well may choose to follow fashion drawing as a career, although I warn you that there is not that much work these days. Colin Beaumont and Antonio seem to be the exceptions."

Mackenzie whispered, "My drawings look like the work of a retarded child on an acid trip!"

Later, they sat with David in the canteen and discussed their careers. Mia, David, and Mackenzie had become a kind of reluctant threesome, mostly due to Mackenzie's insistence on joining them whenever they ate.

"When she talked about merchandising," Mackenzie mused, "I had this flash of being a buyer for some big store, maybe Bloomingdale's. Traveling all around Europe, seeing the new clothes, meeting dreamy Italian and English guys. Fun, huh?"

David laughed. "It's not quite that easy."

"Would you ever go into your father's business?" Mia asked her once. "My mother said he was really nice."

"She did?" Mackenzie looked at Mia carefully. She had forgotten that Mia must have received a full description of her father from Coral, and hoped he hadn't been too crude that day.

"My Dad's a rough diamond!" she finally said.

"Really?" David glanced at Mia. "My dad was just rough!"

They all laughed, and looked at Mia as if expecting her to add some funny remark about her father.

"I still miss my dad," she said sadly. "I can still hardly believe he isn't out there, in California...."

Mackenzie reached over to pat her hand. "Poor baby," she said. "You can have Abe, okay? I give him to you."

Mia stole glances at David as Mackenzie continued to monopolize the conversation, making them laugh, getting them on to wilder and wilder subjects. She was entertaining, but Mia felt regretful that she never got a chance to be alone with David. It would be nice to get to know him better....

Mackenzie was in her element. Spending her entire week thinking and working on what gave her most pleasure—fashion—was almost too good to be true. She kept expecting someone to walk into a class and order them to study math. She got on with all the teachers except their design tutor, Bruce Neville. From the way he wrinkled his nose when Mackenzie approached his table, he obviously disapproved of the way she dressed, spoke, designed, and even smelled.

"He's a prissy, snooty creep!" Mackenzie complained to her friends.

He criticized her exuberant designs, saying, "One would never wear a white belt after five o'clock! Those pants are only suitable for the beach! Red shoes are vulgar!"

She looked at him, surprised at the vehemence of his criticism. "Hey! Loosen up, sir! This is 1964."

He smiled grimly. "That may be, but there are still

certain things a lady doesn't wear. Not if she doesn't want to look as if she's from the wrong side of the tracks."

"Well, hush mah mouth!" Mackenzie cried in a Southern accent, making the class laugh. "Plenty of women like to dress a little slutty now and then."

"Really?" Mr. Neville asked icily. "Nobody *I* know."

Everyone in the class held their breath.

"Well, I *like* white belts and red shoes, Mr. Neville," Mackenzie said, not hesitating. "I'd wear them—even after five o'clock! There *are* no rules in fashion anymore! We're gonna break 'em!"

Mr. Neville sniffed. "Certain rules have changed, perhaps—"

"And how can I design if I'm not true to my own taste?" Mackenzie asked. "What would I have to sell?"

Mr. Neville remained silent. He obviously felt Mackenzie had nothing to sell. The concept of dressing sluttishly for fun was too young, too new, for him to understand.

He was not her only critic. At home her father looked through a stack of designs and then held his head in his hands. "Who would wear this stuff?"

Mackenzie glared at her father. Esther approached them, putting an arm around them both. "Abe, please, it's *shabbos*. I want my family to eat nicely and peacefully together. *I* think this girl is a genius. *I* would wear these clothes, Abe!"

The idea of Esther Goldstein in a gold lamé miniskirt made Mackenzie giggle. "Mom!" she said, and hugged her. "You've always encouraged me. When I'm rich and famous, I'm gonna buy you a beautiful home—"

"Yeah?" Abe sneered. "Don't hold your breath, Esther!"

Esther patted her. "I don't need a beautiful home, darling. I'm happy here. All I ask is that you get on with your father and your brothers."

Reggie and Max bounded in for dinner, clumsy as young puppies, tearing lumps of challah off the fresh loaf on the table, Abe nodding encouragingly at them. The noises of eating took over as Esther served the meal. Later, his hands holding his full belly, Abe continued the argument.

"Look how happy my sons are—and look at the mug on my daughter! How is it I can never please her?"

"I'll be very happy when I get out of here," Mackenzie

cried. "This is all so putrid! I want to spend my time with chic, sophisticated people like Coral Stanton!"

Abe laughed noisily. "Sophisticated? The poor woman looked like she hadn't eaten a square meal in *years!*"

"At least she's intelligent, and she really knows about fashion—"

Abe's face suddenly changed. "Get outta here, then! Who's begging you to stay? I'm fed up with looking at your superior face. Let's see how superior you are when you start trying to earn a living!"

Mackenzie got to her feet.

"Abe, I want she should stay here," Esther said quickly. "I haven't served dessert."

But Mackenzie stalked to her room, ignoring them both. She locked the door, lit a cigarette, pulled out her fashion magazines and leafed lovingly through them. Soon the world of fashion swallowed her up, soothed her, took her to capital cities, smart parties, places far from the Bronx. In this world, everyone called each other "darling," smiled, told each other how divine they were. Soon she would be part of it.

"Who am I seeing this morning?" Coral asked Virginia through the intercom.

"A designer named Howard Austin. Wayland Garrity recommended him."

"Oh, yes..." Coral got up from her table to peer at herself in the full-length mirror, smoothing her short black dress. Dear Wayland, she thought. He had taken Mia off her hands, and he sent her a steady stream of new young designers. She remembered him talking to her about Howard Austin.

"*Claims* to be heterosexual!" He had laughed. "If it turns out to be untrue, you're to send him back *immediately.*"

As usual with any designer or photographer Wayland recommended, he was outstandingly good-looking. Perhaps Wayland thought ugly designers couldn't be talented? She shook Howard Austin's hand and looked warily into the twinkling, warm brown eyes. They were looking at her with awe and admiration. She knew that look well; and she knew it meant nothing would happen that wasn't strictly business. Pity. As he showed her samples of his clothes and fanned photographs across her table, she took in the tousled dark hair and smooth, tanned skin. She was not used to meeting men who attracted her.

She indicated the seat adjacent to her desk, then her eyes swept the dresses and coats he had hung up. Good, clean shapes—no gimmicks, yet fresh and modern. "Very, very nice!" she said crisply. "In fact, *super*! My eyes have been starved for something like this. Give me an idea of the stores you're selling."

"Headquarters, of course," he said, collecting his swatches. "I just got a nice order from Bendel—"

"It's always nice to have Gerry Stutz in your corner."

"And Sakowitz in Texas, Gallay in Beverly Hills," he added.

"I'm impressed, Howard. These are the kind of cool, understated clothes that those of us who are just a few days older than eighteen will crave. When do you present your collection?"

He laughed. "We're not couture. Just humble ready-to-wear. I do five small collections a year. I hope you'll honor me with your presence at the next, in September." He looked directly at her with a personal gleam in his eye, and she lowered her eyes, flustered. No man had looked at her like that in quite a while. Wayland told her she frightened them off. She stole a glance at her reflection in the mirror behind him. She *was* looking pretty terrific.

"I'll be very happy to attend," she told him.

She watched him drink his coffee, noting the well-kept, tanned hands as they held the cup. They chatted a few more minutes, then she helped him gather up his samples and fold them into a garment bag.

As she was showing him out of the room, he turned suddenly to her, asking, "I suppose there's no chance of a date?"

She did not understand him at first, but his gentle touch on her arm and the intent look in his eyes made it clearer. "With *me*?" she said. "Why... nobody's used that term to me in ... God, *years*!"

"Why not?" he said, and laughed.

He had perfect white teeth. Was she imagining it or was there some sexual rapport between them? A glimmer of what could be? She held out her hand, and he took it between his warm ones. She glanced at his full lips, then looked into his eyes again.

"Thank you, anyway, Howard. We're working flat out on this issue. Why not call me in two weeks, when we've put it to bed?"

"I will," he replied.

Later she walked back to her desk, frowning. Could Wayland have set her up for this? It was all a little too pat. Howard was a handsome guy on the make, she decided. Probably all of eight years younger than she. But at least he had been a handsome guy with talent. It felt nice to be asked for a date. Made her feel young again. Back at her desk, she quieted the nagging yearning that had suddenly started up.

Coral lay on her bed, limp as a rag doll. The masseuse had left her supine, relaxed, but she could not stop her brain. It whirred with ideas like an ever-turning giant Rolodex file. Now, in addition to overseeing the junior fashion editors for her Paris, Milan, and London schedules, she was suddenly being bothered by Howard Austin. She had previewed his new collection at his Eighth Avenue showroom and liked it very much. He did elegant, clean-cut clothes—the kind she could be very creative with. He'd have been someone to watch even if he were not so damned good-looking and charming.

A visit to the theater together had followed the showing, but they had still called it work because the leading lady in the off-Broadway play wore Howard's clothes, and *Divine* was doing a feature on her. They shared an after-theater drink at a dim bar at a genteel midtown hotel, where Howard had made it clear he was interested in her as a woman, not just as a fashion editor.

"I have some friends with a house in the Hamptons they hardly use once summer's over," he told her. "Some weekends I pile the car with books and albums and enjoy a kind of retreat. I go on long walks, watch the sea..."

"Mmmm...it sounds like heaven," she purred.

She sat close to him on the banquette. He took her hands and held them. An alarming feeling pulsed through her body. She removed her hands to search for a cigarette, which he lit for her. She considered him through the smoke.

"You're very sure of your attraction, aren't you, Howard?"

He frowned, began to smile, and stopped. "Why I...I

took it for granted there is a mutual attraction between us.
I hoped—"

"I'll introduce you to my daughter one of these days,"
she said, taking a long puff of her cigarette. "You'll like
her. She's pretty! Fresh!"

Howard caught at her wrist angrily, scattering ash: "Are
you trying to provoke me?"

Coral's eyes flickered over the room. "Please, Howard!
People will—"

"Fuck them!" he said.

She noticed a slightly dangerous twist to his mouth she
hadn't noticed before, but his passion excited her. She
looked into his dark eyes, which now burned into hers,
and glanced at his curly dark hair.

"What would we do in Southampton?" she asked huskily.

"Well," he laughed, "we'd hardly drive all the way out
there to play with our Barbie dolls!"

She laughed too, wanting to finger the back of his
head, where the hair grew in fronds that grazed his neck.
She liked his skin, wanted to run her fingers over it, feel
his strong, blunt hands on her.

"You're an up-and-coming designer, Howard," she said.
"I could be very useful to you. . . ."

He dropped her hand, and she reached for his. "No,
listen to me. If you knew of all the times I've been wooed
by eager young designers, photographers, makeup and
hair people. I've made it a rule to never let anyone get to
me."

"Except *me!*" he urged, his shining eyes boring into
hers. "I *know* I've gotten through to you, Coral. I feel it.
Here!" He pressed her hand into his lap, and with an
excited lurch of her stomach, she felt his excitement. She
withdrew her hand, looking at him. He laughed. "You
see, you've got through to *me!* In spite of you being a
big-shot editor, which I wish to God you weren't . . ." He
brought her fingers to his mouth and kissed them quickly.
The warm breath on her hand aroused her. "Sometimes
there's a feeling," he said, "a spark between two people.
They just click! It's chemical, or biological. Tell me you
don't feel it too!"

Yes. Oh, God! If only she wasn't feeling it! The touch of
his thigh alongside hers on the seat. His presence, his
smell—but it was too damned dangerous.

"I have an incredibly full day tomorrow," she said, gathering her purse.

"I'm sure *all* your days are incredibly full," he replied bitterly, then threw a ten dollar bill onto the table.

At the exit a flashbulb suddenly exploded, blinding her. "Who *are* you!?" She shouted angrily at the photographer.

"Don't you recognize me, Mrs. Stanton? It's Aldo, from *Women's Wear*. Whose dress are you wearing, please?"

She glanced at Howard before saying, "It's by Howard Austin. The new young American fashion hope."

In the taxi back to her apartment, he joked, "I hope that makes the cover and not the Fashion Victims page."

She turned on him furiously. "Did you alert *Women's Wear* to be there?"

He flashed her an angry look. "Do I look that hungry?"

Coral shrugged, saying nothing.

"I've been called everything from a gigolo to a hustler tonight," he said. "In an elegant way, of course—"

"I'm sorry," she murmured. "That man gave me a shock."

She reached for his hand, and held it. Just before arriving at her apartment building, she turned and kissed him. It was supposed to be a brief, apologetic kiss, but he quickly planted his mouth on hers, over hers. The feel of his lips and the quick thrust of his tongue was a hundred times better than she had imagined. It triggered a leap of lust inside her, something that threatened to get out of control. When he helped her out of the cab, she swayed and almost lost her balance.

She held his arm for a moment, looking into his face, and said firmly, "Good night, Howard. Thank you," then walked into the building without turning around.

The sophisticated clients of Impressionati, a new Italian restaurant which managed to make simply prepared pasta incredibly expensive, stared at the striking couple seated on the star banquette.

"I never imagined I'd be discussing my love-life with you, Colin," Coral said.

She flicked her cigarette impatiently while the waiter cleared their plates. Colin feasted his eyes upon her. She wore a white Courreges shift in soft wool. He was in his usual black turtleneck and black corduroy jeans. It had become his signature, topped off by a John Lennon black cap found in Harlem.

"I'm attracted to him, Colin," Coral said simply. "If only he were ten years older..."

Colin patted her hand, which was weighted down with gold, silver, and bronze bangles.

"You're the only soul in the world I could tell this to," she went on. "You really should have been a shrink, Colin. Or a Catholic priest. I tell you things I could never tell Wayland. He'd either laugh at me or sulk with jealousy."

"And how do you know *I'm* not terribly jealous?"

She frowned at him. "*Are* you, darling? How perfectly *sweet!*"

Colin had become her new confidant. Now that Wayland was Mia's unofficial guardian, a certain distance had come between them, a distance that had grown when Wayland cancelled HQ's fifty-page advertising supplement the day after Maynard's death. Lloyd now thought she'd invented that story. Besides, she felt responsible for Colin's move to New York and his subsequent success. His fashion sense and knowledge, coupled with the impeccable British accent and kindly manner—not to mention the speed with which he delivered his assignments—had swept him to the very top of the fashion tree.

But by far the best thing about Colin, Coral thought, was that he listened so supremely well. The art of listening was rare in New York. She sought him out to dine with her at least weekly, *Divine* footing the bill. But if she'd had to pay for dinner from her own pocket, she would still have felt it was worth every penny. There was something magical about this tiny, odd-looking person who drew so exquisitely. His kind blue eyes reflected a flattering vision of herself which she liked and was becoming almost addicted to. To everyone else, she knew she was Superbitch or Dragon Lady—they were in awe of her, or afraid of her. But Colin related to her as a human being, and—yes—now that she thought of it, as a woman.

She realized she wanted him to approve of her, that she cared about his opinion. She did not care if they made a ridiculous-looking pair, if she towered over him, if people stared, or if *WWD*, running photographs of them dining out, tagged them "Fashion's Odd Couple."

"It would be my first affair since my marriage ended," she told him.

"My God!" Colin marveled. "You've been a virtual nun!"

"I've poured my sexual energy into the magazine," she said. "I like to think it shows. *Divine is* a sexy book, isn't it, Colin?"

"Positively erotic!" he agreed. "Almost kinky, now that you're using Helmut Newton such a lot."

"Colin, in the sixties all the barriers, the restraints, are being swept away. *I* want to be swept away, too! It's high time *I* acknowledged my natural, animal urges. . . ."

Colin watched her as she convinced herself to have an affair. For him she was now even more unattainable. And even more attractive.

Their double espressos arrived and she held up her white porcelain demitasse. "To love!" Coral proposed, sipping the scalding coffee. "Or at least a reasonable facsimile of it."

"To love," Colin echoed sadly, lifting his cup to hers.

Seven

Mia woke on Saturdays to the sound of Wayland whistling, going about his chores. He liked to wear an old yachting cap to bustle about the neighborhood, picking up his dry cleaning, buying the odd item. He usually liked Mia to join him, but today she felt like exploring alone.

She took a bus down to the Village and browsed in the basement boutiques, fingering Indian shawls, Mexican serapes and ponchos, enjoying the colors. By noon she'd reached the Figaro, her favorite hideout. She ordered a cinnamon cappuccino, and sketched the beatniks playing chess and nodding to the Bach music that filled the cafe. Near her a bearded man read the *Village Voice*.

"You can't sketch in here!"

She twisted around and saw David, smiling.

"I don't believe this! I was thinking of calling you today. I had your number with me—"

A waitress stopped by the table. "Can I get you anything?" she asked David.

"Another cinnamon cappuccino," Mia ordered.

"Thanks!" David said as the girl moved off. "You just used up my food allowance for the weekend." He sat in the chair opposite Mia.

"It's only eighty-five cents."

"Coffee's a dime at a place near me!" he replied.

"It'll be on me, okay?"

As they sipped their coffee they gossiped about Mac-Millans, their courses, their fellow students, the teachers. It was the first time Mia had been alone with David in a social setting, outside of the school. Mackenzie had al-

91

ways forced them into a threesome. It was nice being
alone with him, she felt, gazing into his blue eyes.

He suddenly reached for her hand. "Wanna see where I
live? Bet you've never seen a real slum before?"

When they reached his street in the East Village, she
tried to look casual. It was pretty shabby, she thought.
"Grotty," Mackenzie would have said. One or two junkies
sat propped up on stoops and some kids kicked an empty
soda can back and forth across the street.

He led her up some steps littered with torn newspaper,
unlocked the first door on the right and threw it open.

"My first visitor!" he announced, letting her pass.

The long narrow room had been whitewashed and the
few pieces of furniture painted white. David's bed had a
gray blanket tucked tightly over it. A pile of books and
magazines by the bed included issues of *Divine*. He turned
on a radio and the tinny sounds of the Beatles enlivened
the room. Mia felt herself trembling.

"Is it cold in here?" she asked.

David shrugged. "Could be." He leaned against the
wall, watching her.

She suddenly realized she was cold with fear. She was
alone with a handsome man, and they would probably
touch. She did not know how to behave or how to tell
him of her fear. Nervously, she crossed to where he had
pinned some of his sketches to the wall.

"I love your drawings," she said, trying to stop her
teeth from chattering. "I always peek at them when you
take your coffee break."

He sat down on the bed, looking at her intently. Suddenly he held out his arms toward her. She forgot her fear
for a moment and approached him, leaning into his embrace. She held onto David's broad shoulders as she
looked down at his angular legs in their faded jeans. His
arms enfolded her and her heart began to beat faster. . . .

In the shower Coral scrubbed to shiny red soreness the
body that had not received a man's touch for so many
years. She inspected her nakedness in the long mirror,
trying to see herself as Howard would see her. She was
proud of her appearance, the result of diet, massage, and
discipline.

He was waiting for her in a red sports car. The doorman

opened the door for her, and Howard jumped out of the car to take her bag and throw it in the tiny space at the back. Then he took her hand and kissed it. He inspected her tight blue jeans, enormous white sweater, and white espadrilles.

"So this is what a fashion editor wears for a weekend?" he asked, grinning. "And I break my head trying to design 'traveling outfits.'"

She smiled as he started the car, glancing at his tanned hands on the wheel.

"I'm as nervous as a new kid at school," he told her, revving the engine.

"Don't be." She covered his hand with hers. He leaned over when they stopped at a light, kissing the side of her throat.

"No." She broke away. "Not here. Not now."

They did not touch again during the three-hour drive. She questioned him about his life, and he told her that his father was a coffee importer, his mother a gifted seamstress. He had apprenticed for a coat manufacturer, studying nights at the Art Students League. Hawking his folio from showroom to showroom had finally led to his first small collection, his first write-up in *WWD*, and the sudden arrival of a Bloomingdale's buyer. It was a familiar story, one Coral had heard from many designers, but no one had sounded quite as happy about it as Howard.

"I do five collections a year now, under various labels, and I want to do not just clothes, but *fashion!*"

"And the name of Howard Austin on sheets, luggage, cosmetics?"

He grinned. "Why not? If Pierre Cardin can do it—"

"I agree. Why not?" It only took that bit of luck: an order from an influential buyer, a huge plug in the fashion press. She must try to forget she was editor of *Divine*, at least for today. She rolled down the window and took a deep breath of air as they neared the coast. It was the last weekend in September and still warm.

The house was white with giant plants in all the right places. The sofas were covered in spotless white canvas. The tiled floors were immaculate. The pool, around which was built a wooden deck, was surrounded by lounge chairs and striped umbrellas. Howard slid open the glass doors, showing her the house proudly, as if it were his. Coral could not help smiling.

She peered at the modern paintings hanging in the living room. "Who *are* these people?" she asked.

"Would you believe intellectual *schmatta* folk?" He laughed. "They're in their fifties. Very hip, very chic..."

"Whoever they are, it's sweet of them to lend you their home. I like it."

He took a step toward her and said, "And I like *you*!"

He caught her in his arms, pressing his mouth down onto hers. His tongue was in her mouth, curling, flicking, moving against her tongue. She became almost dizzy, his strong arm supporting her as she bent back. They kissed like two figures frozen in a tango.

She broke away, gasping. "Howard, I—"

He placed his finger gently on her lips and she opened her mouth and playfully bit on it. He half carried her around the room with him as he undid the blinds, letting them down so they shadowed the room with slats of light. At the stereo he tuned in some classical piano music. Then he carried her into the bedroom and gently set her on the bed. Hovering over her, his arms on each side of her, his eyes smiled into hers. Slowly he lowered himself onto her, bringing their mouths together.

She had not realized her body would go crazy, but like the first drink a reformed alcoholic takes, Howard's kiss unhinged her. She thrust her fingers through his dark, curly hair, pulling his head back as he nuzzled her throat. He stuck his hand inside her jeans, unzipping, curving his fingers under her, into her.

"You're wet down there," he murmured. "I knew you would be."

His touch snapped the last restraint. As his lips lightly brushed hers and his fingers moved, sending almost unbearably sensual tremors through her, she pushed up to meet him fiercely, wanting their mouths to kiss brutally, to bruise. Suddenly she needed them both to be naked. She began to pull off her clothes and he broke away to ease off his pants. When she was naked, he made her stand before him.

"Turn slowly," he asked and she did, blessing the grueling regime that had kept her trim.

"You're even elegant without clothes," Howard breathed,

touching her gently. She ran her hands appraisingly over his tanned chest.

"I adore hairy men," she said, and leaned to tease his ear with her tongue.

"What do you like?" he whispered. "I'll do anything you want."

"Everything!" she replied. "I'll like anything and everything you do to me!" He pushed her back onto the bed and knelt beside it. Spreading her legs, he nuzzled his face between them. She mòaned as she felt his nose and mouth rub against her, her head jerking back with a cry of pleasure. It was almost too intense. He tried to lick, to suck, to nibble *there*, where she could hardly stand the feeling.

"*Oh!*" she cried out, "that'll drive me crazy."

He glanced up at her, smiling. "That's the idea."

His erect sex poked up from between his legs, and when she reached down to stroke it, it moved to her touch. He put his face against her thighs, his breath hot and moist on her skin, his tongue flicking.

"Just relax, Coral," he whispered in her ear, his breath sending shivers of delight through her. "Listen to the music," he said, urging her gently back onto the bed, sitting on the floor before her, his face in her lap.

Listen to the music? She was hearing a strange kind of music of her own, a whirligig, honky-tonk rhythm of sexual pleasure that ran in direct counterpoint to the Liszt or Brahms or whatever it was on the radio.

"Lie back, darling," he pleaded.

He held her knees, her legs, then slowly tongued her thighs, kissing, nibbling, biting gently inside them, working his way slowly up until she cried out, twisting on the bed, giving herself up to this voluptuous pleasure. Now he lapped at her most vulnerable part. His tongue was giving her pleasure she had never felt before. She held his tanned shoulders with her white, red-tipped hands. Her heart constricted, she held her breath, felt her pulse pound, race, as her body started to move of its own accord. She felt it thrust against him, push against his head, against his tongue—wanting it deeper inside her. And soon she dragged him up to lie on her, full-length, his sex pressing into her belly as she stroked his back, held his muscular buttocks in her hands, tested the hard thighs. She murmured that she wanted him inside her and slowly, tenderly, he inched in and she lost her breath, teetered on unconsciousness as he began his dance, an almost mechanical, steady thrust that was smooth as velvet inside her, oiled, relentless. She groaned, cried out, kissed his ears, gently biting on the lobes.

"Oh, darling, don't stop . . . don't *stop*!" She ground up against him, rode under him, clung to him as he moved above her, back and forth, faster, inside her, like a wild animal or a bucking young colt. The waves of pleasure began, each leaving her exhausted yet on the brink of another. Wave after wave of orgasm racked her body. Finally she began to giggle, to tell him to come—that this was too wonderful, it was almost starting to hurt.

Only then did he move quicker inside her, lifting his body slightly off hers now as he looked down at her, shuddered, sighed, trembled inside her and then gave a long drawn-out cry which sounded like a cry of torture, or surprised pain, but which she knew was ecstasy. He shuddered for a few long moments, as she felt his release in her. Then he collapsed, his head lolling on her breast, panting, as she ran her fingers reassuringly again and again through his tousled, wet hair as if to calm him.

Soon, the sweat cooling on their bodies, both slept. The best, she thought as she drifted into unconsciousness. The best I've *ever* had. . . .

David and Mia embraced awkwardly on his narrow bed. She could smell the fresh soap on his neck as she nuzzled there. They held each other for long moments, changing positions slowly, hugging tightly. Tensely, she waited for him to do more. But he did not attempt to touch her breasts or to kiss her deeply the way other boys had tried to do at the end of dates. The tension seeped from her body, the cold fear left. He was not going to do more than hug her. Releasing her, he lay back on the bed. He clasped his hands behind his head and smiled up at her. She sat on the edge of the bed, watching him.

"I like you so much, David," she blurted. "Let's always be friends." He sat up and put his arm around her. She rested her head against his broad chest, touching the back of his head with her fingers.

"What should we do?" he asked. "Treat ourselves to a

triple-bill movie on Forty-second Street? Or a hot dog in the park? The budget could just stretch!"

She looked around the room; suddenly, now that she knew David was gentle and shy there was nothing she would rather do than stay there all afternoon. He pulled her to her feet.

"Come see where *I* live," she suggested. "Wayland will be out all afternoon."

They walked uptown for a few blocks before giving in and taking a bus to Fifty-seventh Street. "Very central!" David approved. "I hate to think what your rent must be."

"He owns it," Mia told him.

David whistled. She knew that compared to most of the other students, she was horribly overprivileged. She had tried to keep a very low profile, even with David. Now she was forced to tell him a little about Wayland and the powerful position he held at Headquarters.

In the apartment David stared at the view and Wayland's ultramodern furniture. She got them each a Coke, a little nervous that Wayland might suddenly appear and give David the third degree.

"Come see my room!" She led him along the passage. "Ta *da*!" She threw open her door. David walked in, bending to look at the shelves containing some of her childhood treasures.

"If you hang out that window, you can practically see the street," she told him. He leaned over the bed to press his face to the window. She stood just behind him.

He turned to look at her, his face worried, his eyes intense. "Back then, in my apartment, I wanted to make love to you," he told her in a low voice.

She felt her teeth begin to chatter. "*And?*" She tried to sound cool.

"I guess I lost my nerve. There's something about you that—" Abruptly he let himself fall onto her bed, pulling her down with him, clasping her tightly in his arms. He pressed his mouth firmly on hers, his tongue trying to insert itself between her teeth. The fear leaped up in her immediately, panicking her.

"*David!*" she cried, managing to break away.

His body pressed back to hers; he was very strong. She tried to enjoy this sudden outburst of affection. *Isn't this what you wanted an hour ago in David's apartment?* she asked herself. The nicest boy she'd ever met wanted to make love to her. Just the thought made her body shiver, her teeth chatter. He brought his hands up under her blouse, cupping her soft breasts. He squeezed there, gently, inserting his fingers under the silk bra and touching her nipples. A cold hard lump of dread knotted in her stomach, made her want to scream. He was fingering her nipples, nibbling on her mouth.

The familiar iciness now engulfed her. She lay stiffly as he kissed her neck, pulled off her clothes, unbuttoning, unzipping. *If I just let him,* she thought, trying to calm herself, *if I just leave it all to him and try to feel nothing at all, I'll be fine.*

When he got down to her underwear, she lay still on the bed, watching him as he pulled off his shirt, shucked his jeans. His body was smooth, muscled, like a swimmer's, but it provoked no desire, only fear. He was wearing boxer shorts against which his aroused sex strained. She looked away. This is part of growing up, she told herself. The longer I put it off, the more difficult it will be. She averted her eyes as he took off his shorts. He lay on top of her and she felt his hot sex on her stomach. He moved his hips down to try to get it between her legs, which she tightly squeezed together. It was suddenly so frenzied, so hurried. His chest muffled her mouth. She was going from icy to hot and back to icy. He nuzzled his face in her breasts, freeing them from her bra.

"No!" she cried, startling him.

He sat up quickly, concerned, looking down at her. "What's wrong?"

"I can't!" she gasped, her eyes tightly shut, as she shook her head. "I can't do it, David! I can't. I'm—I'm a virgin!"

He kissed her neck gently. "It'll be all right," he murmured. "I'll be very careful. Very gentle. I won't hurt you, Mia."

"No..." she whimpered.

He pulled her panties down to her knees and she raised her body and pulled them back up. He laughed, thinking she was teasing. He lay full-length on her again, and she could barely breathe.

"You're beautiful, Mia," he told her. "Really beautiful.

Just relax." Her hands automatically held his back, moved down to the twin globes of his buttocks. She could feel him rubbing against her stomach. He ground his hips against hers, placed his hand between her legs to rub her there.

"Oh, I *can't!*" she screamed. "Please! I'm not kidding ...I'm not ready!"

"Oh, God," David moaned. "Oh God, *I'm* ready! Oh, *Mia!*"

He gave a loud shout and a long drawn-out moan, and to her horror, she felt his entire body go into a spasm, an electrified series of jerks. Then spurts of warm stuff jetted out of him over her stomach. Each time he gasped and shuddered, his breath halting in her ear, she screamed "*No!*" as if someone were pouring molten lead over her.

He stopped moving, and the room was silent but for her sobbing. David got up and returned with a handful of tissues to wipe her stomach. She kept her eyes tightly shut. This wasn't happening. Oh, *please*, God, she prayed, let this not be happening! She could not open her eyes, must not see his face. As he reached for more tissues, she got up and ran.

"Mia? What—"

He tried to grab her, but she reached the bathroom before he could, and slammed the door shut, locking it. She tore off her panties and bra, sobbing, running under the hot water of the shower. She let it run over her, holding her face up to its cleansing flow. She would stay there, under that clean water, for as long as she possibly could.

David pounded on the door. "What's wrong, Mia? What's the matter?"

"Get out!" she shouted. "*Please* just go!"

She could not possibly face him. She wouldn't have known how to look at him. When she heard the front door slam, she sobbed with relief.

Wayland returned at five with some friends. They had seen a private screening of outtakes from *All About Eve*, and each was giving his own imitation of Bette Davis smoking a cigarette.

Wayland insisted on Mia joining them, pouring her a vodkatini every bit as large as his. Why not? she thought, gulping down her drink. It went straight to her head.

Soon she was doing the silliest imitation and they were all applauding. After another round of drinks Wayland constructed a kind of shrine to Bette Davis atop his credenza. He lined up a dozen framed photographs of the star and lit some candles, placing them before the photos. They turned off the lights and everyone had to kneel in turn before it, cross himself with a lit cigarette, then stand and say, "What a *dump*!" In the middle of all this camp gaiety, Mia felt tears streaming down her cheeks. She ran quickly to the bathroom, locked the door leaving the light off, squatting on the bath mat, holding onto the edge of the tub.

"Oh, God . . . what's *wrong* with me?" she moaned. "There's something wrong. What *is* it?"

So this was what other women gave up careers for, gave up ambition for?

Coral drifted back into consciousness as Howard slept gently at her breast. Her fingers, still entwined in his hair, let go. Her mind clicked into action. Feelings had been awakened. They stirred uneasily inside her now, awaking other worries, fears, gaps in her life. The intensity of these feelings unnerved her. They were in direct opposition to the rules of fashion. Good taste, great fashion, was all about denial, discipline, making less mean more. Great sex, the wave of sexual pleasure that had swept her body, making her happy to die of it, would give the lie to fashion.

In that world of pleasure, clothes were made meaningless, for what was more beautiful than her naked body pressed up to his? Sex was dangerous—a minefield. But oh, God, it had felt so good! It *had* been the best she had ever had. But if she gave in to it now, it would prove she had lived her life in the wrong way. *I'm not like other women*, she reminded herself. She practiced more discipline, whether with food, exercise, rising at six each morning, cold showers, *any*thing! She would extend that discipline to include this artist of sex—or rather, to exclude him.

His brown shoulder was just below her chin. If she stuck out her tongue, she could taste him. If only he were not sleeping atop her, she could make a stealthy exit, leave a note, take the next train back to Manhattan.

Slowly she nudged him off her, conscious of his warm flesh, the good smell of him. He awoke with a start, smiling sleepily at her.

"I have to get up," she said. She sprang to her feet and ran quickly to the bathroom. She heard his long, loud yawn, and then his call, "That was *wonderful!*"

When she appeared, she was fully dressed, her makeup refreshed, in her usual immaculate condition. He sat on the edge of the bed, wearing his shorts, sleepy-eyed.

"Why did you dress?" he asked, surprised.

"Why improve on perfection?" She leaned over and kissed his forehead. He pulled her to him, but she deftly moved away. "Now don't be angry, but I'm going home, Howard."

"What?" He frowned. "Are you kidding me?"

"Just put me on a train. You stay here," she said, looking in the mirror and giving her hair a quick ruffle.

"I don't understand—don't you feel that what we had back there was kind of special?" He was serious, stepping into his pants, pulling on loafers.

"*Too* special."

"What does *that* mean?"

She regarded him, softening slightly. "Oh, Howard, of *course* it was special! God, it was the best sex I've ever had in my *life!* It's just that this"—she gestured at the rumpled bed—"isn't for me. Don't worry, you'll get your spread—how does four pages sound?"

Howard laughed bitterly, the joy drained from his face. "That reduces me to your level, Coral, and I'm not *on* your level. I really *like* you. Doesn't anyone like you?"

She turned away. "I have hundreds of friends, as you well know. I would have featured you anyway. We need designers like you in America. It's just that at this time in my life, I can't—" She stopped, shrugging helplessly.

"Can't relate to humans?" he asked. He caught her arms, shaking her, forcing her to look at him. "Have you taken so many photographic shoots you can't see real life anymore?"

She broke away. "Don't manhandle me, Howard. I *do* see real life, and I don't always like what I see. Especially when it's a woman *d'un certain âge*, about to make an enormous fool of herself. A woman who cannot afford to be emotional. . . ."

"*Afford?*" he echoed. "We either experience emotion or we don't."

"I protect myself against it!"

"Oh, you don't need protection. You don't *have* emotions, Coral," he said harshly.

"Is lust an emotion?" she asked him. "If so, I plead guilty."

He drove her back to Manhattan with the radio playing, no conversation between them. Just once, she said, "I wish you'd have stayed for the weekend."

"Alone?"

"You'd soon meet some lovely young thing. Or an attractive older woman, if that's really what turns you on."

He glanced at her. "Perhaps you believe in all this sexual revolution stuff, but I liked *you*! I wanted to find out what you were all about, your hopes, your dreams—"

"*They're* no secret!" She twisted in her seat to face him. "I want to stay editor-in-chief of *Divine* for as long as I can! I must devote myself a hundred percent to that!"

He pulled up at the curb when they reached her apartment, turning to her and holding her shoulders. He kissed the side of her neck gently, and she tried not to feel it.

"I know it's scary," he whispered. "It's scary for me too. I expected so much from this weekend, and I got even more than I expected from you. It's rare for two people to feel that good with each other. And I'm not like most of the people in this business. I'm a decent person, Coral. And I'm in love with you...."

She turned to look warily into his eyes. "Love?" she echoed doubtfully. "It's not as easy as that."

"Maybe it *is* that easy? Maybe this is one of those one-in-a-million times when it just clicks—"

"No!" she said, and saw the pain flood his eyes.

"But you *want* me, Coral. I *know* you do! The way you let yourself go back there—"

"It frightened me," she admitted. "These feelings frighten me—I've shut them up for so long. Now I see why. They're overpowering. They're the reason most women let their lives get sidetracked—"

"You think being in love is getting sidetracked?"

"If it means neglecting one's career, yes, I do." She

kissed his cheek, opened the door, then hesitated for a moment.

"Am I going to see you again?" he asked.

"You know how incestuous this business is, Howard. We're bound to run into each other."

He sat and watched her sweep past the doorman with her dazzling smile, holding the little weekend bag she had not opened. Leaning his forehead on his hands over the steering wheel, he tried to collect himself. Finally he straightened and caught a sight of his pained eyes in the rearview mirror. He was damned if he'd give up that easily. Starting the car, he glanced up at her building and said aloud, "Only *au revoir* ... and next time you'll beg me for it."

Eight

All that weekend David kept calling her. Wayland was told to say she wasn't in. But after a night's sleep and the realization that she'd be seeing him on Monday, Mia knew she would have to somehow make her peace with him. When he called at noon on Sunday, she spoke to him.

"Feeling all right?" David asked, concerned. "What the hell happened?"

"David..." She took the phone into her room and carefully closed the door. "I felt sick. I panicked. I just wasn't ready. I don't know what..." She trailed off. "I don't really know what to say to you."

"Well, let's at least stay friends," he suggested. "Do you think you could stand that?"

She heaved a long, weary sigh. "Of course I'd like to be friends. But only if we can pretend that yesterday never happened."

"Okay. Fine by me. It never happened. You sure you feel okay? I mean, I felt like a rapist afterward. I—"

"Stop. Let's not talk about it. We're just going to pretend—"

"Nothing happened. I promise. I'll see you tomorrow, Mia."

From then on Mackenzie was always with her. They became a familiar twosome around the school.

But Mackenzie had her own problems. The Beatles' "She's Leaving Home" became her theme song. It wasn't easy for a Jewish girl to leave home; it would have to be planned secretly. *Divine*'s tuition award covered all fees, some travel, and materials costs. A little was left over for lunches. If she added weekends of waitressing, she might just stretch the money to cover a quarter share of a Village apartment. "It will be a slum," she told Mia, "but my *own* slum!" She scanned apartment-sharing ads in the *Village Voice*. And now she had a new friend to aid her—Alistair.

No one was too sure exactly who Alistair Briarly was. The best thing about him was his British accent, and even that changed from day to day, from very grand to a kind of cockney, to his own brand of New Yorkese. He was tall and skinny, with blond hair and pale blue eyes. He looked like a cherubic choirboy with a wicked glint in his eyes. MacMillans's cafeteria was his hangout, and he knew all the motherly waitresses. Now and then he had been known to pay for designs for a rock group he managed, four Brooklyn boys called The Henry Eighths who pretended they were from Liverpool. He had distributed free tickets in the cafeteria for their first public appearance at a Village club's talent night; Mackenzie had been the only student to show up.

Since then Alistair had been attentive and charming. An English boy was the hip accessory of 1964, so Mackenzie was flattered when he leaned his chin on his hands, stared at her as she chewed on a bagel, and told her, "You fascinate me!"

"Why?" she asked quickly. She wanted to know exactly what a man saw in her so she could enhance it.

"You're so . . . American, I suppose. Like a fictional character from a film I once saw or something."

"You mean, like Marilyn Monroe or Liz Taylor?"

"I was thinking of Shelley Winters, actually."

"Thanks a lot." She pushed him.

He was confident, cocky. "A bullshit artist," Mackenzie told Mia. "Like me!"

"What do you do with yourself all day while we work our behinds off in this jail?" she asked him.

"I do a different kind of work." he said. "I put people together. Contacts. Heard of Vidal Sassoon? I'm helping launch his salons. I promote my group. I have a finger in many pies, Mack."

Alistair didn't talk much about the life he had left behind in England. He obviously enjoyed being a bit of a mystery, but she managed to dig out the information that he was the black sheep of an upper-class family and had been educated at Eton, a school he'd despised. His mother had died when he was a child.

"I never got on too well with my father," he muttered, and suddenly seemed like a cowed little boy.

She felt she understood him so well. The brash, aggressive act he put on was obviously his defense system. Attracted by artists, rock and roll, and "anything American," he had escaped to New York.

"I'm the black sheep too," Mackenzie confided, her dark eyes gazing seriously into his pale blue ones. "I always felt I was, like, *better* than my family. For years I nurtured this *certainty* that my real mother was Gloria Vanderbilt. I mean, it wasn't a fantasy—I really *believed* it!"

She shrugged. "But you *have* to be nuts to succeed in New York. You've also gotta be hungry—hungry for success, or fame, or riches. . . ."

"Which are *you* hungry for?"

"*All* of them!" She laughed, finishing her coffee. "And not just hungry, Alistair. *Famished! Starved!* I want it *all*! But it's funny. It's like I know I'll be famous. It's a feeling I have inside me. When I won that *Divine* contest, one side of me was so thrilled! The other side just shrugged and said 'So? You knew you'd do it.'"

Alistair nodded, watching her. She had an aura of success around her. "Yeah, you have to believe in your dreams."

She loved talking with him. He fed her fantasies. Telling her dreams and plans to a classy guy from England—this was how she wanted her life to be. He never laughed at her. Away from the roots of Abe Goldstein, her crude brothers, and her poor, faded mother—she could blossom, *be* the new Mackenzie she had always wanted to be.

"I'm slowly getting my style together," she told Alistair. "But I sure won't find it as long as I'm living with my family. They destroy my inspiration. I've gotta get out of there! Soon!"

"You'll find a way," he promised, "if you want it enough. Maybe I can help you."

Alistair began to store her belongings in his untidy walk-up on Seventh Street. Each morning she smuggled out clothes, books, magazines or records in her school bag. Alistair would pick them up at school.

Sometimes they bought Chinese food to eat in his

apartment between school and her waitressing. But fighting off Alistair's advances, which increased in proportion to the help he was providing, spoiled these meals. She loved hearing him say he was crazy about her—it was great for her ego—but she did not want her first grownup affair to begin amidst the empty, greasy cartons of chow mein. It did not have the class which she had decided must now pervade every aspect of her life. Alistair did not insist. After the first few tussles, he would get back to discussing money-making schemes—his brain was always ticking. He disbanded his pop group which wasn't getting anywhere, and began to approach the boutiques springing up around New York, offering to do publicity for them. He smelled the potential in Mackenzie, too. Her designs were original, zany, and new. His approval and faith added to her confidence. She began to need his compliments the way she needed a cup of coffee in the morning.

Some nights she arrived home at seven. Since the Goldsteins always ate early for Abe's indigestion, dinner was over by the time she returned. Mackenzie would sit with her mother in the kitchen, eating what had been kept warm for her, discussing her day.

"Your father would like to see the designs you're working on at school, darling," Esther urged one night. It was December and cold, and she had made her famous *borscht*.

Mackenzie rolled her eyes. "Oh, God, *why*? He doesn't like what I do—he doesn't understand it. Even the teachers at school don't all go for it."

"So, why don't you try to please your teachers?" Esther asked.

"I have to please myself first!" Mackenzie snapped.

Esther gave a heart-rending sigh. Her role was to keep the peace, to act as go-between for her volatile daughter and her irritable husband.

Later, Abe Goldstein made the pilgrimage to his daughter's room, knocking loudly and walking in. She turned to the wild pages of her sketchbook, decorated in neon felt tip. Abe took the book, fumbling for his spectacles. He stared at her miniskirts with matching luminous wigs, the skimpy tee-shirt dresses, the disco outfits with holes cut out at the back or above the bosom.

"It's like the Sunday funnies," he remarked, handing the book back.

Mackenzie laughed. "That's a good description, Dad. That's what girls want to look like—pop, op, zany, funny."

"Yeah?" Abe shrugged, unconvinced. "You know what we're selling like there's no tomorrow? House mu-mus."

"What are they?"

"They're like housecoats, but in wild Hawaiian prints. Multicolored. Nineteen ninety-five, and I keep selling out of 'em."

"Well, that's great."

"Think you could design stuff like that?" he asked. "Like house mu-mus?"

Mackenzie shrugged. "I dunno. I suppose so. If someone held a gun to my head."

Abe shifted his feet, then sat on the edge of her bed, facing her. "Your brothers are doing pretty good at the stores. They don't regret coming into the business. *You* used to do some pretty good selling on weekends, remember? My plan was to groom all of you to take over. *I* can't go on forever. I don't have the strength."

"You've been saying that for years."

"And each year I grow weaker." He gave her his "You'll be sorry" look, designed to inspire guilt. "If you ever feel like quitting that school, I'd set you up in your own workshop. When we see something is selling well, you could quickly make a pattern, and we'll get a couple seamstresses. We'll eliminate the middleman. You won't have to do your own sewing, like you used to. What do you say?"

Mackenzie shook her head. "I liked doing that. It was one of the few things I *did* like—designing my own dresses and then making them. I don't want to copy someone's design. I have my *own* designs!"

"*These?*" He closed the sketchbook. "What kind of person would wear *these*? Freaks?"

"Yeah! Freaks like me!"

He glanced at her tiny leather skirt and ribbed white stockings. "It's no joke. In my book, you do dress like a freak!"

She laughed. "Good! I *want* people like you to think I look like a freak! Your Bronx housewives in their Hawai-

ian mu-mus are freaky to *me*! They have nothing to do
with fashion."

"Fashion is the clothes women are wearing!" Abe shouted.

"Uh-uh," Mackenzie replied. "Fashion is ahead of all
that."

"Ahead!" Abe stood, grimacing. "You think you'll make
money from stuff like that? This school isn't teaching you
what's important—how to make a living!"

She stood, too, trying to stay patient. "I'll make a living!
But I can only design stuff *I* think is good."

"In my book that's stubborn!" He snapped, and stalked
out of the room.

Reggie and Max poked their faces around the door.
"Why d'you always have to get him mad?" Max asked.

"Because I don't kiss ass the way you do," she called
out.

"Any pretty chicks at your school, Mack?"

"Sure! Plenty—what makes you think they'd want to
meet you?"

Max grabbed at his crotch. "'Cause we got what it
takes."

"God, you're both so *crude*, you know that?" she
screamed. "You think my friends would even put up with
the way you two *eat*?"

She slammed the door shut on them, sat down on her
bed, and held her head in her hands. Oh, God, get me *out*
of here! she prayed.

Colin had just sketched some of Howard Austin's new
collection for a six-page spread in *Divine*. He had invited
Howard to his studio for a drink, an advance view of the
drawings, and because he wanted to meet another man in
love with Coral.

"You're Coral's best friend," Howard told him. "That's
what *Women's Wear* keeps saying."

Colin agreed. "I adore the woman."

Howard stared earnestly at him. "I'd adore her, too, if
she allowed me to get close to her."

Colin shifted in his seat. "What do you want me to tell
you, Howard?" he asked. "The way to Coral's heart? I'm
not entirely sure she has one. Perhaps it's been generously
donated to the fashion industry? I mean, she *is* giving you
this spread because she loves your clothes."

"Bullshit!" Howard gulped his drink. "This spread is my payoff! She told me as much after Southampton. 'You'll get your spread!' she said, as if I were some escort service."

"You *are* upset!"

"Yeah, she got to me." He finished his drink and frowned. "I don't know why I'm telling you all this."

Colin smiled. Most people said that to him as they confided.

"I guess I like older women," Howard continued in a puzzled tone. "I never realized they could be so sexy."

Colin tried not to flinch. He did not exactly relish hearing how sexy Coral was.

"I usually have quite a defense barrier up around my feelings," Howard was saying. "And the moment I let Coral through, I got it thrown back in my face. This spread should have delighted me but now it just makes me sick to my stomach. I don't even know if I want to continue designing."

Colin shook his head. "You wouldn't throw it all up because of a disappointment. Besides, what on earth would you do if you stopped designing?"

Howard laughed, embarrassed. "I've always harbored a secret desire to mount a rival to *Women's Wear*. I've already been approached with the financial backing. It would be a weekly, mostly gossip and news. Fashion people are gossip addicts, you know. They get their daily fix from the Eye column in *Women's Wear*, but it isn't enough. I'd give them a whole week's worth!"

" 'The Fashion Enquirer'?" Colin suggested.

"I'd call it 'Labels.' "

The title suddenly brought shivers to Colin—as if he had a premonition of the havoc such a paper could cause, especially if it was launched by a man with a grudge against Coral Stanton.

Howard took his sample clothing and left soon afterward.

Colin tidied up his paints and pencils, crumpling the sheets of paper on which he had made false starts, spraying the good drawings with fixative. He'd heard plenty of fashion confessions, but had never expected a handsome young designer to confess to loving and losing Coral. Howard might be one of those people who fall for the unattainable. Wasn't *he* one too? He was as in love with

Coral, but in an even more despairing, hopeless way. But at least he had made Coral his friend. At least they kissed hello and good-bye and Coral had a genuine affection and need for him. In Colin's life he had often had to settle for that kind of compromise. His heart ached when he thought of it: What he would not give for twenty-four hours in Howard Austin's tanned, healthy, *tall* body!

Colin glanced around the studio which he had hardly bothered to furnish. There was just a couch upon which he slept, a large table and the tall director's chair he sat in to draw. A tiny portable TV, a radio, a couple of chairs, and that was it. He simply didn't care about that aspect of his life. He did not propose to entertain here, and the few models who passed by to pose for him were used to bare photographers' studios and thought he lived elsewhere.

He made a supreme effort to cheer himself. He could still be Coral's friend—her very special, closest friend. Short of some miracle, that would have to do.

Howard called Coral a week later. "Champagne in some ritzy bar?" he proposed.

Coral thought for a moment. "But you've never seen my apartment. Come here and we can be private."

She thought it would be good for her ego to see him again. Having immersed herself in work since that Saturday in Southampton, Coral had not so much as even glanced at a man. But she had missed Howard and his attention. That incredible afternoon had awakened a whole host of cravings in her.

One of the pop stars she'd interviewed had casually handed her a joint during a session. Realizing she would appear unforgivably square not to take a casual puff like everyone else did, she'd inhaled and even said a few words in a funny voice while holding the smoke in her lungs. Afterward, everyone else giggled and sent out for ice cream, chocolate, and in one case, sour pickles. But the stuff had had a different effect on Coral. It made her feel sexy. She had taken a few joints home and smoked them, and those evenings when she took a warm bath, drank a glass of wine, she had actually suffered a kind of sexual agony as her body craved something she refused to supply it with: a man.

"We have a lot to catch up with," she told Howard.

* * *

"You gonna work in the store during the summer vacation?" Abe Goldstein asked Mackenzie over dinner later that spring.

Her mother and brothers watched her, wondering how she would get out of this. She took a deep breath.

"No, Dad, I don't wanna work at the store. I have other plans."

"Yeah?" Abe swallowed some Cel-Ray tonic. "Such as?"

Mackenzie dabbed at her lips with a paper napkin, looking around the table. "Don't all faint, but I have a job. I'm cocktail waitressing part-time at a very nice bar down in the Village. They get a real nice artsy crowd—very few drunks—and the tips are *great!*"

"You're gonna work late there?" Esther quickly asked.

"Only on weekends—"

"And how late is that?" Abe asked.

Mackenzie shrugged. "I don't know. Two, two-thirty, maybe—"

Esther gasped. "You'll be out on the streets in Greenwich Village at two-thirty in the morning?"

"Just forget that, young lady." Abe pounded the table. "Because *I* won't allow it."

"It's too late—I've already agreed," Mackenzie said blithely. "I start on Tuesday."

"Oh, yeah?" Abe roared. "And what if I tell you you don't have a home here if you go ahead with this cock-eyed plan?"

"Abe!" Esther cried. "You'd never throw your own flesh and blood out of her own home!"

"If she won't abide by my rules, sure I'll throw her out. Maybe we'd have some peace around here."

"You want peace?" Mackenzie stood up from the table, brushing off her mother's restraining arm. "I'll give you peace right now."

She heard Abe shout "Good riddance!" and her brothers' laughter as she ran to her room. Furious, she began packing the clothes she still kept at home. The timid little knock she heard later was, she knew, her mother's. "Come in," she said grudgingly.

"Darling..." Esther came slowly into the room, shutting the door carefully behind her. "Apologize to your

father. Forget about being a waitress and help out in your
father's store...."

Mackenzie shook her head. "I like *this* job! It's a safe
place. There's nothing to worry about, Mom."

Esther sat down on the bed, gazing up fearfully at her
daughter.

"You're such a smart girl, darling. What's a girl of your
caliber doing in a bar? Remember when you used to think
you were Gloria Vanderbilt's daughter? You think *she'd*
work in a bar?"

"Oh, *Mom!*" She knelt by her mother's side and hugged
the familiar, loving body. It was becoming impossible to
explain her life to her mother. No one in her family had
ever understood her. She kissed Esther good night and
ushered her out the door, then packed her last possessions. She waited until everyone was in their rooms and
at ten o'clock she crept out of the apartment holding a
small suitcase and two Bloomingdale's bags.

She stood a little uncertainly on the Grand Concourse,
looking up at the ugly building. A life of ordinariness, she
thought. I won't be held prisoner a moment longer! You
have to *make* things happen for yourself! The only trouble
is, she thought, setting the bags down on either side of
her, panting, *I don't know where the fuck I'm going!* There
wasn't much choice. The only place a girl could count on
for acceptance was the Village, where being a runaway
was the norm. Alistair's pad for a night or two, and then?
She shrugged; she'd figure something out. She picked up
her bags and plodded toward the subway.

Howard Austin approached Coral's apartment warily.
This happened sometimes, he told himself as he walked
crosstown. An ex-flame feeling horny. Or regretful. Nothing more serious than that. And he would certainly never
trust her again. But he did have a plan, a scheme, a last
idea for winning Coral. If her career was so important to
her, maybe he could offer her a new one.

In her apartment, Coral smoked her second joint and
poured a large glass of sparkling white wine. She refreshed
her makeup. Oh, God, she was glad he was coming. She
lit some candles, then stood naked before her hall mirror,
applying a little rouge to each nipple, a trick her makeup
artist had told her about.

The doorman rang to announce a "Mr. Austin."

"Send him up," Coral said curtly.

His knock at her door was barely audible. She opened the door gently and ushered him in. He glanced at her naked body in surprise. "I'm sorry—am I early?"

His hair was longer, he was less tan, but he was as handsome as ever. "No." She wrapped herself around him, pressing up to his blazered chest, her legs on each side of his strong, gray-panted leg.

"Did you like Colin's drawings?" she purred in his ear. She licked his lobe with little flicks of her tongue.

"Mmmm..." His bass growl stirred her, made her shiver. "I've already had plenty of reaction—"

"There's only one reaction I'm interested in tonight," she told him, her hand snaking to the front of his body, slipping beneath his blazer. She found him, held him through the thin flannel, stroking him until she felt him grow hard beneath her hand and heard him groaning softly in her ear. His fingers had already found their way between her naked legs, gently caressing her, quietly insistent, slipping inside her and making her breath come in short pants.

"Easy..." She moved away from his hand. "I don't want to rush...."

She knelt before him and unzipped his pants quickly. He gasped as she extricated his sex from his clothing, bending down to kiss it, to take the tip between her lips and run her tongue over the sensitive area. Bending forward, he reached for her, taking her small breasts in his palms, cupping them, moving his fingertips over her nipples until they jutted hard, then taking them between his thumb and forefinger and pinching gently over and over again. She thrust his pants down to his feet, rubbing her face in his body hair, clutching his buttocks. He followed her to the bedroom where she had an Italian romantic pop album playing. Her Rigaud candles flickered, giving off their enticing aroma, as she undressed him tenderly, piling his clothes at the foot of the bed. He stretched out upon her.

"Oh God," she whispered. The feeling was incredible. She suddenly knew what sex was about, had finally gotten in touch with her own feelings. She wanted to tell him that marijuana had pulled down the inhibitions, the self-defenses, but she didn't want to put it into words, or take her lips from beneath his. The smoke and the thoughts swirled around her brain. The music was so mellow and romantic, and her body was telling him everything he needed to know. She wanted every part of them to touch: from foreheads to tongues to toes. Now she crossed her legs up behind his back, feeling over his chest with her hands, rubbing across his nipples. He bent to suckle at her breasts, flicking his tongue quickly over them, making them erect again, almost hurting. She felt like sobbing with pleasure. Neither said a word. The bed was silent with their passion, their pleasure. She slid the lower half of her body against his. The new dances were like this, she thought, rotating her groin against his to the beat of the music.

"Inside me," she finally whispered. "Inside me, now. . . ."

"Oh, baby. . ." his sex was straining against her. "That's just where I want to be. . ."

She took him in her hand and helped him glide gently, slowly into her, her cries of arousal getting louder, shriller, more astonished as he sank deeper into her. When he was up to the hilt in her, they froze for a moment of pure pleasure together.

"Oh, no," she groaned. "It can't get any better. . . ."

But it could—it *did*—as he started to move gently inside her. She eased her body in answer to his, up and down against his rock-firm hardness. Oh, God! She bit her lips to keep from telling him too much! That *feeling*! It was worth anything in the world!

"*Wait!*" he cried. He held her body with his hand, and they stayed still. She felt his sex pulse inside her as he controlled himself, not moving, gritting his teeth near her ear.

After a few long moments he nuzzled her: "I'm sorry, but you said you wanted this to last. . . ."

He made love to her over and over again, stopping just before he felt he might climax, and each time she felt herself approach a kind of yawning mouth of pleasure which promised even greater pleasure to come. He broke away to lap at her perfumed, lean body with his hungry tongue. She nibbled parts of him she could reach, gently biting on an ear, a shoulder, even his nipples. His hands continually caressed her, gently moving over her entire body until it seemed to dissolve in a blur of pleasure. Meanwhile the marijuana enhanced everything, honed the pleasure, the sensation, took away the pressure and guilt, allowed her to relax and enjoy him.

Finally their bodies seemed to decide of their own accord that it was time to bring this pleasure to a climax. Howard suddenly held her in a tight grip, his mouth completely covering hers. She clung to him, pushing her body against his each time it moved, and as they moved frenziedly against each other, her cries began, then his, then both cried out as they experienced a perfectly simultaneous climax; Coral gasping; Howard crying out in surprise that his body could feel this much pleasure. She felt she might skim off the bed into some new stratosphere of enjoyment and sensation, so she clung fiercely to his shoulders as if gravity was centered in him, as if he were her touchstone, her anchor to the world.

"Cream?" Coral poured the coffee.

"Yes, please."

She had thrown on a black organza Dior robe, almost see-through, ankle length. Howard wore his pants, his chest bare, and he lay stretched out on the carpet, stroking her ankle.

"You've changed," he told her, as she placed the cup beside him.

"How so?" She sat at a stainless steel table next to him.

"This time you're gentler, softer."

She laughed, holding up a small twisted cigarette. "You have these to thank for that."

He raised his eyebrows as he sipped coffee. "The elegant Coral Stanton turns on?"

"I've thrown out my little white gloves, Howard," she told him, sipping her wine. The pleasure he had ignited in her body still echoed, cocooning her in its warm glow. "I *like* sex! I like the feeling of you inside me! Do you realize what a breakthrough it is for me even to be able to *tell* you this?"

"So you've transformed yourself into . . . what? The new woman?"

"Fashion *is* change, darling. I pitied Maynard for being mired in the twenties. I'm damned if *I'll* be stuck in the dreary fifties."

"So all those *Women's Wear* stories about your rock-concert partying, those little dinners with Mick Jagger and Marianne Faithful..."

She nodded. "Absolutely true. The Rolling Stones, the Beatles: *they* are forming the lifestyles of today. I *have* to get to know them. On their own level. And *this*"—she held up the cigarette—"is one of the keys. When they first met me, they didn't know how to relate to someone like me. They didn't know what elegance was. I had to meet them halfway."

"I'm feeling old-fashioned already—"

"Oh, no, there'll always be a place for your kind of taste. You could be one of the big American names, you know."

Howard shook his head slowly, caressing her ankle gently in his hand. "I think you're too late. I want to tell you this before you read it in *Women's Wear*. I've had an incredible offer for my firm. Over a million. I'm going to take it and quit the rag trade."

Coral sat bolt upright, her eyes flashing. "*Why?* You have so much talent!"

He ran a hand through his dark, curly hair. "I took a good long look at my life after our little...episode in Southampton. It really shook me up. It actually put me off fashion. You told me *you* had to constantly choose between love and fashion. Maybe I'm an incurable romantic, but *I* go for love every time. Actually, tonight, I could offer you both...."

"What do you mean?"

"I'd like to ask you to work for me."

"Are you joking? In what capacity?"

"Same one as you're in now: Editor-in-chief."

"You're starting a magazine? Under whose backing?"

"My own, now that I've got the money. That way, I'll have nobody to answer to. I want to do an upscale, gossipy, fashion version of *Women's Wear*, a weekly. I've done my research; there's plenty of advertising available. We'd go for an initial run of a hundred thousand—all from the trade. Later we could think about attracting the consumer—"

Coral's laugh cut him off. "You expect me to give up the editorship of *Divine* for something like that? *Our* circula-

tion is edging the half-million mark! My salary alone
would—"

"I'll match it!" Howard's eyes gleamed. "I'm putting
every penny I have into this. I'll cut no corners, beginning
with you. And you'll be free to be as avant-garde as you
choose."

Coral finished her wine in a quick gulp, suddenly
angry. She brusquely removed her foot from his grip,
stood, and began to pace the empty living room. "Howard,
let's never mix pleasure and business. . . ."

Howard watched her with narrowed eyes. He reached
for his shirt, put it on and began to button it.

Coral turned to glare at him. "You don't realize the kind
of clout *Divine* has! If I want to photograph Barbra Streisand
wearing Chanel, I just have to lift a phone. If I want that
marvelous Diana Ross to pose in the new American collections, I call her agent, who is only too delighted. You
think they'd do it for—what *is* your paper going to be
called?"

" 'Labels,' " Howard said, darkly. He was pulling on his
shoes, looking so hurt and angry that Coral rushed to
him. She put her hand on his arm, and he ignored her,
tying his tie.

"It's a marvelous name," she soothed. "I'm sure it will
be a great success. It's just, well . . . I *am* the top fashion
editor in the country, perhaps in the world. You *can't* set
your aims that high."

He turned to look at her, his mouth twisted with anger.

She tiptoed to kiss his mouth. "I'm sorry, darling. . . .
Forgiven?"

He threw her a dark glance. "I seem to spend most of
my time trying to forgive you. I offer you an exciting new
job, and you throw it back in my face. Vreeland or Nancy
White would jump at it."

"No." She smiled brightly at him. "Don't kid yourself,
Howard. You simply won't get an editor of that caliber. I'll
try to recommend someone, though. We have some very
bright kids working for *Divine*. Now, tell me about 'Labels'
—do you think you'll really have the clout to take on
Women's Wear?"

Dressed now, Howard turned to her impatiently. "It
doesn't matter, Coral. You're not really interested. You

think *Divine* is the be-all and end-all. I'm interested in another kind of reporting."

"I did apologize," she said, pressing her body to his, and her lips to the side of his mouth. "You're not going to leave in a huff, are you?"

He didn't answer. He allowed her to kiss him. The sexual chemistry, he realized, was there whether he liked her or not. She was fondling him through his pants, and a moan escaped his lips. He took her in his arms once more, and they swayed and fell back against the wall.

"Take those clothes off," she murmured hoarsely. "Let's do it all again."

He broke away from her, his face flushed and dark. "I've got to go." He looked for his jacket, finding it in her white hallway. It suddenly seemed distasteful to him— being humiliated, letting one's body overcome one's pride.

She touched his shoulder, and he turned with his hand on the doorknob. "Will I be seeing you again soon?" she asked.

He looked back at her expressionlessly. "I have to start protecting myself, Coral. You seem to have a special ability to hurt me. So—*no*."

She slammed the front door as he left. Pouring more champagne, she thought, He'll be back. A sexual chemistry like theirs didn't happen every week....

"Mom? It's me! Are you okay?" A week after leaving home, Mackenzie called her mother.

"Mackenzie? Oh, Mackenzie, how *could* you do this to me?"

"I left you a note, didn't I? I told you I'd call as soon as I found somewhere to live. Well, I just found somewhere."

"Yes? Is it close?"

"I'm living in the Village, Ma. I'm sharing an apartment with three other really nice kids—"

Esther Goldstein began to sob. "I never thought my own daughter would become a stranger! No phone number, no address! If we had dropped dead, you wouldn't even have known about the funeral...."

"Well, you didn't drop dead, so are you gonna write down my number?" Esther sniffed, fumbling for a pencil. She gave her mother the address and phone number. "Is there any mail for me?"

"A few letters. I'll bring them down myself on Sunday on the way to visiting your Aunt Fanny. Then I'll be able to see where you're living."

Mackenzie glanced around her cluttered room. Through the open door she could see Luke, one of her roommates, in his underpants, cross-legged, playing the flute. "No," she said. "I'll come for brunch on Sunday, okay? Stock up on lox."

"Do you need an invitation? This is still your home."

"Thanks, Ma, and remember, I still love you the best."

She hung up, sighing. She had stayed with Alistair for three nights, fending off his advances. Finally, she found a household she could fit into. It consisted of two girls and a boy, all around her age. Laura tie-dyed tee-shirts, Loretta was a macrame artist who sold plant holders and hangings at weekend markets, and Luke was a quiet, introspective boy with long, straight blond hair; he did little but practice a flute and stir a pot of vegetables on the stove. They casually accepted Mackenzie into their lives, and she became part of the Village population—an energetic, kookily dressed girl, often seen running down the street to her waitressing job at six o'clock.

The Goldstein home had been sunk in gloom since Mackenzie's escape. Esther's series of anxiety attacks had affected the entire household.

"I don't like thinking of my baby out there, living on her own," she would cry to anyone who would listen. "She's so innocent! What if a man fancies her?" Reggie and Max would exchange glances and snort with suppressed laughter.

"She could probably teach him a thing or two, Ma!" Reggie said.

"I won't be happy until she's back," she told Abe in their bedroom one night. "Darling, give her a job—she shouldn't be in a bar!"

"She doesn't want a job from me," Abe shouted. "My shops aren't good enough for her! She wants *fashion*! She wants skeletons wearing loony dresses—"

"If you gave her her own shop," Esther pleaded. "At least we'd know where she was!"

"Her own *shop*? What do you think—I wanna lose my life savings?"

"Maybe you'd *make* a fortune? She won that contest, Abe. She has talent!"

"Yeah, yeah. . . . I saw her sketchbook," he sneered.

But as the months passed, even Abe Goldstein was forced to notice that something was happening in the fashion world. A recent experiment with some cheap, young 'Carnaby Street' clothes had resulted in his stores being raided by excited teenagers, snapping up the stuff.

"Go see your sister one weekend, I'll give you time off," he told Reggie. "Get a look at how she's living. I'd still like her involved with the Goldstein business. It's ridiculous for her to work for strangers. I'll give her her own store. They call 'em boutiques now. So we rent a little storefront somewhere—it could be your own enterprise. If you break even, I'll be happy. Listen, it'll be worth it—just for the sake of your mother's health."

Nine

Their first year at MacMillans came to an end at the last week of June. Mia, David, and Mackenzie were among the top dozen students of their year. During their last term they had been required to make two garments. David had surprised everyone with two amazingly accomplished outfits: a coat and a suit, both beautifully cut and tailored. Mia had shown genuine talent for revitalizing classic looks: She had taken a suit, making it startlingly contemporary by shortening the skirt and changing the styling of the sleeves and pockets. The unique detailing gave the outfit a fresh, new look.

Although Mr. Neville, the Design Head, had studiously avoided Mackenzie, other teachers hailed the originality and exuberance of her wild, mod clothing. A little encouragement had been all that Mackenzie needed to blossom. She had produced a pair of black, lacy pants covered in spangles, and a round-necked skimpy tee-shirt top to layer over it.

"We're leaving this place in a blaze of glory!" Mackenzie cried as they celebrated their last day at a nearby Italian restaurant.

They were all due to follow their separate paths for the vacations. Wayland had arranged for Mia to work as a temporary sales assistant in the couture department at Headquarters. Mackenzie would work full-time waitressing through the summer. David was returning to Syracuse, where a summer of odd-jobbing would help him save up some money. Their farewell lunch was sprinkled with promises to keep in touch during the long recess.

"I'll pop into HQ all the time to see you," Mackenzie promised Mia. "If Alistair *ever* lets me out of bed!" she winked. She noticed the exchange of embarrassed looks between Mia and David.

"Oh, pardon *me*!" Mackenzie said coyly. "Did I say the wrong thing? I'm sorry, but in the Bronx we lead such rude, crude lives—we tend to let it all hang out—"

"Shut up, Mackenzie," David told her.

Mackenzie's eyes flashed. "Fuck *you*!" she shouted. "Nobody tells me to shut up!" She stormed off to the ladies' room to repair her Twiggy eyelashes, which had run in the steam from the hot food.

Mia sighed, looking at David. "It'll almost be a relief to stop playing peacemaker between you two."

"Well, she bugs me." He blew out his lips exasperatedly. "She's so incredibly insensitive. Until it comes to *her*, then she's a Jewish princess!" He gazed at Mia with an expression that had inspired a mixture of guilt and regret in her ever since that disastrous Saturday of last fall.

"Have you ever really forgiven me?" she asked.

"There's really nothing to forgive. Let's call it bad timing."

She nodded. "I guess I'm what's called a late developer. I still want us to stay friends "

He leaned to kiss her cheek softly. "We are. We will be. You know, that first time I saw you—the first day of school—I felt as if you were someone I'd known before. I can't explain. It's as though . . . if I had to invent the girl I wanted, she'd look like you. You're just . . . everything I'd want."

Mia shook her head. "It's a lovely thing to say, but . . . don't. I don't want to hurt you in any way."

"I know what I want, Mia. I'm willing to wait—"

"No," she said. "Don't wait. I have so many things to work out . . . in myself. I'm just going to throw myself into my work for a while."

"I understand," he said. "But you can't stop me from hoping."

Mackenzie returned to the table waving a fresh bottle of Chianti. When their lunch finally came to a raucous end, they all kissed each other good-bye outside the restaurant.

"*Bye*, darlings!" Mackenzie ran up the subway steps and struck some outlandish poses at the top, blowing kisses back at them. Mia kissed David good-bye, then took a hot, slow bus ride home, her folio of designs under her arm. Wayland was taking her out that night for an "end of year" special dinner at the latest trendy Chinese restaurant.

All eyes were on them when they entered the crowded place, Mia in a black French dress Wayland had borrowed from the store, makeup in the exaggerated way she knew he liked.

"This is a reward for doing so well, pet," he said, and slipped an envelope onto her plate as the waiter poured champagne for them.

She tore it open: It was a round-trip airplane ticket to Paris. She stared, then hugged him in delight.

"It's for August," he told her. He held his champagne glass aloft. "No Parisienne would be caught dead there, but it's the perfect time to sneak *you* into all the fashion showings! We'll say you're an HQ junior buyer-trainee. You'll have the time of your life...."

Mia sat in the salon of Nina Ricci, off the Boulevard des Capucines, awaiting the start of her first Paris showing. She tried to coolly survey the elegant, hushed salon. No one made their salons as imposing and intimidating as the Parisians. The spacious, gray-carpeted area with its tall windows framed in gathered, paler gray drapes, resolutely shut out everyday outside life, creating a fantasy world for its clients. Never before had she realized what a serious business the *couture* was for the French.

Clothes assumed tremendous importance—a pleat, a tuck, a scarf in these surroundings took on the power of a revelation. Mia wanted to destroy everything she was wearing, starting with her dusty shoes. When the first models swung haughtily by, their arrogance gave her an immediate inferiority complex. She felt her makeup was dated and sloppy as she stared at the exquisite shading of their eye sockets, the sculpted contours of their high cheekbones. The directrice of Nina Ricci, Antoinette Darriaux, was a small woman with crisp white hair and sapphire eyes. She stared through Mia while pretending great friendliness. She looked as if she could efficiently kill anyone who crossed her or the house.

Mia forgot she was a student, and imagined herself wearing these beautiful clothes. Designed by house designer Jules-François Crahay, they were sometimes theatrical, overdramatic, and could only be worn by these glorious larger-than-life creatures who modeled them. But between each show-stopping outfit were ten supremely wearable ones.

Sitting at the Café de la Paix near the Opéra after the showing, Mia jotted down as many sketches of the clothes as she could remember. She would be able to use this privileged information to prepare some kind of a report for the first term of her second year at school.

It was humid and warm. She stirred her café au lait while staring at a pile of postcards she had bought, wondering what to write to David. Looking up, she saw a dark, good-looking Frenchman at a neighboring table watching her with interest. He gently raised his eyebrows, and she quickly looked down at the blank card and wrote "David Winters" on the address half.

Now that she was hundreds of miles from New York, she found she could think clearly about him. How romantic it could have been if he were sitting at this outdoor café table with her, holding her hand. He *had* attracted her. She had *wanted* his arms around her, wanted to kiss him. *Why* had it all turned so frightening and horrible? She vividly remembered the feel of his body pushing against her, that stiff sex prodding, the wetness on her stomach. She closed her eyes in the heat of the afternoon, shifting uncomfortably.

Each day she visited a fashion house, using Wayland's name as an invitation. Patou, Saint Laurent, Cardin... she wrote her impressions and made sketches after each showing. One day, after visiting Dior's grandiose salon, she left in a happy daze: It had never before occurred to her to work in Europe, but now she suddenly realized what a wonderful idea that was. Living this far from her mother, she could forget the twinges of abandonment she felt at Coral never calling her. Being on her own in a foreign country brought out all kinds of hidden feelings in her. Lying in bed at night in the clean, small hotel Wayland had tracked down for her, she'd realized that there was still a little girl inside her, yearning for her mother's love, hurt and puzzled at not getting it. She wondered if she would feel up to contacting Coral and mending relations between them back in New York.

One evening she bought a pile of fashion magazines to leaf through at a café near her Left Bank hotel. That was the evening she discovered the name Phillipe Roux. The photographs of the clothes by this new designer sent a shock of recognition through her. They looked like clothes she would have designed in a year's time—as if a time traveler had shown her designs from the future. When she turned the page and saw the photograph of Roux himself, she was even more moved. His dark-eyed, handsome face shone with conviction and happiness. He was rugged, sensual, intense, his presence rebounding off the printed page; it was as if she had known him in some other life. His face, his words, his clothes were disturbingly familiar. Some psychic feeling told her she was fated to work with this man, maybe even become part of his life. She closed the magazine almost in alarm. There was nothing to do about such a crazy notion but forget it, she told herself. She had two years of design study to complete in New York.

After Paris, New York looked crude and tough. The quality and *luxe* of the French clothes had spoiled her. Mia realized that the couture was her real love, her first love, probably because of that first excitement she had felt upon seeing the dreamlike, beautifully made dresses and coats in her mother's closet, glittering with spangles and mystery and something secret, forbidden.

"Don't tell Daddy how much they cost. . . ." The words echoed in her memory. The price of Coral's clothes had been the only shared confidence between mother and daughter.

MacMillans was not equipped to teach couture; few designers wanted to learn the expensive, time-consuming methods of made-to-order clothes. Few designers wished to bother with demanding private clients. Fashion worked quite differently in America—it was more democratic, less privileged.

"Who did you see in Paris you thought really good?" Wayland asked.

"There's a new couturier, Wayland—half Spanish, half French—Phillipe Roux. He used to work at Dior. God, his clothes are beautiful. I only saw them in *Elle* magazine, but each was perfect."

Wayland frowned. "I read about him. *Women's Wear* called him 'promising but unripe'—made him sound like a green fig!"

"I'd do anything to work for someone like him," Mia mused. "I wonder if he needs an assistant?"

"We're selling British fashions like hot buns, Mia," Wayland told her. "The cheaper the better. Maybe you shouldn't think couture?"

"That's just *it*, Wayland—I don't think I *can* work cheap after seeing those gorgeous clothes. My dream is to work in Paris."

"An American in Paris?" Wayland sighed. "They'd hate your guts, but there's no reason you shouldn't try. It was hell around here without you, but Mia, if you really want to work in Paris, go all out for it." He was on his third vodkatini and in one of his sentimental moods, "I'm always here to help you, because I believe in you."

Mackenzie had been living in the Village almost six months when Reggie called on her without warning one hot Saturday morning in August. She had worked late the night before, and they'd had a party too. It was ten-thirty, most windows were heavily draped, and some guests were still sleeping on the floor. Mackenzie peered through the security spyhole and saw her brother making a funny face at her. She opened the door two inches, screening the mess.

"Whaddya want?" she whispered, "Is Mom all right?"

"Don't I get asked in?" Reggie applied a little pressure to the door.

"And have you tell everyone I live in a slum?" She grimaced, pushing back. "Meet me downstairs in the coffee shop. Give me five minutes."

She shut the door on him and stepped over a snoring body on her way to the bathroom. Quickly, she drew on her movie-vamp eyes and streaked her mouth with red. She ran down the block in a short coat over her nightie, her feet in black patent slippers. She found Reggie in a booth, sipping coffee.

"Hi!" She slid in next to him. "I guess you missed me too much to stay away?"

"The place sure is quiet without you. You don't even fight with Dad that much when you come to visit."

"You should be happy. Now, what do you really want?"

"You gonna order some breakfast? My treat."

Mackenzie studied the menu earnestly as the waitress handed Reggie his scrambled eggs. When the waitress served her bagel, she spread cream cheese thickly on it, piling it high with strawberry preserves and taking a savage bite out of it.

"Listen," Reggie began, shifting in his seat to look at her. "Dad really has his heart set on all of us coming into the business—"

She moaned. "Can you see me in that place? I'd rather die."

"You could help Dad change the image."

"That's simple—just burn the whole thing to the ground and reopen under a different name on Madison Avenue."

"What if that's not so crazy?" Reggie said. She nearly choked on her chocolate. "What if Dad let us open our own store somewhere? Somewhere a bit classy? Like a boatique, y'know?"

"The word is 'boutique,' Reggie. It's French. And where does Dad consider classy? Queens?"

"Listen to me: We could use Dad's facilities, Dad's know-how, his warehousing, his machinists. Max and I take care of the business side and you come up with the designs. Dad knows that your stuff is the future, even though he hates it. He's more interested in making money than in fashion anyway. . . ."

"So what?" She had eaten so fast she felt sick. She signaled for coffee.

"He's ready to back us, Mack. You'd be crazy to miss out on this."

"I'd be crazy to have anything to do with it," she said. "He'd always be hanging around, watching, criticizing . . . *you* know what he's like. And anyway, why do you need *me*? We've never got on."

Reggie spread his hands and shrugged. "What are we gonna do? Go out and hire some stranger? This way it's all in the family."

"Ha!" she snorted. "Like the family is so wonderful? Like the family can't screw you as bad as any stranger?"

"Just think about it," Reggie urged. "I tell you, this could be big. Dad is really pretty proud of you, you know. He walks around with that cutting from that fashion magazine—when you won that contest? He shows it to all his customers."

"Yeah, he tells everyone but me how proud he is."

They left the coffee shop, and she took his arm as they

walked to the subway. "If I ever have a business of my own, I'd call it 'Gold!'" she told him. "I'd change my last name to Gold too."

"You're a rebel, Mack. You always will be."

They reached the subway and she kissed him, leaning over the rail to watch him run down the steps. "Tell Ma I'll be there tomorrow! Thanks for breakfast!"

She strolled through the sunny streets to the apartment. Wouldn't all the kids at MacMillans give their right arms for the chance to get their own boutique, designing their own clothing? She pictured the rows of skinny little dresses she'd do, the shirts with long collars and tight sleeves that came to a point over the wrist. Long enough to just cover the tops of thighs, worn over panty hose that matched or clashed in violent colors like pink, lavender, orange, scarlet. Her mind ticked with ideas as she ran up the steps.

Her grueling session of waitressing ended at two in the morning. After her shift, she walked the few blocks to Alistair's apartment. She saw him often. The 'wild affair' she had bragged about to Mia seemed almost ready to take off.

Alistair had done wonders for her ego and was now working on her appearance. He saw through the thrift-shop clothes and trailing shawls to the real Mackenzie underneath, the girl who was supremely confident of everything but the way she looked.

"If you could just lose thirty pounds, Mack," was how he began most of their discussions. She knew he was right. She also knew she fascinated him and made him laugh. He fascinated her, too, with his stream of schemes ranging from their working on an abandoned San Francisco gold mine to starting a bed-and-breakfast joint in Scotland. Despite the certain craziness they shared ("We're eccentrics!" he assured her), Mackenzie thought him the perfect Englishman with his floppy blond hair and pale blue eyes. He was everything she was not: skinny, well-spoken, pale, and classy. She enjoyed being with him. His constant attempts to seduce her were endearing.

She recounted Reggie's visit while he created a low-calorie salad for dinner. "I could design clothes that would sell like crazy," she told him lying back on the sofa, sipping Tab. "I know the colors girls want, the shapes, the details, everything! It's all the stuff I'm looking for and never find."

"Do it!" Alistair urged.

"But they'll find a way to gyp me," she said. "They always do. I never got my share of Halloween candy, or my third of the Hannukah *gelt!*"

"I could represent you if you're scared of your brothers."

"Scared of *those* two lugs?" she cried. "I just don't want to spend the rest of my life fighting them."

Alistair tuned the radio to WMCA, and the Supremes were wailing "Back in His Arms Again!" She relaxed on the couch, clicking her fingers. She had rearranged the cluttered studio for him, filing all his old *Billboard* and *Variety* magazines, storing the stacks of promo records. His apartment was coming to represent a small oasis in her hectic world of shared apartment, school, bar work, and family Sundays.

After dinner they smoked one of his special joints, passing it between them. He flicked off the light and switched on the psychedelic lamp with its tips of colored lights glowing at the end of the plastic fronds. He lit some scented candles, filling the room with the aroma of blueberry, cinnamon, and musk.

Mackenzie giggled softly. "Smells like a goddamn head shop in here!" He sat at her feet and she watched him, knowing that she would let him make love to her tonight. She was drifting into her own world, spaced out. Relaxed, warm, and calm. Life was so simple if you just shared a smoke with someone. She sipped at her wine, breathing the perfumed air, distanced from this scene. She saw, as if she were floating above them, herself and Alistair. Saw him turning to bury his face in her lap, her hand gently stroking his blond hair.

"This is the first blond hair I've touched," she murmured. "Not counting a little girl who lived on the next block. It's so forbidden, so *goyische*."

"What's *'goyische'*?"

"It means my mother wouldn't approve of you."

He glanced up at her with a wicked look that made his eyes twinkle, his proper, crisp accent undermining it all. He flattered her, made her feel good. And just his desiring her made her excited; no one had ever wanted her this much. She watched him remove her shoes, then his. She liked the sensation of his chin moving in her lap. She ran her fingers through that fine blond hair as he unzipped her skirt, peeled down the black panty hose.

"I liked just being friends," she protested weakly.

"We'll be loving friends," Alistair said. She felt him fingering her panties, and she opened her eyes to see him gently pull the elastic leg away from her thigh, inserting his tongue into the gap. She closed her eyes, pretending to be more stoned than she actually was. His tongue moved moistly on her, and some nerve endings she had been unaware of jumped in reaction.

He took her hand and led her to his bed, pinching out candles on their way, leaving one glowing by the bed. She was naked now, lying on the bed, watching him undress. He took off his underpants and grinned at her. The angelic British choirboy certainly wasn't built like an angel. His slim white body was hard and strange to her—the guys she had known in the Bronx had been stocky, hairy, more like her idea of a man. They had grabbed her, had never touched her gently like this. He was stroking her very softly, making her body leap alive under his touch. He kissed between her legs and she stirred, moved restlessly against him. She had never been with a man who was not in a hurry. This was delicious! This was finesse!

"Touch me," Alistair said, and he took her hand and guided it to him. Again this was new to her, this hard muscle that moved in her hand as she squeezed.

She continued to hold him as they kissed, feeling him grow. She caressed the tip of him, making him groan. She watched their shadows on the wall beyond, giant caricatured shapes.

"Put your beautiful British cock inside me, Alistair," she murmured. She had never spoken like that to anyone before; it must be the pot. She sighed as he slowly entered her.

"Oh, you're beautiful, Mack," he whispered. "So beautiful! Oh, this feels so good, love. . . ."

His English voice made her think of the Beatles being interviewed, one of the Beatles making love to her! "Jesus!" she cried, feeling the delight. He began moving inside her, shifting to hover over her. She held onto his hard white buttocks with both hands, feeling them move rhythmically as his sex slid up and down inside her. Which one could it be? Paul McCartney, her favorite? George Harrison? Or that handsome drummer from the Dave Clark Five? He kissed her, nibbling on her lower lip, breaking away to gently bite the tips of her breasts. She caught her breath.

"Oh, Alistair... that feels *so* good!"

He nibbled and sucked, combining that with his machinelike pumping. It was irresistible. She felt the first stirrings of her own pleasure startling her. He thrust his tongue into her ear, breathing heavily into it. His body never stopped moving.

"Oh, God, Alistair, this feels *marvelous!*"

He changed his rhythm and pumped harder, up and down, very quickly. She followed his body, still holding his thin waist in her hands, slipping her hand between his buttocks and tickling him there.

"God!" Something was beginning inside her, a pre-echo of an explosion about to happen to her! It became a low swoon of pleasure, gathering in momentum until a wave of pleasure took her unawares.

"Alistair? It's happening! God, it's happening!" she screamed.

He lost his mind when he heard her. He pumped back and forth at an unbelievable speed, nibbling her breasts, breaking off to stick his tongue in her mouth, returning to her breasts.

"*Fuck* me, Mack!" he cried breathlessly. "*Fuck* me!"

They moved together, against each other, as he held onto her and she clutched him, almost afraid of the feelings they were stirring up. They were on an out-of-control merry-go-round. She suddenly knew, or her body did, what he wanted: He wanted her to squeeze him, to milk him, to grasp at him with her body each time he slid out of her. They were up, off the bed, fucking in midair as the feeling took hold, took over, and the last big wave swept her. She cried out, tears streaming from her eyes, holding his head as he lolled his tongue over her face like a thirsty puppy. Now she felt his body tense, and he jerked as if struck by lightning.

"I'm *coming*, Mack!" he yelled. "I'm *coming!*"

God, she had always thought the British so reserved! Those Bronx boys had clenched their teeth, stayed silent, or grunted. Hearing him cry these words, throb inside her, caused yet another wave of pleasure to crash over her. They froze, clutching each other tightly, holding onto the pleasure until it subsided. Panting, they fell into a deep sleep, the remaining candle flickering out.

She awoke in the same position the next morning, Alistair asleep on top of her. She eyed her watch. "Christ! I have to be in the Bronx by twelve!" She pushed him unceremoniously off her and ran for the tiny shower. A quick wash, and she dressed in yesterday's rumpled clothes.

She left Alistair drowsing, although he had the presence of mind to call out, "No cheesecake, no strudel, no French toast!"

On her way to the Bronx, sitting in the grimy subway car, she realized she was going to say yes to her brothers and father. But she would not allow them to use her. *She* would use *them*! With luck, she'd never have to serve another cocktail again.

The friends met up at MacMillans late in September to start their second year. David was darkly tanned from the outdoor work he'd done in Syracuse, Mackenzie weary and pale from nights of waitressing. She wanted Mia to tell her every detail of Paris and the clothes.

"I'll go there one day," she promised herself, turning the pages of Mia's Paris sketchbook.

One day at lunch in the cafeteria, Mia asked her, "Would you think I was off my rocker if I told you I was thinking of quitting this course?"

"I'd join you!" Mackenzie said quickly. "Against all my better instincts, I'd start a boutique with my brothers, backed by my dad. They've been nagging me to do it. I told them to start looking at locations. They're such cheapskates, it'll take them months to reach Manhattan!"

"I want to work in Paris," Mia told her. "Do an apprenticeship or something. I know it's crazy, but I can't get Phillipe Roux out of my mind."

"Well, *write* to the guy!" Mackenzie cried. "That's what *I* used to do, and look where it got me!" She looked around her, wide-eyed. "The best table in the crappiest cafeteria in town!" They giggled. "No, really, Mia, you'd be surprised at how you get through to people with a really honest, sincere, *flattering* letter!"

"Okay, I will!" Mia promised, then noticed Mackenzie looking longingly at her unfinished doughnut.

"I'm not even going to ask for a bite of that," Mackenzie said.

"Alistair?"

"Yeah. Oh, Mia, I wish I could tell you I was in love. I'd love it to be all romantic. But it's really just . . . great *sex*! I've never had great sex before. It's kind of a novelty."

Mia felt herself blush. What would Mackenzie think if she knew her love-life consisted of a portrait of Phillipe Roux torn from *Elle*, framed at her bedside?

The fall term went quickly enough. David was still the hardest working one, Mackenzie the craziest, Mia the most dedicated to the concept of couture. She wrote to Phillipe Roux. She decided that if he replied in a way she could interpret as even remotely favorable, she would try to talk Wayland into financing a second Paris trip.

It neared Christmas, and she knew Wayland was planning his annual party. But she overheard him describing it on the phone to Colin as a roundup of homeless strays. That includes me, she thought. It depressed her. She hadn't been sleeping well. New York unnerved her now— the wail of sirens, the brick-walled view from her bedroom, the fact that her mother lived a few hundred yards away, and the idea that David was still in love with her. She did not know how to handle that—whether to encourage him to wait, to be distant with him, or what. His admiration was a source of warmth. The look in his eyes was the only kind of affection she received, apart from Wayland's warm hugs, which she discounted.

"You know something, Mia," Mackenzie advised during one of their endless discussions at school, "If you want something bad enough—anything—you can get it. I'm living proof!"

"I want to live in Paris," Mia said yearningly. "I think of it all the time."

Mackenzie lit a cigarette and took a long drag. "If I could escape the Bronx, you can escape Manhattan," she said.

Mia hesitated. "I don't know . . ."

"Oh, *Mia*!" Mackenzie cried. "Go ahead! Do what *I* did! Give your life a kick in the pants! You won't regret it!"

Ten

Mia strode down the freezing cold avenue, hunting for Phillipe Roux's salon. She was in Paris again! It was April. *I must be insane,* she thought. This is what came of giving her life a kick in the pants. Her teachers had tried to delay her, telling her she wasn't ready. Why, then, had she felt so sure, so confident, that Phillipe Roux would want her? She reached into her pocket, touching the letter she'd received from him a month ago.

She had written him from the heart, telling him she recognized something in his clothes, something she understood. His reply had not exactly been encouraging, but he'd professed himself touched by her interest. He told her to call his salon if she ever came to Paris. When optimistic, Mia translated that to mean that he had a job for her; pessimistic, it meant he would invite her to view his collection.

Wayland had been wonderfully supportive, promising to sponsor her if Roux showed any interest. "After all, he's going to pay peanuts even if he wants you," he warned her.

From the vantage point of New York it had all looked so easy. But now that she was actually walking down the street toward the salon, having not slept much for two nights, she asked herself how demented, deluded, and just plain crazy she could have been. How could an American girl who had not even completed her training, who could hardly sew buttonholes, possibly interest a French couturier?

Phillipe Roux's salon was simply a private apartment in a residential building. A brass engraved plaque adorned the large wooden door which clicked open onto a stark stone courtyard when a bell was pressed. The young woman who showed Mia into the salon wore one of Roux's black dresses—very short, cut as strictly as some exclusive school uniform; worn with sheer black hose and low black pumps.

"He will be with you in a moment," the girl said in American-accented English.

Mia placed her folio on a gilt chair and sat, her heart beating loudly. The salon was quiet, hushed, unlike any other fashion house's salon she had visited. There was something soothing, almost churchlike, in this silence and in the minimal decor of white walls, spotlights, and gray velvet cushions tied to the gilt chairs lining three walls.

Phillipe Roux entered the room quickly and lithely. He stopped, the intense stare of his dark eyes flashing across the room to her, striking home.

"Bonjour!" His warm, deep voice accompanied the wide smile that spread slowly across his face. His presence and vitality were magnetic: a source of energy, of well-being. He glowed with bronzed health. He was only about her height, and somehow that endeared him to her. He wore a spotless white jacket, obviously his own design, with a tailored collar, and pockets that echoed his last season's suits. He looked like an artistic surgeon, elegant and sophisticated, but with something earthy and peasant about him too. In contrast to most of the fashion people she had met, there was a humbleness and an air of humility in his bearing. She felt his gaze take in all her clothing approvingly, the new coat Wayland had insisted on giving her, the neat new shoes, the way she'd drawn her blond hair back into a simple black bow, the minimal makeup which allowed her cold cheeks to glow from the Paris wind. He walked across the room to her, took her hand, and she jumped to her feet.

"You have come a very long way," he said. "I hope it was not solely to see me?"

Mia nodded, spellbound, then shook her head. "I was coming to Paris anyway," she mumbled.

He raised his eyebrows slightly, as if awaiting an explanation, but she said nothing else. She had been right to come, she felt. Even a few moments in his presence would somehow—magically—change her life. His warm, sherry-colored eyes seemed to reach down into her. No one had ever looked into her eyes like that, into her soul.

"And I may see?" He indicated her folio. He spoke English with a faint accent, half Spanish, half French. Like everything about him, it was fascinating.

He slowly turned the pages of her drawings. She had edited them down to a dozen of her very best designs. Beautiful coats with huge, oversewn patch pockets and flaps, the coat falling in gentle, gathered fullness at the back. Slimmed-down dresses with unusual necklines or crossover straps. Tailored suits with the concave profile he himself favored. She had included all her design details— the shoulder seams, the oversewn welting outlining pockets and cuffs, the buttoned flaps.

She watched his brown hands as he turned the pages, glancing now and then at his grave expression. He had sculpted cheeks, his dark hair thinning on top but worn long at the back, his skull as brown as the rest of his face. His look of utter concentration, almost childlike, gave him a quality of radiance: It was a face one could never tire of watching.

"*Bien*," he said, reaching the last design. Slowly, he replaced the pages one by one, looking at them again. Now and then he traced a line down a figure with his finger. Once he said, "This is not flattering," indicating a gathering of fabric at the hips. "Women want to be elongated," he told her, looking up. Each time they exchanged looks, they seemed to become closer. She felt that if they could just sit looking into each other's eyes for a whole morning, they would know everything about each other without speaking. She told herself to think in a professional way and not make this so personal, but something about Phillipe Roux made it *very* personal.

He closed her folio carefully, tying the ribbon. She looked at the bow he made. If only she could keep it like that forever.

"You are not at all like your mother," he suddenly said.

Mia started. "How do you know?"

He laughed, indicating that they sit. "*I* know nothing. Stephanie, who showed you in, tells me. It seems I did meet your mother last year. She is very important in America, yes? I like your modesty in not mentioning her to me."

"Would it have made any difference?"

He frowned slightly. "Only your talent and your usefulness to this house matter to me. I like your work very much. As you said in your letter, you design like me... or I design like you." He let his shy smile peep through. "But we are very small. Only twenty girls work in the atelier. Stephanie helps me with the press and the clients. My assistant is Josephine. No sketchers, no assistant designers, no helpers. If I should take on another person, I would need to reflect very carefully on what your duties would be."

"I'd do anything!" she said quickly. "Translation, helping with the press—I know most of the American editors...."

He stood. "Call me in one week, Mia. I shall make a decision."

She floated down two flights of stairs, out onto the Paris street. It looked entirely different. All of Paris seemed hushed with anticipation, awaiting Phillipe Roux's decision! He was the most fascinating man in the world, and he would take her, she knew it, she *felt* it! She didn't mind what they might make her do: fetch coffee, pick up pins. It would be a beginning, and she could say she worked for Phillipe Roux! She would be his disciple, continuing a whole school of elegance. As Balenciaga had been Givenchy's mentor, Phillipe would be hers.

When she called the salon a week later, Phillipe had left a message with Stephanie to ask Mia to come by again. She tried to still her excitement as she waited for the bus that crossed the Seine to the Right Bank. She rang the door of the salon. When Stephanie appeared, Mia thought her ginger-lashed eyes appeared a little friendlier. And when Phillipe Roux arrived in the white salon, wearing his immaculate jacket, a smile on his face, Mia felt a shudder almost stop her heart. In an instant her hopes for fashion, her ideas and fears of men, her search for something to focus her life upon, fused and took shape in the form of one person. For the first time in her life she had fallen irrevocably and very deeply in love.

"*Look!*" Mackenzie waved a postcard under Alistair's nose.

He snatched it away and read it: "Starting work for

Phillipe Roux next week! Delirious! Hunting cheap apartment: *impossible*! Come visit! Love, Mia."

"That lucky bitch!" Mackenzie screamed. "And all because *I* told her to write! If *she* can leave in the middle of the course, so can I!" She flung herself onto Alistair's lap, throwing her arms around his neck. She had lived in the Village for nearly a year. Alistair stayed some nights with her, and she slept over some nights with him.

"Like an old married couple," she told friends.

Her roommates were gentle people who were slowly indoctrinating Mackenzie into their lifestyle. They spoke of "good karma" a lot, and using one's force to change the world for the better. Her instinct told her they were the wave of the future—the "love children" who would soon swamp the world. They attended demos against the Vietnam war, dragging Mackenzie along with them. Standing in Washington Square, protesting, linking arms and singing "We Shall Overcome," Mackenzie would cry at being part of such a beautiful movement.

"One part of me identifies with it . . ." she told Alistair. "I can learn a lot from them."

Mackenzie jumped off his lap, sat on the floor, and gazed up at Alistair earnestly. "I have a family that wants to back me. What the hell am I wasting my time at school for? They all think I'm nuts there anyway."

"You're never there!" Alistair scoffed. "You goof off most of the time!"

"Because I'm bored! If I can convince my family about the location . . . well," she pondered, "if I nag hard enough, I can get anything."

"Yeah," Alistair agreed, rolling a joint.

"And what the hell are you going to do with *your* life?" she asked him.

"The Sassoon salon pays a handy little retainer," Alistair said. "Besides, I'm always scouting around, trying to find new talent to manage, from the clubs and things. . . ."

"And what do you actually live on?" she asked.

"I've told you. My father sends me a small allowance. Every month I go way downtown to some obscure little English bank office and pick it up. I can just about live off it."

"If my boutique really happens, will you do the publicity for me?"

"Of course!"

"I want you to get off your backside and have a *career*!" she told him. "I have to respect you. I can't respect someone who sits around getting stoned all day. I could have Luke for that!"

"Did someone mention my name?" Luke poked his head around her door and Mackenzie threw a shoe at him. She had tried to tell her parents about Alistair, but all they had wanted to know was: "Is he Jewish?" She had refused to say any more about him after that. Her request that they open a store on a decent Manhattan street fell on deaf ears. Reggie had not been completely honest with her. They would *not* be independent of Abe Goldstein. They would each own twenty-five percent of the company, which they had agreed would be called Gold! They could gang up on her and outvote her on any decision, but each time that had happened, she simply threw her twenty-five percent share on the table and walked out. They always relented and called to tell her she could have her way. From the beginning she saw that *her* taste was what the company would succeed on, so it was up to her to impose it.

"I'm giving you kids a *million bucks*!" Abe shouted at stressed moments.

"Bullshit!" Mackenzie shouted, and her father would stamp angrily from the dining room, their designated boardroom. Esther, delighted to see the family reunited, would then bustle in with more coffee and cookies.

Reggie scowled. "You gotta learn how to handle him, Mack."

"Why *should* I let him get away with thinking he's giving us a million bucks?" she cried. "A store won't cost anything like that!"

Reggie shook his head. "Dad exaggerates! Just say, 'Dad, we'll make you *two* million!'"

The meetings exhausted her. Before Abe Goldstein put one cent into Gold!, he was attempting to tie up any possible problems. Her energy was dissipated on trying to win his trust. Meanwhile, as her brothers continued to scout locations, she continued halfheartedly at MacMillans.

Reggie and Max had inherited their father's business methods. They called it "thinking realistically," but she called it cheap. They tried to fob her off with bargain

storefronts in rundown neighborhoods. A realtor cousin
was tipping them off to "real steals" in places like Delancey
Street or Little Italy. Mackenzie refused even to look at
such places. She knew New York well enough to know
that one did not open a fashion boutique just anywhere.
The lower part of downtown did not attract fashion-
hungry girls, and the Village was not yet taken seriously.
The good avenues—Madison, Lexington, Third—were too
expensive. She resigned herself to settling for Second
Avenue. The problem then was how high or low on
Second? Manhattanites were snobs. The cross street placed
you socially and economically. It would have to be in the
Seventies or Eighties, she told them. As Reggie and Max
began to come up with stores in the Twenties and Thirties, she knew she was starting to win.

They finally came up with a deserted grocery in the
upper Seventies, just off Second Avenue. It was spacious
and airy, and the minute she walked into it, she knew it
was right. After a fight with the landlord about erecting a
sign on Second, they signed the lease. The store was
gutted and the endless battles about decor began.

Once again Mackenzie won her argument. She had
them put up pasteboard walls and covered them with
thick, silvered vinyl, inspired by pictures she had seen of
Andy Warhol's studio. The silver reflected colored spotlights, in red, violet, and orange. The effect was glamorous. Chrome rails crisscrossed the store at crazy angles,
notched to hold hangers. Clothes would hang from these
rails as the mood took her, sometimes in rainbows of
color, sometimes all red or all white.

"What would I have done without you?" Mackenzie
said, collapsing on Alistair one night. They were working
sixteen hours a day to get the shop ready to open, and
Alistair was running around town for her to suppliers,
driving a small van they had rented, picking up orders,
helping to install equipment. If Gold! really took off, she
would have to integrate Alistair into the firm somehow.
She felt comfortable with him, and he was proving himself to be a good friend and confidant. Plus they had great
sex together. If it wasn't a "relationship," perhaps it was
as good as one.

"The clothes are what it's all about," Mackenzie had to
keep reminding herself. She had chosen very carefully

from her designs and put together a tight collection of dresses, tops, skirts, and pants. She planned to specialize in a limited range of shapes made up in three sizes and in various fabrics and colors. They would retail at under twenty dollars a garment, so girls could afford to mix and match. Abe Goldstein ferried the samples from the workroom of Goldstein Modes to Manhattan and back. Mackenzie was a perfectionist, spending days with the sewing ladies in the Bronx, altering, changing, recutting until the garments were as perfect as mass-produced garments could be.

"If only Mia were here to help me get through to her mother," Mackenzie told Alistair as she sat on his bed, stuffing hundreds of envelopes with an advertising flyer she had designed. "I've called *Divine* a hundred times asking them to preview my stuff. After all, they did discover me! They're only sending a junior editor."

The editor duly arrived, glanced at the clothes, and made some notes. "Try *Mademoiselle* or *Seventeen*," she suggested.

"Fuck them!" Mackenzie growled, showing her out.

She called *WWD*, and their boutique editor came to take pictures for a story titled: "Gold! New Entrant to the Ever-growing Boutique Scene."

The night her rolls of labels finally came in, Mackenzie threw one across the store like a streamer, whooping with excitement. Then they worked through the night, sewing them into the back of every garment. MACKENZIE GOLD FOR GOLD! they read, in black and white. She was a name designer!

For the opening-night party she invited everyone she knew, from her Village pals to the staff from MacMillans.

She made up very carefully in the bathroom, shouting out her news to Alistair. "*Vogue* may do me a big favor and send someone... today I actually sold out of the window! Girls saw the skirts and just wouldn't stop rapping on the glass until I let them in! I'm going to *love* this! It's like playing shop! I wanted to laugh when I took their money—it was too *easy*! I knew girls would want what I designed! I *knew* it!"

Alistair wore his new mod collarless navy suit, making him look like a blond Beatle. "Let's drink to your instincts!" he said, producing a bottle of champagne. "I've been hiding this all day."

"*Darling!*" She hugged him. "Have I told you how grateful I am for all your support and help?"

He popped the champagne cork, and she screamed as it ricocheted off the ceiling. She fetched glasses, and he ran a critical eye over her outfit. "Is that what you'll be wearing?" he asked.

She twirled around for him. "It's the craziest thing I could find—what do you think?" The harlequin romper suit had huge black pom-poms down the front. It terminated in tight black bands around the calves. She had colored her face brightly to match, sleeking down her hair.

Alistair whooped. "You look fantastic!" He poured them each a glass and clinked his against hers. "To Gold!" he proposed. "The first in a nationwide chain."

She swallowed great bubbly mouthfuls, collapsing into a chair. Alistair sat at her feet, rolling a joint.

"Tonight?" she asked, sitting up and frowning. "Won't you be working the room? There'll be lots of press people to chat up. You should be alert—"

"I want to enjoy myself," he said. "It's not every night I get to meet my in-laws."

"They're not your in-laws yet," she corrected. "And what makes you think they'll be there?"

"You mean you wouldn't invite your own parents to the opening of a shop they're backing?" He finished off the joint with a practiced twirl.

"I told you there could be a *Vogue* editor there," she said. "Abe might end up offering her some wholesale bargains from Goldstein Modes. He won't know how to speak to normal, elegant people."

Alistair swallowed his champagne with a grimace. "Don't be such a little snob!" he said.

Mackenzie made for the telephone. "Oh *please!*" she groaned. "*You've* put the entire Atlantic between you and your family. All *I* want is for the Goldsteins to stay in the Bronx! Bad enough my brothers have to be there. . . ." She began to dial.

"Who are you calling?"

"My parents. I'm going to beg them to stay home tonight."

"Give me that!" He grabbed for the phone and hung up, holding it behind his back. "I'm not letting you do this, Mack. Your father's put up all the bread for this. It isn't good business to treat your backer like that. Aside from it being lousy manners!"

"Oh?" She made a grab for the phone, her eyes blazing. "*You're* going to give me a lecture on manners? You don't even *write* to your father!"

"But he isn't pouring his life's savings into me; if he was, I'd be a little more careful."

"So you're just a hypocrite!" She made several lunges for the phone, but Alistair was stronger and more agile.

"Well, screw you!" She looked around for her shawl and threw it on. "I can use any pay phone on the street." She walked toward the door and called back over her shoulder, "And *you* don't need to come tonight, either, Alistair! I don't need *any* of you there—*I'll* be the life and soul of the fucking party!"

She slammed the door with all her might and ran downstairs, her heart beating with anger. On the street she felt a sick feeling. How *could* he be like this to her on the most important night of her life? But after hailing a taxi and collapsing on the backseat she reconsidered. Of course he was right. It would have been a pretty shabby way to treat her parents. She glanced at her watch. Anyway, it was too late to put them off. They were probably already there—they always arrived embarrassingly early for any event. Esther would be dressed up in some brocade dress left over from a Goldstein's Closing Down Sale. And Abe would be shiny and red from his second shave of the day. They would embarrass her, of course. She would get that nagging, blushing feeling that had been part of her entire childhood! That suspense of praying they would not say the wrong thing, or do something laughable in front of her friends.

The boutique was crowded and noisy—a Beatles record blasting—as she paid off the taxi and stood looking at her windows. *Her* store! Her heart began to pound as she took a deep breath, opened the door and walked in, her eyes shining. Fuck Alistair! She was going to enjoy this evening!

She was greeted by a crowd of students from MacMillans and her roommates from the Village. Everyone was wearing their wildest clothes, colorful scarves tied around their foreheads, wide bell-bottoms, short minis, and frilly, lacy shirts. She pushed through to a table of wines and glasses, pouring herself a large glass of Gallo Chablis while noticing that her parents had installed a huge bottle of Manischewitz red wine. She hid the bottle at the back. In the midst of the painted and bejeweled mob—almost cowering behind the counter—stood the four Goldsteins; Max and Reggie flushed from hard work and wine, Esther and Abe watching bewilderedly. Her parents ogled the young girls and dressed-up boys from the art school, and her brothers stared at the girls who had responded to invitations Mackenzie had sent to modeling agencies. Her teachers stood in a separate group, watching.

It was obviously Mackenzie's role to act as a catalyst to this mixed bunch. She drank some wine quickly, wishing Alistair were with her, then strode to the center of the store. She shouted at the top of her voice, "Presenting: Mackenzie Gold for Gold!," and broke into a crazed frug with a fellow student.

They danced for a few moments, then everyone joined in. She ran over to her parents and hugged them. "I think I'm gonna like this business!" she told them.

"Who are all these people?" Esther asked.

Mackenzie shrugged. "I don't know! I invited anyone and everyone! It's good for business. The more people who know about me, the better."

She dragged her father to a space in the store where everyone was dancing. "C'mon Dad, see if you remember." She did a combination of a rhumba and a tango with Abe, to the cheers and whoops of everyone. "More wine!" she shouted, and held out her plastic cup. Someone filled it for her. She needed to get very drunk tonight.

She was dancing with Reggie when she saw Alistair arrive. She ran up to him and kissed him, chattering, "Oh, baby, I'm so glad you came! I was freakin' out here! Just ignore my family, will ya? Stay with me!"

"I'm so bloody high, Mack!" He laughed, his eyes glazed. "I was so angry with you I smoked another couple of joints. Then I thought, what the hell, and got a cab here."

He whirled her around on the wooden floor to the pounding rock that was making the boutique pulsate. She got waylaid by a Village friend, and when she turned back, Alistair was with her mother at the hors d'oeuvres table. Somehow Esther Goldstein had smuggled in a big bowl of her own chopped liver. She spread some on a cracker and offered it to Alistair. Mackenzie hurried over just as Abe joined the group. "Mom, you *didn't*! Manischewitz wine, chopped liver—people are gonna think this is a *deli*!"

Alistair tasted the cracker, then hugged Esther. "It's *delicious*!"

"You see?" She looked triumphantly at Mackenzie and reached out to her husband. "Abe, meet Mackenzie's friend Alistair Briarly. He *loves* my chopped chicken liver!"

"*This* is Alistair?" Abe put out a burly hand. "From the back, I thought you were a girl—"

"Dad! *Please!*" Mackenzie wailed. "This is how guys wear their hair now!" She dragged Alistair away from them. "Oh, God, I'll *die*!"

Her brother was chatting up a model who was looking at some pants.

"May I take your inside-leg measurement, miss?" she heard him ask.

"Max!" she yelled. She rolled her eyes at Alistair. "I tell you, I'm gonna die!"

Alistair doubled up with laughter. "I've never seen anything so funny, Mack!"

A drunk Reggie grabbed her arm. "Everybody loves it, Mack! And the stuff is selling already! Dad's taken over five hundred dollars! He can't believe it!"

Alistair swept her off her feet, twirling her around until she screamed. Dusty Springfield wailed, "I Only Wanna Be with You!" and the whole store spun around her in a blur of color as she held tightly onto him.

By eleven, most people had left. Mackenzie opened the cash register and counted out nearly eight hundred dollars.

"We'll split it four ways!" she cried, stuffing two hundred dollars into her purse. "Now let's go out and get drunk!" she yelled, grabbing Alistair. "Let's celebrate!"

She had never been so happy.

Gold! took four thousand dollars in its first week, about four times the amount they had forecast. As the weeks passed, the take went up and up until they were selling out of all stock by two p.m. on Saturday afternoons, their busiest time. On that day the Goldsteins would begin a frantic chase around Manhattan and the Bronx, reordering fabric, delivering it to piece workers, picking up garments and hiring extra machinists to work around the clock for them. Reggie and Max brought the new clothes into town in plastic bags by subway until a second van was rented. After three months a dozen girls were working full-time to produce the separates that sold so well.

Esther Goldstein came in from the Bronx each Saturday to act as cashier at the store so that Mackenzie could serve customers and study their needs. Girls began to wait for the Gold! delivery van to drive up on Saturdays, trying to pluck dresses from the racks before they were even inside the store. It was called the London Look, or mod, and Mackenzie's genius was in distilling it, interpreting it in clothes that featured the details customers craved. The skinny, body-conscious clothes had been seen only in magazines or on British pop groups. Suddenly they were not only available, but cheap—an irresistible combination. Gold! struck gold overnight.

The boutique was going to be bigger than Mackenzie's wildest dreams. She kept the stereo system working over-time, blaring Cilla Black, the Stones, the Animals. And she was inspired. She got new ideas every night as she tried to sleep, and would sit up in Alistair's bed sketching furiously in her sketchbook.

They drank champagne for breakfast, mixed with fresh orange juice. Alistair called it Buck's Fizz. He was still working hard for her, running around doing errands, taking photographs of her clothes to use in handouts; and he was always high. It didn't matter in this boom year— *everyone* was high! Mackenzie grabbed handfuls of cash from the register when she needed it. She cut her mini-skirts in vinyl, in gold lamé, in fake fur. Pop groups and stars, and costume designers for TV shows like *Hullaballoo*, descended on the store and stocked up.

And then the supreme accolade: Coral Stanton's secretary made an appointment for Coral to come "when the joint was jumping," which meant around three p.m. on Saturday. Alistair tipped off *WWD* so Coral's visit could be duly recorded for the Eye column. At three-thirty the following Saturday a black Rolls disgorged what looked like three go-go girls in white vinyl skimpy cheerleader dresses. Only on looking closely, however, could it be seen that one of the "girls" was a forty-five-year-old woman masquerading as a cheerleader. Coral had captured the youth look. She stalked in, opened her eyes wide and pronounced, "*Genius!*" Embracing Mackenzie she shouted, "And *I* discovered you! It's the fashion store of the future! We'll get Avedon to photograph Julie Christie, Cher, and Cilla Black, *here*, in this very store: very *reportage*, very *now*, very trendy! A troupe of lithe young dancers, perhaps? *Black! Amy!*" She signaled an assistant, "Find out if Alvin Ailey's troupe's in town! Mackenzie? Will those rails support human weight? I see young bodies with gleaming dark skin hanging in the spotlights, like acrobats, wearing every color of the rainbow! It will be *super!*"

Alistair poured champagne for them all, and Coral toasted their success. Quite a few garments were shoplifted that day because of Coral's distracting presence, but when she grandly swept out, they felt it had been worth it. *WWD* interviewed Mackenzie in depth, calling her "Queen of the Yankee Mods," saying, "At last the British invasion has been halted by a homegrown variety: down-to-earth, bubbly Mackenzie Goldstein. . . ."

When Mackenzie read the article, she tossed the paper across the room. "That's the last time I want to see that yucky name in print! From now on I'm Mackenzie *Gold!*" She took out papers to legally change her name.

"Oh, Mia!" she wrote to Paris, "this is the *best!* Address any future mail to Ms. M. Gold! Come back soon to visit: I'm so proud of my shop! No matter what happens in the future, nothing will mean as much to me as this place!"

She was wrong about that. Gold! had only been operating for four months when her brothers began talking about a second store. This time she put her foot down and said, "It's Madison Avenue or nothing!"

Backed by a half-million dollars from three eager banks, dazzled by the incredible weekly figures of the modest Second Avenue store, it became her new dream—opening on Madison! The money was pouring in. The Beatles sang on and on, and the pot got better and better. She and Alistair took an LSD trip, and she smoked pot to relax her jangled nerves. She started looking at big, expensive, uptown apartments. But dreams coming true, as hers were, still feel dreamlike. The thinner, chic Mackenzie Gold could not shake the fear that she might wake up one morning to find she was plain old Marsha Goldstein, plump, unloved, and still living in the Bronx. Meanwhile, the Goldsteins were on their way to making one of the quicker overnight fortunes of the 1960s. . . .

Eleven

Mia's rooms overlooked a street of chestnut trees and a children's school. It was a cheerful, sunny apartment, although she only saw the sun for an hour in the morning, as she got up. Her working hours were those of the other girls of the atelier who sewed from eight-thirty to five o'clock every day. Getting to the salon on the bus, shopping for food, taking life-drawing classes at a small academy in St. Germain des Prés, filled her days.

The couture was not at all as she'd pictured it. She hated the boredom of the workshop, sitting alongside the young French and Algerian seamstresses as they performed their repetitive sewing and ironing tasks.

She had thought she couldn't be lonely if she saw Phillipe Roux each day. But she had not seen him alone since beginning work. Occasionally he came into the workroom with a jacket or skirt in his hand, discussing alterations with Madame Martine, the supervisor, indicating where he had pinned it—alterations on clothes he had sold to clients. But she only got glimpses of him during three weeks of working in the hot, stuffy room.

The girls were curious about her, plying Mia with questions about America, asking her exactly what was her position in the house. Phillipe had simply told her that she must learn to use fabric and sew. Then he'd dumped her in the atelier, where she was assigned very elementary tasks—pressing hems or tacking. It was like starting over at MacMillans, but without the company of Mackenzie or David.

This must be a test of her seriousness, she decided. The days were so long, so dull! His assistant, whom everyone called Mademoiselle Josephine, often barged into the room in a bossy, domineering way. Out of the corner of her eyes Mia studied her. She wasn't pretty. Tall, in her late thirties, with short-cropped hair that looked as if she hacked it off herself, white trousers and white smock; she bustled in and out with a brisk air of efficiency. Mia hated her on sight. And she soon learned that her feelings were shared by the girls. They whispered that Mlle. Josephine was very hard on them, and very jealous. Jealous of what? Mia asked. Very shyly, they replied, "Of Monsieur Phillipe..."

She listened carefully to the girls' gossip. They said Mlle. Josephine was Phillipe's protector, bodyguard, buffer for the outside world; probably also his mistress, since they arrived together in his tiny car and left together late at night. Josephine screamed at them for their mistakes. Monsieur Phillipe was a sensitive artist, they said, who never used a harsh word. It sounded like a convenient arrangement.

By the end of the third long week in the workroom, Mia's mind felt as dulled and empty as the chatter of the girls around her. She had almost forgotten her intention to be a designer. This was more like a sentence to hard labor, a punishment for daring to harbor illusions about assisting a great designer.

The pressure built up in her mind until she decided she must go to Phillipe and tell him she was leaving. If this was what working in the couture meant, she would return to New York and find a job somewhere—it couldn't feel worse than this!

At the exact moment that she came to this decision, Phillipe stuck his head around the curtained door and said, "Mia? Come in to see me before you leave tonight, please." A warm glow was relit in Mia; he had not forgotten her!

At five o'clock she went to the tiny bathroom in the back and quickly refreshed her makeup. She said good night to Madame Martine, and feeling terribly privileged, walked through the door into the salon. *Had* he deliberately stuck her in the workroom to humble her? She passed an office and Stephanie looked up from her desk, saying, "I'll tell him you're here." Stephanie disappeared through a doorway, reappearing seconds later and beckoning Mia, summoning her to Phillipe's studio.

It was situated at the front of the building, the long

windows opening onto narrow balconies overlooking the bustling avenue. Mlle. Josephine stood alongside Phillipe as they went through a stack of swatches.

"This is my assistant, Josephine," Phillipe said, introducing them. "Mia is doing an apprenticeship in the workroom," he told her, as if they had never discussed Mia.

Josephine stuck out a brusque hand, looking Mia directly in the eye. "Welcome," she said expressionlessly as they shook.

"I hope you two will become friends," Phillipe said, without conviction.

Very unlikely, Mia thought, considering the waves of hostility coming from Josephine. It was a perfect chance to examine her at close range, however. The face she scrutinized was stark, bony, with good features and dark intense eyes like Phillipe's, but without his sense of wonder. She had a mean, thin mouth, and her face was scrubbed shiny clean. The angular body had no breasts or plumpness.

"How are you liking working in the atelier?" Josephine asked. Her fluent French had a slight Spanish accent.

"I was never good at sewing." Mia made a face. "I'm much more of a designer than a seamstress."

"Phillipe Roux is the only designer here," Josephine said quickly. "One must learn to sew before one even considers design. It's like walking before one can run, no?"

"At the time of the collection, she will join us in the studio and do some sketching," Phillipe explained.

"I'd love that!" Mia said quickly.

Josephine turned her attention back to the swatches. "I'd choose this one," she told Phillipe, indicating a beige wool. She busied herself with a pile of receipts.

Phillipe smiled at Mia. "The workroom can't be much fun, but they are good girls. It is the only way you can learn the métier—"

"The only way," Josephine repeated without turning.

Phillipe touched the back of Mia's hand with a warm fingertip. "Come and see me if there are any problems." When he removed the gentle pressure of his finger, it felt as if a life-sustaining force had been withdrawn. She moved to the door.

"Oh, Mia?" he said. "You are sketching—at home and during the weekends?"

"Yes. I always do."

"You might bring me the sketches each week. I'd like to see what sort of progress you're making." She left the salon, feeling only a little better. What Josephine said doesn't matter, Mia told herself. It was only what Phillipe said that mattered. And what Phillipe signaled to her with his eyes was not imaginary. It couldn't be. One did not imagine anything as intense as that expression.

She walked along the Seine that night, lost in thought. When she reached home she took a long, warm bath, Phillipe's face constantly in her mind. Stretching her arms above her head, she looked at herself in the steamy mirror, noting the lines of her breasts, the fullness of them. They were young, upright. She touched the rosy pink nipples, wondering how it would feel if Phillipe touched them. She pictured their making love as very different than the way David had pounced on her. Phillipe would be gentle and sensitive with her, and yet she knew there was an electrifying, animal side to him. It showed in his sensual mouth and in his eyes. For the first time in her life she found herself yearning for a man's touch, for Phillipe's. She went to bed feeling unfulfilled, incomplete.

The Chambre Syndicale de la Haute Couture, a trade body with a lot of pretensions and little power, informed Phillipe Roux that his new collection was scheduled for its first press showing on the last Wednesday of July. They began to make the clothes in early June.

Mia was excited and a little afraid. This collection would define her position in the house. If he even used her sketches as starting points, she would feel part of the house, thus part of him.

The studio began to fill up with bolts of fabric, left on consignment by the top textile houses of Europe. Phillipe Roux would put together a collection of about fifty outfits. The routine of the salon changed. The seamstresses stopped making clothes for private clients and waited for Roux to make up toiles, the canvas trial runs of the garments. These were fitted and cut on live models, then brought into the workroom and taken apart to be turned into flat patterns.

The pattern was only the second stage in his complicated construction of suits and coats and their magical interlinings.

Choosing the fabric was the most important part. Phillipe called Mia into the studio several times to look at fabrics with him. The heavy bolts of wool, twill, or tweed were his raw material, and he treated them with a reverence a master sculptor would give a marble quarry.

"Feel it!" he instructed Mia, making her crunch the fabric in her hand. It was always of the best quality, thick, soft, expensive, with price tags of up to ninety dollars a meter.

She worked constantly on her design sketchbook. Sometimes she left it in his studio. One afternoon she came to reclaim it and found Roux leafing through, peering intently at her designs. He looked up, almost guiltily, when she came in. "These are interesting, Mia," he told her. He handed the book to her. "I am in the habit of working from other people's sketches. I may even see something in a sketch that you did not intend." He touched her arm gently: "Perhaps you should be helping us in the studio as we get nearer the collection?"

Oh, to get out of that workroom with its boring sewing and the meaningless chatter of the girls! She tried to show her enthusiasm in her eyes.

At home she did nothing but sketch her designs.

After the weekend, she took a batch of designs to show him. On Tuesday he summoned her from the workroom, all the girls looking up at her speculatively, wondering, as she left. He took her to a tiny storeroom at the end of the salon corridor. It had been emptied of shelves and stores, and a chair and table placed in it.

"This is your own room. You will sketch here," Phillipe told her proudly. "But you must always close the door, so clients arriving for fittings cannot see in."

She looked at the tiny space, small as a closet, and felt a moment of panic at the idea of being shut in there. He caught her thought and quickly promised, "You will mostly be in the studio with us."

Now she used the front stairs of the building to enter, receiving Mlle. Josephine's snapped *"Bonjour"* in the morning. It sounded as welcoming as "Go to Hell!"

Each time she entered the studio, before going to sit quietly in a corner, Mia glanced at the bulletin board

where Phillipe pinned some of her designs. Occasionally
he attached pieces of fabric to her drawings. Once, she
saw he'd torn certain drawings off the sketch-pad pages
she'd shown him, without asking her. Did it mean he
intended to actually make them up? She did not dare ask.
The atmosphere when Phillipe worked was so hushed, so
reverent.

Another day, bringing some designs into the studio, her
heart skipped a beat. Phillipe was pinning the toile on a
live model and creating one of her designs—a cocktail
dress with swags of fullness floating from each shoulder,
one drifting free, one bloused at the back.

"See this seam?" Phillipe indicated the waistline. "It
was too high on your sketch. Women prefer a lengthened
torso. I dropped it . . . softened it. . . ." He gently gathered
a double thread through the waist, shirring the toile so
that it fell into a flowing, soft line. Mia watched him,
hardly daring to breathe. The best designer in Paris—maybe
in the world—was transforming one of *her* designs into a
dress! She smiled at Elisabette, the model, in the mirror.
She was not pretty, a "second tier" mannequin who was
fitted for clothes but never modeled in the salon.

Before their eyes Phillipe pinned and gathered the canvas, sculpting it in his fingers as if it were clay. He asked
Elisabette to step out of the pinned dress, and carried the
complex structure over to his worktable. He penciled the
toile, deftly repinned a few seams, and tried it on her
again. Now the waistline dipped, curved around to the
front, making her torso slimmer, longer. It showed Mia
exactly how great fashion worked—the magic that sold
clothes. This flattery of the figure, this exaggeration of
femininity, made Phillipe's clothes special. He admired
women's bodies, and this showed in his clothes. That is
what made them unique, and so wearable and wantable.

He touched Mia's wrist. "Would you like to try draping
the back?"

She had never mastered draping at MacMillans. She
made an attempt to pin the long fall of canvas to the
shoulder seam, but as usual it seemed too tough, too
unyielding to float like the silk the dress would be made
up in. Then she tried to arrange its bulk into a graceful
flow but it stuck out, awkward and stiff. When the fullness

was clumsily pinned, she stood back, her hands slippery
with sweat, feeling she'd failed.

"*Quelle atrocité*," she cried, and they all laughed.

Mlle. Josephine entered just then, glancing at the scene
with a tight smile. "Amusing yourselves?" she asked.

"Mia was draping the model," Phillipe explained.

Josephine looked stern. "But she's been posing since
nine, Phillipe," she scolded. Phillipe moved to the dress
and undid Mia's work, then, with a few quick pins, made
it look light and fluid.

"I'll never learn to work with toile," Mia said with a
sigh.

"You will practice until you can," Phillipe told her.

Josephine helped Elisabette out of the dress, peering at
it as she took it to the worktable. "But would these panels
not have been much easier to work if they had been *en
bias*?" she asked Mia, her eyes burning.

Mia frowned. "What do you mean?"

"*En bias!* Cut on the cross!" Josephine made a gesture.
"Surely you know what that is?"

Mia shook her head, dazed at this sudden question.
"Of course I know what it is—but I just used the piece of
material Phillipe gave me—"

"But you should have recut it on the bias!" Josephine
cried. "Anyone would have known that!"

Mia felt tears welling up at the unexpected attack.
Speechless, she turned to look at Phillipe.

"It was a natural mistake to make," he told Josephine
calmly.

"But Phillipe!" Josephine exploded, her hands on her
hips. "How could you employ someone who doesn't
understand the importance of cutting on the bias?"

Mia ran out of the studio, slamming the door behind
her, down the hallway to her tiny room and slamming
that door too. She fell into her chair, sobbing. Josephine
had been right—which made it worse.

There was a soft knock on the door, and she called out,
"*Attendez!*"

"It's me. Phillipe." His voice purred through the door.
She reached out and opened the door. Phillipe entered,
looking at her kindly, smiling. His eyes were filled with
emotion. He closed the door gently behind him. Mia
sniffed, wiping a tear away with her finger.

"There is absolutely no reason to cry," he said. He fished in his pocket and handed her his snowy handkerchief. She dabbed it at her hot cheeks, looking away from him. "She is brusque, I know," he murmured. "But that is her way."

He was so close, she could smell his cologne mixed with his own personal odor, and her nostrils widened. She wanted to turn her face up toward him, so that he would cover it with kisses. She trembled in anticipation of his touch, and as if he had picked up her thought, he gently touched his fingertips to the back of her neck. She shuddered slightly. It was a healing touch, waves of comfort emanating from it. He let his fingers linger for a moment, and she took a deep breath, marshaling all her control to keep from reaching out to him, from kissing his concerned face. It was the first time she had felt this intense desire to kiss a man, and it surprised her. She handed back his handkerchief.

"Thank you. I'll be all right now," she promised.

They exchanged another long look in which she could interpret a hundred things. That he was sorry for Josephine's jealous temper. That he loved her more than he could ever love Josephine. That he was tied to Josephine in some dutiful way. That he was sorry he had ever invited her to join the house. As she searched for more meanings in his serious gaze, he turned away and left her, closing the door gently behind him.

She felt a surge of anger at the way he seemed to know exactly how to handle her, to calm her, to keep her happy with his little touches, his moments of attention, as if she were some pet that had to be artfully tamed. All she wanted was to be held by him. She knew how strong he was, how firmly he could crush her in those brown, sinewy arms. She knew how he would smell, how his skin might taste if she lapped at his neck with her tongue. These fantasies surprised and frightened her. The idea of herself and Phillipe naked, holding each other, was too incredible to even fantasize. Just thinking about it, she began to tremble violently. She suddenly realized that he would be the man to unlock the fear, to set it free. He would know how to make love to her so that she would not be afraid. He was probably the only man in the world who could achieve it, which was why fate had decreed that she gravitate here—a green, young American girl working in a top designer's studio—it *must* have been destined! The looks they exchanged. The extra dimension when their eyes met. It took her into another world, a world that left her breathless, trembling, not caring what happened as long as they ended up together, somehow, somewhere. She leaned her head in her hands. She loved him so much she couldn't think clearly.

When she reached home that night, there was a message to call Wayland collect at the store.

"Your mother and I are coming to Paris on July twenty-fourth," he told her excitedly. "We'll both be staying at the Crillon. She's in fine fettle. All this liberation and revolution has had a good effect on her. She wants you to join us as much as you can while we're here. Dinners and things . . . you *will*, won't you?"

"I don't know," Mia said. "This is the busiest time for us, and this collection is so important to Phillipe. I'd love to see *you*, of course, Wayland."

"Well, your mother's looking forward to seeing you, so try, Mia. We could have so much fun. Colin will be there, of course. We'll double-date and eat ourselves *silly*!"

"Great!" she said, trying to sound enthusiastic.

When she hung up, she felt sick. She had successfully blocked Coral from her thinking for months, and her arrival in Paris could stir up a lot of problems. She would want to see Phillipe, might even expect special treatment from him. The kind of coverage *Divine* allotted to a designer would make a big difference to the future of the house.

"This collection is—how you say—'make or break' for him?" Stephanie murmured to her one evening, when they were both alone in the studio. "It is a pity you joined the house at such a tense moment."

"I'd think most moments at Phillipe Roux are tense!" Mia replied.

Stephanie didn't laugh. "He knows he must fulfill the promise of his first season, or pouf! There simply is not enough backing to keep him going unless he makes some big money."

"American buyers?" Mia asked. "I have a good friend at Headquarters! He'll be seeing the collection."

Stephanie nodded, looking at the list. "Yes, but we also

need Japanese, British, German, and lots of interest from stores, pattern companies, *parfumiers*, all those people."

Mia sighed. "And great press coverage. God, my mother had better like him. . . ."

All the top modeling agencies sent their stars for Phillipe to choose four female models to present the collection. He found four with the proportions he liked best—long-limbed, healthy, sportive types. These high-priced models were used very sparingly. Phillipe continued to use Elisabette, his house model, and a German girl, Rosemarie, to stand for the hours of fittings, their measurements corresponding with those of the star models.

One of the girls Phillipe chose was a beautiful dark-haired New Yorker named Audrey Zelco. She was only nineteen, with an allure and a sophistication far beyond her age. She and Mia chatted as she waited to be measured. Her huge, dark eyes, pert nose, and sensual, full mouth suggested something exotic. She told Mia she had arrived in Paris a month ago and her modeling career had started that same day. She was that rare creature: a photographic model who was also good at showing clothes on the runway.

Audrey had a string of admirers who took her to places like Morocco for the weekend, and to the best restaurants and *boîtes* in Paris during the week. She was stunning, and wore clothes with a European chic, her skirts slashed to the thigh, her beautiful long, slim legs showing. The other models, one of them a black girl who showed off Phillipe's clothes to perfection, hung around the studio, puffing cigarettes, filling the salon with smoke, to Josephine's annoyance. Mia watched her to see if she was disturbed by the presence of these lovely creatures. But Josephine knew that Phillipe was so intent when he fitted the garments that he might just as well be using a dummy.

Audrey took to joining Mia at the local *tabac* where they were watched interestedly by the local businessmen as they lunched on *croque-monsieurs*, and huge cups of *café crème*.

"What about *your* beau?" Audrey asked, after reeling off the dates she had lined up with various men. "You must have one?"

"David was a boy I really liked at fashion school in New

York," she replied. "Since I came here, though, I guess I've lost touch with him."

Audrey nodded her exquisite head. "I hate writing too. I like guys to call me. They usually do if they're keen. The only guy I broke my rule for was Mick Jagger. I had his number once in New York and I called him." She raised her eyebrows. "Nothing happened," she confessed.

Later she told Mia, "You should see the dump I'm living in now. Cheapest hotel in Paris, I'll bet. I want to save every penny from modeling to keep me when I'm old and fat."

Mia laughed. "I don't picture *you* living in poverty— ever! You'll be flying to Marrakesh for the weekend and dining at the Ritz."

"Yeah, and hiding food in my purse for the next morning!" Audrey assured her. "But if you don't have a beau here, what do you do for fun?"

"My work is my fun," Mia said.

"Fun?" Audrey cried. "Working for that gruesome twosome—"

"I only think that about one of them."

"Oh, Phillipe can pour on the charm all right, but the atmosphere is so strict up there. Like, you want to apologize if you say 'shit'! And that *Josephine*, God, she *really* spooks me! I feel embarrassed at showing my tits in front of her! And she'd *kill* anyone who looked at Phillipe."

"What do you think of him?" Mia asked shyly.

"Phillipe?" Audrey pondered, taking a sip of coffee. She looked frankly at Mia. "You're stuck on him, aren't you? I've seen you looking at him."

Mia stared at this new friend. It had been so long since she had confided to a sympathetic American girl of her own age. "I'm in love with him," she finally confessed. "Oh, Audrey, I've never felt like this about anyone in my *life*."

"Oh. . . ." Audrey took a huge bite out of her sandwich and chewed silently for a moment.

"What's the matter?" Mia asked.

Audrey shrugged. "I just think you should start writing to David, fast!" She bent forward across the round marble-topped table. "You know about fashion, don't you? What's right or wrong? I'm that way about *men*! Phillipe Roux is an incredibly sexy man, but he's out for Phillipe Roux.

He'll use all his charm to get there, and he'll make it. But there's something funny about those two—don't you feel it? They have some weird little scene going. They aren't sophisticated. And they're out of their element in this city, really. Listen to Audrey—don't get in their way...."

Designers all over Paris panicked as they approached the dates of their showings. Phillipe was no exception. Tempers were lost, usually over trifles: small disasters like misplaced buttons, an uneven hem, a pin left in a lining pricking a temperamental mannequin.

Phillipe Roux was like a master chess player trying to solve a problem. The problem was elegance and how to give to a woman's body—any woman's body—the shape she desired. Mia sat in her tiny room each morning, concentrating on design, ideas spinning from her. She was bringing together the vitality of street fashion and couture workmanship.

Phillipe saw what she was doing and as he looked through her sketches and talked to her about them, suggesting materials, Josephine left them together. Their conferences became the high point of her day. They seemed to inspire Phillipe also. Soon the bulletin board was entirely covered by her sketches—there was not an original Roux drawing among them. The meaning of this was almost too much for Mia to grasp. The entire Fall-Winter collection of Phillipe Roux, Paris, France, would be based on her designs, her ideas. She said nothing, told no one, kept the unbelievable secret to herself.

Only Audrey, who saw the bulletin board and peered at her sketchbook, questioned her. "Aren't those *your* drawings? Mia, do you mean to tell me *you've* designed the whole goddamn collection?"

"I contributed," Mia said softly.

"You dumb kid—and you're probably not even getting a decent salary."

That was true. Phillipe paid her less than the cost of her lunches.

As the collection shaped under her eyes, she knew they were doing something very new. She knew Phillipe would be hailed either as a madman or a fashion genius. Some of the outfits were so short, so daring, that the models protested when they tried them on. Phillipe wanted them

to walk in a different way, not slowly or languidly, but to
dance or run through the salon.

"I heard them yelling at each other last night," Audrey
told her over a quick lunch. "They thought they were
alone, but I'd come back in for some makeup I forgot.
Josephine was asking Phillipe why he was so American-
influenced. Had he forgotten how Frenchwomen liked to
dress? And he said America was the new leader—even for
fashion! He said he could do designs that American wom-
en would like because they inspired him—and then I
understood, Mia. They *are* all your designs, aren't they?
You inspired him! His cut was always great, but this
season the clothes are so different. You must represent
young America to him, long legs, healthy bodies—that's
why he chose me and the black girl. He wants to be big in
America—he doesn't give a shit about France."

But he had said a hundred times to Mia that they were
all working together for the good of the house and he
didn't care about money. To take any credit when it was
his genius that made the clothes so wonderful would
be wrong. She knew he needed her now, and that was
all she really cared about.

Twelve

"For God's sake, Lloyd, spill the beans," Coral hissed. They were at the best table at La Côte Basque, and even the blasé crowd was staring. Coral looked astounding. Her Chanel suit had been an excellent choice—it was a style everyone believed had gone out forever, and here she was, bringing it back, making the crowd of socialites feel underdressed.

"You look wonderful, Coral, but let's order first."

Lloyd was in a jubilant mood. Why? she wondered. Usually her grapevine—her photographers, hairstylists, and makeup artists—provided a clue to Lloyd's mood: a circulation rise, his wife leaving town for a week—she studied him as his eyes ran greedily over the menu. Coral was worried. The sixties were starting to unnerve her. Maybe it was all that pot she'd been smoking. She felt a new restlessness stirring in her. She had been editor-in-chief for two years, and had led the fashion world into using pop stars as models: Cher, the Supremes, and lately Andy Warhol's Superstars—two of whom, Baby Jane Holzer and Edie Sedgwick, were as elegant as any professional models. Now everyone used them, which meant that Coral had to move forward: What would be the Next Big Thing? And would *she* be the one to discover it, as she had to be?

"Phoebe has agreed to a divorce," Lloyd said, closing the menu with a snap. "Lobster?" he asked.

Coral fixed him with surprised eyes, speechless, her brain racing as he ordered champagne. Was this good or bad news?

"To happiness!" Lloyd proposed when champagne was poured. Coral clinked glasses automatically. The news, helped by Dom Pérignon's bubbles, took a few moments to percolate through her head. She found herself longing for some pot.

She attempted a smile. "How'd you manage it, darling? Did she meet someone?"

Lloyd chuckled. "No. I have my lawyer to thank. It's usually a question of finances, you know. I hung onto *Divine*, don't worry, she's not getting any of my publications."

"And that's why you're so happy?"

"I'm also in love," he told her. "Perhaps for the first time in my life! I wanted to bring the lady in question, but she talked me out of it."

The waiter was serving their first course as Coral cried out, "But *why*?"

"She's a little shy. The kid thought you might not approve . . . she works for you."

"One of my editors?" Lloyd nodded. "One of my *junior* editors? Oh, Lloyd, you naughty boy! Let me guess: Donna Haddon, my clever little sportswear editor?"

Lloyd nodded, beaming. "Isn't she pretty?"

"Charming!" The salad suddenly choked her. She coughed, taking a sip of champagne. Donna was in exactly the position *she* had started out in at *Divine*. A chill of fear made her shiver. "Paris is going to be terribly exciting, Lloyd," she chattered quickly, "I signed up Twiggy in the face of all opposition. Cher will model the American stuff: Twiggy and Cher! Not bad, eh?"

"Better than Sonny and Cher, I guess," Lloyd grunted. "Donna's made 'I Got You, Babe' *our* song! You said pop music would enter every aspect of our lives, Coral, remember?"

"Yes," she mused, eating without appetite. Especially if sixty-year-olds like you start going with twenty-five-year-olds, she thought.

The bad mood this news brought on lasted for the rest of the day. When she left La Côte Basque to attend a shooting, she got so irritated with the multicolored Tovarich Dynel falls attached to a model's hair that she yanked them out, reducing the girl to tears and lawsuit threats. Everything was going to be youth, youth, *youth*! she lectured herself in the taxi home. And where will that leave *me*? Frazzled, she reached her apartment building, longing for a smoke. She closed her eyes wearily, leaning against the

elevator as it climbed to her floor. She had begun to loathe
the sixties. She now had the distinct feeling that they were
not going to lead to better and better things. In fact, she
realized, *the sixties may well go sour on me.*

Inside her apartment, she searched feverishly for her
secret stock of grass. One joint would soon put this awful
day behind her. A few long puffs—*tokes*, as the kids called
them—would relax her. She smiled grimly. You had to learn
the current lingo. It kept old age at bay and made the kids
feel you were one of them.

She lit the joint she'd rolled and kicked off her shoes,
reclining on her bed as she breathed in the smoke and
held it down in her lungs. Slowly, her mood changed.
Nothing really mattered. But she had one thing to do
before she allowed herself to drift off completely.

She called Howard Austin. Maybe she could kill two
fashion-birds with one well-aimed stone? Sacrifice Howard
and get rid of Donna Haddon's threat in one clever move.
Donna was pretty and Howard handsome: Would they be
able to resist each other?

It had been several weeks since they'd met. He sounded
guarded, off-hand.

"Still seeking an editor, Howard?" she asked him.

"Don't tell me you've changed your mind?" he laughed.
The bass of his laugh reverberated in her. It made her feel
like making love.

"It occurs to me that someone on our staff might be just
the person you're looking for. Her name's Donna Haddon
and she's smart as a whip . . ."

He spotted Donna Haddon the instant she appeared in
the small, out-of-the-way bar they had chosen so no one
would suspect she was job-hunting. It was a week after
Coral's call and Howard was exhausted from the business
of selling his dress firm and renting new offices, seeing
printers, establishing a publisher and a small staff in the
cramped, garment-district rooms he'd rented. He watched
as Donna strode confidently into the room like a refugee
from the pages of *The Great Gatsby*. Tall, thin, with a
longish face and dark bobbed hair, her perfect grooming
and immaculate clothes marked her as a fashion editor.

He jumped up and approached her, holding out his

hand and smiling. She stopped, smiling back, taking his hand. "You're so young!" she said.

"You too!" he laughed. They locked eyes and a definite frisson passed between them. He guided her to a table, holding the chair as she sat.

"Who told you about me?" she asked as he sat opposite her.

"Colin Beaumont," he lied easily, as Coral had requested.

"A very special man," she said.

"He's a great fan of yours," he assured her. "What'll you drink?"

A waiter hovered near. "I'd love a glass of champagne," Donna said.

Howard ordered a bottle. He'd studied the girl appraisingly as she had approached the table. She had one great advantage over Coral, he realized: She was about fifteen years younger, she was fresh, and she was beautiful. Dressed in a classically styled cream-colored linen suit, her understated elegance was a refreshing contrast to Coral's typical wild outfits. He allowed his eyes to feast on her, and she smiled frankly back at him.

The champagne arrived and they talked fashion. He described *Labels* and his intentions for it.

Donna was politely interested. Ice cool. He mentioned salary, and she raised one eyebrow slightly. Obviously money was not her objective. After her third glass of champagne, she leaned toward him.

"You know, Mr. Austin—"

"Howard."

"Howard. If you had told me about this a few months ago, I would be expressing a lot more interest. But to be honest, I'm not interested in moving from *Divine* right now. I'm complimented that you're even considering me, and I appreciate it. But things are happening at *Divine*—I can't go into details, but it's pretty important that I stay put for the moment."

He frowned. "I don't really understand. Do you get on with Coral?"

She shrugged. "As well as anyone."

"Is she difficult?"

"I'm not one to tell tales out of school, Howard," she said, smiling. "It's my strict Nantucket upbringing. Let's just say that Coral knows how to use power—"

"You're after *her* job?"

"I wouldn't be so presumptuous. . . ."

"Okay, I give up. I smell a scoop, but I guess you're not about to hand me one. Will you call me if there's any news? I'm going to need all the contacts I can get."

She remained sitting, smiling at him. "I'm not able to take the job," she said crisply. "That doesn't mean I'm not interested in *you!*"

He opened his eyes inquisitively. "Is that what strict Nantucket upbringing does?"

She held his eyes with her frank, cool stare. "You turn me on. This is a hotel, isn't it? Why don't you get a room?"

"Are you kidding?"

"Aren't we in the sixties?" she asked challengingly.

He did not need any more urging: she was gorgeous. Her suggestion was unexpected, but he wanted her too. He excused himself and went to make arrangements at the desk, sending Donna a written message and room number via silver platter and page boy. He waited in the suite for her. When she entered, she walked straight into his arms. Mouths pressed together, they fell back on the bed. She adjusted her clothing, unzipped him, and he was inside her as she sat astride him, her skirt falling over his knees.

"Oh, my God!" she cried as she moved up and down on him, her dark hair bouncing on her shoulders. He reached to hold onto her, steadying her as she undid the rest of her clothing and pulled it off. Soon she was naked, and without leaving him, worked on getting off every piece of his clothing, tearing some of it, popping buttons.

Once their naked skins were rubbing against each other, they lost any last shred of restraint. He buried his face between her legs, licking and lapping there until she begged him to stop. She had perfect, round semispheres of breasts, and he nibbled the tip of each until they were hard and swollen, thrusting themselves at him. She whispered dirty words in his ear, caressing his body with her soft, gentle hands until he clambered onto her. Then he made plain, hard love to her until they both cried out with pleasure, climaxing at the same time. When it was over, they lay alongside each other on the rumpled bed.

"That was the most intense sexual experience I've ever had," Howard said, still breathing heavily. He clasped her hand and squeezed it. "I demand it at least once a week for the rest of my life!'"

He turned to watch her, and she smiled and said, "I don't know about once a week. But any time I can slip away..."

A warning note in her cool voice stopped his happiness dead. "Slip away from what?" he asked. "Your busy schedule at—*Divine*?"

She nodded. "Among other things." She stood and began to dress as he watched her, feeling a stab of disappointment.

"Other things like what? A husband? A fiancé? A boyfriend?" He couldn't stop himself from asking. Damn these *Divine* women. She was very quickly, flawlessly dressed, retouching her makeup in the mirror, a hand on the doorknob. She looked so icily cool that no one would possibly believe that she had just had fifteen minutes of sexual pleasure.

"You're trying to create a mystery," Howard said, looking for his clothes.

"You read *Women's Wear*?" she asked him. "Tomorrow's edition will have all the answers...." She opened the door, blew him a kiss, and disappeared.

The next morning he couldn't wait to get his hands on the paper, coming into his office early. He leafed through to the Eye, running his eye down the column until he found the item.

Lloyd Brooks of Brooks Publications, publishers of the super-success glossy *Divine*, announced his separation some weeks ago from Phoebe Brooks, his wife of thirty years. Last week he was seen with the chic sportswear editor of *Divine*, Donna Haddon. "A business meeting," Mr. Brooks insisted, waving our photographer away from the entrance of "in" spot Divertimenti, where he dined his young (26) staff member. Her Fashionness Coral Stanton had no comment for Eye other than that it was a free country, but insiders say Mr. Brooks (62) is serious."

"*Shit!*" Howard swore, throwing the paper across the room. "I'll be my *own* fucking editor!"

* * *

He got through to Donna's secretary the next week.

"A secretary? For a sportswear editor?" he marveled.

"Mmmm . . . we're building up the sportswear section," she told him.

"Over Coral's dead body?"

"Something like that."

"I wanted to congratulate you. And tell you how sorry I am for myself at our lousy timing."

"Howard," she said softly into the mouthpiece, "*I* think the timing is perfect!"

"Aren't you about to marry your boss?"

"So what?"

"You mean, it's not exactly love?" He shook his head to himself. How naive could you be? Had he actually thought a girl as smart as Donna would be some simpering little angel?

She laughed throatily, and he imagined her long, slender neck arching as she threw her head back.

"Lloyd and I will be very happy, Howard," she assured him. "I'll *make* him happy. But that doesn't mean you and I can't make each other happy, too."

Howard smiled grimly. "I underestimated you, Donna, forgive me," he said. "I don't think I've ever met anyone quite like you . . ."

"I'm pretty unique," she agreed. "And I hate to be compared to anyone, Howard, especially someone like Coral."

"Who's comparing you to her?"

"*You*, for one. And everyone in the fashion world who knows I'm aiming for her job."

"So you admit it?"

"Why shouldn't I have it? And it will be a hell of a job, too, undoing all the crap she's built into the magazine over the last couple of years. I *loathe* her attitude to fashion—it's anti-female. Women can't *move* in the clothes she photographs. *That's* why she loves rock stars and Warhol freaks—they're too stoned to move! I *love* clothes, and I see the future very clearly: We'll have clothes we can *move* in! Sportswear, health, *action*! That's what the seventies will be. Coral won't be able to stand all that fresh air."

He heard her out and gave a low whistle. "So! A girl with a mission! You're really pretty ambitious, aren't you?"

"Enough to want my cake and to eat it. That means *you*, Howard! I loved the way we felt together. Our skins are compatible—couldn't you feel it?"

Howard felt himself weaken. "Oh, God, could I feel it, Donna. I'm hard just hearing your voice, baby. . . ."

"And I'm soft just hearing yours, darling. Soft and wet . . ."

"But I'm not going to be satisfied with snatched half hours in hotel rooms," he told her firmly.

"We'll work around that," she promised, "and we do have the same aim, don't we?"

"*Do* we? *What?*"

"We'd both like to see her get her comeuppance, for being such a bitch, wouldn't we, Howard?"

"What makes you say that?"

"Howard, you're *still* underestimating me! I know you had an affair with Coral. I know it was more serious for you than for her. I know you offered her the editorship of *Labels* before me. . . ."

"How do you know all that?"

"I'm smart," she replied without hesitation. "I asked around. I guessed." She laughed. "And I'm on excellent terms with her secretary, Virginia."

"It sounds like you could get what you wanted without my help."

"I *could* persuade Lloyd to fire her when her contract's up for renewal, but that would make *me* look bad. It would be so much—cleaner—if she merely resigned. *You* can help me with that, Howard. I'll feed you information you can attribute to an unnamed source. I won't ask you to publish anything that isn't true. You'll just be reporting the facts. And you yourself said you needed contacts. You'll do it, won't you? It'll make your 'Tittle-Tattle' page hot!"

He glanced at the telephone. She was using him, but sometimes it felt good to be used. Sexy. He thought of the hurt he'd felt after that Southampton weekend with Coral, when they'd made love so supremely well together and he'd still been an innocent, naive, somewhat immature good guy. Coral had made him cynical, guarded. He remembered her maddening, denigrating laugh at his suggestion that she work for him. Her glib dismissal of his new paper. He thought of Donna's body, of her mouth, of the thoroughly abandoned way she made love. . . .

"Sure I'll do it," he promised Donna.

Coral sat between Wayland and Colin on the velvet banquette at Impressionati, basking under the spotlights. It was their pre-Paris dinner. "We *will* all be together on the first Sunday evening?" Coral asked them. "La Coupole? It's a tradition! Perhaps my daughter will even consent to join us?"

Wayland beamed. "You'll become friends again? I'd be so happy!"

"She *is* my daughter," Coral said, lighting a cigarette thoughtfully. "I've been getting in touch with my buried feelings. It's a little ridiculous for us to be enemies. I've made mistakes. This is the age of peace and love, they keep telling me. I haven't shown Mia much of either. I'd like to make an effort this time to . . . to *reach* her. I'm proud of her for getting this job with Phillipe Roux. *Women's Wear* has dropped a few hints that his new collection will establish him. She stared intently at Wayland, then Colin. We could certainly use a new direction in fashion—the sixties don't appear to be going anywhere. You should see the stuff we're photographing for October. Everything is vinyl, transparent, *wild!* My discovery, Mackenzie Gold, will be America's biggest designer! It's suddenly made me long for the return of *elegance*."

"If anyone can bring back elegance, it's you," Colin assured her.

"Oh, maybe this isn't the time for elegance," Coral mused. "We have to get through the Swinging Sixties—that's what *Time* is calling them—before we reembrace the old values. I understand this era so well and I'll have to go along with it, but"—she gave a little shiver—"I hate it!"

She could not voice her greatest fear: that Donna Haddon would soon marry Lloyd Brooks. If she demonstrated to the world's press that she knew who or what the Next Big Thing was to be, she could save herself by becoming indispensable to *Divine*. Then Lloyd wouldn't dare replace her. She *must* discover a new fashion hero in Paris!

She held up her fresh cocktail when it arrived and proposed: "To the return of elegance! And lots of fun in Paris!"

* * *

"Children! *Chil*dren!" Abe Goldstein pounded the table for order. The family had gathered for a meeting in the dining room of the Bronx apartment. Mackenzie put her mouth to her wrist and blew a rude sound. She refused to take these family meetings seriously, seeing them as nothing more than ego displays for her father. Even Max and Reggie burst out laughing at their father's stern expression.

"Will you please listen!" Abe shouted.

Of course, he loved this, Mackenzie thought. It reinstated him as the head of a family. But these noisy hours were often not much more than family quarrels. It fell to Mackenzie and Reggie to battle it out as Abe sat back with a resigned expression. Although he had backed Gold!, he did not understand the modern fashion scene. Neither did Reggie, but her brother at least had enough business sense to see that what Mackenzie fought for usually worked.

Abe stole glances at the week's receipts like a dirty old man sneaking looks at a porno magazine. The figures were ten times what he was used to, and he could never believe his eyes. But when midtown rents were discussed, he clutched his heart and cried *"Yoy!"*

Mackenzie was holding out. "Our second store *has* to be on Madison!" she said for the hundredth time. "And I'll be even more specific: in the Sixties, Seventies, or Eighties, on the west side of the avenue. We must really *showcase* Gold! Believe me, I'm right—have I steered you wrong yet?"

Abe made a face and shrugged as her brothers glumly agreed that her choices had worked so far. The details she had insisted upon—the opening hours, the displays, the sales staff, even the design of the shopping bags—had all worked well.

"Okay," Reggie said grudgingly. "I guess we'll have to start looking along Madison. Now, what about this friend of yours? This . . . Alistair?"

"I want him to become part of the company," Mackenzie stated. "If we open on Madison, we need press coverage and promotion. That's what he does. He should start attending our meetings, too."

"Since when is he one of the family?" Abe asked.

"He's *my* family, okay?" Mackenzie snapped.

Reggie grunted. "Just because you're shackin' up with some guy does not make him part of *my* family, Mack."

"You're living with this man?" Abe asked. "Is he Jewish?"

"Oh, for God's sake!" Mackenzie shouted. "Let's leave my private life out of this."

"You expect a salary for this boy?" Abe asked.

"No, he'll work for free!" Mackenzie's eyes flashed. "Honestly, Dad, he's worked his butt off for us running around town, helping with this shop. It's time he was on salary—it's long overdue."

The three men looked at each other resignedly. Finally Reggie said, "Okay. Work out what kind of salary he expects, but keep it to the minimum. I don't need all these extra payrolls each week. And we made a rule about family meetings, didn't we, Dad? *Only* family. He cannot attend our meetings."

Abe nodded. "How come a stranger should know the kind of money we're taking?"

Mackenzie shook her head. His adamant tone told her she wouldn't be able to change his mind.

"It's better this way, Mack," Max said. "He doesn't need to know every detail. This is a family-run business, and we have to keep it that way. . . ."

"And what if I marry him one day?" Mackenzie burst out.

"One day is one day," Abe said and nodded sagely.

"We'll cross that bridge when we come to it," Max promised.

She left these meetings feeling drained and exhausted. "They know nothing at all about fashion," she complained to Alistair. She did not tell him of her fight to get him officially accepted by the company. "Everything I say is questioned. But they have the money, and I have to get on with them. Just for a little while, anyway."

She knew enough about business to realize that their accountant, a cousin of Abe's who had always handled his business affairs, was not equipped to deal with the kind of turnover Gold! produced. Reggie agreed with her and proposed an old school friend, Ed Schreiber. As sales boomed and negotiations got under way for the second store, they proposed setting up a twenty-seamstress work-room in the Bronx. Ed Schreiber attended a meeting—

Mackenzie hardly noticed him, her head buried in her sketchbook, drawing new ideas for the next collection.

She did not have one moment to herself, but between designing and supervising fittings, she looked for a new apartment as a backdrop to her new, successful life. The spacious Madison Avenue apartment she eventually found could just be called a penthouse—"a walk-up penthouse," she quipped to her family. "It makes sense to charge this new rent to the business," she told them. "I'll design there instead of renting a studio. It can all be tax-deductible." Her brothers and father had stared at her, eyes wide. It had not even occurred to them that Mackenzie would ever need a design studio.

"And they let me get away with it!" she told Alistair afterward, triumph shining in her eyes. "I never have to step into that crappy Village apartment again, and the place is huge! I tell you, it's a damn penthouse, Alistair!"

She dragged him there, bringing a huge sack of Doritos and the largest jar of caviar she could find in Bloomingdale's gourmet shop. The top-floor duplex was in a refined small apartment building with doorman and very proper residents. "I'll be the token weirdo," Mackenzie said, spreading out her picnic in the center of the bare living room. Alistair walked around the echoing large rooms and peered into the kitchen and bathroom. He returned as she held out a chip to him.

"You're the only person in the world who could eat Beluga caviar off a Dorito!" he marveled.

"Well, I feel so damn rich, I can eat just about anything I want!" She laughed. "And when the Doritos run out, I'll use my fingers!" Alistair squatted down near her and she fed him snacks.

"They'll never respect me," she told him, "but I can see by the way they treat me that they think I'm the goose laying the golden fashion eggs." She frowned at the caviar: "I don't even *like* this!" she said, "but I'm going to acquire the taste for it. *And* for anything else that's expensive."

"You'll outgrow me, Mack!" Alistair said. "You'll be bigger than I dreamed—"

"You should be happy for me, you believed in me," she said, slipping her hand into his lap and stroking him, making him grow.

His eyes grew soft and drowsy as he watched her. She giggled, unzipping his pants and pulling him out. Alistair never needed much encouragement, he was already hard. He lifted her sweater and began sucking on her breasts. As a joke, at first, she spread some caviar on his sex and slowly licked it all off. He put some on his forefinger and gently spread it over her nipples, bending his head to gently lap at it. She squealed in delight, "Oh God, Alistair, this is *really* living!" Ready for him, she pulled off her clothing. "My sweet Alistair," she crooned, closing her eyes tightly as he entered her, moving his groin slowly against hers as if they were dancing. Her fingers combed his thick blond hair. He took his time, slowly building her excitement. He never failed. It was so delicious. When she felt her pleasure climaxing, she sighed long, shuddering sighs, and he took them as his signal to come. He moved so fast then that he gave her another orgasm; they invariably climaxed together. Spasms jerked his body as he groaned aloud and she relished his pleasure, too. It was the best feeling in the world, to know she could give a man such pleasure. Some minutes passed, and their breathing slowed to normal. They heard the sounds of city traffic seep back into the room.

"I want to buy the most beautiful furniture, Alistair," she murmured, "Italian, clean, way-out stuff. Bloomingdale's is open late—will you come with me?"

They went via the boutique. At five that afternoon they watched the customers browsing the racks.

"There's something we have to talk about," Alistair said quietly. "Do *I* work for Gold! or what?"

"You're always here, aren't you?" She tickled under his chin. "Whaddya wanna be? General Manager?"

He frowned. "Shouldn't you speak with your family before you start handing out titles?"

She straightened a pile of neon-bright sweaters in their acrylic cube. "What d'you think I've been fighting them about all week?"

His face fell, and she saw how important it was to him. "So they *don't* want me?" He tried to sound casual.

"Oh, baby!" She rolled her eyes at him. "I have to fight for every single thing, so I fought for *you*! And *we* want you, Alistair!" She hugged him impulsively, and a browsing customer giggled.

"Okay, but I want a proper contract, Mack," Alistair warned. "And a decent salary."

"Oh? Suddenly you're so proper? I don't like taking it so seriously. It's still like playing shop to me! What is it? Do you need money?" She leaned over the counter and rang up a No Sale on the register, extracting a handful of twenty-dollar bills, pushing them to him. "You know you only have to ask me, darling. Christ, I know you've worked your butt off for me. *Here...*"

He glanced at the money she held out, then at the shoppers around them. "Mack," he said, "this isn't the way to do it...."

"Oh, don't be so stuffy." She tucked the bills into his blazer pocket.

She dismissed the salesgirls and locked up the store herself. Alistair straightened up the stock and turned out lights. As they stood in the darkened store setting the security alarm, he held her close to him.

"Let's get married, Mack," he whispered.

She returned his hug, then said brusquely, "No!" He broke away from her, hurt. "Let's just live in sin for a long, long time." She took his arm and walked alongside him toward Second Avenue. "Marriage is such an ancient, barbaric practice, darling, and I have so much living to do first! I have to see the world!"

"Married people travel, too," he reminded her.

"Come to Bloomingdale's and help me choose furniture." She kissed him on the cheek. "We can talk about this when I get pregnant," which I won't, she finished mentally. Not one minute before I'm thirty, she remembered vowing. It still held true.

"If only you were here," she wrote Mia in Paris. "We'd lunch at all the ritzy places—and I love having money to spend, Mia, to just *blow!*"

And she blew it each Saturday, at Bloomingdale's, where they were starting to know her as the crazy customer who bought the largest bottle of perfume they had in stock, or the biggest magnum of Dom Pérignon after a nonstop day of selling at Gold!

"When you take two and a half thousand dollars and your feet hurt and your back aches, what's forty dollars for a bottle of booze?" she told Alistair, laughing. They would drink and make love in her new penthouse, now redecorated in white and laid with a thick, nubbly gray carpet. You could sit on the soft floor, eat, make love, sleep. It was the best, the most fantastic feeling in the world. Not just the champagne or the sex, but the knowledge that what you had created was something people wanted to buy! Success gave her the magic ingredient—confidence. She wore her own clothes but doctored them—cut them shorter or lowered the neck to make them a little more outrageous. It was all too easy, too much fun!

When they found the perfect space on Madison Avenue, in the Seventies, and on the right side of the street, the store was signed for and then gutted, backed by a huge loan from the Goldsteins' bank. She spent her time in the shell of the new store, watching workmen attach giant mirror to the walls or hang the chrome rails that zigzagged across the store, counterpointed by strips of neon lighting.

By the time Alistair moved into the penthouse with her, it contained the very best Italian furniture, elegant and expensive. Mackenzie was working on her own appearance, too. Hard work and dieting had made her slimmer, more attractive, more sophisticated.

On one of their first evenings in the new apartment, she called out, "Look at me, Alistair!"

He was smoking a joint. Since demanding a salary that provoked Abe Goldstein into simulating a heart attack, Alistair bought a finer quality of grass, which gave him a more elegant high. He stared into the television screen with a more fastidious expression these days.

Mackenzie stood before her reflection in the black-and-white bathroom. Alistair got to his feet shakily and made his way to her. Her hair had been cut very precisely by Vidal Sassoon into an asymmetric bob. The new makeup accentuated her large brown eyes, narrowing her face. She had learned to cut long eyelashes, and had applied two sets to the upper lid, one to the lower. She looked chiseled, sophisticated. Alistair stood behind her, appraising.

"I don't look like Marsha Goldstein anymore, do I?" she asked.

"Of course not. You're Mackenzie Gold!"

She giggled, turning her head this way and that. "Now I know how Frankenstein felt."

She led him back to the living room, holding his hand,

then poured more champagne and watched as he rolled a fresh joint. "I'd prefer it if people didn't know I was connected with the Goldsteins in any way," she said.

She took a sip of champagne. "I've never had much in common with them. They *embarrass* me, if you want to know the truth...." She perched on the edge of one of the giant Italian sofas, watching him. "Do you know what it feels like to be ashamed of your family?"

He shrugged. "I was never actually *ashamed* of mine— just terribly bored by them!"

"You never tell me about them..."

"Oh, I was shunted off to boarding school when I was eight. That's how the English upper class solve child rearing!"

"So you *are* upper class? Is that why you have such a posh British accent?"

"Yeah, and it's why my father runs a stately home. It's crumbling and shabby, but it's on a list of preserved buildings, and it's been in the family for centuries."

"Oh, Alistair—could *we* stay there?"

"I don't know. I'm rather distant from the family. And it's not very comfortable!"

"I'm tired of apologizing for my crummy brothers," she told him. "I don't need them. I don't want to be associated with them."

"Well, calm down, it's not that important."

"It is to me." She found him irritatingly calm, distant, high on marijuana.

"Mack, it's just a grudge you're holding—an obsession. Why don't you let it go?"

Her temper suddenly exploded. "Fuck *you*, Alistair, you haven't listened to one word I've said! Will you quit turning on for two minutes while I try to talk to you? You're becoming a pothead, you know that?" She stalked off to the bedroom and slammed the door.

Later, he knocked softly. "C'mon, Mack. Let me in."

She knew she would let him in, sooner or later. They would make love. It was always fantastic after they had had an argument.

Thirteen

"We're here, darling!" Coral's crisp voice crackling down the phone made Mia's spine tingle. She could almost smell the cloying aroma of the Rigaud candles. "Wayland was about to call you, but I wrestled the phone out of his hand. I said, 'I want to hear my daughter's voice.'"

"So I'm suddenly your daughter again?"

"Don't be silly, Mia, you were always my daughter...." There was an awkward silence. To fill the gap, Mia asked lamely, "How was your flight?"

"Gin rummy and champagne all the way—we behaved rather disgracefully. I won twenty dollars off Wayland! *Now!* When are you joining us? La Coupole tonight is a *must*, of course! *Everyone* goes! Oh, Mia, we have so much to catch up on! Why don't you come here around eight, and then we'll meet up later with the boys—Colin and Wayland."

Mia held her breath, listening unbelievingly. "Mother," she finally said, "are you trying to pretend nothing's happened? Am I supposed to forget that you threw me out of my home two years ago?"

"Oh, really, Mia." Coral's tone was impatient. "Surely if *I* can call bygones bygones, *you* can? You *did* nearly cost me my job, remember? Let's have a truce, darling! Let's forgive, forget, and start a fresh chapter, here in Paris. Remember how I used to say we were a little family of two? Well, I've missed my family, Mia."

Mia held onto the phone. She was surprised and devastated to feel two tears rolling down her cheeks. "Have you?" she whispered.

"Of course I have! So spend some time with me. You

must have enormous talent to work for Phillipe Roux. He *does* like you for your talent, doesn't he?"

"What do you mean?"

Coral laughed her tinkling, maddening laugh. "We'll have to have that long overdue talk we never got around to having about men."

"Mother," Mia sighed. "We haven't even met and you're already making insulting little digs. Phillipe *did* hire me for my talent."

"So you're *not* having a marvelous affair with him?" Mia felt her face flushing, but she said nothing.

"Well, *is* there a beau in your life?" Coral insisted.

"I'm in love," Mia blurted out. "Let's leave it at that."

"With Phillipe Roux, of course. He's extremely handsome, isn't he?"

Mia swallowed. She could not find the right joking tone with which to fend off her mother. She cleared her throat.

"Listen, Mother," she began. "We never really got on, right? I always longed for your support—for your love, I guess—and when I really needed it, after Daddy died, it wasn't there. Why should it be any different now?"

"Because we've both changed," Coral replied easily. "These last two years have changed me enormously. I'm more in touch with my feelings. Maybe it took the Beatles and pot to bring it out, but I've admitted to aspects of my life that weren't right...."

"Such as?"

"Our relationship, for one," Coral said. "Don't you think I wish it had been storybook perfect? I'd like to try to make it up to you...."

Mia was silent. She could hear Coral lighting a cigarette and inhaling. Don't trust her, she begged herself. *Don't!*

"The sixties are liberating us," Coral said. "I don't intend to miss out on any part of them. That includes being a mother, Mia. *Your* mother. You can't deny me that—it's a fact. Now, tell me, is Phillipe Roux in love with you?"

Something warned Mia not to say more. But what Coral was saying did have some truth in it. Maybe if she opened up to her, they could really be close, be friends? The familiar tug-of-war inside her ached: the dual urge to be accepted by her mother, but also to avoid the possibility of more hurt, more betrayal.

"Phillipe is the most wonderful man I've ever met," she said finally.

"I *knew* it!" Coral's triumphant tone made Mia immediately regret confiding. "And you're having a wild affair, of course?"

"It hasn't reached that stage...." Mia faltered. "It's still just a...wonderful kind of understanding between us. It's so powerful—"

"I see," Coral said flatly. "Well, don't let it continue that way for *too* long, darling. He's bound to have *scores* of women chasing him."

"He's not that kind of man," Mia protested. "He lives for his work."

"Then I can't wait to meet him again!" Coral cried. "*I* live for my work too! Bring him with you to La Coupole tonight?"

"You don't understand!" Mia laughed. "We're working flat out! We only have four more working days until we show to the press. We're at the studio *all* day, *every* day. I'm on my way there now."

"Is any of your work actually in the collection?" Coral asked. Mia hesitated, then burst out: "Oh, Mother! the *entire* collection is based on my designs! Can you believe it?"

Coral gave a strangled little laugh. "It does sound almost too good to be true."

"Phillipe will show the best clothes in Paris," Mia promised.

Another silvery peal of Coral's laughter echoed over the phone. "You wouldn't be the tiniest bit biased, would you, darling?"

"You'll see...."

"I can't wait. Well. Come and see me as soon as you can. Love and kisses, darling."

Mia hung up, feeling her mother had somehow got the better of her.

The weekend before the main week of Paris collection presentations, thousands of journalists and buyers from all over the world poured in to report on and choose from the new clothes. They jammed hotels and restaurants for ten days, spilling over into the streets in excited little mobs after especially successful collections. Around thirty

designers, in salons scattered like jewels across Paris,
from top names like Dior to struggling new couturiers like
Phillipe Roux, would show the prototypes that would
influence the clothing of millions of women. Sometimes
the designs were so far ahead of street fashion that, they
took years to filter down to the average woman. Balenciaga's
designs were considered so avant-garde that they were
usually copied by his fellow designers seasons later, thus
ensuring them a life of several years. In any profession
one or two geniuses lead the way, and Balenciaga was
almost above fashion as its seer, prophet, and inspiration.
Givenchy, his equally gifted pupil, was on the same level.
Those two houses no longer needed press coverage. They
had enough devoted clients and buyers to guarantee the
success of their business for life. As an afterthought, they
allowed the press into their salons some weeks after store
buyers and private clientele had selected clothes.

The other designers were resigned to the press tram-
pling all over their elegant salons in their eagerness to
report to the world what half its population would be
wearing—sooner or later. Styles would be copied quickly
by Seventh Avenue "schlock shops" and would appear in
chain stores within weeks, especially if *WWD* ran a detailed sketch. For that reason big houses jealously guarded their new fashions, shrouding the models in sheeting
as they ran through the mazelike buildings housing the
maisons de couture; forbade press photographs for up to six
weeks after the first showing; and only grudgingly allowed artists like Colin Beaumont to do "tendency sketches"
which showed a vague silhouette without revealing details. *WWD* alone sometimes broke the embargo by sneaking a photograph (shot through telephoto lenses trained
on a couturier's window) or a detailed drawing. Paris
houses needed the publicity too much to do more than
tut-tut when a publication broke the rules.

Some of the clothes shown were exaggerated and not
truly intended for sale; they were included to attract
publicity or to wake up a drowsy audience or amuse it.
Many clothes in the collections were dull and conventional; intended for private clients, rich women of a certain
age who did not want to look too different, just elegant. A
collection had to include some clothes for everyone—
wearable clothes for clients, newsworthy clothes for the

press, and clothes that were different enough from last season's to make the big chain-store buyers and New York stores want to buy the toile or pattern, rush it to New York, and copy it by the thousands in a cheaper fabric. Some outfits would not even sell one copy, and others sold hundreds of times over. Sometimes this meant two of the world's best-dressed women bought the same dress or suit and then tried not to hate each other, each complimenting the other on her exquisite taste, each believing she had made the outfit quite different by the way she had accessorized it. Some zealous clients changed details of the outfits they had ordered, requesting no pockets or removing sleeves, ensuring that their outfit was unique. This was sometimes done without the designer's knowledge, aided furtively by the *vendeuse* selling the outfit and a pet tailor at the house. If a client was a particular favorite of the designer, he might add a little design detail to delight her and make her feel special.

Most designers bitterly resented their clients changing one centimeter of their creations and were furious to discover the deed had been done when they spotted the damage in some magazine coverage of a society event.

A collection could make a house famous overnight, boosting the sale of its perfumes and makeup around the world, generating millions of dollars. Within this hysterical, emotional week, thousands of photographs would be taken, millions of words written, dozens of tantrums pulled, hundreds of cups of espresso gulped to heighten awareness, and the fortunes of a handful of top designers assured or ruined or allowed to simmer on the back burner of opinion for one more season. Paris had to reinstate itself as fashion capital of the world for another six months, despite growing threats from Rome, Milan, London, and New York. Paris relied on the Collections Week to do this.

Phillipe Roux's studio looked as if an avalanche had hit. Fabrics and bolts of wool, boxes spilling with buttons, feathers, hats, costume jewelry, and shoes littered the room, overflowed from chairs and desks onto the floor. Everything was kept out for the countless rehearsals of the *défilé*—the fashion showing. Phillipe wanted it to move fast, his clothes making an instant, dramatic impact, then disappearing before the audience knew quite what had hit them.

The Roux collection looked startlingly new. Everything had been made up in the softest pastel wools, over skimpy, fitted dresses. The hemlines had to be the shortest in Paris history, Mia thought. The colors and fabrics were unbelievably flattering. Because the models' average age was about twenty, every woman in the audience would believe she looked twenty when she shrugged on one of the luxurious jackets or coats. Phillipe believed in simplicity, and would eliminate most jewelry, hats, or scarves. Stud pearl earrings were the only jewels worn with each outfit. All the girls wore light-colored hose and pumps dyed to match the pastels of the collection. Hats were no more than tiny ornaments pinned to the side or the back of the sculpted hairstyle.

Among Paris insiders, the fabric people who scampered from house to house, the little "button ladies" who matched button and thread, and the *fournisseurs* who supplied accessories like belts, shoes, jewelry, the word was out that Phillipe Roux was the one to watch. Glimpses of the clothes had been caught by visiting suppliers. These people were so attuned to fashions that they could sum up an outfit from out of the corners of their eyes, moving onto the next couture house and gossiping with supply people there. In this way the underground fashion network was au courant with the trends, and thus the same design or look sometimes turned up in two different houses, causing the fashion press to sagely note that two designers were "mysteriously in tune," a nice way of saying someone copied someone.

Stephanie turned down all requests for previews. The press wanted tendency sketches. *WWD* demanded to see some models for their preview roundup eve-of-collections feature, and were turned down.

"But you must cooperate with *Women's Wear*!" Mia tried to tell them. "If you offend them, they could hurt you!"

Phillipe and Stephanie just laughed. They said it would build an "aura" around the collection if they kept it secret. But finally, grudgingly, they agreed to show a few atypical models to *WWD*'s publisher, John Fairchild, and his editor, James Brady.

"A fashion intellectual," *WWD* wrote of Roux. "A refreshing antidote to courreges' strict tailoring..."

The fashion world was ever ready for a new hero. And if anyone was ready to discover a fashion hero, it was Coral Stanton. Donna Haddon had given her a wonderful motive. Nervously, she sharpened her nails on a little silver file in her Crillon suite. The cypress scent of her Rigaud *bougies d'ambience* was now augmented by the sweet smell of the pot she had smuggled past Customs in her Louis Vuiton wallet. She placed the lit candles at strategic points around her suite, counting down the minutes to the curtain lifting on the newest Paris fashions—her lifeblood, her raison d'être.

At nine that first Sunday night in Paris, a caravan of black limousines and taxis carried the big money of fashion across the glittering Place de la Concorde, over the Seine to the beckoning Left Bank. La Rive Gauche was the anti-establishment side of Paris—the students and artists' side. The fashion caravan pulled up at La Coupole, a huge artist's café whose heyday had been the 1920s and whose decor still echoed that era.

The cars disgorged their cargos of models, editors, photographers, stylists, and the few designers not rehearsing their collections. Tables on the sidewalk were crammed, and the sound of high-pitched chatter rose with each carload. French and British colleagues were greeted by newly arrived Americans. Friends who had flown on different flights from New York reunited as if they had been parted for years. Kisses were thrown and blown. During these eight cramped Paris days, everyone became just friendly enough to scrape cheeks, kiss air, then scamper back to their own tables to gossip.

Coral swept past the fashion riff-raff into the depths of the café where the fashion aristocracy had staked out its territory.

"English *Vogue*, French *Vogue*, American *Vogue*," she murmured to Wayland and Colin, waving at them all as she passed. "Oh! Who are *those* extraordinary folk?"

"Australian *Vogue*," Wayland murmured dryly.

They settled at a table near the end of the huge room, the men flanking Coral on the leather banquette, keeping up a steady stream of comments into each ear. Between

the two of them she could be sure of not missing so much
as an earring. Wayland glanced at the parade walking the
long aisle from the front to the back of the café and said,
"If you dropped a bomb on this place tonight, the fashion
world would disappear. Tomorrow everyone would wear
potato sacking."

"And there would *still* be competition among the
women to see whose sack was more elegant," Coral
predicted. She peered around, her short red hair sticking
up spikily from her head.

"Coral, *darling!*" The first Paris kiss was planted on her
cheek by Alix, an assistant Paris photographer they booked
to back up David Bailey.

"What do you think, Alix?" she asked him. "A vintage
season?"

Alix gave a marvelous Gallic shrug, his long lank hair
swaying. "They say Phillipe Roux's collection will be..."
He hesitated, *"inattendu."*

"Unexpected!" Coral translated. "Could Mia have backed
a winner?"

Wayland sighed. "I wish she had joined us tonight."
The waiter bowed low to them and listened patiently as
Wayland explained exactly what a vodkatini was.

People from the front of the café made their pilgrimage
to Coral's table to welcome her to Paris. She waved to the
faces she was on good terms with, ignored the other
curious faces turned in her direction. There was a lot of
kissing and toasting. Gossip exchanged hands. By the end
of the evening, hardly a designer, model, or editor had an
intact reputation. Only Phillipe Roux's name was spoken
with respect. At midnight, Coral had reigned long enough.
Giddy with jetlag and vodka, she clutched Wayland's arm
to steady herself as they made their way through the
chattering crowd to the waiting car. They dropped off
Colin at his modest hotel in La Madeleine and drove on to
the Crillon.

"God, Paris is so beautiful, so romantic," Wayland said
in her ear as they skirted the boulevardes. "It's a crime
not to be having some mad love affair."

"Shut up, Wayland," Coral snapped. But she felt the
same way. It *was* a crime. She was beginning to sense, for
the first time in her life, that fashion was not the only

thing in the world. She stared out of the window at
Paris's glowing lights, startled, feeling suddenly lonely.

Most collections have one or two outfits that give a lot
of trouble. Phillipe Roux had unpicked a cream tweed suit
six times, putting it back together again and still feeling it
was not quite right. It served as a convenient focus for the
panic every Paris designer feels when it is too late to
change the collection. In spite of this and the fact that
models were running around the salon in skimpy underwear—to Mlle. Josephine's evident disapproval, extra gilt
chairs crowding the rooms, the workroom misty with
overwrought workgirls, Phillipe seemed to be in his element. He had put in inhuman hours, having been in the
workroom or studio before the first arrival, Madame Martine,
at eight in the morning. And he was still in his studio
when Mia popped her head around the door to say good
night at ten or eleven, bent over some stubborn jacket
which his strong brown hands coaxed into shape, battered
into submission with a steam iron, or simply moulded
and pinned. He was fresh-faced and happy, and Mia's
heart went out to him. Everyone in the house was willing
the collection to be an enormous success, but they were
all too close to the clothes to even guess whether they
were right or not.

Phillipe sought out Mia three days before the collection's debut. "Your mother telephoned to me this morning," he told her. "Stephanie was not here so I was
obliged to answer the phone. She asked me to take three
suits to her hotel this evening."

"Oh, no!" Mia felt her face flush. He regarded her with
a mixture of interest and amusement. "I haven't even
seen her yet!" How typical of Coral to expect special
treatment. "She had no right to ask you that, Phillipe.
Please don't think you have to do it for my sake. Should I
call her?"

"I telephoned to Stephanie while she was still in her
home. She says your mother's magazine is the most
important in America. If she likes my clothes, we have a
success. I shall go. I am flattered by her interest in me."

Mia's eyes suddenly blazed, and without meaning to,
she clutched Phillipe's arm. "Oh, no! No, Phillipe, don't

you see? It's not your clothes she's interested in! It's her way of interfering with my life."

He frowned. "Could people be so petty? Is this possible?"

She let go of his arm, embarrassed at her outburst. "We haven't even been talking for two years," she confessed. "She called me when she arrived here, saying she wanted us to be friends again."

He shook his head sadly. "Maybe this is your mother's way of being friends—to be interested in me, your employer?" He patted her arm, and she looked at his eager, happy face as he smiled his wonderful smile at her. He moved on, his mind already on some other matter.

As soon as she could reach the phone in Stephanie's office, she called Wayland, paging him in the Crillon restaurant where he was breakfasting alone.

"What's she doing, Wayland?" she cried. "Is she trying to show how powerful she is? Treating Phillipe like some kind of delivery boy?"

He calmed her down. "She does that with everybody, especially new designers. She wants to scoop the other magazines. Fashion means a lot to her, pet. It's everything, remember, her whole life!"

"I don't know..." She toyed with a pile of invitations on Stephanie's desk. "Somehow I feel if I wasn't working here, she would never have dreamed of bothering Phillipe."

The day passed very quickly, and at six o'clock Phillipe passed her in the corridor, holding three suits wrapped in plastic garment bags. She watched through the salon window as he loaded the garments into his little black *deux cheveux* car, parked outside on the Avenue. Maybe she should go with him, she found herself thinking, to protect him against her mother's mocking smile.

"I'll be back in one hour," she had heard him tell Josephine, but two hours later the four models were sitting on the floor of the studio, waiting with Stephanie, Josephine, and Mia, yawning, drinking coffee. The run-through of the collection had been scheduled for seven that evening, and dozens of small details awaited Phillipe's touch. Josephine was getting anxious; hurting with jealousy, Mia knew. She did not like Phillipe to be beckoned by a powerful American fashion editor, and it didn't help that the editor was Mia's mother. But there was nothing to do but wait....

* * *

Coral sat on the blue velvet couch with Phillipe Roux, staring at him. Never in her life had she met a man she so instantly, physically, desired. She was pulled into his gaze, falling into those wide, warm, sherry-colored eyes that held such a quizzical look and yet were so completely sincere. She did not want to think about Mia. *This man*, she reminded herself, *is in love with my daughter.* But that only seemed to make him more desirable.

This was her second meeting with Phillipe Roux. The first, a hasty encounter backstage congratulating him after his first collection, she hardly remembered. Possibly she had been less aware of men in general then. Anyway, meeting Paris designers had never before come under the category of potentially romantic encounters.

Her hand trembled as she poured them each a tulip-shaped glass of champagne. "To your success!" she toasted him. "I can't tell you how much I appreciate your coming here. I heard so many rumors about your collection that, frankly, I couldn't contain my curiosity. If it's as good as people are saying it will be, I'd like to be first on the newsstands to feature you."

Phillipe nodded, smiling, hardly understanding. It was only with great control that she managed not to touch his face, not let her hand dart between his shirt and his chest to feel if the rest of him was as bronzed, as smooth, as the skin on his neck.

He spoke of his collection as the scent of Rigaud candles wafted around them. She hardly heard him. The tone of his voice was so bass, so musical, it seemed to stir something very deep and hidden inside her. As this little-known feeling came to life within her, it was curiously painful. She sipped at her champagne quickly, hoping to deaden the sensation.

"Let me see your clothes!" She jumped to her feet, refilling their glasses, gesturing at the garment bag. "I live for fashion, you see, Phillipe. I can't wait!"

He carefully hung each suit on the edge of the mantel-piece that underlined the huge mirror.

Coral silently considered the suits from all angles, held them to the mirror, then against herself.

"God! The smell of brand-new Paris clothes!" she

whispered. She threw the suits over the backs of three chairs.

"Of course this is the way fashion had to go, Phillipe!" she nodded to him.

"It's . . . *genius*! You took pop culture and the streets and the feeling of today and you melded them. It's witty, it's right, it's total, total *chic*!"

Phillipe beamed. He held a jacket toward her. "Please! I would like to see an American woman in this."

She eased into the jacket he held for her. They both looked at her reflection in the mirror. The new proportions did wonders for her: She looked ten years younger.

"My God, you're going to have some success!" she told him. "They make one so young!"

Phillipe threw back his head and laughed with delight. A brilliant act, she thought. A sophisticated man acting naive and innocent. She refilled his glass.

"I'm so happy to have your opinion," he said. "Sometimes one is too close to one's work. . . ."

As he made certain points, he touched her hand with his warm fingers. It sent tremors through her. The very idea of his hands working on a garment she would wear next to her body made her shiver. She stared at his hands: brown, strong, the hands of a peasant. Clean, but with something rough about them, as if hewn from wood by a brilliant carver. She imagined them cupping her breasts, the index fingers just grazing her sensitive nipples, and her nipples grew hard at the thought, under her woolen shift. He watched her, silent, as if reading her mind. She quickly drank more champagne.

"I want to see the entire collection," she said.

He nodded, calmly smiling. "In two days—"

"*Must* I wait that long?" she begged. "By then I'll have seen Saint Laurent, Courreges, Ungaro, and I only have a limited number of pages, you know. . . ."

She raised her eyebrows hopefully, staring wide-eyed at him. Phillipe gave a weary shrug. For a quiet few moments they sipped their champagne. She was glad she had worn one of her sexiest outfits, a black knit shift by Sonia Rykiel, slit up the thigh, a little silk shell beneath it, lacy black stockings, sexy Vivier pumps. She ran her fingers through her hair nervously.

Phillipe stood up. "There is still much to prepare.

Everyone at the salon is waiting for me, and the mannequins are very expensive."

She stood too, holding his arm. "Take me with you.
Show me your collection. We'll take Wayland Garrity with
us while he has his entire budget to spend. You've heard
of his store Headquarters, of course? It's like Galleries
Lafayette and Printemps put together. His store will *make*
you!"

"If he is a buyer, he must pay the premium, like every
other buyer," Phillipe warned.

"He *has* paid the goddamn premium!" Coral snapped.
"So let him see your stuff tonight! He'll go crazy for your
clothes!"

"And if he does not go crazy?"

"He'll go crazy if I go crazy," Coral promised. She
linked his arm with hers. "Craziness is contagious, Phillipe."
She was getting electric shocks through her arm touching
his. She tried to imagine his torso stripped. What would it
feel like pressed up against her breasts?

He disengaged his arm. "Madame Stanton, your interest is flattering. But I treat everyone of the press equally. It
is only fair. If I cooperate with you in advance of the
showing, all the other editors will be angry with me." He
stared at her, unbending.

She held his eyes for a moment, then burst into a wide
smile. "All right! Return to your salon! Keep me in suspense! I can see you will amaze Paris on Thursday. Go!"

He bowed over her hand, kissing it with just a trace of
irony. He might not quite understand her, she thought,
but his peasant stubbornness and cunning were a match
for her. She closed the door on him and leaned back
against it, sighing. She *must* have him, somehow! There
must be a way a top fashion editor could get a man like
him. She poured the last of the champagne and drank it
quickly. Only then did she remember that she hadn't even
asked Phillipe about Mia.

Fourteen

Mia never witnessed such scenes as on the night before their press showing. The French called them *crises*, and everyone in the salon seemed determined to have at least one. It usually involved screaming at someone in an inferior position, making that person cry, then begging forgiveness and ending up in each other's arms.

They rehearsed until after two in the morning. The models, bleary-eyed and exhausted, threatened to walk out, were charmed by Phillipe, and the offer of a cash bonus, into staying. Boyfriends waiting in cars on the street below wearily pressed their horns to remind everyone of their presence.

"I'll sue Phillipe if I lose this guy," Audrey threatened, hanging out of the window and waving to someone in a black Mercedes.

A suit had its armhole sewn up by mistake. Another sported buttons that refused to stay sewn on. In each case the culprit was hauled out of the atelier and yelled at. Josephine did most of the shouting; she was particularly good at it. Madame Martine was reduced to three fits of hysteria during the evening. Stephanie, in turn, screamed at Jean-Jacques, a milliner friend of Phillipe's. Only Phillipe stayed calm.

The oversized *faux* pieces of jewelry were returned to the supplier: They were wrong for the clothes, after all. The look was to be uncluttered, Phillipe insisted. A model, discovered to be wrong for the clothes, was sent sobbing and disheveled into the night, clutching a fistful of hundred-franc notes. Another model replaced her, quickly briefed by the others to demand five hundred francs extra for the long night's work.

Everybody left at three, the models standing around as Josephine unlocked the safe and doled out cash to eager hands. The girls ran to kiss Phillipe, ignoring Josephine.

Mia treated herself to a taxi home. She left Phillipe hunched over his worktable, steaming shape into the jacket of a suit. He hardly noticed her leaving.

Coral called her early next morning. "We've an hour between Laroche and Patou," she said briskly. "It would be too ridiculous not to see you at least *once* while we're here. Can you be in the Crillon bar at twelve-thirty?"

Phillipe had said they should start at two in the afternoon, to give them time to catch up on their sleep.

"I'll be there," Mia said.

She wore the dress she had bought from the salon's *soldes*, clothes that had been worn in the last seasons' collections. She felt marvelous in it—a simple shift in a delicious sugar-almond pink. Its expert cut skimmed the body narrowly, stopping above the knee to show off her long legs. She did her makeup slowly, knowing it must pass the critical review of her mother.

When she reached the Crillon, she took several deep breaths before peeking into the bar. Her mother was talking animatedly to Wayland. Wayland spotted her and ran over, hugging her tightly.

"My *darling*! You look *sensational*! *Super*! Boy, does Paris agree with *you*!"

"Wayland! Darling!" She hugged him, looking down at Coral. "Hello, Mother."

Coral jumped up and took Mia in her arms, then thrust her back to scrutinize her. Mia bent forward to kiss her mother. The familiar fragrance beckoned her back to her childhood.

"Doesn't she look super?" Wayland cried.

Coral stared at her, smiling. *"Super!"*

"He's not overworking you?" Wayland asked. "You look a *tad* tired!"

Mia sank into a chair. "We worked late last night," she admitted. She glanced around at the bar, which was full of fashion people. "What's the season been like so far?"

Coral patted her hand. "Nothing mindblowing yet. Most people are raving about Saint Laurent. Not me! Let me really *look* at you!"

She stared back at her mother. Coral had gotten a little

older. Certain lines appeared around her eyes when she smiled. Her *visagiste*, however, had done a great job: The skin was still pure white alabaster.

"What's it like, working for the Monk, Mia?" Wayland asked.

She laughed. "Only *Women's Wear* calls him that!" She turned to Coral. "What did you think of him? He's very special, isn't he?"

Coral reached for an olive from a dish, chewing very slowly, her eyes narrowed.

"She wants to photograph all his clothes," Wayland blurted eagerly.

Coral shot him a swift, lethal glance. "I'd like to *see* them first!" she snapped.

"Isn't he special?" Mia asked again.

Coral stared at her daughter's hopeful face. "He's a first-rate . . . *tailor*," she pronounced, dragging out the word like a poor consolation prize.

Mia tried not to show her disappointment. "He's much more than that," she said.

"What are you drinking, pet?" Wayland asked.

"Just tomato juice, please." She stared at Coral. "His color sense, the way he works fabrics, sculpts them, molds them . . ."

"Impressive," Coral agreed, lighting a cigarette. She took a long drag. "I'm sure I shall adore the collection. Remember, I only saw three suits. But they were better than Courreges."

"And as a person?" Mia insisted.

"Buckets of charisma!" Coral enthused. "An attractive, attractive man . . . the ladies must go wild for him. I can see why you fell head-over-heels, darling."

The drinks arrived and Mia sipped at her juice.

"How is the romance going?" Coral asked interestedly.

Mia looked levelly back at her. "He's actually more of a teacher to me than a romance. Anyway, he has an assistant he's very close to—"

"Who?" Coral tried to sound casual, but they both picked up the urgency of her question.

"Some girl from his hometown—they worked at Dior together for years before he started this house."

"Pretty?" Coral asked idly.

"Not really. She looks like a boy . . . an urchin."

"Maybe that's what he'd really like?" Wayland suggested quickly. "Sometimes a repressed queen will—"

"He is *not* a repressed queen!" Mia protested.

"Absolutely not!" Coral agreed. "Not from what I saw. *And* heard!"

Mia stared directly into her mother's insinuating eyes. "What have you heard?"

Coral shrugged. "Darling, you *know* the fashion world produces more gossip than clothes!"

"Tell us, Coral," Wayland clamored. "Tell *all*!"

Coral took a sip of her drink, patting her lips, making them wait. "They say Phillipe Roux is *the* Casanova of the haute couture. He *loves* the ladies, and vice versa. Do you know how rare that is? His fittings at Dior are legendary! The fitting-room door was often locked when he was in there with a client—"

"To protect his methods!" Mia cried. "He uses steam and ironing pads to mold the suit or coat while it's actually *on* the person."

"*Really?*" Coral laughed. "I think his methods are a lot more old-fashioned than that! You *are* protective of him, aren't you? I'm only telling you what the *'on dit'* around town is. He has enough Dior clients wild about him to follow him to his own house. Few couturiers can do this because most of them—as you know—do *not* like the ladies. Jacques Hay at Patou wouldn't even *touch* a woman— he wore kid gloves for his fittings... imagine!"

"Why *do* they call him the Monk?" Wayland asked.

Coral smiled. "I'm sure I'd rather my daughter worked for a monk!"

"What do you mean?" Mia asked angrily. "What are you getting at?"

"Really, Mia..." Coral glanced coolly at her. "First you say you're in love with him. Then you get angry because I say the ladies love him. Now you're angry because I say he's a monk. Is there no pleasing you?"

Mia shook her head. "Since I came here you've been trying to bait me in some way." She stood up.

Coral stood, too, and put an arm around her. "Just teasing, darling." She kissed Mia's cheek. "Don't mind me—I'm probably jealous, if you want to know the truth. I'm also terribly nervous for you today...."

"I'd better go." Mia gave Coral a quick hug, then bent

down and kissed Wayland's cheek. "We're showing at
five, but we start preparing at two. I hope you like the
collection. . . ."

Wayland insisted on walking her to the street. "Don't
mind her, pet," he said. "You stood up to her—that made
me so proud."

She hugged him, stepping back, her eyes full of tears.
"Don't ever try to excuse her to me, Wayland. I don't even
know why I let her get to me. I don't need her anymore. . . ."

He saw her into a taxi and leaned in the window. "All
the luck in the world for tonight, darling. I'll be applauding
loudest!" She pressed his hand, and then the cab sped
away, getting lost in the traffic.

By the time the press and privileged buyers crowded
into the tiny salon of Phillipe Roux that afternoon at five
o'clock, there was a fervent buzz of excitement and anticipation. The apartment across the way had been comman-
deered for the afternoon, a large room draped in white
cotton and lined with gilt chairs. The models were to pass
across the landing on which spectators sat. Journalists
who had not been assigned a seat stood on the stairs,
craning their necks.

Wayland sat next to Coral on a seat card reading maynard
cowles, which he stealthily removed so as not to upset
Coral.

"It smells like something is going to happen," Wayland
whispered.

"It *is*, darling, it *is*," Coral said. She moved her knee
slightly as the British editor of *Vogue* sat down next to her.
They ignored each other.

"You know that on the basis of three suits?"

"I tell you they had something *new*! Never-before-*seen*
new!" she hissed.

"It's a question of proportion, perspective, *je ne sais quoi*;
a whole new way of seeing women. If the rest of the
collection is as good, he'll be the premier designer in the
world by tonight."

Wayland's eyes bulged. "I'm *beside* myself," he told her.

More and more journalists squeezed into the room.
People were shunted up against each other, arch rivals
grinding knees, old enemies breathing down each other's
necks in the three tightly packed rows. The overflow of

people jammed the entry hall and corridor. The air was thick with perfume. They had started that morning so fresh, so well groomed. Now, six collections later, mascara ran, sweat stained, hair was sticky. Only the very top publications could afford to limousine fashion editors from one collection to the next, allowing them to stay cool. A plump German editor draped a silk scarf flatteringly over her knees.

Mia was alert, in the studio to dress the models who would run in and out of the room at breakneck speed. Audrey was her special charge: exquisitely madeup, her big brown eyes lined and shadowed with graduated gray and brown. She peeked through a crack of the studio door and watched as the journalists pushed their way in. By five o'clock, fashion had become such a matter of life and death that most of them would rather have died than miss the possibility of an important collection.

They were thirty minutes late. "Walk fast!" Phillipe was telling the models. "If someone reaches out to feel a fabric, don't linger—move on! Turn only once in each room." He was worried that the sharp-eyed artists and buyers could copy the unusual new details on the yokes and sleeves.

The heat was suffocating, the studio hushed, the four girls dressed in their first outfits, ready to walk out on a signal from Phillipe. He peered through the crack to watch for the sign from Stephanie at her desk. When John Fairchild of *WWD*, Nancy White of *Harper's Bazaar*, Diana Vreeland of *Vogue*, and Coral Stanton of *Divine* were all seated, the signal came.

Phillipe turned to his staff: "*On commence!*" he said.

Mia had one moment to take in Audrey's exquisite face as she left the studio; the agonized, taut face of Josephine, white and strained, with dark eyes darting everywhere making last-minute checks; and Phillipe, pale and drawn under his tan. She wanted to take him in her arms and assure him everything would be wonderful.

Audrey walked down the corridor into the main salon. The chatter abruptly stopped in each room until the entire floor of the house was hushed, hundreds of pairs of eyes concentrated on the new details, the new proportions, the new colors, the fashion of Phillipe Roux.

Soon all four models were out and Mia waited with

Audrey's next suit in her hand. The collection was shown
in total silence, punctuated by bursts of applause—often
led by Coral. Women reached out to finger the soft,
luxurious wools. For the first dozen outfits the reaction
was shocked, then, "they got their eye in" as an English
editor put it, and it all started to look right, inevitable, and
exciting. The clothes were different from those of other
Paris houses, the collection a surprise. A French *Vogue*
editor turned to her neighbor saying, "He has outmod-
ed the others."

Through the rush of changing Audrey, Mia heard the
surprised murmurs, the delighted applause, saw the radiant smiles on the models' faces as they ran back into the
room to be stripped of clothes, standing like stiff stick
figures as new clothes were hastily buttoned or zipped
on. Mia held onto models as they stumbled in, kicked off
shoes, pulled on dresses as the hairstylist teased a strand
of hair or tucked it behind an ornament.

The look of the collection was due to her. She had
provided this surprising combination of exuberant young
American fashion and... haute couture. She had influenced Phillipe to drop the formal, large hats he had used
last season. Now the clothes stood out on their own—the
freshness of cut, the short skirts, and the wide shoulders
and sleeves giving extreme youth to the models. The clear
bright colors suggested a nursery—a relief from the navys,
grays, and blacks of the other houses. Here, all was light:
pastels, whites, candy colors. It was like having one's eyes
washed with soothing lotions. All the agonizing over the
cut of the suits and coats had paid off. Once the toile had
been reworked until it resembled a dirty rag, it had been
freshly cut in the real fabric with a throwaway chic that
made it look as if the garment had been created whole,
with a wave of the hand. It looked magical, fresh, unlabored.
Phillipe never wanted his clothes to look too "wanted," too
worked out. Like an acrobat or juggler, he wanted his
craft to look effortless, easy.

They sailed through the cocktail dresses with draped,
bloused backs that had sprung from her drawings. They
were so perfectly cut that every woman wanted one.
Low-cut bodices over perfect, crossover skirts, in fuchsia
or black silk. His little black dresses—the test of any
designer—received much applause. They had been de-

signed so many times that if a designer could make them look fresh, it was a sign of genius.

The wedding dress with which every couturier ends his collection could not have been simpler: a classic, sculpted shape in white silk with long, pointed sleeves, molded torso, and a perfect, gathered dropped-waist skirt.

The bride had to fight her way back into the studio, amidst the screams and cheers. Coral was standing on her chair, pulling Wayland up on his chair, screaming *"Bravo!"* They wanted an appearance.

Pandemonium broke out as the photographers began looking for Phillipe. The press was calling for him. In the noisy confusion, Mia saw Stephanie beckon Phillipe to acknowledge the applause. He shook his head emphatically, closing the studio door, busying himself by opening a magnum of champagne and pouring glasses for the models, the hairstylist, Josephine, and humbly serving them himself.

The models threw off their last outfits and clutched their little white salon coats around them, lighting cigarettes and sticking their feet up on the makeshift dressing tables. Mia was on the floor, sorting shoes, and Phillipe bent down to hand her a brimming glass of champagne. They locked eyes—eyes sparkling with excitement and relief.

"To your success, Phillipe." She held up the glass.

"*Our* success," he whispered. "You should go see your mother. She is an influential woman. . . ." Mia continued to sort the shoes, lowering her eyes. "Mia . . ." He smiled down at her. "Thank you for all you've done. Don't think I am unaware of all you've contributed. I want to negotiate a new salary, a new position for you in the house. . . ."

He needed her!

At that moment the door of the studio burst open and two French *Vogue* editors rushed in, making straight for Phillipe. They threw their arms around him, kissed his cheeks, and dragged him to the door. Phillipe looked embarrassed and weary. Josephine was darting up and down the racks of clothes, furiously checking them off her list. Mia guessed she was overcome at losing Phillipe to the world—she even felt a little like that herself. She took some gulps of the champagne and the alcohol went straight to her head. The collection had been shown: It was a success! It was also the most terrible anti-climax.

She followed at a distance as Phillipe was swept off into the salon by a group of well-wishers. The reflected flashes of the cameras heralded the pictures that would appear in the following day's papers. "Phillipe Roux, whose new collection yesterday changed the course of fashion..."; "Unknown designer challenges Dior, Saint Laurent, to present collection of startling originality...." And even *WWD* grudgingly conceded: "Outsider surprises Fashion Press and Buyers with clean-cut youthful clothes!" Mia watched as her mother threw her arms around Phillipe and kissed him on both cheeks; the ultimate accolade had been bestowed.

For the next week the salon was mobbed. Phillipe was booked for fittings from eight o'clock in the morning till past midnight. The chic women of the world had heard the message and wanted to be dressed by him. There were toiles to be made up for delivery to American stores, patterns to cut, fresh supplies of fabrics to order. Mia enjoyed being out of her cramped room, mingling with people from magazines, television news crews, and an assortment of fashion vultures who descended on the tiny salon. Buyers returned to see the collection again. *Vogue* sent their junior editors. Each day they showed the collection, Mia helped to dress the models. Clothes lent at night for photographers had to be checked upon return, cleaned and pressed. It was marvelous to be so busy, although she missed working directly with Phillipe.

Mademoiselle Josephine had a wistfully sad expression on her bony face. "She is losing Phillipe," Stephanie muttered to Mia as she passed her in the hallway. "Not to another woman, but to the world."

Phillipe passed her in the crowded corridor with just a quick, preoccupied nod.

"Tell me what you need quickly, Coral darling, before I pass out." Gilles ran quickly past Coral into the bathroom, setting up his cosmetics and brushes. "I've had a sixteen-hour session making up prima-donna models for prima-donna photographers," he muttered.

Coral followed him into the bathroom, shrugging off

her silk robe. Gilles flicked a professional eye over her, wagging a finger. "Don't lose another ounce, Coral! It's not *true* what the Duchess of Windsor said—you *can* be too thin! Men like a rounded body."

Coral posed before the mirror. "How would *you* know what men like?"

Gilles frowned. "They tell me."

"Then make me irresistible for tonight. I'm seeing a man...." Gilles began brushing foundation on her face as she closed her eyes, leaning back against the cold white-tiled wall. She had commanded Phillipe Roux to visit her tonight to iron out "last-minute details of her coverage." Totally unnecessary business, but how else could she see him alone?

"Who did your hair?" Gilles murmured, a lipstick brush in his teeth.

"Alexandre." Coral sighed. "A hundred dollars to get my hair dried with his own breath. He's been blowing on it for half an hour! No wonder only Elizabeth Taylor can afford him! But it *is* a miracle!"

"*Divine!*" Gilles breathed.

"And here..." She indicated her groin. "Give me some fantasy."

Gilles gently lowered her panties, peering thoughtfully. "There is not enough to braid, but I shall make an amusing little shape for you." He rummaged in his Louis Vuitton carryall and extracted a tiny razor and shaving cream; he sprayed some on her, then deftly shaped a heart outline with the razor.

"Is *that* what men like?" Coral stared at the reflection.

Gilles giggled. "All the tranvestites of the Bois de Boulogne are doing it!"

"Gilles!" She reached for a hairbrush and whacked him on his buttocks. She noticed his pants were skintight white cotton, and his shape stood out appealingly.

"*Ah, non!*" he cried as she struck him again. He went bright red, and she saw that he was aroused, his sex straining hard against the front of his pants.

"So *that's* what turns you on?" she cried, attempting to pull him over her lap.

He stood up straight, saying "Coral!" and pretending to be embarrassed, but she could see he was admiring himself in the mirror.

She outlined his sex with her forefinger. "What a waste," she said. "If I didn't have definite plans for tonight, I believe I'd show you how to use this."

"I *do* use it! Often." He smirked, sweeping his makeup into the bag, zipping it shut. He adjusted himself with a shrug. "I must run now, darling. I have to do makeup for—" He bit his lip, sending her a mischievous glance.

"*Who?*" she cried. "Who else is *Bazaar* using? Is it the Vicomtesse de Ribes? I'll scratch her eyes out. She promised me she—"

"It isn't her." He gently touched her arm. "It's for ... the 'other collection'...."

"Oh, Gilles ..." She clutched him pleadingly. "Tell me what it is? I know it's men only, but whose fashions are they? Are they *wonderful*?"

Gilles's eyes glinted. "They are for the boys—all the artists and designers who like to appear *en travesti*, eh? In womens' clothes. Their own designs, of course. They are all beautifully made up by me to look like star models. Some have beards or moustaches, so it is ... stylized, you know?"

"I should think it *is*! But why don't they invite *me*?"

Gilles pulled a face. "It starts off *comme il faut*, very distinguished. Then it gets a little rough. They start to undress, all that. It ends up an *orgy*! They are some of the most famous designers, you know? They don't want to be watched by fashion editors!"

She raised her eyebrows. "One day I shall smuggle in a camera and blackmail all of you."

She saw him out, flinging open the balcony doors of her suite for a quick gasp of air. It smelled of Gauloises, garlic, furniture polish, and cheap gasoline fumes. "Paris oxygen," she murmured, closing the window.

Pausing at the giant mirrored mantelpiece, she ran a hand through her short spiky hair. She liked the colors Gilles had brushed on her eyelids, the heavy-lidded look his charcoal-bronze pencil had added to her gaze.

Phillipe was late. Perhaps he would not even keep this late-night rendezvous? She had photographed all his clothes: If he expected her to splash them over the pages of *Divine*, he had better turn up. She was naked under a billowing black silk shift made for her by Balenciaga last season. She shivered at the idea of Phillipe's presence in this room. He was unpredictable, proud. Now that he was designer of the moment, he might simply laugh at her seduction plans.

She paced nervously, straightening a cigarette box, a pile of papers, impatiently expecting his soft knock. When it finally came, she took a deep breath and went to the bathroom to spray her throat and arms with Joy. Then she opened the door.

Phillipe stood before her, very erect and formal in a navy suit. His face took her breath away. He had gained something in the last week, some new self-knowledge. Success had added to his looks. He glowed with vitality.

"Please come in," she said. He stepped in.

She had left the bedroom door ajar. a Rigaud candle flickering in there. The table lamps glowed, lighting this room that hovered over the glittering Place de la Concorde like a giant air balloon.

Phillipe walked toward the windows, smiling. "You must find Paris very beautiful, staying here with this view?"

She laughed. "I've hardly had a moment to look out: twenty-eight collections in six days is so ridiculous!"

He raised his eyebrows, turning. "Were they all good?"

She sank to one knee on the thick pile of the rug. "Only yours . . ."

He looked in surprise at the kneeling woman, the most powerful fashion editor of the American press, then reached out for her hand. "Please," he urged. "I am not the pope. . . ."

She took his hand but held onto it, remaining on the floor: "I want to offer you this homage," she said. "You are the high priest of fashion. Your clothes will start a new religion! They will resurrect good taste, quality, elegance!"

She looked deeply into his eyes, showing her sincerity. Finally she allowed him to pull her gently to her feet, indicating that he sit next to her on the velvet settee. There *was* something almost holy about him, as if he were so disciplined that he had become almost untouchable.

She had a bottle of Taittinger icing in a bucket. He poured glasses. She glanced down at the shape his knees made against the navy blue of his pants. They looked straight, square, strong. The brown skin of his neck, his wrists, made her wonder which stupid rules had decreed

that a man like him should wear a double-breasted navy
suit. He should have been naked, as she was under this
Balenciaga. She wondered if he realized it. The silk of the
dress just lightly grazed her breasts. She glanced down
and noticed they were very obviously pushing out the
light fabric, plainly outlined for him to see. At that moment she would have given anything in the world for him
to gently lift the dress and lightly run his tongue over her
hard nipples.

As he turned to stare, fixing her with dark, serious
eyes, she nearly abandoned the entire plan. She suddenly
realized this man *was* for real!

"What should we drink to?" she asked, holding her
glass.

"To fashion?" he said, lightly touching her glass. "That
is all I am trying to achieve."

"You are also going to make a lot of money," she told
him, sipping. She held out her glass. "More, please! Much
more!" As he refilled her glass, she said, "Tell me something, Phillipe. Mia told me she designed most of your
collection. Could that possibly be so?"

He nodded. "She was my collaborator. She is very
talented. I am inspired by her drawings. I was a cutter at
Dior. I was in the habit of working from someone's
sketches. . . ."

Coral shook her head sadly. "You should not have told
me that, Phillipe. I want you to answer my question
again, but this time give me the right answer. The right
answer, Phillipe, is, 'Only *I* design!' "

He frowned. "Why?"

"Oh, *dar'ing*! *Never* share credit with *any*one! Don't you
know that's one of the secrets to becoming a top name?
Women don't want clothes designed by some young American *girl*! They want clothes designed by Phillipe Roux—
the exciting new Paris talent!"

Phillipe stared at her for a moment, and suddenly his
eyes sparkled. "Only *I* design!" he said imperiously.

She laughed delightedly, throwing back her head and
crying "Bravo!" Draining her champagne glass, she held it
out for more. "*That's* it! You're learning! You'll be dealing
with America and we don't appreciate modesty!"

Phillipe laughed with her, a little puzzled but willing to

learn the strange ways of Americans. He sipped at his champagne, refilling her glass.

"Mia," he said softly, turning the name into something French and romantic. "She is a beautiful girl. You must be very proud of her...?"

Coral frowned. "Proud?" She considered. "We were never close, Phillipe. I'm not really the motherly type. *Am* I, do you think?"

Phillipe looked at her appraisingly. "You are certainly not like *my* mother!" he said.

Coral burst out laughing. He *is* a peasant, she thought. But a charming, *sexy* peasant!

"Tell me about her, Phillipe," she pressed. "What is she? A darling little Spanish señora? Very dignified?"

"Dignified, yes..." he answered thoughtfully. "She is dead now, but she was a humble, simple woman. She made dresses for the rich ladies of our town. That is how *I* learned."

"*Very* Balenciaga!" Coral approved. "It sounds *charming*, and I do so want to hear all about it some day. I admire people from modest backgrounds who manage to rise above it all. We actually have that in common, Phillipe...." He raised his eyebrows. "But let's talk about when you are coming to *my* town," she went on, quickly. "To New York!"

"I have many, many fittings to do for my private clients..."

"Among whom I aim to be." Coral sipped more champagne. "I'll need at least six outfits. *I* shall need fittings, too, Phillipe!"

"Call Mademoiselle Stephanie," he suggested. "We will accommodate you before you leave Paris."

"But I don't want to miss any fittings!" she cried. She had heard from a French *Vogue* editor, Ina Mellindorf, that fittings were Phillipe's specialty. The mirrors of the fitting room reflected every angle of his handsome head. The atmosphere of dedicated attention to the client's body, the way he examined it like a doctor or masseur, produced an intense excitement. Some customers found his touch so arousing that as he lightly touched their rib cage, their shoulders, their knees, they reached thinly disguised orgasms....

"I give two fittings," he said. "If you stay on another week, I could make you some outfits."

"Do you have a tape measure with you, Phillipe?" she asked.

"No." He frowned.

She disappeared to the bedroom for a moment, finding a tape measure on her dressing table. She glanced in her mirror, running a nervous hand through her hair. *Now or never!* she told herself. She would not wait until he decided to come to New York. She undid the shoulder buttons of the chemise. It fell to the floor and she stepped out of it. She came to the door of the bedroom naked and put her head around the door, watching him sit formally on the couch, one leg crossed, absently tapping his ankle with a finger.

"I want you to fit me, Phillipe," she called.

"For what?" He turned his head slightly. "A dress? A coat? A suit?"

"How about two of each?" She walked into the room. Phillipe looked up at her naked body and quickly got to his feet. His eyes widened slightly. "Here!" she threw the tape measure to him and he caught it. She stood in the center of the room, gazing at him. It was wonderful to be naked before him. Thrilling! The candles glowed around her.

"Fit me!" she commanded.

The seconds passed. *I don't care what he does,* she thought, *as long as I hold his attention.* She waited, patient and impatient at the same time, the sound of her own pulse throbbing in her head.

"You're terribly in love with him, aren't you, pet?" Wayland asked Mia. They were at the hot restaurant of the moment, Quadrille, a romantic candlelit room on the Isle St. Louis.

"Yes," she confessed softly. "And he has Josephine, so I haven't a chance. Yet somehow I'm happy just being near him . . . helping him, being a part of the house. It's wrong, isn't it?"

"Oh, don't ask me, pet," Wayland said, swallowing the rest of his wine. "I'm biased when it comes to you. I think you should have everything! I saw Josephine. Any man who finds her more attractive than you is *not* someone I would buy a used car from."

Mia burst out laughing. "You're a great boost to my ego, Wayland."

He shrugged. "One thing's for sure: Your mother is going to give him the most incredible coverage. She's photographed everything in his collection. And at least four cosmetic firms are longing to move in on him."

"Phillipe's in no hurry to be taken over," Mia said firmly. "He always says he doesn't care about money—"

"Oh, *please*, Mia, they *have* to say that! But it's people like Roux who actually want it the most. And are *you* getting a little credit, my dear?"

She shook her head. "I don't care if people know about me. Phillipe knows he needs me, that's what matters."

"Mia, this is your *career*! Let me call James Brady at *Women's Wear*—he'll be fascinated to know that an American girl is behind Roux's success."

"No!" She clutched his hand. "*Promise* me you won't do that—Phillipe would never forgive me."

Wayland shook his head in frustration, calling for the bill. "I didn't want to tell you this, but I have tried to call you at the *maison* several times this week and been told each time that no Mia Stanton works there."

Her eyes clouded and she frowned at him. "Maybe they didn't understand you. It's been so crazy these past days—"

"I spoke to three different people, Mia. Would they all make the same mistake?"

"I don't understand, but I'll check it." She shrugged lightly, indicating her lack of concern, but something ominous nudged her stomach. She realized now that she had given her name to several journalists and manufacturers and had been surprised when no one had called.

"When will I be seeing you again, pet?" Wayland asked in the taxi home.

"I'll pass by the hotel to say good-bye," Mia told him. "I don't want to continue being Mother's enemy, but she sure makes it hard to be friends. I think she can't help feeling competitive with me now. It was lovely being alone with you tonight, though. How did you give the others the slip?"

"Colin's working flat out in his hotel room. Coral's dining with your boss, tonight, as you know."

Mia's eyes widened. "I didn't know," she admitted. She sat in silence for the rest of the drive. Why hadn't Phillipe mentioned it to her?

At the door of her building Wayland kissed her. "Hold back something of yourself, Mia. One little piece. I don't want to see you get hurt."

Phillipe Roux smiled an enigmatic smile that allowed Coral, for a moment, to indulge her wildest fantasies. Surely this reticence, this control, was a prelude to the wild animal about to burst out of him? He slowly removed his jacket without taking his eyes from hers.

"You Americans are always in such a hurry," he said softly.

Coral smiled. "No," she said, "I'm in no hurry at all. You may take your time."

He moved toward her, dressed in a spotlessly white silk shirt. She closed her eyes as he approached. But there was no touch, no embrace. She simply felt his jacket—still warm from his body—thrown across her shoulders. Opening her eyes wide, she glared at him. He was watching her calmly.

"I am a very simple man, Coral," he said. "I am not a sophisticate."

"What are you trying to say?" She clutched his jacket to her.

Phillipe cleared his throat. "I don't understand any of this! You're an attractive woman, you are very respected in our profession: Why behave like this?"

"This is not the way I normally behave," she said. "I hardly recognize myself. It's just that I want you so much I'd do anything! Hold me, Phillipe, please hold me!"

He held her arms, shaking her a little. "But I am not free. This is not the right time."

"When will it be the right time? Oh, darling, in New York?"

He shrugged, his eyes darting about the room. "I don't know. . . ."

"Oh, Phillipe. . ." She put her hand behind his neck and stroked him. "I'll dedicate the entire Paris issue to you! I'll build you up in New York as the greatest designer they've ever seen. Together we'll bring back elegance—"

"Perhaps. We shall see." He moved away from her.

"But for now I do not intend to play the gigolo." He held out his hand to her and she took it as if in a trance, naked under his jacket. In a second he had turned and left, closing the door gently behind him, leaving her alone in her suite.

"No!" she cried as the door closed behind him. She threw off his jacket, staring at her reflection in the mirror. Her body had been tensed, expectant, awaiting his touch. She picked up his champagne glass and hurled it against the wall, where it shattered into crystal shards. Furious, she ran to the bedroom, reaching for the telephone to dial Wayland's room.

"It's me!" she said when he answered.

"Coral? What's the matter? You sound so angry. How'd your evening go?"

"A disaster! Phillipe just left! I'm so incensed I could—" She bit her lip. "Tell me something, Wayland. What does a terribly frustrated lady do in a city like Paris?"

Wayland giggled: "I just asked someone *exactly* the same question! You know Jean Christian's agency, Beau Monde?"

"We use them sometimes, why?"

"Write down their number: Passy 5805. Ask for Claude. Say you want the takeout service. It's especially for visiting Americans, and you can charge it. They do look-alikes, darling! Describe the man of your dreams—anyone you like—"

"You're *bananas!*"

"Try it, Coral. I've just spent the last thirty minutes with the nearest thing to Charlton Heston you've ever seen!"

"Good night!" She slammed down the phone and sat naked on her bed. I'll never get to sleep, she thought. Impulsively, she dialed the number. She was starting to lose control, do things she would not normally do.

Claude sounded quite blasé.

"What did you have in mind, madame?" he asked.

Coral smiled, moving a pillow behind her so she could lie back comfortably. "Let's see . . . someone about five feet nine. Around forty, forty-five. Slightly balding. Dark, olive-skinned. Slim, with very intense dark eyes. Fiery: Spanish- or Italian-looking. Very, *very* virile!"

"*All* our escorts are virile, madame," Claude reprimanded.

"How else could they work? I think I have what you seek, but he may not have the English tongue—"

"Just as long as he *has* a tongue!" Coral said.

She replaced the receiver and took a warm bath to relax herself. She would turn off the lights and call him Phillipe. He had probably received stranger requests. . . .

At seven-thirty the next morning Coral stretched luxuriantly. She moved a small pillow under her neck and sighed. Paulo had not stayed the night, but he had performed very well—God, *too* well! Her body still seemed to throb from the intense orgasms she had experienced. Her buttocks ached, her pelvic area felt bruised from grinding against his. The agency had come up with as near a lookalike as one imagined could be found in one hour in Paris. He was better-looking than Phillipe in many ways, and he had certainly performed to her fullest expectations. Later, by the time she was dressed in a gray silk pants suit, she had almost come to believe that it was Phillipe who had made love to her the night before. Somehow she would get him to fall in love with her.

Now that the first hectic week of showing the collection daily was over, Mia went about her chores at the house in a subdued daze. The expensive magazine models had departed, replaced by less glamorous models who showed the collection twice weekly. Mia had dutifully sketched every item in the collection, showing front and back views, for the house archives. She had dealt with the dozens of artists, photographers, and journalists who had requested photographs, biographies of Phillipe, interviews with him. Suddenly there was nothing for her to do. It was much too soon to think of designing for the next collection, which was five and a half months away. And she did not feel she could rejoin the seamstresses in the workroom, where extra girls had been recruited.

Phillipe handled the fittings for private clients, and even Josephine seemed to be puffing up her work of supervising the workroom and greeting clients into something more important than it actually was. Mia took longer lunch breaks. She called the Crillon and heard that Coral was staying another week to be fitted for her new Roux outfits. That afternoon, as she was wondering whether she would dare ask Phillipe about Coral, he approached her in the corridor.

"Mia, you and I will be going out to dinner next week."

"We will?" She had nurtured so many fantasies about him, she almost had to pinch herself to see if this was real.

The house bell rang to announce a client, and he touched her arm quickly. "Choose a restaurant you like, and let me know. Will Thursday be convenient?"

She had arranged to have a farewell dinner with Coral that night, but she would have broken a date with God to be free for Phillipe.

The days until Thursday were interminable. She kept trying to picture their evening together and failing. Was this simply the gesture of a grateful employer toward a hard-working employee? Phillipe's way of saying thank you? She called her mother and arranged to see her on the Friday morning of her departure, the day after she dined with Phillipe.

There had been a bonus of a thousand francs added to her pay that month; the explanation had been "extra hours worked." Sooner or later they would have to discuss what her position in the house was to be, what the salary would be, for she could not allow Wayland to support her forever.

The evening with Phillipe finally arrived, and she told him she wanted to dine at Quadrille, the romantic place Wayland had taken her. Phillipe had not heard of it. He would arrive at her apartment at eight, he said, and she agreed to wait outside.

That night she made up as carefully as she ever had. She had bought two more dresses from the previous Roux collection. She wore the cornflower-blue dress with matching panty hose and a pair of white boots. Her long blond hair newly washed and shining, she had never looked so beautiful. The sparkle of love made her glow, gave her eyes a secret expression. She was convinced that tonight would change everything.

Fifteen

She was waiting for him when he drove up in his modest, small black car and leaped out to open the door for her. He was very formal and polite. She wondered how she would get through an entire evening with this serious, sober person. Would she be able to make him laugh? Her feelings for him gave her a confidence, a protective feeling toward him. He seemed so awkward now, so constrained. His brown face was freshly shaved, his hair slicked down so that his forehead gleamed. There was a hesitancy in the air, as if they were teenagers on a first date. How had he accounted for this evening to Josephine? she wondered. Had he said, "Just let me have dinner with the kid—she deserves it!" or, "I'm taking Mia to dinner—I don't care *what* you say!"

At Quadrille they were ushered to a corner table glowing with tiny table lamps, the waiters fluttering around them as if they were a pair of lovers. Most pretty Paris restaurants turn two diners into a pair of lovers, Mia thought, warning herself not to get carried away. But it was impossible not to. After a few sips of the sparkling white wine, she began to float. She was with the most beautiful man in the world, dining in romantic surroundings in Paris! And she was in love.

"What sort of childhood did you have, Phillipe?" she asked when they'd ordered.

He gave a short laugh. "One you cannot imagine. Usually I was hungry. . . ." He did not enlarge upon that, and as if to make up for his lack of conversation, he took her hand and held it lightly. It felt like the hand of an affectionate father. His eyes bored deep into hers. She felt he wanted her to read something in his eyes that he could not say.

"I know it hasn't been easy for you," he suddenly said. "I am trying all the time to find a solution."

"A solution?"

"For running the house. So we can all work happily together. It is so small, we are bound to have clashes sometimes. I have had offers this week from American firms to make us big. I shall eventually accept an offer, but for the meantime we can learn so much more if we stay small. Josephine is not easy to work with, I know—"

"Are you going to marry her?" She blurted it out.

"We are very close," Phillipe replied, and his words struck her heart like a blow. "Closer than you can ever understand, because of our shared childhood. We grew up together in the same village."

"I know you think I'm a spoiled-rotten American who only knows luxury," Mia said.

"I do believe you are used to luxury," he admitted. "I spent an evening with your mother last week. You and she would find it hard to picture where I came from or to understand what real poverty is. Have *you* ever been hungry, Mia? Not for dinner or lunch, but going to sleep hungry, with that gnawing pain?"

"Were you that poor?"

"Yes," he said. "We were. And the only way out of that was work." The waiter placed the hors d'oeuvres before them, and she suddenly saw the appetizing platter through Phillipe's eyes, saw how wasteful a trendy restaurant must seem to him.

"But if you sell thousand-dollar suits, you cannot be against luxury," she said.

"I'm not against it," he replied. "I'm just trying to explain Josephine's attitude to you."

She tried to eat, but she had no appetite at all. Just looking across the table and seeing his face, his eyes, played tricks on her body. The longing she felt for him, the disbelief she felt at being with him, all made her feel too excited for food.

"I shall see your mother in New York," he told her.

"She feels *she* has discovered you," Mia said sadly.

"Mia..." He laid his hand over hers again. "I understand your mother so well. We have had many private clients like her. Lonely women. Do you know, I've had rich lonely clients who ordered one outfit a week, through the year, just to see me?"

His bass voice rumbled through her as he spoke. The steady gaze of his dark eyes combined with the heady wine to hypnotize her. She wished some *WWD* photographer would snap their picture so it could be published with an insinuating caption for everyone to see.

"Will you come up for coffee?"

They were in his car, outside her building. Dinner had passed like a dream. She was almost impatient for the evening to be over, just to see what would happen at the end. From the way he touched her arm as they took a short walk in St. Germain des Prés on their way home, she felt something was impending, some feeling, some action. He had guided her along dark streets, and she had again had the illusion that they were lovers, that at any moment they would duck into some doorway and kiss.

He glanced at his watch sadly. "I have appointments starting at eight tomorrow. It is already eleven-thirty."

It wasn't possible. She could not just leave his car and go home. Something had to happen! "I'd like you to see where I live," she said softly.

"Just for a minute," he replied, getting out of the car reluctantly, as if against his better judgment.

In the tiny elevator they stood close, but she made sure they did not touch, even though she was sensitive to his body so near to hers, and his spicy, heady smell. She unlocked the front door and they crossed the darkened hallway to her room. She switched on one lamp, keeping the room dim, closing the door behind him.

Now Phillipe Roux was in her room! Her eyes were seeing the man of her life slowly walking around the spacious room, examining the framed photographs, the sketches on the wall, the rooftop view, but she could not really believe Phillipe was there—with her.

"It is a very pleasant place," he told her, sitting down on her bed.

She was in a chair, opposite, watching him. There was a sadness in his expression as he looked at her. Why? she wondered. His worried expression was an enigma to her: Why didn't he do something? She was not going to make the first move and risk a rebuff. It had to come from him—it *had* to! She tried to show him this in her eyes, make him feel what she was thinking. But he knew. He knew only too well, she suddenly realized. That was why he now looked so worried. He did not know what to do with her love.

So she sat there, watching him, excited about this evening and from the wine. She sat in a haze of happiness mixed with a terrible sadness that he might never be hers; enjoying the novelty of his presence in her own familiar surroundings, fearful that he would leave suddenly.

And then she must have somehow drifted off, lost consciousness for a few moments, because she lost the sense of what was happening. She so much wanted it to happen that she saw, or dreamed, Phillipe leaning forward and taking her into his arms. It was so real she could feel his closed eyes as she kissed his eyelids, feel his sensual lips brush her cheek and move to her neck, sense his strong arms around her, holding her. . . .

Her eyes fluttered open. Phillipe was watching her, smiling.

"You are tired," he said. "I shall let you sleep."

In this moment of half waking, half sleeping, she held up her arms to him dreamily. He took her hands, holding them lightly, sitting on the edge of the bed, piercing her with his intent stare.

"I love you, Phillipe," she said. She would never have forgiven herself if she had not found the courage to tell him. "I'm in love with you."

Oh, God, the relief to have said it! It no longer mattered what he answered—for her it had gone beyond that point. She had expressed *her* love. It was a huge hurdle cleared; it made everything simple.

His eyes dilated slightly as he bored into her gaze with that stare for a long minute, not speaking, still holding her hands. Then he leaned forward and kissed her. It was the sweetest kiss a man and a woman had ever shared. It *had* to be, she thought, there could be nothing sweeter than this. His lips against hers—and they were as full and as soft as she had imagined—the bliss of it, the impossibility of it happening, and then there was a last pressure of his mouth and he broke away. . . .

When he spoke, it was in a different tone. "I love you,"

he told her. "You're the all-American dream I've had since my boyhood. The beautiful American golden girl I would watch in the films at our local cinema." He smiled. "I would sneak in through the back door to watch *you*, Mia, the woman of my dreams...."

"Oh, darling," she breathed. "*Darling!*" Tears began to roll down her cheeks. Her eyes were sparkling bright, sad, happy.

"My dream is *you*!" Phillipe told her. "How do I keep this dream for the moment I can enjoy it—*we* can enjoy it?"

"*Which* moment? *What*, my darling?"

"I don't know how to fit you into my life, Mia." He spread his hands helplessly and she held onto them. "Everything was planned. Everything but this."

"Josephine!" she cried.

He nodded. "Whether it is possible in an honorable, caring way to..." He made a hopeless gesture and trailed off, staring at her.

She stood and flung her arms around him, pressing his head to her breast. "Oh, kiss me, Phillipe! *Love* me, darling!"

He stood stock-still as she kissed his face, kissed the eyelids she had promised herself she would kiss. His face was warm, a muscle clenched in his cheek as she softly brushed her lips over it. Was this part of her dream? She dug her nails into her palm and felt them: This was no dream! Finally his hand came up and he caressed her neck, her throat, his touch so hesitant, so tender, that in spite of herself she moaned.

"Oh, God, *touch* me more, Phillipe! *Hold* me! I'll *die* if you don't!"

Things were happening to and in her body that had never happened before. Desire... it stirred restlessly in her, surprising her. He turned her head with his hand, using the softest pressure, so that their mouths just touched. His mouth hovered against her lips, and then he pressed firmly against her mouth. The feel of his lips against hers was so magnified, it was as if she were sitting at a movie, looking at a giant close-up. The tip of his tongue moved against her lips, and she eagerly parted her lips, letting him thrust his tongue into her mouth, brush against her tongue. She slumped in his arms, giving herself to the kiss. But suddenly he broke away, his eyes wide open, afire, staring at her as if she were the devil sent to tempt him, to disrupt his life.

"What is it?" she cried. "What's wrong? I *love* you, Phillipe! I want you. And you want me, too. I know you do—"

"Never have I wanted anyone so much—" he told her. He reached out, taking her hand and pressing it to his lips. She could feel him trembling. He shook his head. "I knew I should not come up here tonight, but I am only human. I was unable to resist being with you."

"I loved you from the moment I saw your face in a magazine," she told him.

"And I loved you from the moment I saw you in my salon," he confessed. "I had to deny it, Mia. I still deny it! I cannot do this to Josephine. I owe her too much—everything! I could not live with myself if I did this to her. I *must* find some solution. I want to find some way that will not hurt anyone."

"You're hurting *me*! Right now."

"I'm sorry, Mia. So sorry. Understand that—"

"I understand that if you love me, you'll stop thinking and worrying and just take me, here, now, while we have the chance."

She reached up and pulled him down on top of her, onto the bed. For a moment Phillipe lost his self-control and buried his face in her hair. Then he pulled down the top of her dress, removing her bra, and lingered on her breast tips with his warm mouth, sucking gently on the nipples. His hand came to rest between her legs and he kneaded her, rubbed her there.

"Oh, God, don't! *Don't*, Phillipe!"

Could you have an orgasm from kissing? she thought wildly. From a man's hand between your legs? He had slipped his hand down into her panties now, and she moved against his fingers, moaning. Oh, God, she *was* going to have an orgasm! What she had read about and thought about for years was now happening to her! A mounting wave of pleasure was gathering in her body, and she grasped his neck, the hair at the back of his neck, clutching him, wrapping one leg around his body so that she could push against this insistent hand, this unstoppable feeling.

Silently, gasping, loving him, she came against his kneading hand. She held onto him as she trembled, held on with all her strength, eyes tightly shut, streaming tears. She could feel his hot breath on her neck as he clenched his teeth, straining not to move. His sex, inside his clothes, was rigid, pressing against her. He stayed still. The smell of him, his body and his scent, intoxicated her. She nuzzled her nose around his ear, down the side of his neck. Still he made no move. As the wave of pleasure left her body, she let go of him. He broke away, panting.

They stared at each other, breathing heavily. Her face was flushed, her lips swollen from his kisses, her eyes heavy with sensual weariness.

"Well?" she challenged. She opened her eyes wide, suddenly feeling more in control. She had experienced her first real orgasm. She had come with a man. He had not been inside her—that would be the next step, but at least she was this far. And she now felt like a woman. "I said if you really cared about me, you would do something—"

"*Do* something!" he laughed harshly. "That is so American! That is the big difference between Europeans and you, Mia. Always instant results, instant action for you, yes? If you had a gun, you would kill someone. Or take a car and drive somewhere, very fast, anywhere, without thinking. To sex. To marriage. To hurt someone, maybe, without meaning to? Without planning? Did you not hear what I've been telling you? *All* my life has been planned! It was the only way I could improve it. I asked you if you had ever been hungry? A man has to make very solid plans if he has been hungry. That's how *I* grew up. That's why I hesitate before I do anything important—" He stopped, looking around the room. "Is there anything to drink?"

She fetched a bottle of brandy and two glasses, pouring a full measure for him and a tiny amount for herself. He swallowed his quickly, with a grimace. She poured more and he swirled it around his glass. He stood and went over to the window, throwing it open and letting the cool night air in, breathing in great shuddering gasps of it. He came back to her and caught her hand, holding it tightly.

"Mia, try to understand what my life has been like up

to this week. Up to this moment!" She had never seen his eyes so full of passion. She longed to be simply held in his arms, for him to quieten her with calming caresses, but she could see how important it was for him to talk.

"Mia, I told you about hunger because that gave me ambition. First, never to be hungry again, and then, to *be* somebody! *Somebody*, Mia! You cannot imagine how great this need is! I knew I had talent, Mia, just as *you* know you have it! But my talent means so much more to me. It meant a passport to a better world. So I worked hard, harder than you can ever know, to finally be accepted in Paris. To open my mouth and not have everyone laugh at me. I knew nothing when I came here. I was a common *ouvrier* in a workroom, as green as those girls you've worked with. But always, that memory of being poor kept me going. And work—nothing but work!" He took another sip of cognac.

She put her hand on his knee, wanting to touch him, but she could feel he did not want to be touched. She felt him slipping away. He was trying to explain to her why they could not be lovers, and she did not want to hear it.

"Josephine joined me as soon as I had a position at Dior," he went on. I found a cheap *chambre de bonne*—you know what that is? A little maid's room on the top floor of a building—it didn't even have running water. Josephine arrived and she gave her life to me. She arrived as green as I had been, and I was able to show her the way. She knew me so well, Mia. Through and through. And she loved me, Mia, she had always loved me. She watched as I became more sure of myself. She had to live with the idea that I might outgrow her one day, because we both knew *I* had the talent and she at best would be a seamstress. To counteract that, she gave me all her love, all her attention, and she became everything to me—my mother, sister, lover, daughter. I had been so lonely in Paris, and I welcomed her love, needed it. It nurtured me. But we were not the same—I did not love her in a romantic way. I was saving that love for *you*, Mia, do you understand? Perhaps I hoped she would meet other men, but I must have known that for her I am the only man in the world. She would die for me. I cannot ever leave her. . . ."

She caught his hand and brought it to her mouth, feeling the warmth of his palm with her lips. Yes, she could imagine Josephine dying for him. *She* would willingly die right now! She wanted him so much her head buzzed and her heart ached.

She threw herself into his arms, crying. "What about me, Phillipe?"

He kissed her on the mouth once, then pushed her away. "Don't you understand?" he cried angrily.

Why did life do this to her? Now that he was holding her, looking at her in the way she had always dreamed of, she was still not allowed to enjoy it. He was promising her nothing at all. Because he had once been hungry, and poor, he could not be hers? His entanglement with Josephine sounded more binding than a marriage. She let herself swim in those burning eyes for another marvelous minute. She must take hold of herself before she went crazy. She counted to thirty slowly while resting in his warm arms, next to his chest, enjoying, regretting every second.

"Leave me, then." She broke away, pulling her dress back on, standing. She opened the door to her room. "You'd better go."

He stood, staring at her. "Yes. Yes, I shall go. But you will give me time. You will not forget what we—"

"Oh, *Phillipe!*" she guided him out the door, suddenly strong. "Forget? You're all I ever think about, don't you know that?"

By the front door, he turned and kissed her once more.

With the feel of his lips still on hers, she ran back to her room. She sank into an exhausted sleep the moment she lay down, her mind awhirl with dreams and nightmares. Phillipe was in them all, reaching out for her but never able to touch her. Something stopped them from being together, some glass wall, missed train, or stalled elevator. She awoke at dawn the next morning, her head throbbing. He would never be hers, she could feel it. A deep ache inside her warned her. Maybe he did love her, but he was too controlled, too disciplined, too much under Josephine's strange spell ever to be free, ever to be hers. She turned over and buried her face in the pillows, which still held traces of his cologne. The scent twisted her inside, made her want to burrow into the bed until she reached somewhere safe, somewhere protected, where no hurt could ever reach. . . .

* * *

Later that morning she dressed carefully for her mother's critical eyes. She had borrowed a black dress from Audrey, and she threw a purple cashmere shawl, a gift from Wayland, over it. She bathed her eyes with cold water and made up lightly. She must banish Phillipe from her mind that morning, she told herself, so that her mother could not upset her.

When Coral opened the door, the overpowering smell of Rigaud candles hit Mia with a sickly nostalgia. Coral leaned toward her, presenting her cheek to be kissed. "What a season! I sent Virginia back to New York yesterday," she said. "She was getting on my nerves. Wayland and I leave this afternoon—he stayed a week extra for me, wasn't that sweet of him? He makes the flight go so fast—we play cards and giggle."

Mia glanced at a pile of contact sheets by the bed. "Can I see what you photographed of Phillipe's?"

"Virginia took a lot of stuff with her." Coral quickly placed a makeup bag on top of the photographs. "What are you wearing? Isn't black a little old for you?"

"I like wearing black. Were the photographs wonderful? I heard you shot a lot of stuff. . . ."

"I sent some to Phillipe—surely he showed them to you? I thought you and he were so close?"

"Stephanie probably has them—she handles the press side."

"Oh, yes, I forgot: You're the designer," Coral said mockingly.

Mia started to protest, then thought: Let it go! Nothing she says makes any difference. I love Phillipe and he loves me. That's all I need to know.

Coral zipped closed a black crocodile bag, gathering up various scarves and earrings from her dressing table. Mia sat on the unmade bed, which reeked of Joy.

"Will you show many of Phillipe's clothes?" she asked.

"As much as I can!" Coral said simply. "The other houses will be furious. Saint Laurent will probably ban us from ever crossing their threshold. But this time I just don't care! I have to do what my heart tells me to—"

"Your heart? Or your fashion sense?" Mia asked. Coral was behaving oddly—simpering coyly, sending her arch little glances.

"Both!" Coral said. "He is devastatingly attractive, isn't he? I don't think I've ever met a more beautiful man."

Mia stared at her mother, speechless.

"By the way..." Coral looked at her accusingly. "He absolutely denies you had anything to do with the designing, so I wouldn't tell that story to many people, darling."

"And you believe him?" Mia asked.

"Why would he lie to me?"

Mia stood. "Then I'll go. I couldn't eat lunch with someone who thinks I'm a liar. Especially my own mother."

"Now, Mia, I'm not calling you *that*!" Coral caught her arms and held her. "I just think you get fact and fantasy a little confused sometimes." She let go of Mia and flicked at her hair in the mirror. "He's a genius, though, I must say that."

"I agree. But he still needs my ideas."

"Let's not argue about it!" Coral cut her off. "He'll visit New York soon and I'll get the truth out of him. I'll get to know him a lot better on my home ground."

Mia stared at her. "He's not staying with you?"

"I think we can afford a hotel room for him. Even a suite! After my coverage, he'll be a superstar!"

"What are you trying to do? *Own* him?"

Coral pursed her lips at herself in the mirror, going over the outline with a dark red pencil. "They do a divine *salade Niçoise* here. I shall either have that or one of their marvelous omelettes...."

Mia watched her carefully. "Is Josephine going to New York with him?"

"We didn't discuss the details...."

"You didn't?" Mia laughed mockingly. "Then I suppose you don't know they're practically married?"

"Really? *That* I doubt." Coral glanced coyly at Mia. "Even in liberated France it's highly unlikely."

"Why?"

"Isn't it against the law here to marry your sister?"

Mia felt the room spin. She reached out a hand to hold onto the wall. "You're crazy!" she cried. "You don't know what you're talking about...." But even as she spoke, something inside her felt it must be true. It would explain everything: Phillipe's awkwardness last night, the strange tension between them, Josephine's fierce, protective jealousy....

"I'll ask him," she whispered, almost to herself.

"Mia, I'm a fashion reporter. I have spies everywhere. Take it from me, Josephine Roux is Phillipe's sister. If he wants to be big in America, he'll have to be very, very careful. He'd be well-advised to leave his sister behind when he visits. He can be *my* escort!"

"Why are you making such a big play for him? You must realize I love him!" Mia cried. "Does it give you some kind of twisted kick?"

Coral glanced sharply at her. "Could you really love him after what you know now? He's a very complicated and unusual man. Not a man one can pin down, I'd say. Grow up, Mia. I'm going to launch him on to the American scene in a big way...*if* he plays ball."

"That's the only way you *could* get a man—promising him something."

Coral strode over to her and grasped her arm. "I don't like you speaking to me like that, Mia. It's not the way a daughter should speak to her mother!"

"You think I think of you as my *mother*?" Mia laughed in her face. "You're more like some deadly enemy I'm tied to. I'd be so glad if I never had to see you again! You're trying to steal Phillipe from me. Isn't it enough that you killed my father?"

"*I* killed him?" Coral shrieked. She grasped Mia tighter, shaking her angrily. "Is that what you've been blaming me for all these years?"

"Yes! I do blame you for it. He wouldn't have been in California if you knew how to be loving."

Coral flung Mia aside, then stood with her hands on her hips, pale with rage. "I never thought of you as a daughter, either," she hissed. "Do you know what *you* represent to *me*? A missed chance to be editor-in-chief of *Divine* years ago! Being pregnant cost me that! You've also been a constant reminder of a lousy marriage! I'm sorry I ever *had* you! And I'm not in competition with you over Phillipe—he's *way* out of your league! You think he wants some virgin with a phobia?"

"He loves me!" Mia cried. "And I love him!"

"Do you agree with me that he's as good in bed as he is at making clothes?"

"How would *you* know?" Mia cried. "Phillipe hasn't been to bed with you—" A rage surged up in Mia that

shocked her with its force. It was uncontrollable. She
suddenly wanted to hurt Coral in the fiercest possible
way. Words could not hurt her enough—she felt her
fingers close over a heavy lead-crystal ashtray.

Coral walked quickly to the living room and found
Phillipe's jacket.

"Take this back to him." She held it aloft. "He left it
here the other night after the most passionate, wonderful
lovemaking I've ever—"

"*Liar!*" Mia screamed. "You *liar!*" Coral was just passing
the mantel mirror that dominated one wall of the living
room. Mia hurled the ashtray with all her strength. Coral
screamed as the crystal missile sailed across the room. It
was meant to frighten her, to just miss her face, and it did
miss. But as it smashed into the mirror behind with a
tinkling crash, a shard of glass flew out, embedding itself
deep in Coral's face. The mirror collapsed, showering the
room with glittering icicles.

"You *lunatic!*" Coral stumbled, her hands to her face,
blood dripping through the fingers. "What have you *done*
to me!"

Mia stared at her uncomprehendingly, eyes wide with
shock. Coral took a few faltering steps into the bedroom
and fell, her nails ripping through the silk of the bed's
valance. Her head hit the floor, and Mia ran over to her,
staring down horrified at the bloodied face. Even someone who knew nothing about injury or plastic surgery
could see Coral would be scarred for life. Mia panicked,
running to the door of the suite.

"*Wait!*" Coral cried. She lifted herself with a supreme
effort, one hand clutching the bed, glaring at Mia with
pain-glazed eyes. "You're *finished!*" she called after her
daughter. "*Finished!* You'll never work in the fashion industry again—I'll make goddamn sure of *that!*"

Mia shook her head, words forming on her lips as she
soundlessly mouthed an apology. Then she turned away
from the nightmare scene and ran. She ran as she had
never before run in her life—down corridors, tripping,
stumbling into maids' carts, through emergency doors
then down service steps. Down flight after fight of stairs
she ran, sobbing, breathless. She wished the stairs would
never reach an end, wished she could run and run until
she reached hell itself....

* * *

Somehow she got into a taxi and gave her address. At her apartment she ran into the bathroom and saw a wild-eyed madwoman staring at her from the mirror. As much as she despised Coral at that moment, she could not allow her to bleed to death on the Crillon rug. She dialed the hotel, asking for Wayland Garrity. Thank God he was in.

"Wayland?" she stammered, almost incoherent. "Please get a doctor to my mother's suite! There's been an accident!"

She hung up as he asked, "What kind of accident?"

She knew her landlady used sleeping pills, and she found the brown glass bottle in the bathroom cabinet. It was one-third full. Please, God, make them be enough! She emptied the twelve pills into her mouth, swallowing them with water. She could not live through the rest of that day. The night before, she had believed she had everything she'd wanted in life: working with the top designer, being in love with him, hearing he loved her, too. Today it had vanished into the Paris air, in the sickest, most horrible way. She threw herself onto the bed where a few hours ago Phillipe had made love to her. Oh, let the pills work, she prayed, please God, *let me die!*

Book Two

Sixteen

"But you lived to tell the tale," Wayland said gently, sipping his drink.

"Yes," Mia whispered. "But I don't call this living—I call it existing."

Wayland stared at her for a moment, then laughed. "Of *course* you lived! *I'm* lucky if twelve sleeping pills get me to *sleep*! Welcome back to the land of the living," he said, hugging her.

Three months after her suicide attempt they sat in Wayland's apartment, watching the last rays of October sun. It was Friday evening in Manhattan, and the city was becalmed, awaiting its weekend. Wayland's apartment had been redecorated in coral marble slabs and dark gray velvet sofas. White roses perfumed the air. Mia had arrived that morning from Paris. Now, her ears buzzing with jet lag, she forbade her mind to think ahead. Better to keep it blank—as blank as it had been since that horrible day in Paris.

Wayland gazed curiously at her. "Did you really expect total oblivion?"

Mia shrugged. "I thought that never having to cope with the problems of living would be wonderful. . . ."

She leaned back against the soft upholstery as Wayland fetched more ice. In a way, it was a great relief to be back in New York. She thought back to that day when her landlady had found her and called her own doctor. He had stomach-pumped her. It was the most incredible experience, coming back to life when one had hoped, had prayed, to die. Afterward, Mia had begged him not to report the incident. Madame Della had slipped the doctor a folded ten-thousand-franc note. "That is the way things

are arranged here," she explained later. Mia had stayed in
bed for a few days, weak and sick. She had refused all
phone calls from Phillipe or Stephanie. They were told
she had flu.

"I couldn't even face Phillipe after what my mother told
me," she told Wayland. "I just wanted to get out of there,
but I knew I had to confront him. It would have been so
cowardly to just run away."

"Poor baby..." Wayland soothed, and added a handful
of ice cubes to a fresh drink.

"You were the first person I called. To find out about
Mother. I was so sick with worry—"

"Oh, *she* survived." Wayland took a long gulp of his
drink. "*I'm* the one you should have worried about. I
never want to go through something like that again.
Getting her onto that plane! Ugh!" He shuddered. "The
American Hospital shot her full of painkillers. She was so
heavily sedated *and* so heavily bandaged, she could hardly
see where she was going. It was worse than Joan Crawford
in *A Woman's Face!* Before we left Paris she made me call
this Japanese plastic surgeon here, in New York—he's
supposed to be the best in the world. He told me he was
booked for three years, but Coral grabbed the phone and
talked her way in for that *day!* The flight was a super
nightmare! We took a cab from Kennedy to his private
clinic and he operated immediately. She keeps saying
she's going to do a piece on him in the magazine."

"And?" Mia pressed. "What sort of job did he do?"

Wayland shrugged. "She spent two weeks in bandages,
taking megadoses of vitamin C. Everyone thought she'd
had a face-lift. Then the dressing came off. It doesn't look
too bad. A neat zigzag near the hairline—"

"Oh, *God!*" Mia put her face in her hands.

"The main trouble is that *she* doesn't think she looks
good. She keeps saying, "I'm imperfect now, Wayland,
and you know what the fashion world thinks of imperfect
goods." She's always touching her face, fussing with a
scarf or hat, asking if the scar shows."

He reached for the cocktail shaker and poured the
remains of his drink into a glass. "She'll adjust...." He
refilled her Perrier.

Mia shook her head. "This was just what our relationship needed. She'll really hate my guts now, and she'd be justified. I'll never forgive myself."

"Oh, I'm sure that deep down she knows you didn't mean to hurt her," Wayland said, trying to reassure her. "She's smoking a lot more pot—says it calms her nerves. She's so determined to be of her time—sometimes I think of her as a little forty-five-year-old cheerleader in her miniskirt and boots, getting high and hanging out with all those wretched pop stars. Colin Beaumont gives me pep talks and lectures on fashion and keeping up with the sixties, but frankly, it all seems tacky to me. I *hate* today's clothes."

Mia lifted her face to him. "Wayland, she told me I was finished in the fashion industry. I know how powerful she is. I'll need a job here: What am I to do?"

"Calm down, pet." He reached over to pat her knee. "Coral's big, but she isn't God. There'll always be a place for you at HQ, especially now that you're a qualified Paris designer."

"She'd kill you if she thought you were helping me, Wayland."

"She doesn't have to know everything, does she? Now let's stop talking about Coral for a moment. Tell me more about you. Did you actually quit Phillipe Roux? Is it *really* all over with him?"

"Of course! Absolutely over!" She tried to sound definite, but even hearing Phillipe's name produced a dull ache. Could it ever be all over with Phillipe? Could you tear out a piece of your heart? She had relived her last meeting with him many times.

She'd finally forced herself to see him. Feeling sick, she slowly walked along the Avenue Marceau to the salon. What were her reasons for leaving? She tried rehearsing them in her mind. "Phillipe, I can't work for a man who commits incest." No. "Phillipe, I could never love a man who made love to my mother." No. She would simply tell him he had disappointed her on every level. She carried his jacket, though she couldn't remember taking it from Coral's suite.

Stephanie opened the salon door. It was nearly five o'clock, the house was quiet and calm.

"You are leaving," Stephanie said, ushering her into her small office. "I am right, yes?"

Mia nodded.

"I do not know the reasons, but I am very sad. Working for those two is not easy, I know, but..." Her pale-lashed eyes gazed at Mia ruefully, expectantly.

"One day perhaps I can discuss it all with you."

Stephanie shrugged. "Nothing to discuss, really. He has a devastating effect on people. I should say on women. One either devotes one's life to him or..." She raised her eyebrows. "Or one escapes. Will you be joining another house? Courreges, perhaps? Phillipe will be so jealous."

When Phillipe called her into his studio, her knees wobbled and she felt close to fainting. To her relief, the studio was empty. Her sketches were still pinned to the wall, fabric cuttings stapled to them. Phillipe closed the door behind her, smiling tenderly.

"This influenza—it is all over? You look well."

She swallowed, staring into his bright, warm eyes. He approached her, touching her arms with his warm hands. She took a step back.

"Mia, we are having an enormous success! We have dozens of new private clients—even the Duchess of Windsor has expressed interest: I told her secretary she will have to pay the full price, like everyone else. Your mother ordered six outfits, the Begum Khan has ordered eight! We have taken on extra workers, and I am negotiating with the apartment next door so we can build a new studio and turn this room into a second atelier. For you, I am redecorating a room on the top floor so you will have a place to yourself—not just a cupboard. I need you to start work at once on a knitwear collection we agreed to do for Japan. Headquarters in New York want us to—"

"I'm leaving, Phillipe," she said.

His face changed entirely. "What are you talking about? Do you need a vacation?"

She shook her head slowly, her eyes on his. "No, I mean I want to leave you. This house."

"But... why?" he asked, very gently. His eyes bored straight into her soul, their innocent, intense expression so guileless. His effect on her was the same as it had always been: She felt like throwing herself into his arms. He looked so hurt, so surprised, she wanted to beg forgiveness for even daring to think of leaving.

"Another house has offered you a position?" he asked.

She looked at him furiously. "Is that what you're afraid of?" She met his eyes. "No, it isn't that. I think you know very well why I must leave...."

He shrugged, beginning to get angry. "But I do *not* know! I only know that I started creating a room for you to work in, to be comfortable in. I intended to offer you a better salary, which reflected the success of this season. I know that in our evening together we reached some new understanding between *us*! Mia, did we not tell each other the most important words a man and a woman can exchange?" He covered her hand with his.

She pulled her hand away. "You told me you were tied to Josephine!" she cried. "Honor bound! What am *I* supposed to do? Hang around here and adore you?"

"I see..." he said slowly, looking grave and worried. "*That* is why you are leaving? You will let emotions come between you and your work?"

"That's only one reason." She reached down into her carryall and produced his jacket. "This is another."

He took the jacket, frowning. "Your mother gave you this?"

"Now you know I know all about that."

"Nothing happened between your mother and me, Mia," he said. "I think it was very embarrassing for her. But none of this matters. It is just gossip. She admires my clothes, her magazine will feature many outfits, and they will all be available from Headquarters. I signed an exclusive contract for New York with your mother's friend, Monsieur Garrity—"

"That's great," she said expressionlessly. "I'm happy for you."

"Oh, Mia..." He sighed sadly. "Why are you so angry? Because I want progress?"

She took a deep breath. "I'm trying to explain all my reasons for wanting to go. People who call me up here are told I don't work for the house...."

He looked guilty immediately. "There, I am at fault. You see? I admit it. I listened to Josephine and your mother. They said it would lessen the interest in me if I shared designing credit—"

"That's disgusting!" she said. "You used all my designs!"

"Yes," he said. "But first we *must* build up the name of the house. Later we can give credit where it is due."

She shook her head. "That's so unfair—"

"I don't think so. It is understood in this business. Some houses have ten or twelve young designers working in the studio. If they are any good, they rise to the top."

"I don't want to work for someone who lies to me." Mia stood and made for the door, but he caught hold of her arm.

"Mia! Even *you* have lied some time in your life—is that not true?"

She shrugged off his grip. "But not to *you*, Phillipe." She opened the door.

"You think you will just walk out of here?" he cried. "Out of my life? He glared at her, holding her as fast as if he were gripping her shoulders. "I shall not let you go!"

"I *am* going," Mia repeated, as if to convince herself. With an effort, she turned away from him.

He followed, his hand on her shoulder. "Maybe you will return to America, but—" he tapped his forehead— "*here*! and *here*!" he put his hand on his heart, "I will never let you go, Mia."

She walked out of the studio, forcing herself not to look back at him.

"In the most important way, you will always be mine!" he called after her.

She walked down the corridor, tears streaking her face.

He caught up with her in the corridor and held her. "You cannot leave me." He nuzzled the side of her neck. She steeled herself as his lips softly moved against her cheek. Her entire body trembled. Oh *God*! she cried, why do you give everything to people only when it's too late? She knew she would carry the touch of his lips forever, for her life. She broke away from him and ran, fast. Down the stairs and across the courtyard. On the pavement she stumbled and nearly fell, imagining she heard him chasing her, calling her name. She was swept up in a crowd heading for L'Étoile and the metro. She let the crowd carry her along, not caring where it took her, and was swept into the metro and onto a train. Wherever she ended up, it would be better than going home. She got off at Montparnasse, and as she walked the wider, less crowded boulevards, she realized she was approaching La Coupole.

The café was bustling, the interior brightly lit and inviting. Mia threaded her way through the outside ta-

bles, past rows of interested faces, some turning as she
passed. She walked through the noise and lights into the
women's room. Other women examined themselves in
the wide mirrors above the marbled basins, their expressions showing dissatisfaction with lipstick or hair. Mia
fumbled in her purse for a brush. Glancing up at her own
face, it looked as if she were in shock. She closed her eyes
and swayed slightly, and a girl with piled-up blond hair
caught her arm and asked "*Ça va pas?*"

"*Non. Ça va. Merci!*" Mia murmured, forcing a smile.

She wandered out. He had said he would never let her
go. One part of her was disappointed that he hadn't
somehow forced her to stay. Now, she told herself, you
start a new life. A life that is not built around him. But she
wasn't sure she could do it. She sat at an empty table and
ordered hot chocolate, thinking its sweetness might revive
her. Each time she tried to think of her future, her mind
felt as if it had gaping holes in it. Two hours later she took
a taxi home, exhausted.

She had expected Phillipe to call, but after a few days
she realized he would not. He was probably too incredulous to believe she could leave him. She prepared to move
back to New York, but allowed herself a few more weeks
in Paris; resting, enjoying the city which now had such a
bittersweet flavor. Each time she left the apartment, she
expected Phillipe to be there, waiting for her. Even when
she climbed the metal steps to the plane, she half expected
him to be blocking her way. At the door she turned for a
last long look at the Paris sky, at her hopes, her illusions,
her soul.

"And now you're back where you belong!" Wayland
said, gulping the last of his cocktail. "I wish you would let
me give you a *real* welcoming-home party! Mackenzie
Gold could come, and David and Colin and all the pals
you knew from MacMillans."

"I want to be very quiet and see no one for a while."

"Oh, don't you fret, pet!" Wayland said. "It's always
the ones from humble beginnings like Roux who want the
most."

"Well, he has it now," Mia replied, indicating the *WWD* on
the coffee table, with its headline: FASHION GOES ROUX-CRAZY!

"Let him have it, my dear," Wayland sighed. "The white
Rolls and the villa on the Côte d'Azur and the Passy

penthouse. He'll still have to look across the dinner table at that beastly woman Josephine—*ugh*! God, when they visited here, Coral and I had to use superhuman control not to strangle her on the spot."

Mia twisted around on the couch to look at him. "You'd better tell me the whole story of Phillipe's visit," she said.

Phillipe Roux had arrived in Manhattan in late August to the biggest publicity barrage ever afforded a visiting French designer; "since Dior!" Coral swore. Twelve pages of his designs in *Divine*'s Paris issue had established him as "Designer of the Sixties," eclipsing even Mary Quant and Yves Saint Laurent. The press decided he was responsible for every sudden shift in fashion, the miniskirt, the Mod Look, the Skinny Look, and the Majorette Look. It was so much simpler for them to credit one person: Phillipe thus became *the* Fashion Celebrity.

Headquarters, sole outlet for Roux clothes in New York, advertised him on whole pages of newspapers, on buses and posters around town. Photographed on the lithe bodies of ballerinas, the campaign blasted the name of Phillipe Roux into public consciousness.

New York socialites had ordered clothes from Paris. Jackie Kennedy and the Duchess of Windsor were photographed in Roux outfits. Women of all ages seemed to love the clothes, and models begged Coral to use them for the gala New York presentation of the Roux collection she had planned.

Coral, still self-conscious about her face, worked herself into a nervous state. She'd gone through a list of makeup artists and hairdressers for ways to avert attention from the pink zigzag scar. For her reunion with Roux, she chose a black angora beret, clipped to her short hair with diamond barrettes. It gave her a fresh, youthful look to accompany the new gray Roux dress and jacket. An hour after he'd checked in at the Pierre, she hurried over.

Phillipe, waiting in the bar, spotted Coral and walked into the foyer to greet her. She felt herself grow breathless as he approached.

"*Phillipe!*" she cried. "*Darling!*" She threw her arms around him and bestowed the fashion kiss—generous kisses in the air to each side of his cheek. Phillipe's back was straight, a faint smile on his face. He guided her to the bar, his hand lightly holding her elbow.

"I don't need a drink, darling," she said. "Let's just go straight to your room—we have *so* much to discuss."

"We are in the bar, Coral," he said, continuing to steer her toward it.

"*We?*" she echoed.

He took her to a table where a serious, dark-haired woman sat. "My assistant, Josephine," he said, introducing her.

Coral's smile froze for an instant, then returned in its full, intense glory. "Welcome to New York!" She took Josephine's hand as Josephine stood to greet her.

"*Enchanté*," Josephine replied.

Coral sat between them, looking at Phillipe. "What a *lovely* surprise, Phillipe!" she said brightly.

"Josephine wanted very much to see New York," Phillipe replied.

"Congratulations on your *incredible* success!" Coral cried. "Did you see the posters on your way in? Did you see the models? Members of the New York City Ballet, no less!"

"I owe a great deal to you!" Phillipe bowed his head.

"*My* twelve pages?" Coral tried to look modest. "They *are* some kind of record, I suppose. . . ."

The tiny bar was dark and intimate. A waiter approached. Coral eyed their glasses of Perrier. "A triple martini!" she ordered.

Josephine watched with dark, suspicious eyes. A curious mixture of unease and confidence, Coral decided. She acted as if she owned Phillipe.

"Er. . . *Voulez-vous voir le* Empire State Building?" Coral asked.

"*Je veux bien, madame!*" Josephine's eyes opened wide, animatedly. "*Quand est-ce que vous pouvez l'arranger?*"

"*Je*—" Coral frowned, then burst into laughter. "This is ridiculous! *C'est ridicule!* Phillipe, I really don't know enough French—you'll have to translate!" She fluttered her hands over her beret, pulling it to one side, leaning her face on her palm. Before he could begin, she said, "We have quite a schedule lined up. There's a charity gala of your clothes Monday—that's when we present you with the first *Divine* Award. Interviews. We've booked Irving Penn to photograph you!"

"Yes, and *Vogue* and *Harper's Bazaar*—*they* photograph me, too. Why so much interest in *me*? It is the clothes they should photograph."

She laughed. "We like *personalities* in America. And that's what *you* are now, Phillipe. Make sure you get an early night on Tuesday. Don't be bleary-eyed for Penn—his focus is deadly! Can someone baby-sit for your... assistant?"

Phillipe frowned. "I do not understand. . . ."

Coral gave him a meaningful look. "So *we* can have some time together, you and *I*!" Her drink arrived and she held it up, looking into Phillipe's eyes and saying, "To you!" as Josephine glared at her.

Coral took a long sip; she was very good at ignoring people close to her; she'd had practice in New York and Paris, sitting knee-to-knee with enemies at collections, all the while gazing serenely into space. Finally she glanced at Josephine. "I'll make an appointment with one of our top makeup people for her," she promised Phillipe. "Just in *case* she gets into any photographs."

Phillipe protested: "We think American women use too much makeup."

Coral laughed coldly. "The trick is to use just *enough*." Josephine obviously used none at all, and nothing irritated Coral more.

Phillipe carefully translated all the dates and times Coral gave them, and Josephine made tiny notes in a diary. Coral noticed *Vogue*, *Town and Country*, and *Andy Warhol* written in on various days.

"I shall give the main reception in my apartment," she told Phillipe. "On Tuesday. I've asked eighty close friends—the most important tastemakers in the city. Be there early, Phillipe—so we can rehearse a little presentation—"

"We shall be there," he promised, his brown eyes twinkling

"*We?*" She touched his arm. "Why do you keep saying *we*? Don't you go anywhere without your assistant?"

He laughed.

They were paging "Mr. Roux," and facing the prospect of being left alone with Josephine, Coral made a curt "*Au revoir*" and accompanied Phillipe to the phone booth. "I'll be in constant touch," she promised, and tried to kiss him again. But he turned his face so that once again she gave the fashion kiss into air.

She left the hotel, furious. He *couldn't* be sleeping with that woman, he just couldn't be! Sister or not, she was a peasant!

"I guess they're closer than you thought," Wayland consoled when Coral called to complain.

"Just keep her out of my sight!" Coral snapped.

The *Divine* awards at Headquarters were presented with all the fanfare and glitter the magazine and the store together could muster. Coral had joined forces with a charity committee to turn the event into a hundred-dollar-a-plate event, all proceeds to go to the Garment Industry Retirement Fund for seamstresses. The champagne reception took place on the fourth floor of the store, mobbed by fashion press and photographers, attended by the top names of fashion and their acolytes. Donyale Luna, first black cover girl, was there, adding new meaning to Roux's clothes. Coral was on tiptoe among the crowd, craning her neck to see who was arriving. The murmuring chatter swelled to screams and cries; perfume and cigar smoke made the air heavy. Flashbulbs popped, blinding subjects who, ignoring the cameras, tried to look disinterested.

"You know what I adore about his clothes?" one society lady in a knee-length Roux confided to another. "His *seams*! His marvelous seams!"

Wayland smiled at everyone. "I thought his clothes wouldn't sell because they made everyone look like they were still in kindergarten," he babbled. "But that's exactly what *sells* them! I just saw the Shrimp *and* Twiggy in the elevator! It was like seeing the future! Both in tiny little minis, all legs and eyes...you really should rush over and catch them!"

The crowd watched entranced as the clothes were paraded by to the music of the Kinks, Herman's Hermits, and the Four Tops. Finally Coral walked out alone onto the stage. She wore Roux's glittering purple sheath, cut simply and stopping short four inches above the knees, her legs pailletted with sparkling hose. The *Times* reported the next day that she'd been totally poised before an audience made up of "everyone who counts on today's fashion scene, from fashion groupies to what *Women's Wear* calls 'fashion victims.'"

The audience hushed, and Coral began: "*Divine* awards this new honor to a designer who has stood fashion on its head, who has changed the very *course* of fashion! Phillipe Roux has done just that in his Fall-Winter collection. I would like to present this award to you, Monsieur Roux, for your brilliance in the art of clothing women, and for ensuring that from today fashion can never be quite the same. . . ."

She held out the stylized female figure in bronze as Phillipe stepped onto the stage to receive it, kissing Coral gravely on both cheeks as the crowd stood to applaud.

"It was the nearest she came to sex with him," Wayland acidly commented later.

Phillipe made a charming, halting speech. "I owe much of my success tonight to a woman who has helped me so much," he concluded.

Coral, standing in the wings, stepped forward to acknowledge this tribute, only to find Wayland grasping the back of her dress, holding her back. "What the—" She turned around to hiss at Wayland as Phillipe beckoned toward the front row of seats.

"Josephine?" he said. "*Presente-toi!*"

Coral watched unbelievingly as Josephine awkwardly walked up the steps in her high heels and out onto the stage, clasping Phillipe's hand.

"I would like to use this happy moment to announce our marriage!" he said.

"My *God!*" Coral gasped, but it was drowned out by the applause.

"I only wish I had words to describe Coral's face," Wayland said later. "It almost matched her magenta gown!"

Her mouth set in a grim line, Coral had run straight to the models' dressing room and begged some uppers from Maxine d'Arbeville, her favorite model. She swallowed them with a glass of champagne and ran around greeting guests, avoiding the happy couple whenever she could.

"Of course, she wasn't his sister after all," Colin told Wayland later, "they were just kissing cousins."

"Fucking cousins, I'd say. Josephine Roux looks like a woman who can't get enough! Those eyes! A plain little country girl . . ."

"They're the ones who know how to hold their men.

Did you see all the shoes she bought? She knows how to spend the money he's making."

Coral's party for Phillipe, catered by La Grenouille, boasted hundreds of candles around the rooms, flickering their romantic light on the ceilings. Phillipe arrived early, Josephine in tow. Waiters took their coats and Coral quickly briefed Colin to whisk Josephine away for a quick "portrait."

Phillipe wore a beautifully cut dinner jacket ("A favor from a cutter at Balenciaga," he told people) and looked very handsome, his hair lightly dampened and combed back. He had developed, Coral noticed, an air of polite interest in all the curious customs and ideas that were being pressed upon him. She was irritated to find he was using that air with her, following her urgent invitation to her study as if this were yet another strange rite he was obliged to go along with.

They brushed past waiters assembling trays of hors d'oeuvres, flower arrangers putting final touches to huge urns of fall flowers, photographers sprawled around awaiting their cues. She closed the doors to the study and turned to face him. She longed to throw herself into his arms, but something told her to keep her distance.

"Now, what *is* this all about? Are you trying to involve *Divine* in a scandal? Ina Mellindorf told me it was well known at Dior that you and Josephine were brother and sister. You come from the same little Spanish village and you have the same name...."

Phillipe nodded. "Yes. We are cousins."

"That's still not so wonderful. Your children could easily—"

"We do not want children," Phillipe stated.

"Why didn't you tell me about Josephine in Paris?"

"You did not ask! I told you Americans are always in such a hurry. Before I could speak, you walked naked into the room...."

"Right!" she agreed, squeezing his arm. "Never have I wanted sex with any man so much! I thought we'd be together on this trip—why have you made it so difficult? Did you forget this trip was *my* idea! *I* invited you! I *invented* this award!"

"Yes?" His intense eyes focused a ray of dislike at her.

"*Why* did you do all this? Because you liked my clothes, no?"

"But also because I like *you*, Phillipe!" She stroked his arm. "God, you're the first man I ever met to have this effect on me. I want to touch you. I want you to touch me. All *over*! Don't make me *beg*. . . ." She caressed his cheek, his mouth. He moved his face away from her hand.

"I don't understand!" she snapped. "How can you be so cold?"

"But I am not at all cold. I am a passionate man."

"Then show *me* some passion!" she whispered near his ear. She brushed his cheeks with her mouth—he was freshly shaved, the skin brown and smooth.

Darting away, she locked the study door and returned to him. She raised her arms to him, but he stepped away again, leaning back against an armchair. She held out her arms imploringly; her whole body felt afire, swept by a horrible yet strangely thrilling feeling of rejection.

"You are spoiling that jacket," he told her.

Coral reached back to find the little jacket and threw it at him. He caught it and smoothed it gently. She watched as his brown hands lovingly stroked the fabric, then cried, "I do believe that fucking jacket means more to you than I do!"

He looked back at her, smiling softly. "But of course! It's my métier!"

She felt a wave of fury pass over her. Struggling out of the dress, she kicked it at him. Wearing only her white slip, she grabbed the dress from his hands and ripped it apart.

"But, Coral!" He watched in horror as she split the seams, clawed the lining out. "You ordered this outfit—you owe a thousand dollars for it," he reminded her.

"Worth every cent!" she cried, opening some sliding doors into her bedroom and routing through her closet. She found a Saint Laurent from last season and quickly put it on, walking grimly back to him. "Zip it up!" she commanded.

He zipped the dress closed. "I did not say I am the only designer, Coral. *You* said that. . . ."

"I've changed my mind. Overnight I can bury you, Phillipe."

He shook his head sadly and walked toward the door of the study.

"And where is Mia?" she asked. "Does she still work for you?"

He had unlocked the door, and now turned back. "She left some weeks ago."

"Really? She left?" Coral checked herself in the mirror, smoothing down a silk collar. "Did you lay a hand on her? Did you make love to her?"

His eyes flashed. "Why are you so interested? Ask her. . . ."

He was about to leave when she called "Wait!" Again he turned back. "I've made a great mistake with you, Phillipe," she told him. "I thought you had talent, but I also thought you knew the ways of the world a little better than you do. Do you know Andy Warhol?"

"He is doing my portrait. . . ."

"He predicted that in the future *everyone* would be famous for fifteen minutes."

Phillipe raised his eyebrows.

Coral's eyes flashed: "Your fifteen minutes are up, Phillipe!"

By the middle of his trip Phillipe had become too big for Coral to control in any way. Donald Kramer had increased his offer to take over the house. It would serve as a little Paris jewel in the crown of Kramer Communications, a giant conglomerate with fingers in almost everything except the Paris couture. Bendel, Bloomingdale's, Bonwit Teller: All wanted little talks about his next collection. When the offers got too big to resist, Phillipe agreed to Kramer's backing. A new cologne called Phillipe was immediately announced.

"By the last evening Coral and Josephine did not even acknowledge each other's existence," Wayland said. "We all flew to Washington to pick up yet another award—a trade award, from the French embassy. . . ."

The French embassy had been persuaded by Coral to use her pages from *Divine*'s Paris coverage, blown up as background for their reception. Coral had agreed to introduce Phillipe to the specially invited group of VIPs. They treated Phillipe and the question of fashion as an invasion

of their diplomatic world, adding their own pomp and
ceremony to the presentation.

Arriving in Washington, Phillipe and Josephine went
straight to the consulate for a luncheon. Coral, pleading
exhaustion, rested in her room, witch-hazel pads on her
eyes. That evening they met in the receiving line at the
embassy. In his first flush of success, Phillipe had bought
Josephine a pair of diamond earrings from Tiffany's. She
wore Roux's white sequined sheath, which skimmed her
body without a curve. Her hair had been cut short by
Sassoon, making her and Coral look disturbingly like
sisters with a twenty-year age difference. Coral wore the
new pale gray two-piece Phillipe had brought over for her,
a cut-out top over a gathered skirt, accessorized with
emerald clips and her signature black shawl. She was
expertly made up by a stylist, her piercing eyes emphasized by large lashes and dark shadow.

"You could have inhaled enough Joy, Chanel, and Dior
to keep a small aircraft aloft for hours," Wayland said.
"Nobody can crush like the French." The Washington
crowd mixed with the flown-in New Yorkers in a dazzle of
scent and smoke. Catherine Deneuve made a surprise
appearance. She'd recently ordered clothes from Phillipe,
and they posed for the shattering explosions of flashbulbs. Donald Kramer, the man who had "bought" Phillipe
Roux, assured everyone that *Phillipe* cologne would ce-
ment Franco-American relations forever. He had hurriedly
made up large cut-glass flacons of the cologne to serve as
previews for the eventual launch. Each bottle had *Phillipe*
scrawled across it in gray glitter, long silk gray tassels
dangling.

"All the men too cheap to buy Chanel for their wives
will buy this," Coral predicted. "Thanks to me, Phillipe's
name suggests luxury."

Wayland had removed the stopper, taken a sniff and
groaned. "I'm renaming it Dead Ballerina," he said.

They sipped vodka in the corner of the consulate's
private drawing room at the exclusive party after the
party. Wayland watched Coral watching Phillipe: "Getting
anywhere at all, darling?"

"I can't prise him away from that human paper clip!"
she complained.

By evening's end, after the flight back to New York and

the drive into town, Coral was angry, tired, and drunk. She sat in the back of the Rolls that HQ had provided for the week, shrinking from the French couple, crowding Wayland. Everyone clutched their flacon of *Phillipe* cologne.

"Mine goes to my cleaning lady," Wayland whispered to Coral, kissing her as they dropped him off. He shook hands with the Rouxs, wishing them bon voyage for the next day. The car started up again toward the Pierre, Phillipe and Josephine staring out at the streets, tired.

Coral placed a detaining hand on Phillipe's sleeve. "Send her in and come back with me for coffee," she said. "We have a hundred things to discuss before you leave."

Phillipe gave her a weary look. "There is nothing to discuss, Coral. And I am very tired. Perhaps we could breakfast together tomorrow?"

"*Fuck* breakfast!" Coral shouted.

Josephine climbed out of the car, the driver holding the door. She hesitated, looking back for Phillipe, a half smile on her drawn face. "*Tu viens?*"

"Send her to bed!" Coral cried. She grasped for Phillipe's hand.

He tried to pull away. "Coral, I think you are very tired—"

"I *am*! Of this treatment!" Coral leaned forward, half out of the car, and pushed Josephine with all her strength. Josephine cried out, stumbled and fell, sprawling on the sidewalk.

"*Mais qu'est ce qu'elle a?*" she cried, getting up. "*Elle est folle?*"

"And *bonne nuit* to you, too!" Coral cried. She slammed the door shut, trapping Phillipe and motioning quickly to the driver. "Take us home!" The driver froze, stunned. Josephine's eyes were wide with surprise as she stared into the car.

"Get behind that wheel!" Coral ordered in her steeliest voice.

"Coral, I must get out here!" Phillipe protested.

"Driver!"

The driver got into the car, turning around to her. "The gentleman wishes to get out here, Mrs. Stanton—"

"And *I* say drive on, if you value your job."

The car moved forward with a jerk, Phillipe turning to

look back after Josephine as her lone figure dwindled on Fifth Avenue.

"But Coral, this is absurd!" Phillipe gripped her arm. "You are surely not trying to kidnap me?"

Coral twisted to face him. "Let's you and I come to a little understanding. If this is going to be the last time we meet, at least let me see what I'm missing." She held his arms, dragging him around to face her, clambering over one leg. Astride him, her back to the driver, she deftly unzipped his black pants. "I want to see what the great Phillipe Roux is witholding!"

"Coral!"

She thrust her hand through the opening. Triumphantly she held him while, with the other hand, she ripped open the snowy white shirt, exposing his smooth brown chest.

"You see? I do excite you!" she crowed as he grew in her hand. She turned her head to watch the driver, closing the glass door with a flick of her fingers. She slid to the floor, burying her face in his lap.

"Make love to me, Phillipe! You owe it to me!" She was very drunk, very high, very attracted to him. She held his heavy sex in her hand, stroking it until it grew to its full size. "My God, you're built like a goddamn bull!" she cried. It explained his arrogance, his confidence, his incredible attraction. No man with a thing like that between his legs needed to skulk around.

Coral crammed him in her mouth, trying to bring him to orgasm by stroking and licking him. She lapped at his shaft with her tongue, mouthing the very tip of him. Meanwhile Phillipe was trying to pull away from her, his eyes wide with surprise, his face flushed. He was also trying for the driver's sake to pretend that nothing was happening. Then he moved his legs to one side, pushing her away from him with the flat of his hand. Her head struck the glass partition with a crack. He tucked himself in and zipped up his pants before she could recover.

"Love?" He laughed. "You do not understand the word. There is no owing in love."

She clambered back onto the seat beside him, glaring at him. "*You*'re marrying Josephine aren't you?" she spat. "Isn't *that* because you owe her? You couldn't possibly find her attractive."

Phillipe pounded on the glass separating them from the

driver. "*Stop!* Stop this car!" He turned back to her. "How do you know what I see when I look at Josephine? You are so sure what is attractive and what is not? Look!" He pulled up the seat mirror from the back of the seat before them, reached out and grasped her face with two hands, then twisted her toward her reflection. "You think *this*—a woman hungry for a man—is attractive? You think it is attractive to tear open a man's pants? You know who is beautiful? Your daughter—inside and out, but not like her mother. . . ."

Coral suddenly became cold sober. She stared at him for a moment, then slid open the glass partition and yelled to the driver. The car pulled up with a shriek of brakes.

She turned to him. "I'm going to make you old hat so quickly you won't know what hit you! Next season I'll promote a new designer! The year after, no one will even remember your stupid name. All that will be left of you is this cheap, stinking cologne!"

Phillipe opened the car door warily, frowning. He turned to her and his expression caused her to flinch. His face had darkened, the veins in his forehead standing out as he fought his instincts. He suddenly placed both hands around her throat in a viselike grip. He squeezed gently.

"I should kill you," he said quietly, through his teeth. For a moment she was very frightened and her eyes bulged slightly. She let out a strangled moan. "But death would be too good for you, Coral. I wish you instead a very *long* life. For you to get old, very quickly and very ungracefully, as you surely will. To become totally undesirable to men, and . . . frankly, Coral"—he put one foot out of the car and let her go—"that will not take long. . . ."

He stepped out, slamming the door shut. Her eyes narrowed, she stared at him with an expression of pure hatred. The car started and she wound down the window, hurling her flacon of *Phillipe* at him. He sidestepped elegantly as it smashed with a luxurious splash on the sidewalk. Phillipe continued walking.

Coral wound up the window and fell back on her seat, exhausted, almost afraid of herself. She had an unbelievably strong desire to rip all her clothes to shreds—to run amok in her closets and set fire to everything.

"Home, Mrs. Stanton?" the driver asked gently.

She frowned, shaking her head. "No!" she cried.

She delved into her purse and extracted a tiny enameled pillbox. An Andy Warhol superstar had given her an LSD capsule, advising her to try it when she felt like an interesting experience. She swallowed it. To return home tonight without Phillipe would be to accept failure. She tried to quell the furious anger and frustration that bubbled inside her.

The Rolls cruised silently up Fifth Avenue as she flicked through her address book. Someone had told her of an amusing place downtown.

"Take me to the End of the World!" she called to the driver.

Seventeen

Coral's driver eyed her warily in the rearview mirror. He couldn't wait to get home and describe to his wife what he had seen that night. A famous fashion editor giving head to a French designer! Maybe he could call the *Daily News* and sell the story?

"Where is the End of the World?" he asked her. "Or is that a stupid question?"

"Here." She passed her address book to him. "It's somewhere between here and Chinatown."

He pulled the car over to the curb, frowning at Coral's handwriting. "This looks like the East Village, Mrs. Stanton. It's after two, wouldn't you be better off at home by now?"

"Certainly not!" She waved a twenty-dollar bill at him and he took it. "I'll need to stop at the Chelsea Hotel. I have no intention of going there on my own," she warned him.

A few minutes later Coral stood on a dirty Chelsea street, shouting through an intercom, "I'm on an acid trip!"

"Groovy! I'll be right down!"

She had used Neon as a model in some layouts: Her frizzy mop of hair and kohl-rimmed eyes combined interestingly with a beautifully molded face. Neon bounced out in a tiny mini dress, a feather boa trailing over one shoulder. She spotted the limousine and leaped in, muttering, "Neat!" As they drove toward the Village, she popped a handful of uppers, grinning at Coral.

Twenty minutes later, after asking a number of people where it was, they pulled up at a seedy disco whose crooked neon sign spelled out THE END OF THE WORLD. It looked enchanting to Coral. She followed Neon down the steep, dark stairs and froze in wonder at the entrance to the club—strobe lighting and deafening rock mesmerizing her. She asked for a corner table and ordered champagne. Neon was pulled off to the dance floor by a tall black man and Coral sat back, watching, as the LSD started to perform tricks. The champagne turned into the most delicious wine she had ever tasted—just one sip of it sent gallons of the most subtle, bubbly stuff roaring down her throat, almost choking her. She scrutinized the label— could California have finally mastered the process? The dance floor itself was the most fantastically beautiful thing she'd ever seen. Somehow the club had achieved the effect of the floor rippling, breathing like some living organism. Since it was glass-tiled, she wondered how they did it. The dancers moved, danced, jived like professionals. Their makeup and clothing were way ahead even of *Divine*. She had never seen such colors and styles: brilliant acid neon colors clashing and matching, the eyes painted with psychedelic rainbows or flowers, patterns on cheeks and foreheads catching the flashing light.

Many different people spoke to her. One or two seemed to know her. She told the story of her life to various listeners. She asked the name of the group playing, because never had music sounded so meaningful and evocative to her. She vowed to bring Wayland and Colin to the club.

When her driver came to find her at three o'clock, she dismissed him. She could not dance—the place was too overpowering to do anything but sit and gaze about her in wonder. At times she believed she was paralyzed, but if she exerted a terrific will, she found she could move.

Kissing her new friends good-bye, she left the club at four-thirty. The dark street was no less extraordinary than the club: Streetlights seemed to be breathing, living creatures. A dog undulated by, several inches off the sidewalk. She hailed a luminous yellow taxi.

Getting in, she tried not to let the driver see that his melting face disturbed her in any way. "Marco Raminez," she said, reading his nameplate. "Charming!"

He looked at her suspiciously: "You got any money, lady?"

Coral frowned: Her sequined purse had vanished.

"You got five dollars, lady? I don't like to take passengers this late who ain't got no money."

Coral bent to remove her spangled pumps. She held them up.

"See these?" she asked. "Just got 'em in Paris. First time I've worn them. They cost a hundred fifty dollars. They're yours if you take me home—"

"I don't need no shoes."

"These are Roger Vivier—see the label? Don't you have a wife? A girl?"

"Don't you need your shoes, lady?"

"I need a ride more," she said, leaning back, closing her eyes.

The cab was moving; he must have agreed to the trade. She would run into the apartment building feeling the cold tarmac on her bare soles. As they sped up Second Avenue, New York had never looked so sharp, so clean, so lovely.

In its next issue, the Tittle-Tattle columnist at *Labels* had a field day:

Which renowned fashion editor has let the Sixties Revolution go to her head? She recently took a change from hobnobbing with the fashion greats to slumming at a notorious acidhead dive in the East Village. Was it fashion fatigue or the aftermath of a capsule that made her look "spaced out" of her Sassooned head? The Psychedelic Look has found a strong foothold in the most unexpected quarters...

Ed Schreiber, the stocky, cocky accountant of Gold!, rapped on the glass storefront of the new Gold!, peering in, shading his eyes to see through.

Mackenzie was sitting at the counter, talking animatedly into a phone cradled at her shoulder. He had been told he would find her there if he came early. He glanced down at his watch: eight-thirty. She unlocked the door, peering out at him.

"We're not open until next week!" she told him.

He stared at her, fascinated. "Hi!" he said. "Remember me?" He had never seen her dressed like this. He had never seen anyone dressed like this. Mackenzie wore her best-seller mini, made up in fake leopard skin, over thick black panty hose and leopard ankle boots. The black-ribbed top clung to her full breasts, layered with a black vest, carelessly undone. One fall of hair hung dead straight over one eye, lending a coy peeping quality to her usual frank stare. Bright blusher and luminous pink lipstick completed the look.

"Who *are* you?" She shook Ed's hand, her face screwed up quizzically.

"So much for my unforgettable charisma!" he said. "Ed Schreiber? Your accountant? Didn't they tell you I was coming?"

She ushered him in, locking the door behind him. "I'm sorry—my mind's full of wide-wale corduroy right now. You don't know anyone who could supply a few hundred yards pronto? In every color?"

"Uh-uh." He shifted awkwardly on his feet, looking into the shop. "It looks great!"

"Doesn't it?" She broke away from him and ran whooping down the central aisle like a little girl. "It was decorated in record time—I've been practically living here, making sure they didn't screw up. I'm so happy with it." She stared around delightedly at the mirrored walls, the acrylic cubes stuffed with merchandise. "Look!" She switched on some spotlights. The new store followed the ideas of the first one, but upgraded them. The pink, purple, and white spots were the same, ricocheting off the mirrors to give the excitement of a theatrical set or a movie premiere.

She peered closely at him. "Oh, yeah, I remember you. You were at one of our family meetings, trying not to fall asleep."

"Around *your* family? Are you kidding?"

She giggled. "I guess we aren't the quietest folk." She took a moment to study him carefully. He was short, with a powerful, stocky build. His animated, mobile face often pulled a wry expression or creased for a joke. His floppy brown hair was just starting to get longer. He was the type who grew his hair a year after everyone else had started to do it, she thought. The best thing about him was his bright blue gaze from startling, almost purple eyes.

She peered closer. "Navy!" she decided. "Why do men get the best eyes and the longest lashes?"

"Yours aren't too bad, either."

"Yeah, but they're painted on."

There was something very sexy about him, she thought. In fact, he was the first man whose maleness had struck her. There had only been two kinds of men in her life up to now: the Bronx Brutes and the Village Hippies. And Alistair. Ed Schreiber was definitely a new category. Alistair had introduced her to sex, but she had never really found *him* sexy—just what he did to her. She had never desired his body, never really liked the white skin, the skinniness. Eyeing Ed, she realized she'd always liked chunky men. It would be a new experience to make love to a man whose body she liked.

She had never looked around at other men. Her lack of confidence about her looks had made her feel fortunate in having Alistair. It had not occurred to her that she could find a man more attractive than him. Or that an attractive man would even notice her. And yet Mackenzie had blossomed. Her manners and voice had improved from being with Alistair; she was less strident, softer. Her constant dieting had finally thinned her to a plump but appealing shape. Her expertise with makeup, plus the best hairstylists in the city, had given her a glossy, well-groomed appearance. Without realizing it, she was now an attractive, sexy woman.

Ed sat down with her and explained some accountancy terms, telling her that she must keep all personal receipts from now on, pay with checks and save them for his files. "We're going to whip the financial side of the business into shape," he told her.

"Yeah? Good luck." She grabbed a handful of price tags and started to write $19 on each one. "I don't do so well with numbers. I've kind of left that to my brothers. What do you think? Think they're screwing me?"

Ed shrugged. "The way you people grab handfuls of cash from the cash register when you need it, I can't see who's screwing who! Once I install the Schreiber system, no one will get a chance to. Anyway, don't you trust your own brothers?"

She peered at him sideways. "No."

He laughed. "I don't blame you."

"Hey!" She burst out laughing, too. "I could get you fired for that!"

"I'm just being honest with you."

"So you're not so straight after all?"

"Underneath this three-piece suit is a crazy, wild animal!"

"Prove it!"

Impulsively, she gave him a kiss on the cheek. To her surprise, he pulled her to him and kissed her on the mouth. It was a long kiss, and she didn't resist the pressure of his lips, nor his tongue.

"Wow!" She pulled back, gasping for air, eyes opened wonderingly at him. "This isn't very professional, Eddie," she said, as a new kind of thrill swept her. "You're a very sexy man!" she told him, amazed.

He looked as surprised as she did. "So are you!"

She wrote out some more tags, and they were silent for a few minutes.

"So?" he finally said. "What kind of a chance does a straight square like me have with you?"

She looked up at him. "With those navy eyes? Better than average. But I have a boyfriend."

"And he lets you go around kissing strange accountants?"

"Oh, *no*—you kissed *me*, remember?"

He watched her seriously, his desire evident. She looked away, suddenly uncomfortable. "So how big do you see this thing getting?" he asked, breaking the silence.

She shrugged, looking at him. "Nationwide? World-wide? Galaxywide?"

"Gold! boutiques on the moon?"

"That would be groovy!" she squealed. She grabbed a black fuzzy jacket, saying, "C'mon, I'll buy you a coffee, Eddie."

She turned on the burglar alarm and carefully locked the plate-glass door behind them. There was a cold March wind, and she huddled close to Ed, holding his arm. He felt big, strong, protective.

Over coffee at the nearby deli he listened intently to her plans for the new store. It was nice to have someone really listening to her. With her brothers, conversation always turned into arguments. And Alistair had a faraway look in his eyes as she confided in him, as if he were almost jealous that his creation had gotten so far.

"You'll have to move your manufacturing base if you get much bigger," Ed advised. "It's more economical to make up in California. Or even Hong Kong or India."

"Why?" she asked.

"Cheaper labor."

"But I always want my samples made up here," she said. "I *love* my sample ladies. They're big mamas—Puerto Rican or black or Jewish! They think I'm bananas!"

"I think you're bananas, too."

"But I know exactly what I'm doing," she said, and winked.

"I agree."

"Listen." She swiveled in the booth to face him. "I know you have to deal with Reggie and Max, but you *are* on my side, aren't you?"

"Sure!" He grinned.

"Will you always level with me? If you smell anything wrong, will you tell me? I don't want any bad karma in this company. I don't want my brothers to make a fool of me or do anything crooked in my name. I'm every bit as streetsmart as they are—"

He held up his hands to stop her torrent of words. "Ease up! You talk as though you think you're working with the Mafia!"

"I do feel like that sometimes," she admitted. "Let's shake on it, Eddie, okay?"

She held out her hand. He took it in his warm, enveloping one. She could feel better about the business now. She would cultivate little spies—she had already asked a couple of Queens seamstresses to call her if they were ever unfairly treated.

"May I have my hand back, please?" she asked Ed.

He laughed, paying the bill and walking her back to the store. Leaning up against the front door, she had the sudden fantasy of pulling him inside and making love with him in a fitting booth. She let him kiss her politely on the cheek, promising herself, "some other time."

"I don't *want* a gala opening!" Mackenzie insisted. "If I have to watch Esther Goldstein dispensing her chopped liver and my father's cut-price kosher wine, I'll die!"

She was at home with Alistair, planning the opening of the new store. He frowned at the list of top press ladies and editors. "What about inviting selected groups of them to personally conducted tours? We could set up tables and chairs in the middle of the store—get the meal catered by

Le Croissant. Give them a couple of glasses of champagne
and they'll go away feeling very exclusive and happy."

"Super! Can we get away with it?" Mackenzie said
approvingly. Alistair so rarely came up with really good
ideas these days that she always went overboard encouraging him.

The new Gold! was hailed by *WWD* as "a new concept
in retailing," a tired little phrase that was wheeled out
each time a store opened with a different-looking counter.
The bitchier *Labels* had called it "nothing more than a
five-and-dime brought up to mod times." The layout had
indeed been inspired by Mackenzie's childhood memories
of Woolworth's.

In realizing that the total-look concept—from hair to
makeup, shoes to gloves—now mattered as much as the
dress or outfit, Mackenzie was a fashion innovator: Her
head buzzed with future visions of Gold! beauty parlors,
shoestores, and makeup lines. Her new clothes had gone
to the limits of her wild creativity, and could be mixed or
matched in numerous combinations. The acid, luminous
colors—lime, fuchsia, yolk-yellow, and electric blue—were
cut to mini lengths and mixed with fake fur, fake leather,
and vinyl. She quoted from the Mod Look, the Hippie
Look, the Red Indian Look, in a delirious mixture of
time-capsule and ethnic styles which all added up to the
outrageous Mackenzie Gold Look.

She had tried out these new styles in limited-edition
runs at the first store, and they had been snapped up. Her
wavelength was directly in tune with the wants of her
fashion fans. There was no limit to the potential of Gold!

Coral Stanton was unable to ignore it. The summons to
her *Divine* office came six days before the opening.

"Why would Coral Stanton suddenly remember me
now?" Mackenzie wondered, in bed with Alistair the
night before her appointment.

"She's heard that you're the next First Lady of the
fashion revolt," Alistair said. "She wants to get you while
you're hot!"

She laughed. "Oh, I'm hot, all right, baby—are you?"
She threw her magazines to the floor and looked over at
him. He was inhaling a joint. On the bedside table was a
large goblet of champagne and a handful of pills. She

eyed them worriedly. Alistair had become pale and even thinner recently.

"Do you have to smoke that stuff in bed?" she asked.

"Helps me relax. I've been working like a madman this week. When I get to bed, sometimes my brain doesn't turn off, and this stuff helps."

She switched off her light and snuggled down next to him, reaching under the covers to feel between his legs. He was naked as usual, but there was no reaction to her caresses.

"This isn't like you, Alistair," she teased. "I used to fight you off, remember?"

He wriggled out of her embrace, turning away, and they lay in the dark, silent.

"Look, none of this is any good if you're unhappy," she told him. "I know you want to be a hotshot for my brothers and me, but it's not worth it if our life together goes down the drain."

He said nothing, and after running her foot gently up and down his calf, she fell asleep.

In the morning she turned in bed to rouse him. He was an unhealthy gray color and lay breathing quietly. She sat up and pushed him, then placed her hands on his shoulders and shook him.

"Alistair, what's wrong? Are you sick?"

A groan escaped his pale lips.

"Oh, God, baby, *please* don't get sick! Not today! You have a lunch and I have Coral!"

She ran to the kitchen to make strong coffee, bringing it to him and spooning it between his lips.

"Alistair! Darling!" She cradled his head in her lap, trying to pray. "Oh, God, I know I never called on you since I won the contest, but please, let him be all right!" She had seen this kind of thing in the movies. She knew what to do.

She pulled Alistair out of bed. She could just support his weight, dragging him under the shower, directing the cold water onto his head. He gasped, his lips began to move, soundlessly at first, and then articulating, "Why the fuck are we in here?" He tried to sit down in the stall, but she grabbed him under the arms and moved his head directly under the shower head. The cold water was making her shiver. Finally, after what seemed like hours of torture, he mumbled, "I'm okay. I'm okay, Mack."

She turned off the water and threw a robe over his shoulders.

"This is ridiculous!" she said as he sat sheepishly in bed, sipping coffee. "Don't you *ever* give me a fright like this again, Alistair! I'm not your fucking nurse! *I'm* the one that needs attention around here! I have an important appointment with Coral Stanton, dammit, and I'm late now!"

He laughed softly. "You're all heart, Mack! You should go far. . . ."

She whipped the coffee away from him. "Don't try to make me feel guilty, Alistair. My career *is* the most important thing to me—I never bullshitted you about that, did I?"

"Leave me alone now," he muttered.

She stared at him, furious for a moment, then hurried to the bathroom to dress. She wanted to look different, original. She knew Coral's fashion eyes would not miss a thing. Carefully, she painted on her eyes in the approved London manner. A layer of white lipstick beneath the red gave her almost fluorescent lips. She had split apart and resewn two pairs of panty hose to give her one pink, one orange leg. Her skirt, a mere wisp of zebra-patterned vinyl, was laced down the front with a striped shoelace. Her black sweater was skintight, and she had sewn a giant Peace badge to one shoulder, finishing off the outfit with an antique fringed shawl and a giant pink plastic shoulder bag.

She wondered whether the gossip about Coral was true. Had her face really been disfigured in an accident in a Paris elevator while having sex with a well-known designer? That's what *Labels'* Tittle-Tattle column was hinting in its blind items.

When she was ready, she popped back into the bedroom to see Alistair.

He gave her an appraising look. "You look fantastic!" he said.

She kissed him, calling down to the doorman to hold a taxi. At her front door she grabbed the atomizer of L'Air du Temps and sprayed her neck for a twenty-second count. Smelling like a million dollars, she took the elevator down to the foyer.

Coral's office was darkened, the flickering candles wafting their woodsy scent around. Mackenzie noticed that Coral sat with her back to the light. She could just make out the zigzag scar on her face.

"My discovery!" Coral trilled as Mackenzie planted a kiss near her cheek, their perfumes clashing almost audibly. "So sweet of you to come!"

"Could I resist a summons from you?" Mackenzie sank into a chair opposite. "*Women's Wear* calls you 'Her Fashion Highness'!"

Coral laughed dryly. "The day I take any notice of *them...*" she said.

Mackenzie took in Coral's face without staring. The makeup was vivid, the scarlet mouth outlined carefully, her eyes defined with kohl and eyeshadow, her face carefully rouged and powdered. She was so exquisitely madeup, she made Mackenzie feel cheap and blowsy.

"You're changing the look of American fashion," Coral leaned forward to tell her. "I'm so very proud I discovered you, Mackenzie. Not everyone here thought you a suitable candidate for contest winner. They would have preferred the old-fashioned twin-set and pearls girl who usually wins."

It was a dig, but Mackenzie knew how to fight back. "That's so passé now, isn't it, Coral?" she asked. "These days fashion can be anything but musty and fusty."

Coral nodded. "You're right, of course. What I like about you is that you're an American, and how many American designers are there today? Okay, we have Bill Blass, Geoffrey Beene, Halston—but no one's taking any *risks!* If you knew the risks I take here, and fight for!"

Mackenzie laughed. "Well, I hope you're right about me." She crossed her legs carefully so that Coral would notice the panty hose.

"Bicolor!" Coral nodded. "Absolutely brilliant!"

"Exclusive to Gold!, in ten different combinations. Two dollars," Mackenzie said.

"Send me ten pairs of every color—they will revitalize the skinny shifts everyone's doing," Coral replied. "And now I'll tell you something exciting, Mackenzie. We're doing a pop issue of *Divine!*" She leaned toward Mackenzie conspiratorially, dropping her voice. "A fashion reportage watershed. It will *define* Fashion! It will define Pop!"

"Oh, wow!" Mackenzie squealed, on cue. "Too much! Far out! Super!"

"Yes!" Coral nodded seriously. "All of those things. *Vogue* and *Bazaar* will be kicking themselves for the rest of the year. Sonny and Cher! The Mamas and Papas, Dylan, Janis, Jimi Hendrix, the two Julies—Christie and Driscoll! All wearing the most switched-on American clothing." Her voice dropped to a whisper. "Have you taken a trip yet, Mackenzie? You must, it's mesmerizing! I've never had so many inspirations for layouts, for features! Do you know a place called the End of the World? I'll take you there—maybe we could do a feature. Do you have a beau?"

"Yes. An English guy."

"What's his name?"

"Alistair. Alistair Briarly."

Coral knitted her brows, chewing on a pen. "Briarly, Briarly..." He must be Lord Briarly's younger son, no? Divine, tweedy man, Lord Briarly."

Mackenzie shook her head. "I think you got the wrong Briarly. His father's not a lord...."

Coral widened her eyes and smiled. "*Ask* him! He probably wanted to stay incognito in America. After all, *he'll* be Lord Briarly one day!"

"But why wouldn't he tell me?"

Coral clapped her hands. "It's the new inverted Mod snobbery!" she cried. "This issue will be special, so naturally I thought of you. A friend took me to a rock and roll show last week. Dusty Springfield, Cilla Black, Petula Clark—all in the latest mod gear, singing their hearts out! I love 'Downtown,' don't you? I've booked them for sittings, and I want *you* to dress them, Mackenzie. Come up with the wildest creations! We may even get the Beatles; I'm speaking with Brian Epstein this afternoon."

"*Groovy!* I'm doing a Unisex collection that boys can wear."

"Do you mind if my staff see what you're wearing?" Coral buzzed the intercom. "Bring in *everyone*! And serve coffee!"

The room was soon twittering with fashion editors and

their assistants, a secretary with a cart was serving coffee, and some photographers and models, hearing the noise, wandered in.

"Stand up, Mackenzie!" Coral ordered.

Mackenzie giggled, standing on her chair, flinging her arms wide open.

"Pay attention, everyone!" Coral cried. "This is *today*! This is *youth*! This is mod, fab, *gear*! This is what your eye should be getting into!"

They stared. Some looked admiring, others as if a wedge of overripe Brie was being held under their noses. Donna Haddon, the sportswear editor, took notes.

"I feel like an idiot!" Mackenzie complained, striking some mad poses. The editors scurried around her, reaching out to feel her vinyl skirt or finger her shawl.

"Corinne!" Coral summoned the beauty editor. "See her makeup? Bright, doll-like colors. Eyes are outlined, eyelashes almost painted on. Take a Polaroid, someone! *This* is the look I want for April. Check the hair! The head is getting bigger!"

"It'll explode in a moment," the beauty editor murmured into Mackenzie's ear.

"I gotta go!" Mackenzie decided, getting down. "You're making me feel like an animal in the zoo."

She floated out of the *Divine* offices on a cloud of happiness. She walked back up Madison Avenue. This was what she had always wanted, wasn't it? Attention, praise, support— It almost seemed too easy now. Those fashion editors would have applauded if she'd worn a boot on her head. Or made her dresses from newspaper. Something was due to go wrong. Fashion was so fickle. What if they found out the emperor's new clothes were not going to last?

Alistair was at the store, getting ready for his first press lunch party. She could see him in the back, supervising the flower arrangements on the pretty pink tables.

She walked toward him, threading her way between electricians and workmen. He looked up, smiling. "Sorry about this morning. How'd it go?"

"Is your father a lord?" she asked.

He frowned, looking back at the flowers. "Interfering old bitch," he muttered.

"Who?" She put her hands on her hips. "Me or Coral?"

"Her, of course. Oh, Mack!" He turned, hugging her hard to him. "You found out my family secret."

"Don't tell me you're really a millionaire and you're letting me work my ass off like this?"

He laughed. "My illustrious heritage doesn't have a fortune attached, I'm afraid. It's just a few green acres with a drafty old house that Father refuses to sell. When he dies, it all goes to my brother, and when *he* dies, I'll inherit debts and headaches! Impressed?"

"Huh?" She stared at him, disappointed and impressed at the same time. It was a lot better than most girls from the Bronx managed to find for fathers-in-law, she thought. *If* they ever married.

The ecstatic press coverage Gold! attracted in its first week of operations ensured that it opened to nonstop selling. It was heralded as the first boutique to open on Madison Avenue with affordable prices. The hundreds of "lookers" treated themselves to a bangle, a pair of earrings, a lipstick—impulse buys that added hundreds of dollars to the daily take, backed up by the steady clothing sales.

"No one's *seen* a store like this before," Abe Goldstein boasted, as if it were his idea.

Mackenzie waited for congratulations from her family, but none came. "Not one of them patted me on the back and said, "Well done, kid," she complained to Alistair. He shrugged, singing "I can't get no satisfaction" from the Stone's song until she told him to stop.

Esther Goldstein was the only member of the family who gave her support and listened to her. "Are you happy, darling?" her mother asked, peering closely at her. They were in Mackenzie's living room. She had issued an always-open invitation to her mother to drop in whenever she was in town, but it was rarely used.

Mackenzie groaned. "Don't ask me if I'm happy, Ma." She handed her mother a big mug of tea. "It gives me that old, depressed feeling I used to get at home."

She stirred her tea. "I'm ninety-nine percent happy, Ma. I think that's pretty good."

"So what's wrong with the one percent?" Esther asked worriedly.

"Oh, *Ma!*" Mackenzie sat on the arm of her mother's

chair and leaned over to hug her tightly. "I miss you so much!"

"You left me in a household of men," Esther said. "I miss my daughter, too." She hugged Mackenzie, and the familiar smell of Jurgens hand cream and soap wafted her back to the days when she could run to her mother with every little problem.

"I love my work. I adore the new shop. I love this apartment," Mackenzie announced.

"I didn't hear you say you loved your... friend. And you're living with him like husband and wife." Esther leveled her most guilt-provoking expression at her daughter.

"Oh! *I* get it!" Mackenzie cried. She blinked at her mother. "*This* is the expression that says, 'If only she'd settle down with a nice Jewish dentist!' Well, I'm sorry Alistair isn't a dentist, Ma!"

"And I don't suppose he's Jewish, either?" Esther tried feebly. Mackenzie hooted with laughter. "You *know* he isn't! I just found out he's the son of a British lord!"

"Do you love him, darling?"

Mackenzie sat on the floor, letting out a long sigh of confusion. She could no longer confide in Esther: how could she tell her the sex problems, the drug problems? She watched her mother gazing around the apartment, trying to smile approvingly at all the empty space but mentally adding drapes and plastic covers.

Esther got to her feet stiffly. "Show me your kitchen. What sort of food do you cook for this skinny Alistair?"

She led her mother to the gleaming, scarcely used kitchen. "We eat out most of the time, Ma."

That was the best part about making money: never marketing or cooking. They experimented with Japanese, Mexican, Thai places. Sometimes they dined at very proper, posh places, just to shock people. Alistair would reserve a table and they would turn up wearing their hippie gear or outrageous outfits from the shop. They would order the best champagne and the most expensive food before proceeding to Max's Kansas City or The Scene and frugging or jerking the night away.

The whole thing was so funny, so weird, Mackenzie thought. Two successful kids with money, naughty schoolchildren whom everyone held in too much awe to report to the principal!

Money meant raiding the stores, too. Mackenzie had always been a compulsive shopper. Now she visited Capezio's, and when she couldn't make up her mind about which colors to choose, she simply bought *all* the colors! Shoes in all colors of the rainbow, and tights to match, notepaper engraved at Tiffany's, food shopping in the gourmet section of Bloomingdale's—all the things she had dreamed of doing and buying. But it was funny: Once she got the stuff home and put it away, it didn't seem to mean anything. It only looked good in stores, not in her home. Later, when things began to go wrong, she would say, "Whoever coined the phrase about money being the root of all evil was incredibly right-on." Without money Alistair would have been unable to afford the better, more expensive drugs that someone with his tastes invariably progressed to. . . .

For a week after her return from Paris, Mia moped around Wayland's apartment, hardly venturing out except to shop at the nearby Gristede's for meals that would take her most of the day to prepare. Sometimes she sat at her old desk and designed new clothes for an imaginary collection.

"You're too pretty to become a recluse, pet," Wayland warned during the second week. They were eating the complicated meal she had cooked. "The dinner is fantastic, but it's a waste of your talents. Why the hell don't you design a small collection for HQ?"

She looked up at him hopefully. "If my mother found out you're helping me, she would cut you dead."

Wayland shrugged. "So you design under a different name. Something French or Italian . . ."

"So you are afraid of her?"

He glanced down at his plate. "Only for the store's sake. If she starts ignoring us, we'll lose money. When *Divine* features something we're selling, you'd be amazed how many orders we get."

Mia stood to clear the table. "I feel like ignoring fashion forever, sometimes. Learning an entirely new career . . ."

"Like dental hygiene?" Wayland deadpanned. "You're my investment, remember. I expect a payoff."

She stood behind him, her hands on his shoulders. "You've been so incredibly generous. But if I start design-

ing now, under a new name, I'd need more money for
fabrics, samples, machinists—"

"Mia . . ." He swung around to look up at her. "Mother
left me half a million dollars. I'm willing to invest in you. I
believe you helped Roux to this season's breakthrough.
His clothes are selling like mad."

Mia took the dishes into the kitchen. When she came
back, she bent down to hug Wayland. "Okay," she told
him, "I've got to do something. I'll think about it."

By the next morning she'd thought up a name for her
collection. Anais—after her favorite writer, Anaïs Nin—Du
Pasquier, after a beautiful half-Swiss girlfriend at school.
Anais Du Pasquier suggested a world of beauty, luxury
and extravagance.

Now that she had the name, the designs naturally
suggested themselves to her. She pored over her drawing
board for days, and all her love for fashion returned and
flowed out of her. These were the designs that she would
have been doing in her room at Phillipe Roux for next
season's collection, if things had worked out between
them. But these would be hers—not taken and used
under another name. It gave her an even greater pride,
and she was thrilled when Wayland enthused over them.

He put her in touch with someone who would guide
her to the right patternmaker and sample maker, so that
she could start to visit fabric manufacturers and really put
together a small collection of clothing for the spring.

She had not yet called David or Mackenzie to let them
know she was back. She easily followed Mackenzie's
progress reading *Labels* and *WWD*. She stared at the
photographs of Mackenzie and Alistair taken at openings
and restaurants; it was hard to connect the sophisticated-
looking woman in the photographs with that gauche,
plump girl she had met in a coffee shop down the street.
God, how long ago *that* seemed! Before she saw them she
had to get her story straight, have the answers ready for
all the questions they would hurl at her.

She also needed a little more time before she met
David. Later, perhaps, when the dull ache she felt each
time she thought of Phillipe was finally gone. When she
could stop reliving the evening with him that had brought
her to such excitement, such pleasure. When she could
stop dreaming of him holding and kissing her; his face,

his burning eyes, his deep voice all so vivid that her
mornings became a time of intense disappointment as she
lost him each day to her dreams.

Sometimes she felt she had to take a break from designing, and then she walked the familiar streets of the city,
stopping in at a coffee shop for a hot chocolate as if it
were Paris. She brooded about her mother. She wanted to
make contact, apologize. She was bitterly ashamed of
having injured Coral; she longed to face her, confront her,
get yelled at, blamed, forgiven. Maybe then they could
move on to a new understanding.

When one of her walks led her to her mother's building
late one afternoon, she glanced at her watch. It was six
o'clock; just possibly Coral was home, changing after a
day at the magazine. On an impulse, she decided to try to
see her.

The old Irish porter, Jimmy, was still on duty. "Miss
Mia!" he shook her hand warmly. "How have you been? I
heard you were living in France?"

She smiled. "It's nice to see you again," she said. "I just
got back. Is my mother in?"

"Just back ten minutes ago." He pressed the elevator
button. "Why don't you go on up?"

Mia hesitated, a sudden flutter of fear in her stomach.
"Maybe you'd better call her, Jimmy? Tell her I'm here...."

Jimmy walked to the phone and picked it up. "Mrs.
Stanton?" Mia heard him ask. "I have Mia down here. All
right if she comes up?" He held out the phone to Mia.
"She wants to speak to you."

Mia took the phone, and Jimmy walked out to the street
to help someone getting out of a taxi.

"So you're back?" Coral's voice crackled over the phone.

"Hello, Mother. How are you?"

"Oh, I'll survive. What do you want?"

"I was just passing by. I thought it would be nice to—"

"See me? Take a good look at my scar?"

"I really wanted to—"

"Say 'sorry'? No, Mia. I'm not giving you the luxury of
forgiveness. I'm glad to know you're back. This way I can
warn everyone I know—including Wayland—not to extend any kind of assistance to you."

"Oh, Mother, you can't be that vindictive. I didn't mean

to hurt you. Surely we can talk things over? You provoked me terribly, you know. You told me a lot of lies—"

The line went dead with a click, and Mia stood in the foyer, tears running down her cheeks.

Eighteen

Mackenzie was in her design studio, surrounded by boxes of jewels, fabric, glitter, and glitz, when Mia called.

"*Mia!*" she screamed when she heard the familiar soft voice. "Where the hell *are* you? Paris or New York?"

"Just a few blocks away—I'm staying with Wayland."

"*Groovy! Fab!* When did you get back?"

"About two weeks ago. It's taken me that long to get over jetlag . . ."

"And what about motherlag and Phillipelag and culture shock and all that?" Mackenzie laughed. "Oh, Mia! What happened to your mother's face? Everyone has a different theory. *Labels* hinted that she was having an affair with a Paris couturier! Was it Givenchy? Who else *could* it be?"

"I'll give you three guesses," Mia said.

"Oh, *no!* Oh, *God!* I wanna hear *everything!*"

"It's a very long story, Mackenzie. We'll need a very long lunch!"

"At someplace ritzy? It's on me, okay? Except that I don't take long lunches anymore! I just never stop working! My brothers are pushing me to take on assistant designers but, I mean, why did I get into this business in the first place? To design, right? So why should I let anyone else design?"

"I guess you have to learn to delegate—"

"Yeah, I *do* have an empire now, Mia. Max and Reggie want to open a whole chain of stores."

"When can we get together?"

"Tomorrow I go to a meeting—I'm politically aware now, Mia. We're occupying Washington Square to protest the war. Why don't you come?"

"I'd rather meet you someplace quiet, where we can talk...."

"At Serendipity, then, my favorite place. Welcome home, darling."

Mia hung up. Just like Mackenzie—she didn't even ask about my plans—completely wrapped up in her own life.

Mackenzie drew her quick, sketchy designs in luminous Pentel on a giant sketch pad. She had protested since her ex-roommates had taken her with them to a Central Park demonstration. Protesting was such a sixties thing to do! Her presence at these events was always duly recorded by the *Labels* photographer, and the resulting shot splashed over features with titles like "Rebels *with* a Cause!" *WWD* sometimes slotted her under their Flower Children category. It was all good publicity.

For the last few months, meetings of the Gold! board had been held in her apartment. The disadvantage of this arrangement was that her father and brothers expected lunch. They were due today in an hour.

She jumped up from her designing table to look for Alistair. He had never accepted the fact that he was excluded from these meetings. While it had been family only, it had been bad enough, but Ed Schreiber had recently been added to the board as financial director, causing a lot of resentment. She found him in the kitchen, sipping coffee.

"Going out?" she asked casually, pouring herself some coffee.

He glanced up at her. "I know you have a meeting scheduled, if that's what you mean."

"Sometimes I think Abe only comes for the sandwiches," she said, trying to joke, but Alistair only grimaced.

The meetings had always bored her, but now that they had the magic ingredient of Ed Schreiber's presence, she found them a lot more exciting. Ed took notes, shooting her looks of undisguised interest, concern, and—yes—desire. She realized she was flirting and she couldn't help herself. Ed was the first man she had desired who desired her, too. It was totally different from the way she felt with Alistair. This was animal, uncontrollable. She made a special effort to look attractive for him, and there was always some reaction—slightly widened eyes, or a flush of

color in his face. Once she caught him adjusting his pants,
and she got an echoing thrill of desire, catching his eye.

When Alistair left that morning, she hurriedly hid a
bowl of grass, setting a big pot of coffee on the stove.

The four men arrived promptly at noon, and Reggie
began complaining before removing his coat.

"There's a photo of you in *Women's Wear* with a goddamn peace band around your head," he told Mackenzie.

"So?"

"You sure it's such a good thing to be seen at these
political things? Kids are getting busted for burning draft
cards and all that—"

"So what? The day I'm too chicken to march for peace, I
may as well give up and go to Russia."

"Yeah? Well, our company policy oughta—"

"Oh, piss off, Reggie! Since when did we have a company policy?"

They went into the living room, where they covered the
basic issues as quickly as they could. Her brothers had
developed a sulky way of dealing with her. It made her
want to scream, but she told herself to be cool and ignore
it. "You're smarter than them," she kept reminding herself. Her father was getting old and a little absentminded.
He only enjoyed the parts where they discussed incoming
money. As the only nonfamily member, Ed was a calming
influence on them all.

They were always talking about expansion: where to
open the next Gold! branch. "What about Boston?" Reggie
asked. "I read where Cambridge is really opening up. You
got your students, your young people..." There was an
expectant silence and Mackenzie tore her eyes away from
Ed's to find them all awaiting her comment.

"I've been saying Boston's next," she agreed. "Let's get
a report. Send someone to clock the passersby at different
locations—" Abruptly she stood. "Isn't anyone hungry?
I'm starving!"

As she loaded the cart in the kitchen, Ed approached to
help. "I gotta see you," he whispered urgently. She peered
into his worried eyes. "Come back after everyone leaves."

She couldn't wait for them to finish the damned pastrami. They seemed to be chewing extra slowly, asking for
more coffee. When they left, she ran to the bathroom to
repair lipstick and coat her lashes. You don't get a guy

with pastrami stains on your blouse, she thought, changing it for a slinky, silky black one. She stopped short, about to aim a generous spritz of L'Air du Temps at her throat. *Am I trying to get Ed?* The excited feeling in her stomach should have told her. She fluffed her hair. How would she like it, she wondered, if Alistair was chasing some chick? She tried to feel guilty, but she just couldn't.*Oh, shit*, she thought, *I may as well enjoy it...I won't do anything.*

He rang the doorbell five minutes later. "I walked around the block twice—nice neighborhood you live in." He grinned. "Did you change your outfit for me?"

"You noticed?" She giggled, letting him in. "I thought your mind was totally on the figures."

"Including yours," he laughed, and moving toward her he took her breasts in his hands. Her breasts were the part of her body she was most proud of. They were full, firm, and round, and in Ed's hands they felt even riper. She jerked her head back in surprise and broke away, glancing down at the blouse sticking out.

"I look like something out of the 50s!" she cracked to cover the thrill of forbidden pleasure.

"That's because I attract you almost as much as you attract me," he said.

"Let me get you some coffee," she offered, disappearing into the kitchen.

In the kitchen she caught her breath, struggling to regain control. She felt that thrill she would always get when a man desired her, but for the first time, she desired the man!

Ed waited for her in the living room, looking out the windows. "Business meetings are now a kind of sexual torture," he told her as she came in. "Sometimes I get so hard looking at you, it's painful."

She put his coffee cup down on the table. "Don't, Eddie," she said. "I might like it if you go on."

"I thought you people were sexually liberated?" He turned back to the table and took the coffee. "You're just teasing me, huh?"

"You turn me on. Okay?" she admitted. "Like crazy. But I told you—I don't fool around."

He nodded. "I admire your integrity, but maybe you

won't feel so loyal when I tell you what I've got to tell you."

"What is it?"

"It's about money, what else? Some money drain I can't fathom."

"How thrilling..."

He shook his head. "Don't say that. A business running properly should be able to account for every nickel. This is a regular amount that's missing each week. Someone's helping themselves. I know it's not your brothers...."

She laughed. "When *they* screw me it won't be for loose change."

"Two hundred fifty bucks a week is more than loose change," he corrected her. "I'm checking out the sales helps' references at both stores, which isn't my job."

"No, it's Reggie's, but he's too busy reading the gossip in *Women's Wear*."

"I don't mind." Ed shrugged, his dark blue eyes twinkling. "Makes me feel like Bogie."

"Only Reggie, Max, and I have cash-register keys," she told him. "Dad hardly goes to the stores anymore."

"What about Alistair?"

"Sometimes he clears the cash for me, yeah—" She stopped. "You don't like him, do you?" Even as she asked that, she knew Alistair was taking the money. It explained the better quality grass, the lack of ready cash, his whole attitude to money. They had quarreled fiercely about his salary when he was officially put on the Gold! payroll. No sum would have satisfied him, she realized. He had very unrealistic ideas of what he was worth.

"I'll do a little sleuthing, too," she told Ed. "Maybe one of the salesgirls has a pal coming in, taking clothes without paying?"

"It's possible," Ed said doubtfully.

"I'll put in a little more time at the stores," she promised. "I've been too busy lately, but I like to keep contact with the customers. If only I had a little more energy..."

She was so exhausted when Ed finally left that she called a new doctor someone had recommended to her, threatening suicide if she was not seen that very afternoon. It was unlike her to feel this tired. She left the building, walking toward Park Avenue.

* * *

Before Coral was aware of it, a new designer, Anais Du Pasquier, was selling from a corner of Headquarters' designer floor. The clothes were like no others in New York, their inspiration obviously Paris. A customer felt the quality of the woolen cloth and pronounced "Phillipe Roux, Courreges, Ungaro, mixed together by an angel!"

Wayland, lurking near the display, smiled.

Mia had been inspired. She had worked incredibly fast—delivering a small collection to Headquarters just two weeks before Christmas. Wayland, impressed and delighted, took a whole page in the Sunday *New York Times* to announce "a special new department for a special new designer..." Anais Du Pasquier was described as a Parisienne bringing "couture details to ready-to-wear." The twelve-garment collection, the luxurious, beautifully made clothing was young, sophisticated, classy, and what thousands of females who were neither Beatles fans nor aging hipsters wanted. The clothes sold out in a week.

Wayland was ecstatic. Mia set up a deal with a coat manufacturer in New Jersey, and the garments were delivered directly to Headquarters. Wayland reordered a gross in various colors and worried about Coral. The fashion world was too inquisitive to allow Anais Du Pasquier to go unreported. Headquarters' press office got calls from reporters at *Labels* and *WWD*. He knew someone somewhere would talk, and Coral would hear about it and never speak to him again. Wayland invited her to dinner and tried to sound her out about Mia.

"To err is human," he reminded her as they reached dessert, "to forgive..."

"Divine?" Coral laughed throatily. "*Who* do you want me to forgive?" she asked.

They were at Rumors, a burgundy-velveted restaurant in the East Eighties, where French cuisine and a camp pianist playing obscure Broadway songs had attracted a fashion crowd. Coral sipped at her espresso.

"Isn't it time you forgave Mia?" Wayland asked gently.

Coral replaced her tiny cup. "If you'd seen the piece of mirror that embedded itself in my..." She shivered. "I do not intend to turn the other cheek. I might get *that* ripped, too!"

"She did not mean to hurt you," Wayland insisted.

Coral stared at him. "If you were my friend, you'd stop

plea-bargaining for that murderous brat. She's lucky I didn't file charges—she could be in jail. And I know she's here—she had the nerve to call me from my lobby the other day. I refused to see her. . . ."

Wayland dropped the subject, and they finished their coffee, reviewing the current gossip.

They ended the evening in Coral's apartment, sipping neat vodka. Coral asked, "Are you helping Mia in any professional way?"

"Do you think I would?" he hedged.

"Yes." She found her cigarettes and lit one. "You've always had a soft spot for her, and she's milked it for all it was worth. If you let her use you now, and I find out, you'll be off my books forever."

Wayland shot back his vodka in a petulant gesture. His lip stuck out defiantly. "What makes you think it's so wonderful being *on* your books?" he snapped.

Coral took a long drag on her cigarette before answering. "I think you could say it doesn't exactly *hurt* business to be featured on our cover, with full credits—"

"Oh, don't try to make me feel grateful!" Wayland snapped. "You owed me after those awards we put on for Roux. You talked me into a two-year contract with *him*, and now you're consigning him to oblivion because he didn't fuck you!"

Coral's eyes widened. "What a crude way to put it!" she said, but she could see Wayland was drunk, and she couldn't help a wry smile. "And let me tell *you* something, Wayland," she continued, "if you'd seen Phillipe Roux's. . .equipment, you'd think being fucked by him was somewhat of a mixed blessing!"

Wayland giggled in spite of himself, but resumed his petulant expression. "What makes you think you'll represent *Divine* forever?" he asked. "*Labels* keeps printing blind items that everyone knows are about you—they might as well rename the Tittle-Tattle page 'Calling Coral'. . ."

Coral lit another cigarette and took a furious puff. "That's Howard Austin getting at me. He's never forgiven me for not falling in love with him. He must have god-damn spies all over Manhattan. If I have an innocent evening out at a club, it's in his damn rag!"

"Innocent? That night after the awards? You *did* get loaded on acid, didn't you?"

"And I can't *wait* to take another trip—it was *fabulous!*"

"Yes? Do it again and you'll come into work and find Mrs. Donna Brooks behind your desk."

"He hasn't married her *yet!*" Coral snapped.

Wayland got unsteadily to his feet. The liquor made him brave. "You know, I'm tired of your vendetta against your own daughter," he told Coral. "She's a good kid, and very talented. Instead of hating her, you should be proud of her."

"*Proud?*" Coral echoed, turning to a wall mirror and pushing her hair up from her forehead. "Proud of this brand I carry like some prize steer?"

"Oh, you hated Mia long before that fucking scar," Wayland replied. "Thank God she's always had me. *I'll* champion her."

"Adopt her legally, if you wish," Coral shrugged. "Just don't expect any more credits from me. I ousted Phillipe Roux from the magazine, and I can do it to Headquarters."

"And don't expect any advertising from us," Wayland snapped, then strode down the corridor to the front door. "Good *night!*"

Coral nodded curtly as he closed the door.

Wayland almost flew with fury along the short blocks to his apartment. He dialed Colin Beaumont before removing his jacket. "Colin," he said, "you're simply not going to believe this!" He gave a drunken, dramatized account of their quarrel. "Headquarters practically pays her salary— we advertise so much. I was so mad when I left her place, I felt like going to the nearest bar and beating up somebody."

"I'm glad you didn't," Colin said soothingly. "So, has war been declared?"

"*You* take care of Coral for a while. I grant you exclusive visiting rights!"

Christmas was very subdued that year because of the feud. Mia and Wayland invited Colin for a drink. Most of the excitement centered around the January 1967 Pop issue of *Divine*. Hailed as a milestone in fashion journalism, it sold out on the newsstands and quickly became a collector's item. For it, Avedon had roamed the streets of London, posing decadent-looking aristocrats in dripping-fringed brocade waistcoats and black satin elephant pants. Mick Jagger had given a particularly ferocious snarl at the lens, and in New York the Andy Warhol Factory crowd posed naked, looking over their shoulders at the camera. A Broadway revue featuring nudity was announced. Coral was in her element: She had no time to miss the attentions of Wayland, being too busy going to "happenings," art-gallery openings, off-Broadway previews, and fashion show after fashion show.

One of her skinniest models had mentioned a Dr. Robbins's Park Avenue practice for energy-booster shots. Pressed as to what these miracle shots consisted of, she'd added, "The B-complex, you know." Since no one actually knew what composed the B-complex, they were satisfied. After her first treatment, Coral flew back to the magazine, arranging an amazing amount of features, marrying contributor to subject to photographer in such a whirl of activity that those in the know said only speed could give that kind of high. She liked the effects so much that she took to dropping by daily, before work, for a shot.

Dr. Robbins was a wiry, nervous little man in his fifties, with a shock of white hair. He was a man with a mission—determined to save the world from what he called "low energy." No one seemed to question the fact that his practice only attracted affluent fashion and media types, with the odd business whiz kid and society hostess thrown in. In the high-tech waiting room, with its metal and suede armchairs, Coral flashed only the briefest of glances from behind her Givenchy sunglasses. Sometimes she had to wait up to thirty minutes for her shot, and now, during one of these waits, the office door opened and Alistair sidled in. They exchanged glances, then he sat down beside her, jiggling his fingers nervously on the narrow arm of the Breuer chair.

Finally he leaned over, his hand outstretched, "Alistair Briarly," he said, removing his dark glasses and kissing Coral's hand. "I work with Mackenzie Gold."

"Of course," Coral murmured. She kept her sunglasses on.

"Is this doing the trick for you?" he asked softly.

"What? The B-complex shots? They're a miracle!"

"Congratulations on the Pop issue. Mackenzie loved the way you used her clothes. We don't see you around too much—don't you do the clubs anymore?"

"*Divine* is a jealous master!" she said. "Uses up every second of my time!"

She was called in by the assistant, and bade him a gracious good-bye. They were just embarrassed enough by the meeting to keep it secret, but there were enough fringe people from the fashion world to have seen both of them at the surgery and report to friends and contacts.

Coral's fashion ivory tower was still visited by the top names of world fashion. Hubert de Givenchy still spent an evening with her when he was in town, bringing his muse, Audrey Hepburn, with him. Yves Saint Laurent came with his manager, Pierre Bergé. All Coral's enemies forgave her the moment she gave them a generous spread in *Divine*. That was the way of the fashion world.

"But the days of her power are numbered," Donna Haddon said on the phone to *Labels*. "I give her, oh . . . six more months if she doesn't get her act together."

"You think it's time to print what we have on her?" Howard Austin asked.

"Go ahead," Donna Haddon replied.

"Anais Du Pasquier!" Coral said into the telephone. "*Someone* must know who she is?"

"I'm sorry, Mrs. Stanton," the press assistant at Headquarters replied crisply. "We are unable to provide Mademoiselle Du Pasquier for interviews. She's in Paris most of the time."

"Well, call me the minute she's in town," Coral instructed. "I want an exclusive interview." She slammed down the phone. Her morning shot did not seem to have taken. Possibly it was because her lunch appointment was with Donna Haddon.

"I get such a threatening feeling from her!" Coral told Colin on the phone. "She doesn't *look* ambitious, but what other reason would a young woman have for sleeping with Lloyd?"

"Can't you send her on an assignment to Alaska?" Colin suggested.

"It's that or take her to lunch and try to be friends."

Coral had stipulated a "working" lunch to Donna when proposing it. Even so, Lloyd's Rolls Royce and driver awaited them as they left the building together.

"He insisted!" Donna laughed, ushering Coral inside.

"He's so thrilled we're lunching. Sometimes he's like a little boy!"

Coral bit back an acid remark. She surveyed Donna's outfit. It was a brilliant sartorial put-down. A denim pants suit with a red kerchief tied over her head, and a floor-length mink-lined raincoat, carelessly open against the January cold. Touché, Coral thought dryly. And on *her* salary. It was a wonder she hadn't left on the gift tag.

Donna leaned back against the leather seat as the car pulled away from the curb. "This *is* fun," she enthused. "I have so many ideas for sportswear features to talk to you about."

Coral briefly closed her eyes. She was wearing a white wool suit with a violet silk shell under it, her stockings tinted violet to match. Her white coat was loosely belted, her fiery red hair fashionably sleek. Donna smelled of fresh air and Hermes cologne. Her frank gray eyes glowed from her healthy, shining face.

"You don't mind that it won't exactly be La Grenouille?" Coral smiled dazzlingly at her.

Donna smiled back. "Oh, Lloyd and I go there far too often. They don't do that many things for a vegetarian like me, anyway."

Coral stared at her for a moment. "Hamburger Heaven!" she announced to the driver. Turning to Donna she said, "I'm sure they'll make you a salad. By the way, I liked the Hyannisport shoot—the tennis and golfing backdrop. Your photographer is quite a find."

"I'm so glad you like her—I'm crazy about her work!"

They reached the restaurant and Coral bade the driver return in an hour. She allowed Donna to hold the door open for her. "This will have to be short and sweet, Donna. I have a shooting at two."

They both ordered the Lo-Cal plate and ate hardly any of it, sprinkling Sweet 'n Low into their iced tea.

"Coral, all this pop-star, movie and theater stuff in *Divine* . . ." Donna began. "Aren't you scared we're starting to look like *Photoplay*? Can't we feature more sports stars instead of those tacky kids?"

Coral played with a lettuce leaf, knitting her brows: "Tacky kids?" she enunciated slowly. "You're not lumping Julie Christie and Mick Jagger and people like that into

that category, are you? We must feature people who
influence *fashion*!"

"I think sports and sports personalities will be influenc-
ing fashion more," Donna said.

Coral shuddered. "How *could* they? Warm-up suits and
running shorts and singlets? I don't feel that in the air, at
all."

"Ah, but *I* do!" Donna replied. "At least, couldn't we try
using very athletic models?"

"But *why*?" Coral lit a cigarette. "When there are exotic, unusual people like Andy's superstars around? Viva is
sensational. Edie Sedgwick wears clothes marvelously—
use *her*! Neither of them could run a marathon, perhaps,
but they have *chic*!"

"Olympic trainers usually tip me off when an especially
photogenic girl is in training," Donna persisted.

Coral raised her eyes. "This reminds me of how I used
to plead with poor Maynard Cowles to be allowed to
feature rock stars!" She dissolved into peals of laughter.

For the balance of the lunch Coral gave a monologue on
her plans for *Divine* and how good a designer she thought
Anaïs Du Pasquier was. "It's rather embarrassing not to
cover her, but I'm not on speaking terms with Wayland
Garrity," she said.

"Anything I should know about?" Donna asked casually. "I'm always featuring clothes from HQ. . . ."

"Try not to, dear." Coral flicked her ash. "It's an entirely personal matter between Wayland and me."

"Is that why HQ canceled its advertising? Lloyd was
very surprised."

Coral shrugged. "We'll get other advertisers. We're not
dependent on HQ's billings."

"But what about the *Divine* Fashion Awards: Don't you
expect to do them again next year?"

"Mmm. I'm sure we'll be friends again by then. You
know what the fashion world is like, Donna." She paid
the check and then leaned toward Donna to confide, "Let
me tell you something. There *is* a place for sports and
sportswear in *Divine*. There always will be, Donna."

Donna smiled, her eyebrows slightly raised.

Coral lowered her voice almost to a whisper, forcing
Donna to lean closer. "But that place is at the *back* of the
book. . . ."

Donna's eyes narrowed. Round two to Coral. "What about Paris?" Donna asked, her teeth nearly gritted.

"I don't know if I should go this season," Coral said airily. "It might do them really good to be ignored for once. They're all so arrogant. That Phillipe Roux and his ghastly assistant! Balenciaga and Givenchy are the true creators, and they won't even show to the press."

Lunch ended politely. Coral felt she had sized up the competition. Amateurs usually pushed sportswear because it was so much easier to understand. Stick a couple of headbands on the models and go on location to some snooty tennis club. She ushered Donna back into the Rolls. She had nothing to worry about, she decided: The girl was not equipped to handle *real* fashion.

Later that afternoon Lloyd summoned her to his office. "Thanks for taking Donna to lunch," he said, beaming. "She thinks so highly of you, Coral. I want to see you two get closer together. She'll be replacing Amy Horton as fashion editor next month."

Coral gasped. "She *will*?" She held onto the desk. Amy Horton was a glorified assistant she had promoted to fashion editor while never granting her any real power. Amy just followed Coral around on shoots and provided the odd accessory.

"She's a sweet kid, isn't she?" Lloyd said.

"Charming," Coral managed to say. "Absolutely adorable..."

"Now, what's this about Paris?" Lloyd asked. "Did you really tell Donna you might not go this season?"

She sank into a chair, fumbling in her purse for a cigarette. "It came around so quickly this time," she said. She touched her scar nervously. "You know what a traumatic time I had last season, with my... accident. I'm not sure that Paris is so important anymore."

Lloyd tapped his pen on his hand, watching her. "It would set a dangerous precedent. Readers expect *Divine* to attend and comment on the Paris collections."

"It's time we shook up the French!" Coral laughed lightly. She lit her cigarette and took a deep puff. "They do *not* rule world fashion anymore, Lloyd. There is London, Rome, New York.... If we missed out on Paris, it would be a marvelous put-down. Our readers would understand."

"This has nothing to do with your little feud with Phillipe Roux, has it?"

"Don't tell me you read those scurrilous columns in *Labels*, Lloyd? Why, I'd never let *any*one get between me and the pursuit of *real* fashion—it would go against every principle!"

"Hmmm..." Lloyd frowned, thinking. "Our French advertisers won't like it. You know, you're starting to antagonize people with this high-and-mighty attitude, Coral. *Divine* is hot right now, but we always want to get on with our advertisers. Perhaps you could tell me why Headquarters canceled their ten pages a month?"

Coral exhaled smoke impatiently, waving her hand. "That's Wayland Garrity—he and I have had a falling out. They'll be back...."

Lloyd shrugged. "Wayland Garrity," he said, ticking off on his fingers, "Phillipe Roux... and Howard Austin at *Labels* obviously has some kind of vendetta going—"

"I should sue him!" Coral spat.

Lloyd shook his head. "Coral, *Divine* isn't a forum for *you*. It's a money-making publication ... one I'm very proud of."

Coral flashed a hurt look at him. "You've never spoken to me like this before, Lloyd. Is this a preview of what life is going to be like around here when Donna becomes Mrs. Brooks?"

"I don't want things to get out of control," Lloyd said sternly. "Now, if you won't cover Paris, let's call in Donna now and tell her she can do it. She's *dying* to go!"

"A *sportswear* editor?" Coral cried, cursing herself. She should have been one step ahead of him. "Lloyd, my love, that would *never* do! That would add insult to injury.... Perhaps I *had* better go, after all. I could edit the showings down to the six most important. Stay a bare week..."

Lloyd grinned, pushing back his chair and standing to put an arm around her. "I thought you'd listen to reason, Coral," he said approvingly.

She recoiled from him, brushing a hand through her hair. *Why wasn't that shot working?* She longed for another. "I must go." She got up abruptly. "Paris reservations and all that..."

"They're all arranged, Coral," he assured her. "Your usual suite at the Crillon—"

"*No!*" she cried. "I won't ever stay there again!"

He stared at her as if she were crazy, and she touched his arm lightly with her hand, trying to control her sudden trembling. "It'll have to be the Ritz, Lloyd."

He shrugged. "Okay with me. I want you to be happy, Coral. And next season I want you to take Donna with you—show her the ropes and all that."

Coral shuddered. She was at the door when Lloyd called out, "Coral?" She froze, looking back over her shoulder. Lloyd held up a copy of *Labels*. "Did you see this issue yet?"

Coral shook her head, walking back to his desk. "It's not the first thing I do when I get in . . . why?"

He handed her the paper, opened at the Tittle-Tattle page. Under a black, silhouetted shape of a woman's profile, the blind item read:

> Which elegant editor owes a lot of her speed and dash to a Madison Avenue quack whose celebrity clientele all share the same characteristics? They are all super-successful, super-confident, super-skinny, and twitchily hyper! They are also super-broke: "Doc's" shots don't come cheap. Insiders say they are so far removed from the vitamins they purport to be that a Food & Drugs enquiry is overdue. . . .

Coral read the item quickly, without blinking, then threw the newspaper onto Lloyd's desk. "Why did you want me to read this?" she asked, her voice ice cold.

Lloyd reached for the paper, his eyes on hers. "I don't want anyone, on any of my publications, involved with drugs. Especially publicly involved—"

"But you're not insinuating . . ." Coral's eyes suddenly blazed with fire. "Oh, Lloyd, you *wouldn't*! Why, there are any number of editors in this city . . ."

"*Do* you attend this doctor?" Lloyd asked.

Coral drew herself up to her full height, towering over the seated Lloyd.

"Let *me* ask *you* some questions," she said icily, leaning over him. "Was our last issue not one of our very best?

Are we not setting advertising records? The circulation *is* on an upward curve, is it not?"

Lloyd sighed. "Yes," he said. "Yes to all that, but Coral..." He stood too, bending over the desk to take her arm. "I don't want you running any risks with your health. This is a very gossip-driven industry. You're too thin, you don't look well, and your behavior while Phillipe Roux was here made a lot of people talk...."

Coral stared him out, her angry eyes sparkling. "This is a totally unnecessary conversation, Lloyd," she finally said.

Stalking out of his office, she angrily returned to her room. *A brilliant performance, if I do say so myself,* she congratulated herself. She dialed the number of Dr. Robbins's office the moment she was seated behind her lacquer table.

"Natalie?" she whispered urgently to the receptionist. "That shot I got this morning doesn't seem to have taken. I'll be by at six for a booster."

Mackenzie left the doctor's office very slowly, moving in a daze toward Fifth Avenue. Bewildered, cold, she brushed past the crowds, waiting for the WALK signals, tried to think. How had she forgotten to take precautions? Often Alistair had been in a hurry for sex, but she had always, *always*, pushed him away. This must have been during one of their champagne-soaked, pot-drenched Saturday nights when she'd hardly known what was going on. She cursed her carelessness. Waiting for a light to change, jostled by the people around her, she instinctively protected her stomach with her arms. This involuntary action changed her mood. Nature was already ensuring that the baby was unharmed. She felt alone with her new secret. "Why should it be so terrible?" she said aloud to herself. She had promised herself not to give birth before thirty, but perhaps this child was fated to be born?

Her Village friends would call it karma and tell her to welcome the child who grew inside her. Her natural urge, if she swept aside all the objections she knew her mother would raise, was to love this child, cherish and care for it. To bring it up lovingly. It deserved a father, too. But a father who was stealing from his wife?

She reached home and systematically searched through

Alistair's pockets. Suddenly she stopped, sat back on her heels in the closet, and laughed wryly. What do I expect to find? she wondered. "Itemized receipts for pot?"

When Alistair arrived home that evening, she threw herself into his arms.

"Hey! What's the occasion?" he asked, pleasantly surprised.

"I missed you, you big lug!" she cried. "I even defrosted some dinner."

"Wow! Living history!" He pulled her into the living room. "Listen, Mack, what d'you say to a Gold! sports glove?"

She groaned. "Haven't we licensed enough stuff by now? I don't wanna design wallpaper and toilet seats, Alistair."

"These are gloves, not toilet seats. They only involve a thumb and four fingers!"

"*And* the right fabric, the right closure. I won't use leather, either. I just joined a movement against skins."

Alistair slapped his forehead, glaring at her. "Who made you do that? Luke?"

"No one makes me do anything—don't you know me by now?" Mackenzie snapped.

Alistair shook his head. "Sharing an apartment with those sweet little flower children was the worst thing that ever happened to you."

"Why?" She turned on him. "Because they made me more aware, more humane? I don't want to be responsible for more animals being killed. Can't you just respect my beliefs?"

"It's only a glove, for God's sake." He found a bottle of wine and uncorked it, pouring a glass. She nearly joined him, then remembered the baby and shook her head. "You're becoming such a perfectionist!" he complained.

"Yeah, if I wasn't, you wouldn't be looking out at that great view over Manhattan and sipping Château Rothschild," she said, and sat on the floor, watching him as he expertly rolled a fat joint, lit it and took a puff.

"Smoking and drinking," she said. "You'll be unreachable in five minutes, and we won't be able to talk...."

He shrugged, lying back on the couch. "What's there to talk about? You just closed off about five potential deals, if we can't ever use leather and suede. I run around all day, and when I come home you demolish everything."

She shook her head gently, watching him, hugging her news to herself. She knew that this was the moment in her life when everything could change. If he showed her the slightest sign of understanding, they might well share their lives together. If he simply turned on and tuned out, drifting away from her, her child was about to lose its natural father.

"We promised each other to always be very honest," she reminded him quietly. "That includes telling each other when we're dissatisfied with anything. . . ."

Alistair set his wineglass on the big black coffee table. "I am dissatisfied, I suppose, Mack." He reached out to switch on the table lamp. Their reflections sprang up in the window opposite. "Your father and brothers do their best to ignore me, so I don't really feel part of the firm. And lunching with fat glove manufacturers isn't exactly my idea of fulfillment, either."

"Who asked you to lunch with them? Do you think I care if we do gloves?"

"Aren't I supposed to be promoting the company?"

"There are plenty of ways to do that. You could think up a publicity campaign for us—direct shooting sessions of the clothes, finding some way to attract all those *Seventeen*-type goodie-goodies who think our clothes are too way out for them. . . ."

"Yeah . . ." Alistair sighed, taking a long drag on his joint. "In other words, be your flunky."

"*Don't!*" she snatched the joint from him. "You're gonna float off, and this is serious: Let's discuss it!"

He jerked the cigarette back from her, taking another long drag. "I may become your flunky, but I'm damned if I won't still have a smoke when I feel like it."

"Look, baby . . ." She sat up on the sofa next to him, making an effort to reach him. "I couldn't have done this without you, honestly. And none of this will be any good unless *we're* good together." She held his face between her hands, looking into his pale eyes, marveling again that anyone could even *have* such eyes. They were so alien to the Bronx. They signified class to her. Could classy guys steal? This was the time to say it. The words sounded in her head: *You're stealing from the store! You're stealing from me!* But she could not say them. It was beyond her to accuse a man who professed to love her.

"I wanted so much to be a creative person," he was saying. "Instead, you're the creative one...."

"You're jealous of my creativity?" she asked. "You can be just as creative, if you want."

He looked mournful now, holding out his arms to her for a hug.

"Oh, Alistair!" she cried. "You know I can never resist your little-boy-lost routine, damn it!" She fell into his arms, and he held her closely. For a minute or two she had the illusion that she was in the strong arms of a man. She longed to tell him her news, and suddenly felt she had to.

"Actually, you've been much more creative than you think...."

"How?"

"You've created a baby in me!"

"No! Mack!" He pushed her up above him so he could look at her, his face alight with a smile. "This is incredible! When did you find out? When's it due?"

"Today. This afternoon! And it's due in August. A summer baby..."

"But—oh, darling!" He kissed her face, her lips. "Why on earth didn't you tell me the moment I got home?"

She stared at him. "To tell the absolute truth, I was considering an abortion."

His expression changed. "Oh, you *wouldn't*, Mack. We'll have this child. I'll be a wonderful dad! You'll have to marry me now...."

She jumped off the sofa and ran to the kitchen. "I forgot the dinner! I must have burned it! I thought Mommy and Daddy should eat in...oh, God..."

He followed her into the kitchen and held her from behind as she peered though the oven door. "I said you'll have to marry me now," he repeated, nuzzling her neck with his nose.

Slowly, she straightened up and twisted around to face him. "You think I'm the type that feels they have to marry the moment they get pregnant?" she asked. "There's plenty of time to marry one day, if we're still speaking to each other...."

He broke away from her, hurt, and tried to cover it by

hunting in the refrigerator. "This demands our best champagne!" he cried.

She watched him, sensing something wrong about his forced gaiety. But when he proposed a toast, she held him close to her, pressing her lips into his soft blond hair, the same hair she hoped her baby would have.

"Don't shut me out of this, Mack, please. Let me be a real father. . . ."

She held him, stroking the back of his head. "That depends on you, baby," she said softly.

The champagne led to sex. It always did. On the living room sofa, once the wine was finished, he was tender, careful, softer with her. He spent a long time caressing between her legs, gently, then with more insisting fingers, until she was groaning. He brought her to one orgasm like that, then quickly lay on top of her, easing his body into hers. Instead of his usual pounding, he rocked gently inside her, and she came to a more intense climax. But there was a bittersweet edge to her pleasure tonight. She cried out a long lingering moan as he shivered inside her and released. This child-to-be tied them together as seriously as they had ever been. Whether they were married or not, she and Alistair would from now on be parents of a child. Guiltily she thought of Ed, and for the first time in her life, she felt regret.

As soon as Alistair left the next day, she summoned Ed to the apartment. Tired from the emotions of the previous evening, she said softly, "I don't want you to do or say anything to anyone about the missing money. I'll make up the difference."

Ed leaned back against the sofa, his brows raised. "You're not pressing charges?"

"Oh, Ed! How can I?"

"Just accompany me to the nearest police station. . . ."

She ran a hand through her disheveled hair. "No . . ."

They stared at each other for several seconds. Finally, he asked, "Don't I get coffee?"

Smiling, Mackenzie led him to the kitchen. "Tried to cook last night," she said, indicating the mess as she filled a kettle. "I should never do that."

He watched her spoon coffee grains into two mugs. "He's strung out, isn't he?" he asked. "He has a reputation as a pothead. He'll graduate to harder stuff—they always do—especially when they can afford to."

"I don't wanna hear this, Ed!" she said, pushing a plate of cookies at him.

"Can you take some advice? I don't care if he's British and has the grandest accent in the world. They're human, too. They throw up a bad one now and then."

"He's not *bad*, Eddie," she said softly.

She saw the concern in his dark blue eyes, and longed to have him hold her and give her strength, support, all the stuff she didn't get from Alistair. He sat at the steel kitchen table and she stood behind him, placing her hands on his shoulders.

"I'm going to have a baby," she told the back of his head.

He twisted around, looking up at her. "*Mazeltov,*" he said sadly. "I *guess.* You'll marry?"

Mackenzie shrugged. "*He* wants to. *I'm* not sure. All I know is that I'm having this baby. *That* comes first!"

"Really?" Ed smiled wryly. "Most people would say marriage came first, *then* the baby...."

"Yeah, well, I'm not *like* most people, Eddie. Don't you know that by now?"

He jumped up and faced her. "You have exactly the same background as me! Don't pretend you don't!"

She laughed. "There's a revolution going on in this country, haven't you heard? You're so uptight, so staid, Eddie! We don't have to do things in the same old-fashioned way anymore."

He held out his hand. "Well, lotsa luck!"

She took his hand, enjoying the warmth and the reassurance of it. He gave her his helpless infatuated look and moved closer. Before she knew it, she was kissing him, clinging to him. She allowed his tongue to enter her lips, and she sucked on it, pulling it into her mouth. A small groan escaped her. He pulled her tightly to him, their bodies touching from shoulder to thigh, a wonderful electricity flowing through them.

"Oh, God," she moaned.

She opened her eyes and stared into his eyes, now clouded with concern and his own desire. The restless sexual energy of his wanting her was hard to ignore. She shut her eyes as they kissed again, more urgently. Was *this* love? Could it catch you so unawares? Was this what it felt like? His hands gently held her breasts. She was growing moist down there, throbbing! She ached to press naked against him, to have his hardness rub her, between her legs. Enter her. This was *crazy!* She broke away before anything else happened, clinging to him for one last moment, one last kiss.

"No!" she said. "No, Eddie...I won't be responsible for what I do in a moment...."

"Isn't that the idea?"

He looked seriously at her.

She shook her head. "No, it isn't. You think I'm a kook, but I have my own set of morals...." Then she giggled and said, *"Damn* them!"

He didn't smile as he walked to the front door. She followed him, and he turned to her as he placed his hand on the doorknob. "I'm not going to play the caveman and hit you over the head with my club—but I sure feel like doing it! Someone needs to knock some sense into you." He took her hand and pressed it. "You know and I know that we'll be together one day. You *know* it, don't you?"

Yeah, she thought. *I know.* I don't know how, but there's a pull like magnets! She shrugged. "I don't know *what* I think, Eddie. But I am grateful for you coming over here—"

"Grateful?" he echoed angrily. He gave her a hard look, then closed the door between them.

He loved her more than Alistair ever could, she realized, walking back to her design room.

"Relax, baby..." She patted her stomach. "Mama will find a way to make it all right. I promise!"

Nineteen

It appeared in *Labels'* Tittle-Tattle column:

Lunching at Serendipity were two "old school chums," according to Her Modness Mackenzie Gold and Mia (Coral's daughter) Stanton. La Gold startled patrons in her shocking-pink fringed vinyl jerkin over tight black jeans, worn with the usual amount of Disneyland accessories and Halloween makeup. Both ladies ordered the chicken curry salad and drank Perrier. Their two-hour animated gab fest was, according to Ms. Gold, "about everything *but* fashion!"

"Did you have an orgasm?" Mackenzie asked. "That's all I wanna know!" Mia sighed, shaking her head, glancing around the tables of people staring at them. Her reunion with Mackenzie could hardly have been more public. Their entrance had caused mayhem, from the moment a *WWD* photographer had blinded them with flashbulbs.

"Darling, how groovy to see you again!" Mackenzie had squealed. "You're so skinny, you bitch!" It had taken her six weeks to squeeze this lunch into her hard-working schedule. It was a cold February day, too cold to snow.

They were swept to a conspicuous table. Mackenzie threw mounds of cashmere shawls onto the back of her chair.

"Oooh," Mackenzie sighed blissfully. "I love it here." She beamed as a complimentary bottle of French cider arrived. Leaning toward Mia, she said, "See the freebies they give you when you're successful? I coulda used this when I was starving in the Village."

Taking the menu from a smiling waiter, she swept it with her eyes. "The chicken curry salad is the best thing here," she said, snatching the menu from Mia's hand. "We'll have two of those! Oh, it's so good to be able to eat without Alistair glaring at me. He has me on this rigid diet—I have to sneak my treats now!" She took a deep breath, staring at Mia, examining her clothing. "That *his*?" She indicated Mia's suit. "God, it's elegant. It's on a different wavelength to my stuff, but I love it!" She clinked her glass to Mia's, "And now it's your turn! Are you talking with your mother? How did she do that to her face? Your friend Wayland suggested I open a boutique within Headquarters, but I'm holding out. Have you ever met Diana Vreeland? I wanna hear *everything*!"

The arriving food stopped her from asking more questions, and Mia had a chance to answer some. Mackenzie attacked her salad like someone starved for days, demanding more bread, more butter, more dressing. She ate with little moans and cries of "Mmmmm, yummy!"

Mia recounted the entire story of Paris, condensed to fit into a one-course lunch. Mackenzie kept her eyes fixed on Mia's face, her expression becoming more incredulous as the tale progressed.

"And last month I passed by her apartment," Mia finished, "and she refused to see me! She didn't even acknowledge my Christmas card."

"Were you surprised? You did disfigure the woman!"

"She told me so many lies about Phillipe . . . I just lost control."

"And it sounds like he screwed you!" Mackenzie cried. "Out of a job, I mean . . ."

"My mother swore to finish me in this town."

"But you'll be Anais somebody—how will she ever know? Oh, Mia, I can see I'm going to have to get your life and career and sex life *together*—you're a mess, darling." She peered into Mia's plate, saying, "Are you finishing that?" and speared a chunk of chicken.

"Now let me tell you about *my* life! It *should* be perfect, right? I mean, you should see the apartment I got! But I'm tired of saying it *should* be perfect, I want it to *be* perfect. You think *your* mother's a problem? My mother will give me the biggest dose of Jewish blackmail ever recorded when she hears I'm pregnant."

Mia's eyes widened. "Alistair? Are you getting married?"

"*Mia!*" Mackenzie looked at her pityingly. "People don't *do* that anymore. I don't even know if I love him. What does being in love feel like?"

Mia bit her lip. "To me it's a kind of desperation, a longing—"

"That's exactly how I feel about Eddie Schreiber. I haven't told you about him yet. He's our business manager. A sweet guy. I swear my father's getting senile and my brothers never stop trying to rip me off—Oh, and what about David, Mia? Have you seen him?"

"I can't face that yet," Mia groaned. "I liked him so much, but..."

"What happened? God, I used to be so jealous of you two...."

Mia stared at her friend. Such a display of interest was hard to resist. And being across a table from the expansive, extroverted Mackenzie made her feel almost equally bold.

"*Tell* me!" Mackenzie commanded, blotting up her salad dressing with a piece of baguette.

"Something was wrong," Mia began softly. "When we went to bed, I was frightened of sex with David. Disgusted by it..."

"Oh, my *God!*" Mackenzie cried. "There's absolutely no excuse for that these days! Have you tried masturbation? Alistair gave me a vibrator for my birthday, God, you should see the size of it! After that, no man could ever scare you. Was David incredibly well hung?"

Mia shook her head dazedly. "I honestly don't remember, I mean I—"

"How *weird!* That's the first thing I notice. When Alistair and I—"

"Mackenzie!" Mia hushed. "Would you please lower your voice? Everybody's listening!"

"Well, what about Phillipe Roux?" Mackenzie asked, her voice just a little quieter. "Did you have an affair with him?"

"Not really an affair..."

"Did you have an orgasm with *him?*"

"Yes," Mia admitted. That part was true, she thought. But we did not *really* make love. Not naked in bed, Phillipe inside me. No man has ever come inside me. *I'm a virgin.* She couldn't tell Mackenzie that. It would be like denying her own femininity. Like admitting to herself and her friend that a very important part of her was *stunted*, retarded.

Mackenzie glanced at her watch. "I gotta go!" she said, springing up, throwing a twenty-dollar bill on the table. She gathered her bags and led the way out, kissing waiters good-bye as she passed them. "Are you officially back?" she said over her shoulder. "Should I tell David? We talk on the phone all the time, you know."

"Is he doing okay?"

Mackenzie spun around to confront her. "So you *do* care? Well, for your info, *Miss* Stanton, David has a very well-paying job with a coat and suit manufacturer. He's ambitious in a quiet way, but he'll go places, you'll see."

At the entrance everyone's eyes were on them. Mackenzie relished the attention. "I'm really glad you're doing well," she told Mia. "I'll try to get to HQ and look at your stuff. We could never be competitors, could we? We're so different. I mean, *look* at us!" There was a mirror by the entrance and she struck one of her outlandish poses before it. "We'll open in L.A. next year," she continued with hardly a pause. "Gonna manufacture out there, too. My brothers say it's cheaper. Leave it to them! Ciao, darling!" She kissed the manager at the front desk, hailing a cab as she stepped out onto the sidewalk. "You wanna lift?" She embraced Mia and got into the cab before hearing Mia's answer. "This was wonderful! Like old times! Call David! Let's always stay friends, Mia, okay?"

As the cab made a U-turn Mackenzie waved frantically, her fringed sleeves fluttering.

Mia walked slowly down to Fifty-seventh Street, then across to Lexington. If she ever opened a store, she thought, it would be the very antithesis of Gold! It would be cool, bleached, with walls of white or the palest gray. Beautifully cut clothes would be spaced generously apart, uncrushed, before large floor-to-ceiling mirrors. Classical piano music would set the cool mood. The clothes would be boldly shaped in the softest, most feminine quality fabrics the world could offer. New details, pockets and sleeves, would slowly evolve. A woman would be able to *collect* these clothes, build a wardrobe. *Anais Du Pasquier.* That name set a mood, a lifestyle. *I can do it*, Mia thought.

I can be ambitious, too. It was better than sitting around missing Phillipe.

Wayland bolstered her self-confidence. He swept her back into Manhattan's fashion scene. She attended openings with him, viewed designers' collections from the chair next to his. There was no risk of bumping into Coral: She now only viewed clothes from the privacy of *Divine*'s offices. After Paris the clothes seemed to Mia to be pale imitations of couture: skimpy, machine-made copies of French inspiration.

She could not stop herself from reading the trade gossip columns. Phillipe and Josephine had been reported honeymooning in Morocco, then remodeling an entire Paris *hôtel particuliere*, looking for larger premises for the salon, signing with various manufacturers for Phillipe Roux sunglasses, earrings, shoes, colognes. Like most designers who sell their names, he would have little to do with the actual design: The manufacturers just wanted his signature, and he would pocket the royalties.

Mia stared at the picture of a smiling Josephine Roux standing alongside Phillipe at Orly Airport. Husband and wife.

"I won't let you go," he had told her. If only she could stop those words of his from echoing around her brain. He had bound her to him with those words as surely as any hypnotist. Had he really meant them? She switched her mind off the subject.

Reaching Lexington, an aroma of freshly baked pizza hit her. A record store blasted Petula Clark through a giant outdoor speaker. Mia wandered into Bloomingdale's, eyeing the displays, a lost soul in Manhattan.

Coral flew to Paris bubbling with excitement, a travel kit of disposable syringes from Dr. Robbins in a specially made alligator case under her arm. The "vitamins" would help her face Paris with confidence.

She kept her Paris coverage secret, but her head was brimming with a novel way to present the season's fashions.

Todd Bundy, a new-wave photographer and discovery of Coral's, flew with her to Paris. He was bald, black-leather-clad, and grunted agreement to her ideas.

In Paris she avoided Wayland and hobnobbed solely with Bundy and her Paris assistant photographer, Alexis.

Coral dressed to match Bundy, in sinister black leather
skirts, studded motorcycle jacket and boots. She stayed at
the Ritz and became a fixture of the Ritz Bar, sitting
excitedly in a corner with her chosen few cronies—a Texas
store buyer; her visagiste Gilles, working exclusively for
Divine that week; and the odd visit from Colin Beaumont.

WWD photographed her one evening chatting with Chanel, during one of Mlle. Chanel's rare descents from her
salon across the Rue Cambon. Mlle. Chanel had long
admired Coral's strict, disciplined look, and she agreed to
Coral's request that she pose for this new avant-garde
photographer. The *WWD* photograph showed Chanel in
tweeds, pearls, and chains, and Coral in black leather,
complete with motorcyclist's studded cap.

"A delicious confrontation of styles!" *WWD* crowed.

Coral was *the* talking point of Paris, as she took fashion
into a new, perverse direction. At the few showings she
deigned to visit, attention was riveted on her entrance,
stunning, strict, and faintly sinister, her photographer
accompanying her like a silent bodyguard.

She booked young actresses from the Comédie Francaise
to model the clothes, first swearing them to secrecy.

"They'll do it for nothing!" she assured Colin. "Just for
the exposure. They're not dumb, these French cookies!
You think they don't remember that Lauren Bacall, Suzy
Parker, and now Lauren Hutton were all discovered in
fashion magazines?" She got them to pose in return for
crediting their names in the magazine, meanwhile pocket-
ing the thousand dollars she had been allocated for Paris
modeling fees. It would go toward joints for Bundy and
herself in Paris, and the bills for the stronger shots Dr.
Robbins now offered at thirty dollars a hit.

"I had dinner with them at the Ritz Grill last night,"
Colin reported to Wayland in an early morning call. "We
were constantly interrupted by calls from Parisian morti-
cians and casket makers! What can she be up to?"

Wayland laughed. "Maybe she's organizing a search for
Anais Du Pasquier?"

"When I saw her to the front desk for her key, her
pigeonhole was stuffed with messages from embalmers,
funeral parlors, and florists!"

"Oh, *God*!" Wayland gasped. "She wouldn't be arranging some kind of spectacular *suicide*?"

"No." Colin shook his head sadly. It grieved him to see that the elegant, bright woman who had discovered him was now ravaged, almost a caricature. "I'm afraid poor darling Coral is living through a very long suicide right now. Those awful speed shots . . . it breaks my heart to see the effect they have on her."

The next day, while Colin was waiting to meet an Italian editor outside Dior's salon, a black hearse pulled up and Coral clambered out.

Colin gasped. "What on earth! Do you feel all right, my dear?"

"Never better!" she called, and waved the driver on. "This is one of our props. I thought I may as well get a lift to Dior in it," she said, giggling. Colin was mystified. "You'll understand when you see the magazine," Coral promised.

One thing was certain: *Divine* had not requested many clothes to photograph.

"We'll tell the Paris story in six edited layouts," she said airily. There were rumors, in *Labels* and *WWD*, that Coral had not been invited to Phillipe Roux's showing. She did not turn up at the collection. "Evidently, I didn't miss much!" she said over dinner that night, reading the *WWD* mimeographed report, circulated exclusively to the buyers and press. "A rehash of his last collection!" she read triumphantly. Howard Austin's biting report in *Labels'* Paris edition called it "the most disappointing collection of the decade. . . ."

Coral couldn't help but wonder whether his lack of inspiration had anything to do with Mia's departure. But she knew it would not hurt Roux. There were plenty of old-fashioned editors in the rear guard who needed a season or two to catch up with fashion. They still thought Roux was brilliant.

Wayland called Mia to tell her of the critical flop. "Your mother's become a fashion celebrity unto herself!" he told her. "She's a rebel—a Paris fashion beatnik!"

The secrecy surrounding the *Divine* shoots exploded when Coral returned to New York, carrying a briefcase of contacts. The art department took one look at them and complained to Lloyd Brooks. A scandal erupted. Coral Stanton's Paris coverage had been entirely shot on "corpses" —models pretending to be dead. Realistically made up to resemble cadavers, wearing black dresses from Dior, Nina Ricci, and Cardin, the Comédie Francaise actresses were draped over coffins, laid to rest in freshly dug graves, or collapsed, in one shocking two-page layout, on a mortuary's embalming slab.

She was summoned to Lloyd's office, Donna standing beside him as he turned the pages of the rough layout. Finally Lloyd looked up. "It's morbid, Coral! It's *sick*!"

"It's also my statement!" she cried. "Paris is *dead*!"

"Coral," Donna chirped, "you can't be serious about this?"

Coral froze, glaring at Donna with the frightening, wide-open eyes she could use so chillingly. "I'm unaware that *you* have any say over my editorials, Donna. Or have you been promoted again without my knowledge while I was away?"

Lloyd reached for Donna's hand. "I'll want Donna to have a lot more say in what appears in *Divine*. We're getting married very quietly next week."

Coral swallowed with difficulty, then smiled dazzlingly. "Congratulations, my loves! But you two should be planning receptions and honeymoons and things. You really shouldn't be spending time on my little divertissement!"

"Work comes first!" Lloyd said grimly. "And *this* . . ." He gestured at the picture of a chalk-faced model wearing a black-draped Gres gown as mourners in black Yves Saint Laurent pants suits scattered rose petals over her open coffin.

"It's *fresh*! It's *witty*! Kids today have a deliciously macabre sense of humor! They'll *love* it!" Coral assured them. "Oh, don't you two get the *subtext*?" She slammed her hand down on Lloyd's desk. "It's what every girl is going to *long* to look like—pale, interesting, ethereal. . . ."

And she was right. The healthy, innocent, childish mid-sixties look was about to be eclipsed by the old-time movie vamp look that, if one stretched one's imagination, could be glimpsed on the "corpses'" cheeks.

Divine's Paris fashion issue was a sensation, reasserting Coral's hold on the magazine. The issue also launched the career of Todd Bundy, who had more requests to photograph people madeup to look dead than he could handle. It became a collector's issue, and took away a little of the importance Paris had hitherto held. Coral had triumphed.

But the triumph did not do her much good in the trade. Coral-watchers—and that included most fashion people— said the Paris Is Dead issue would lead to her own decline and fall.

As *Divine* became more brilliant, more unpredictable, and more successful, Coral became more erratic, imperious, maddening. Her antennae were tuned into every fashion and underground event. Her coverage of theater, film, pop, art, and lifestyles was unrivaled, and translated quickly into the fashion coverage she reigned over. She took to flying to the West Coast, touring Haight-Ashbury as it became the hippie acid capital of the world. She was arrested for smoking pot at a famous San Francisco party which moved to a local jail for a few hours, almost as to an annex. She photographed Andy Warhol in Brooks Brothers, Julie Christie in Zandra Rhodes, Twiggy in anything. She persuaded socialites to don political sweatshirts, tamed Black Panthers to escort her to literary and political events, did the Skate with jazz-dancers at discos, wearing Mackenzie Gold's twenty-five-dollar vinyl dress. In an era when boutique-owners and hairstylists were becoming celebrities, Coral was the celebrity fashion editor, photographed everywhere, peripatetic, a gaunt caricature of her former self.

"And thin, thin, thin!" Colin complained to Wayland. "Those shots are going to kill her. I've got to talk her out of them."

She was inspiring *Divine*'s photographers to do the craziest things: hosing down models with water while they were wearing evening dresses, or dragging them into indoor swimming pools wearing flimsy Diors, for ethereal, underwater photography. She threw a handful of high-fashion girls into the sleazy pit of a Forty-second Street movie house and snapped them next to raincoated, amazed patrons. Coral was talked about and *Divine* was bought and discussed; *WWD* and *Labels* nearly ran out of innuendo in their hints that all was not quite right with the editor of the chicest publication.

"It isn't simply fashion anymore, Colin," Coral said, gesturing excitedly at their weekly dinner. She had taken to wearing lots of rings, and her quick, nervous gestures gave her conversation the sparkle of fireworks. "It's the whole shebang! It's protest, art, society, drugs—and *Divine*

is finally selling to people under thirty! Lloyd loathes
what I'm doing, but figures don't lie, and Lloyd likes
figures!"

Colin nodded understandingly. Having dinner with Coral
these days was like riding a roller-coaster. The moods
swung from high to low. At least she was on a high for
the main course, he mused, which was nice. They were
sitting at the back, insiders' table of Il Giardino, attempting
to eat pasta so al dente they needed knives and forks. She
regarded him fondly, knowing she must look odd sitting
opposite this tiny man but not caring. They had an
unspoken agreement—she never mentioned his lack of
height, he never mentioned her scar.

"You'll always be ahead of everyone," Colin said,
smiling. "But I'm concerned about the campaign Howard
Austin seems to have launched single-handedly against
you."

"Oh . . . *him*." Coral grimaced. "Everyone has enemies
in this world—he seems to be mine."

Later, Colin watched her as she wound a cashmere
shawl around her body. "You're not planning on losing
any more weight, are you, my dear?" he asked.

"Mmmm . . . Dr. Robbins likes me trim."

She swept through the doorway as he held the heavy
plate-glass door for her. They breathed in the cold night
air of Manhattan as he walked her home.

"Coral, darling, you know that they're calling your Dr.
Robbins Doctor Feelgood. . . ."

She clapped her hands. "But that's a wonderful name
for him! He *does* make you feel good."

"I see quite a few models who use him, too. None of
them seem very healthy to me. . . ."

"Are you crazy?" She turned to him with glittering eyes.
"Those B-complex shots are keeping half the fashion
industry going."

"But Coral, don't you know what's *in* those shots?"

She stopped short on the sidewalk, looking at him, her
eyes alight with manic energy. "Colin, in the fifties we
were all such little ladies. Remember? I was never without
my white gloves. In the sixties we frug, we protest, we
attend happenings, and we dabble in drugs. Suppose the
stuff *does* contain drugs? Aren't doctors *supposed* to
prescribe?"

"But it's making you manic!" Colin protested. "Your...
behavior is being talked about. And it breaks my heart,
Coral."

She took his arm silently and they continued to walk to
her building. "I appreciate your concern, darling," she
finally murmured, "but please don't worry about me. I've
never felt this positive, this energetic. And I need all that
energy to fight Donna Brooks, Colin! She wants my job as
badly as I want to keep it! What happens when an
irresistible force meets Coral Stanton at the door marked
editor-in-chief, Colin? Something has to give, right? Well,
she has a fifteen-year headstart on me. Oh, Colin, darling..." She turned to look beseechingly into his eyes.
"Don't hate me! This is all I've *got!*"

"I've never seen you like this before, Coral," Colin said
wonderingly. He groped for words to get through to her.
His heart was thumping. They stopped at her apartment
house and he took her hand.

"Come up for a nightcap, darling," she asked.

He shook his head. "I have some advertising to finish
tonight. But listen to me, Coral. I'm not going to stand by
and watch you destroy yourself. You're getting sick. I
know I've been called a skinflint, and it's true. I must pay
less rent than your cleaner, but there's a purpose behind
it. I'm going to buy a little house in France, and if you
came, I'd pamper you back to real health!"

She laughed delightedly, her breath showing in the night
air. "And what'll you do when I leave? Expire of boredom?"

He gave a secret smile. "I'll garden!"

"Nonsense!" she cried. "You're more of a fashionaholic
than I am!" She bent down to kiss him. "But out of all my
friends, I really do believe you're the only one I can really
count on. You can't know what it means to me."

He stared at her sadly as she swept into the building,
turning around to wave as she reached the elevator. As he
walked home, he had a feeling of enormous waste, loss.
There had been a look to her face that night of someone
on the brink of something terrible.

"I'm pregnant, Ma!"

Esther Goldstein stared dumbly at her daughter across
the table at Serendipity.

"*Well?*" Mackenzie cried. "Aren't you going to congratulate me?"

She put her hand out toward her mother's, but Esther edged her own hand away. "Are you married?" she asked, quietly.

"Oh, Ma, you *know* I'm not! Wouldn't I have invited you to the wedding?"

Esther Goldstein turned pale. She shook her head to herself. "To tell the truth, nothing you did would surprise me anymore. If you married secretly, if you give birth to a—is Alistair the father?"

"He *will* be, yes, but you don't sound excited."

Esther swayed in her chair. Her head nodded and she began to slump.

"*Ma!*" Mackenzie cried, quickly dipping a napkin in ice water and holding it to her mother's forehead. Neighboring tables watched in alarm, and two waiters ran to her side.

"It's fine . . . I'm fine . . . I'll be all right," Esther moaned. She struggled to get to her feet. "Take me to the ladies' room, please. . . ." Half-supporting her, Mackenzie somehow managed to get her to the rest room. It was a private cubicle and she sat her mother on the toilet lid and locked the door behind them.

"I'm fine. . ." Esther said, and sat up straight, staring at her daughter.

"Are you going to pass out? Do you need to throw up?" Mackenzie fussed around her, holding the damp napkin to her forehead.

"I'm all right, I told you," Esther said calmly. "I just put on a show so we could get away from all those people around us—they were all listening and watching you."

"So what?" Mackenzie shrugged. "God, you gave me such a fright—why can't you be happy and excited for me? Don't make me feel it's something to be ashamed of . . ." She ran her fingers through her hair, fluffing her bangs, looking intently at her eye makeup in the mirror.

Esther impatiently clicked her tongue. "Maybe you'd like me to throw a neighborhood party to celebrate that my first grandchild will be half *goy*, and illegitimate to boot!"

Mackenzie groaned. "So you're gonna be like that?"

"What did you expect? That you can treat your family

like slaves and that we'd be pleased when you drag us down into the dirt?"

"*What* dirt? You mean because I don't follow the conventions of straight, uptight society? I make my own conventions. Except for you, my family doesn't care about *me*. They only see me as a money maker for them, that's all."

"Your father and your brothers *love* you," Esther insisted.

"Oh, *please*, Ma! *Love*? They have never once even *thanked* me or congratulated me on our success."

"Why don't you talk to them? Have a little chat with your father now and then. Try to help us understand why you're going to throw your life away like this."

"Did I ever give you any reason to believe I was the keeper of the Jewish faith? Besides, the religion goes through the mother—you can think of this baby as Jewish if it makes you happy."

Her mother shook her head wearily. "Nothing about this baby makes me happy. Not the way it's been conceived out of wedlock, not the father's religion, not—"

Mackenzie suddenly exploded. "Okay, then, can we get out of this fucking toilet and finish our lunch?"

Esther gasped. "You'd say those words to your mother?"

Mackenzie was fumbling with the lock. "Look, Ma, I invited you to a celebratory luncheon to announce that you'd be a grandmother in five months. I didn't expect to celebrate sitting in a toilet together." She banged at the lock in desperation.

"Are you all right, Miss Gold?" a waiter called from the other side of the door. "You're not locked in, are you?"

Mackenzie wrenched the doorknob, and the door suddenly burst open. The waiter looked in anxiously. "Everything all right?"

"Fine! Great!" Mackenzie swept out graciously, followed by her tightlipped mother. "It's called a rest room, isn't it? Well, we were just resting."

They finished their lunch in an offended silence, Esther hardly eating, Mackenzie blinking back unexpected tears. Afterward, Mackenzie put her mother in a taxi, thrusting a ten-dollar bill into her hand. It was regurgitated through the window and fell onto the sidewalk. She kissed her mother's cheek quickly, and the cab sped off. *Damn!* Mackenzie bent down to retrieve the money. Just as she'd

begun to think she'd dragged her family into the twentieth century, her mother had to pull this kind of thing.

Alistair was supervising fashion shots for a Gold! color
poster and catalog, so she hailed a taxi to take her downtown to the shooting location. She had expected to spend
the afternoon shopping for baby things with her mother.
Now she could surprise Alistair and they could do the
sitting together.

Patrick McCallister, a hip young photographer, had transformed an old Village church hall into a whitewashed
studio. Loud rock music blasted down the sleepy Village
street as the taxi pulled up in front of it. She had to hold
her finger on the bell for a full thirty seconds before she
was heard.

"I'm freezing to death out here!" she gasped when
Chrissie, Patrick's assistant, finally opened the door. She
pushed past her into the reception area, shivering. "You
can hear this music midtown!" She laughed.

"Anything wrong?" Chrissie was staring at her with
painted lashes and a worried, surprised expression.

"They *are* still working, aren't they?" Mackenzie asked,
walking toward the swing doors that connected to the
studio.

Chrissie darted in front of her, barring her way. "Don't
go in there!" she said.

"*Why?*"

"He's . . . Patrick hates to be disturbed. . . ."

Mackenzie fixed her with a withering gaze.

"Look, kiddo—I'm paying through the nose for these
sessions. I can at least *see* them!"

She pushed past and strode into the large studio. Everyone was clustered at the far end. The Mamas and
Papas album abruptly ended while screams, cheers, and
laughter filled the silence. Flashes were exploding every
few seconds, and the sweet smell of pot hung heavily in
the air. Someone put on "Dancing in the Street" by
Martha and the Vandellas, the beat blaring deafeningly
through the loudspeakers.

"*Yeah!*" Mackenzie cried approvingly, clicking her fingers and doing a couple of dance steps toward the group.
She loved the atmosphere in fashion photographers' studios—
always so creative and crazy! One or two stylists and
makeup girls saw her and ran toward her, kissing her,

holding her arm as if to head her off. There was another explosion of cheering from the group. A Sassoon stylist she knew, a redheaded girl, grabbed her and gushed, "What *fab* earrings! Where'd you get them?" and tried to steer Mackenzie to the side of the studio, away from the group clustered around the subject of Patrick's flashing camera.

Mackenzie whirled away from her. "Where's Patrick? Are you all trying to hide something from me?"

Pushing away the stylist, she walked to the noisy circle and edged her way into it, peering down at the floor. She found herself staring straight at pink, humping, male buttocks. It was Alistair—no one else could move that fast just before an orgasm. He was performing his famous speeded-up finale in public. Underneath him, her legs up and crossed behind his back, was the girl she and Alistair had chosen to represent Gold!'s new look for next fall. Janice Allen's eyes were shut tightly and she uttered little squeaks as the group counted her down to orgasm. Mackenzie took in the scene in one split-second, a wave of humiliation and nausea sweeping over her. She couldn't help noticing Janice's long toes and painted toenails. Patrick's camera flashed relentlessly.

They all seemed to be standing there forever. Never had an orgasm taken so long, and yet she knew she would have to stand there, waiting for it to climax, before her own scene could begin. How cool could she be? Mackenzie had no idea how she was going to react. Right now she was as curious as anyone else to see what happened. And she was very aware of a stream of boiling anger slowly building up in her.

"Ten! Nine! Eight!" they chanted, in time with the beat and Alistair's thrusts. Janice's eyes fluttered open, focusing on Mackenzie. People looked from Janice to Mackenzie, as if at a tennis match.

"Oooooh! My God!" Janice cried. She banged Alistair hard on the shoulder.

"Yes! Yes, baby, I'm coming!" he cried.

He went into his familiar convulsions, his buttocks squeezing rapidly together, his loud cries audible even over the blaring music. Mackenzie watched as his body shuddered to a standstill, Janice staring up in dismay at her.

—

"Alistair . . ." Janice said warningly. The music stopped. There was silence.

"Whatsa matter? Did you come?" Alistair's voice was muffled in her hair. He slumped over her, his buttocks gently moving as he ground out his last moments of pleasure. Now everyone stared at Mackenzie.

"Did you get it all, Patrick?" Alistair asked.

"Yeah! All of it!" Patrick, a tall gangly man, said.

"Did I break my record?"

Mackenzie answered him this time, saying, "Yes, Alistair. I think you broke it."

Alistair sat up quickly, looking at her. "Oh, hi, Mack!" He pulled up his pants hastily, throwing a sweater to the naked, sprawling Janice.

There were about twelve people present at this, the hippest scene in town. Alistair and Mackenzie were one of the hippest couples around: How were they going to handle this?

"Wanna joint, Mack?" Patrick held out a reefer. "We've taken some great shots—"

She ignored him. She looked over at Alistair, who was quietly, carefully dressing. He looked blank, determined not to be apologetic. So she didn't know him at all! The pain was unbearable, especially as it could not be shown. She looked around for someone to attack and chose Janice.

"How many times has she been fucked today?" she asked, hating herself. "Have you had her, too, Patrick?"

"Look, Mack . . ." Patrick placed a hand on her arm, which she shrugged off angrily. "I don't like your insinuations. I was just taking pictures, that's all. I love your new stuff, by the way—"

She snapped her fingers. "Give me the film!"

Patrick stared at her for a moment, then motioned for an assistant to unload the camera and hand the roll to Mackenzie. She placed it in her purse. Patrick looked irritatedly at the hangers-on. "C'mon, break it up, everybody, will you? The fun's over." He put his arm through Mackenzie's. "Since when did *your* values become so bourgeois? I thought you were one hip chick."

"Yeah, well this hip chick is about to have a hip little chicklet," she said dryly, "and it changes you."

She broke away from Patrick and approached Janice, who was sulkily getting dressed on the other side of the studio. "I've changed my mind about you!" Mackenzie said. "You don't have quite the look I want. I was after something a little more wholesome."

"You're still gonna pay me!" Janice yelled at her, stumbling as she put on some high-heeled shoes. "I've been here since eight! I've worked six hours. . . ."

Mackenzie stood her ground, aiming a killing look at her. "You send in a modeling invoice, Janice, and I'll have you arrested for prostitution." Janice burst into tears, and Patrick crossed the studio to comfort her. "I've changed my mind about you, too, Patrick," Mackenzie told him.

Patrick turned to face her. "C'mon, man, be cool!" he said.

"I've had it with being cool." Mackenzie was now alongside Alistair. She forced herself to look at him. He had an uncaring expression on his face, one she'd never seen before.

"Don't you have anything to say, Alistair?" she asked softly. He was bending down to relace his shoes.

"I thought I was in charge of publicity," he muttered.

"I just relieved you of that."

He looked earnestly into her face. "Look, Mack, we have to make these sessions fun or they'd turn out like boring catalog shots. . . ."

"Oh, it's in *my* interest, is it? Is that what you were doing—improving the quality of the shoot? Funny, it looked to me like you were screwing your little butt off."

He stood up straight, a spasm of anger passing over his face. "Do you mean to say *you've* never screwed around?"

She looked to either side; a few people were eavesdropping, pretending not to. Suddenly her eyes filled with tears. A picture of Eddie Schreiber flashed into her mind, and she remembered how she had stopped him last time, pushing him away when she'd been longing to make love.

"No, I've never screwed around," she whispered. Then she glanced at the others and shouted, *"I've never screwed around!* Did you all hear *that*? I wanted to be virgin-pure for my Alistair, because I was carrying his baby! Ever hear anything so *dumb*?"

Patrick had his arm around Janice. He looked across at Mackenzie and said, "The dumbest thing I've heard is you taking this campaign away because of a bit of fun—"

"Alistair screwing a girl in public?" she cried. "That's fun?"

"Bu we're all friends!" Patrick groaned. "Peace and *love*, man! Share the karma—where have you *been* for the last two years?"

Mackenzie shot another look at Alistair, then walked toward the door of the studio. Her heels clattered loudly against the floorboards as everyone watched her. She stopped just before the doors and called back, "Fuck *you*, Patrick! Fuck *all* of you! You're just a bunch of tacky, shallow—" She bit her lip and ran out into the street before they could see her cry.

Outside, she dumped the exposed film into a garbage can. As if to punish herself, she walked for blocks and blocks in the cold wind, reliving the scene. More fool you, she told herself. From now on you grab any bit of sex, any fun, you can get. She wanted to call Eddie and see him that evening. But she became so cold she hailed a cab and went straight home, feeling very sorry for herself. Her mother *and* Alistair had both let her down on the same day. She started to cry again in the backseat of the taxi, avoiding the eyes of the driver n the mirror. If she had ever been in love with Alistair, this was the day she fell out of it.

Twenty

"Anais Du Pasquier has *arrived*!" Wayland poured a very large vodkatini for himself and an orange juice for Mia. "My press office is frantic!" He handed her the glass. "They keep getting requests to interview her! Maybe we should hire a French actress to portray her?"

Mia laughed. "Couldn't Bette Davis do it?"

"With one hand tied behind her back," Wayland agreed, and gulped at his cocktail. "But I was thinking more along the lines of Catherine Deneuve."

It was seven o'clock, and they were going out that evening. March was bringing biting winds down from Canada into Manhattan. Mia was now earning large sums of money from the clothes. She knew she'd soon have to start thinking of getting her own apartment and that she'd miss Wayland.

"You'd better come in and at least meet our buyers, pet," Wayland suggested. "They'll swear an oath of silence. It will be good for you to get some input." He placed a dish of peanuts before her. "They're ready for a larger range, skirts in different lengths. We have tie-ups with stores throughout America, all of whom seem very interested in our little Anais. You'd better get an advertising agency to think up some brilliant advertising for you."

Mia shook her head. "Isn't it funny that all this happens when I don't care anymore?"

"That's *when* things happen, sometimes." Wayland wagged his finger at her. "So *start* caring! You're talented, your clothes are selling, what's *with* you?"

She sipped her juice. "I guess between my mother and Phillipe, I've used up all my energies on people."

He peered at her anxiously. "You're not having some

kind of nervous breakdown, are you, pet? I felt pretty hopeless when that window-dresser walked out on me last year. I mean, I thought it was the end of the world. But..." He shrugged, swallowing his drink. "You have to get yourself out there and meet more people, pet. Who are you seeing tonight?"

"Mackenzie, I *think*...."

"Why do you only *think*?"

"She said for me to be at the Russian Tea Room at eight, and to be slightly dressed up—maybe she'll have some people with her, I don't know."

That evening she wore her own purple two-piece in wool, with thick textured hose and calf-length purple boots. She pulled on a black fake fur coat, tied a bright yellow scarf around her hair, and walked down Fifty-seventh Street to the restaurant.

Giving her name to the maitre d', she was directed to a corner booth. The man sitting there rose as she approached. Her heart lurched.

She gasped. *"David! So you're the surprise!"*

He swept her into his large embrace. She should have guessed Mackenzie could hardly wait to play matchmaker! His clean, soap-fresh smell took her right back to their first days together.

"I'll murder Mackenzie!" She laughed as they sat down, then tried to collect her thoughts.

She'd forgotten how handsome David was, his fine blue eyes so honest and unflinching. Phillipe had filled her thoughts for so long that she'd been blind to the fact that other men could be attractive. She hadn't seen him for a year, and the year had improved him. His fair hair was longer, fuller, and the blue eyes seemed a shade deeper.

He grinned happily at her. "God, it's good to see you, Mia. You're more beautiful than ever. Why didn't you let me know you were back?"

She pulled off her scarf, and touched the back of her hair. "I don't know," she said simply. "I've felt so odd since I came back. Wayland swept me into designing a small collection—I do it under the name of Anais Du Pasquier. I have no social life at all, beyond what he drags me to...."

He looked disappointed. "Are you going to tell me everything?" he asked, his eyes sparkling with curiosity.

They ordered blinis and coffee.

"First tell me what's happened to you, David," she said.

He shrugged. "You and Mackenzie stole all the honors our year. I was doing some part-time work with an Eighth Avenue firm last year, but now I'm designer-cutter for a coat and suit firm at 1440 Broadway. I work damn hard, and I'm paid well, but I'm bored to tears. I have to fight to get every pocket flap approved. My creative juices are..."

"Blocked?" she supplied.

"'Damned' would be a better word." He laughed. "I planned to pull my act together in the evenings, at home. I've been working on a kind of seamless dress made from jersey tubing. When I get it right, it could be a new classic...."

"So?"

"I need to walk or swim or play squash in the evenings, too!"

"Still the outdoor type?"

"This is New York—only the walking is outdoors!"

They sat back as their food was served. She got a sudden glimpse of what a "normal life" would be like for her with a man like David.

"Why did you leave Paris?" he asked her gently. "I know how much it meant to you, to be working for Roux...."

She sipped at her coffee, looking at his strong, square jaw.

"I don't know—you're such a sane, solid person...it would all sound so melodramatic to you."

He shook his head. "Listen, Mia: I've waited a long time for this. I want you to tell me. Slowly. In great detail..."

The waiter refilled her coffee cup, and she took a deep breath. She did not want David to know she'd been in love with Phillipe, so she edited her story, describing Phillipe as a manipulator, a dictator. She said Coral had refused to believe she'd designed the collection, which was why she'd thrown the ashtray.

David almost choked. "But *I* recognized your style the moment I saw the photographs. I recognized the pockets and collars—all Mia details...."

"Thanks!" She smiled, spreading her hands. "So here I

am! Living in luxury at Wayland's apartment. Designing a collection. Able to afford my own life and not able to visualize it."

She took a sip of water. "Wayland's like my family. I must introduce you to him. I'd like him to see your clothes. I'm sure they're wonderful."

He made a dismissive gesture. "Clothes mustn't be too wonderful today. Look at Mackenzie. She turns out such junk. It sells because of the way it's merchandised—all those colored lights, that rock music . . . Kids would buy anything . . ."

"I got spoiled in Paris with the finest craftsmanship," she told him. "You cannot believe the trouble they go to in order to make a garment perfect—inside as well as outside. Everything is hand-stitched. . . ."

"Tell me about the clients—are they rich, spoiled bitches?"

"Some of them are." She finished her blini and folded the napkin. "Some of them expect a lifelong commitment to a suit or dress. They pay up to three thousand dollars for it, so if a button falls off, or there's the tiniest imperfection in the lining, they bring it back. Even years later, they want refittings if they lose or gain weight, alterations . . . Phillipe would go crazy when some suit he made five seasons ago at Dior was brought back to him for repairs. He has to be patient and charming to everyone. Of course they don't expect to be charged."

"Do they pay their bills promptly?"

Mia frowned. "He refuses to deal with the actresses and politicians' wives who have a reputation for not paying. Some of them haggle over the price, or agree to pay only the price of the fabric. They feel the publicity they give the house is worth money."

David sipped coffee, studying her. "Didn't the guy ever make a pass at you?"

"He's married," Mia said crisply. "When you work for Roux, you're expected to give your life over to the house. It's like some cloistered religious sect. Fashion is 'bringing order and style to the world'—like some divine mission."

"Maybe a top designer *has* to think like that?"

Mia shook her head. "Phillipe's as commercial as the next man. He couldn't wait to sell out. Kramer Industries bought his name—they're bringing out some tacky cologne. . . ."

"You sound a little disillusioned." David smiled. "Did you part amicably?"

"You *can't* walk out of a Paris couture house amicably! He was convinced I was joining some rival! Honestly, when I think back to it, it all seems like some overheated melodrama!"

"And your clothes at Headquarters?" He signaled for the check. "Why aren't they under your name?"

"It has to do with my mother." She smiled at him. "Another long story, for another day...."

He walked her home afterward. "I'm starting to get hungry for recognition," he confessed. "I have as much talent as Halston or Bill Blass. I've just got to find a way to launch it."

"You just need contacts," she said. "Mackenzie told me she has a brilliant accountant—Ed something—who put their firm in shape. A talk with him wouldn't hurt...you need a brilliant accountant for costings."

"Yeah, she's very good about offering advice. I'm stubborn, I suppose. I want to do it on my own."

At the entrance to her apartment building, he kissed her cheek. "You'll stay in touch?" he asked.

"Yes. Thank you for a nice evening. I'm truly glad to have seen you again."

She watched him walk down the block. He hadn't asked for her phone number.

Donna Haddon Brooks ran her fingers through Howard Austin's curly dark hair.

"I missed you," she confessed. "I didn't think I would. I'd forgotten how smooth your skin is here...." She stroked his side, just under his rib cage.

"I didn't forget what *you* felt like!" he told her hoarsely, his mouth pressing her throat, his hands covering her breasts. "Mrs. Brooks...."

"Don't ever call me that," she warned. "Not you. Especially not you..."

It was two months after "the fashion marriage of the year," according to *WWD*, and Donna had that week become fashion editor of *Divine*.

They were both naked, lying in the bed of one of the larger Plaza suites overlooking the park, the occasional whinny of a horse sounding beneath their window. As

Labels had attracted more and more advertising from the manufacturers who could not ignore its enormous appeal, it was achieving the unbelievable feat of almost equaling *WWD*'s circulation after only a year. Fashion in the sixties was still a huge growth area.

"Even Lloyd reads your Tittle-Tattle page every day," Donna told him. "And not just to find out which drug Coral's taking."

"Do you ever feel guilty about her?" Howard asked. He twisted in bed so their bodies could press against each other. He loved finding new ways to touch her. He now nestled between her legs, his nose buried in her clean-smelling hair.

"The day will never come when I feel guilty about Coral," Donna said, absently tracing a finger down his stomach, coming to rest on his sex, which she cupped gently. "You don't know the havoc she creates at the office. If I do get rid of her, it'll save Lloyd an awful lot of money."

He pressed his lips against hers, silencing her; they could both feel the excitement stirring his body. "Let's not talk about her today," he murmured. "She always seems to be with us, like an invisible third person."

"Howard, we always said this would be just sex. But when Lloyd makes love to me, I feel so different. He'd do anything for me—kiss me, tongue me all night if I wanted him to. And I have an orgasm—I'm not going to lie to you. But, God, it's so different from what I have with you. It's more . . . clinical somehow. Detached. With you—"

She stopped as he quickly clambered onto her, entering her. "Oh, God," she groaned.

He made love to her with a new confidence. They had met many times since their affair began, each time at a different hotel; only Donna's honeymoon in New England had interrupted their meetings.

"You know what I'd really like today?" she said. "I'd like to surprise you." She pushed him off and jumped up.

"Hey!" Howard cried. "I was just starting to get going there—"

"C'mon!" she urged him, dressing quickly. "You get dressed, too."

They had only been in the room for half an hour, but he shrugged and dressed.

It was a marvelous spring day, a warm day that a New York April can suddenly conjure. Outside Donna ran toward the first horse-carriage waiting by the curb and clambered in.

Howard frowned. "This *is* a surprise! What if someone sees us?"

She laughed, catching his hand and pulling him in alongside her. "Do *you* ever look closely at people in horse carriages? We'll look like any out-of-town couple or honeymooners. . . ."

He regarded her bright pistachio Halston ultrasuede dress worn with matching pale hose, her hair tied back with a bright violet scarf. He laughed. "You don't look like an out-of-town anything."

The carriage was trotted gently into the park. Under the blanket they'd been given, Donna's fingers explored him busily. She unzipped his pants and held his sex in her hand until it grew to its full length. Gently caressing him, she leaned her head against his, looking up at the bright blue sky. He slipped his hands under the blanket, up between her legs, and was delighted to discover she was wearing stockings and a lacy garter belt. He reached into her panties and kneaded her. Their moans as they circled Central Park were politely ignored, or perhaps unheard, by the old driver. Howard slipped to the floor of the vehicle, at Donna's feet.

Later, any onlookers, if they peered right into the carriage, would have seen the shape of a man kneeling on the floor, his head and shoulders beneath the blanket, a woman sitting alone on the seat with her head thrown back, legs spread apart, gasping and moaning with pleasure. He made her come quickly, using only his tongue, alternating soft licking with stiff little jabs. Her hands held and guided his head, clutched his shoulders as waves of pleasure shook her, and the carriage seemed to add to the excitement—the danger as it bumped over the uneven roads, the horse clip-clopping, lurching around a curve.

Donna lay exhausted, fulfilled, on the seat next to him. She extracted a small tube of hand cream from her purse and, under cover of the blanket, held him in her slippery hand, caressing him to his peak of pleasure, feeling his sex pulse and release in her hand. Howard's eyes were tightly shut as he lay back, abandoning himself to her touch.

When the ride ended up back at the Plaza, their legs were trembling from the pleasure they had given each other. Howard tossed the driver a fifty-dollar bill.

Donna took the nearest waiting cab, blowing him a kiss. He shook his head as he walked back to his new offices on Madison. A blind item about the chic fashion editor of *Divine* and the publisher of *Labels* making out in a Central Park carriage would have pepped up tomorrow's Tittle-Tattle page; too bad he couldn't run it.

"Shit!" Mackenzie swore. She was sitting up in bed reading *Labels*, having turned straight to the Tittle-Tattle page, the column everyone in the trade read first.

> Which designer decided to surprise her boyfriend at a shooting of her clothes, only to discover that no one was wearing any? And that the high jinks were being photographed for ... er ... posterity! We're not telling, but the story's worth it's weight in ... gold!

She flung the paper to the floor. One of the assistants at the shooting must have blabbed. She'd show it to Alistair that night. She sipped her coffee, thinking. Her life was changing, and so was her relationship with Alistair. Just when she thought she had some kind of control over things, her life had turned upside down. Being pregnant was different enough, and after the events at Patrick's studio, there had been a week-long silence between them. Alistair had finally apologized and begged forgiveness, but she had the uneasy feeling he'd done it not because he loved her, but because life would be a lot more convenient with her. He had humiliated her, and she wasn't sure whether she could ever trust him again. He'd been a kind of Svengali for so long, however, that she was afraid of losing him. If she hadn't been carrying his child, she would probably have thrown him out. Forgiving him had been a major compromise in her life. She had only made it because she could not shake the conviction that her child should grow up with its father. She was fighting to establish her own philosophy of life, her own morality, uninfluenced by her mother's conventions or by her Village friends' Peace and Love philosophy. Life was much more complicated than she had expected: You couldn't always do exactly what you wanted to do. She had imagined that once she had money and fame, everything would be so easy. And now she knew she had to work out her own pure, honest, truthful way to live.

Eddie was very much on her mind, but now that she was pregnant and not even considering marriage, he obviously did not approve of her. He was keeping his distance now.

On top of everything else, there was the business to run and plan and try to maintain control of, and her brothers to keep up with and outwit. She didn't trust them either. She knew they would go to any lengths to cut costs, which meant her keeping an eye on them; they were even capable of switching to cheaper thread and cheaper buttons, behind her back. As Gold!'s production became so much bigger, as more clothes were manufactured to supply the demand, the unions and the labor force had to be dealt with and she tended to leave that to her brothers, knowing that she shouldn't. Now that they were manufacturing in California, they might contract some sweatshop in Los Angeles to sew the stuff under terrible conditions, paying less than basic wages and using illegal aliens as machinists. Her social conscience, developed in the Village days, recoiled at the idea, and made her even more wary in her dealings with them.

In fact, Mackenzie had come to dislike her brothers, Reggie in particular, since Max merely followed his lead. Instead of becoming more sophisticated as they became more successful, they had regressed in style and attitude. Every step away from the Bronx Mackenzie had taken, seemed to inspire them to embrace their roots. They shared an apartment a block away from their parents and Esther still cooked for them, did their laundry and generally babied them. Reggie was fat and they both dressed in a dull, dated way as if to spite Mackenzie's new chic image or to show her that they would never get personally involved in the fashion business by even attempting to dress stylishly. They made it very clear that for them fashion was purely a money-making racket.

As her pregnancy slowed her down, she worried about the baby's health. She went to bed early and refused to

eat in smoke-filled restaurants. It distanced her further
from Alistair, since he liked to go out every night, keeping
in touch with the in-crowd that haunted Max's Kansas
City, the Scene, and Arthur. "It's work, Mack," he assured her. She knew it was also a way for him to score
drugs.

Her workload finally became too much for her. She had
launched a jeans and denim line which was selling to
stores around the country under the Gold! label. There
was a knitwear range, a children's label, and various deals
with manufacturers making tights, berets, and shoes. She
was forced to surrender her reign as sole designer. Con-
ferring with the dean at MacMillans, she interviewed the
top graduating students, picking four to work for the
company.

"I'll train them to design in my vein," she told her
brothers at the next meeting neither Ed nor her father
attended. "I won't pass any garment that doesn't have my
stamp on it."

They regarded her bulging figure, now clothed in specially made smocks of bright corduroy with contrasting
braid trimming. "What about the opening of the L.A.
store?" Reggie asked her. "Think you'll make it?"

She sighed. "In this condition? They'll think I'm opening a tent store!"

"Maybe if you married your boyfriend," Reggie suggested,
"you'd look a little more respectable."

"You just stick to negotiating with truck drivers and
labor unions!" Mackenzie snapped. "That's what you're
best at. Leave the morality questions to me!"

"Children! Children!" Max said, imitating their father.

Reggie sneered. "What's with that guy anyway? He's
living off you, you know."

"No, he isn't!" Mackenzie denied hotly. "He does a
damn good job of getting us into the media. You think
that stuff just happens? Alistair charms them into it. They
love the fact that he's British—it give Gold! a good image
and—"

"Do they also love the fact that he's a pothead? A
British pothead?" Reggie laughed, his round, shiny face
gleaming.

"Our turnover is pushing a million, Mack," Max told
her. "This is not kid stuff anymore. Business people at

the bank are urging us to expand before other stores get there—places like San Francisco, San Diego—"

"I don't wanna get too big!" Mackenzie cried.

"Well, then you'd better quit right now, because this is gonna get *very* big!" Reggie warned. "And we can't afford anyone on the staff who isn't one hundred percent professional. I'm a square, right? But I read the papers. The comments on your protests, on Alistair screwing around and turning on—they are *not* good for our image. We sell to young girls—we need a clean, all-American image!"

"Fuck you!" Mackenzie shouted.

"Max and I own fifty percent of the company, we have a big say in what goes on. Make Alistair shape up or we'll fire the guy."

Mackenzie stared levelly at him, hating him. "Do that, and you lose your designer."

"There are other designers around," Reggie said darkly. Mackenzie laughed. "You think you're so indispensable?" Reggie asked. "No one's irreplaceable. Your stuff sells because of the label—not because *you* design it—"

"That's how little *you* know!" she shouted. "I sweat blood to come up with the right designs. I look at a thousand fabrics before I find just the right one. I—" She shook her head. "Oh, piss off—both of you—before I throw something at you."

Their meeting broke up early that day. Mackenzie complained about her brothers to everyone she could call that afternoon and evening, from Ed, to her father, to Alistair, to Mia.

"The figures are starting to frighten me now," she confided to Mia. "It's like I created a monster. It's going to get bigger and bigger and gobble up everything before it. I have four designers under me now, and it's so *weird*! I'm terrified of hurting their feelings if I criticize their designs! I wasn't cut out to be an employer."

"I know what you mean," Mia said. "I'm making more money than I ever imagined I'd make. It's really dumb to continue to live here with Wayland, but I haven't found the energy to start looking at apartments."

"I've *had* to look for offices and studios!" Mackenzie said. "I've found a floor just around the corner from Madison, on Fifty-ninth Street. Alistair will have a small office there, too. Oh, Mia, there are openings to attend,

talk shows to appear on, out-of-town stores that sell my
stuff where I do promos. . . ."

They commiserated with each other and groaned about
how tired they were.

Alistair had a family event to look forward to. Mackenzie
arrived home from a day in the studio later that week and
found him waving a letter at her. "My father's coming!"
he said, looking happy. "He got roped into promoting a
tweed factory! He gets a first-class plane ticket and three
Savile Row suits. Guess the old boy's a bit strapped for
cash—he never could resist a freebie!"

"So I'll get to meet him?" Mackenzie said, and collapsed
on the oversized couch, kicking off her shoes and sipping
apple juice.

"You two will get along well, I'm sure," he said, hugging her.

"If only he'd stay to see his grandchild born," she
replied wearily. "Lord Briarly, is that what I call him?"

"Well, since you won't marry me, you can hardly call
him Dad."

"Alistair, he won't have to meet my parents, will he?"

"Oh, don't start that up again! Afraid they'll offer him
chopped liver? He'd love it!"

She propped a cushion behind her head, closing her
eyes. She could hear Alistair roaming the apartment, opening and closing closet doors. She knew what he was
looking for. Finally he returned.

"Mack, where did you hide that bowl of grass?"

"I didn't hide it," she murmured, her eyes closed. "I
threw it out."

He stared at her. "*Why*? That was the best stuff we've
ever—"

She opened her eyes and looked directly at him. "I
don't want it around. When the baby's here, I don't want
it trying to eat the stuff, or breathing in the smoke, or
even growing up in that atmosphere. So get used to doing
without it—at home, at least."

"Do you know how much that stuff cost? It's the best
grass you can—"

"I don't care if it was Queen Elizabeth's fossilized *shit!*"
Mackenzie yelled. "You're too goddamned dependent on
it! I mean, okay, turning-on can be fun once in a while.
But between that and the speed shots and the booze, I

feel like I'm living with some fucking *addict*! I'm having your *child*, Alistair. You said you want to share the experience—well, are you going to *be* there for the kid or what?"

His face paled with anger. "I have a right to spend my money on whatever I choose!"

She sat up abruptly. "You think you're paying for this?" She gestured at the apartment. "You think your salary buys this kind of life? Those daily speed shots from that quack? Bowls of the best grass? Vintage wines? Let alone the rent on this place, which the company pays. You know better, Alistair. Now this is hurting me, and it's going to hurt my child."

"*Our* child!" he corrected her.

"Only if I agree to that. You're making my life very difficult. . . ."

"Mack, for God's sake, I love you. Please don't let's fight."

She shook her head. She put her arms around him. "Oh, Alistair, you're like a naughty schoolboy sometimes. What's happened to you? I used to be in such awe of you. You were Mister Everything to me. . . ."

He groaned, muttering something that was muffled in her shoulder.

"You say you love me, but you have to show me by the way you live that you love me. Your father's coming—try to get in shape, Alistair. Stop seeing that quack doctor for a while. Put on some weight. Walk a couple of miles in the park every day. . . ."

He lifted his head to kiss her. "Okay, I'll try, Mack, I promise."

He clung to her, slipping his hands down the neck of her dress and caressing her swollen breasts. Then he made love to her slowly and tenderly on the couch. He brought her to a climax, then to another and another. He was good at it, she had to admit. He clasped her to him as he came, and she felt his body release and go into its spasms inside her. But something was missing now. They went to bed early, and she was jostled by his cold, thin body as he slipped into bed beside her, hugging her from behind in his usual embrace before they fell asleep.

I guess I'll have to be the strong one, she thought. She was starting to think longingly of Ed, and hated herself for

that, but she had to try to make *this* relationship work—
she owed it to her child.

She left Alistair very early the next morning as he slept,
and hurried downtown to view proofs for the new advertising campaign. Their color catalog had meant working
months ahead of her usual schedule, producing advance
models. She had to beg fabrics manufacturers to release
advance yardage of fabric she'd chosen for her models.
Her designing now seemed to be one long fight against
time, racing against other designers and firms trying to
copy her styles.

The one aspect of her life she could control was not
seeing Ed. They tried to avoid each other, rarely attending
the same meetings. She had hardly allowed herself to
think about him—it was too confusing. Her mother kept
reminding her in their regular phone calls that she could
still legitimize the forthcoming grandchild if she chose to.
Instead, Mackenzie chose to throw herself into her work. It
was a great escape, keeping her too busy to brood.

She was still the hub around which Gold! turned. After
the employees left the company offices above the first
Gold! boutique that evening, Reggie and Max called a
meeting with the architects of the new Los Angeles Gold!
Her brothers had flown out several times to scout locations and supervise the construction. They had chosen a
large space on Melrose Avenue, just outside Beverly Hills.
While they were there, some of the Hollywood style had
rubbed off on them: They were starting to wear louder ties
and more obtrusive pieces of chunky gold jewelry. Mackenzie
had to bite her tongue not to tell them what she thought
of their new style.

From what she could see of the photographs and sketches,
the L.A. Gold! would be a deluxe version of her original
ideas for the first store, overlaid with Hollywood glitz. It
looked very exciting and colorful, but it was as if it were
happening on the moon. She hadn't had time to fly out
herself and look at it, and couldn't summon much interest
or energy in the project. This was unusual for her, for
she'd always taken an interest in the smallest detail of her
business. She put it down to her pregnancy and its tiring
side effects.

There were numerous details to wrap up before the
architects flew back to L.A., and Mackenzie was exhausted

when the meeting finally broke at eight. She tried calling Alistair at home, but no one answered. Having an uncontrollable craving for Mexican food, she decided to get takeout.

"Mom isn't well, you know," Max told her as she pulled on her coat.

"Yeah?" She looked concernedly at him. "I spoke to her last night and she didn't mention anything."

"She doesn't want you to know."

"Oh, God . . ." She hugged her coat around her. "Jewish secrets again? I suppose it's all the aggravation over me?"

"You guessed right. She cries herself to sleep nights. Dad told me. She'd like you to marry this guy, even though he's not Jewish."

Mackenzie walked toward the door. "The more you all nag me to marry, the less appealing marriage seems," she called back over her shoulder. "If *you* are all so keen on marriage, there must be something wrong with it."

She took a taxi to her favorite Mexican joint on Eighth Avenue and picked up containers of chile rellenos, burritos, and tacos. The driver waited and drove her back uptown as the meter went over twelve dollars.

She left the food in the kitchen and walked through the living room and studio, calling, "Alistair? I'm home!" She poked her head up the twisted staircase that linked the upstairs floor, then ran up it to their bedroom. The drapes were tightly shut—a strange sight: They never closed them, preferring to watch the sky. An ominous chord struck inside her. She ran into the bedroom. Alistair was crouched in a corner, on the floor, shaking.

"Alistair!" She ran over to him, crouching down next to him. "What is it? What have you taken?"

Alistair's haunted eyes simply stared at her as his lips tried to form words. He let out a soft moan.

"*What?*" she screamed, "For God's sake, *tell* me!"

"They're dead. . . ." His eyes were wide with disbelief. "My family is dead!"

"What d'you mean?" She clutched him, shook him. "*How?*"

He made an effort to pull himself together. "My father and brother took a helicopter to London. They were going to stay there a few days before they came here. The

helicopter crashed just outside London—everyone in it
was killed!" He fell into her arms, crying.

"Oh, God . . . no!" The horror coldly engulfed her body.
This was it . . . success! She hugged him fiercely, as if she
could squeeze the bad news away. For some reason she
felt as guilty as if the accident had been her fault. "I'm so
sorry, darling . . . so terribly sorry. . . ."

"I was never close to him," Alistair murmured. "Nor to
Ian. But you always hope to be friends one day. I thought
this visit would give me a chance to get to know them
better."

"How did you find out?"

"My sister rang me from London. I couldn't take it in.
I've been sitting here trying to believe it. The phone's
been ringing, but I couldn't pick it up."

The phone rang at that moment, startling them.

"Let it ring—I can't talk to anyone." He turned to her
and wrapped her in his arms. "Mack? I need you more
than ever now. . . ."

"Okay. Okay, darling," she soothed him, trying to think.
Things happened for a reason. It was part of the cosmic
pattern, her Village friends would say. Maybe this had
happened to help her decide to marry Alistair, to give *her*
child a father?

They sat in the corner of the bedroom for a long time.
The phone rang several times. She felt responsible for
Alistair, somehow, as if it were now up to her to redress
the balance, make life better for him.

Alistair finally said, "I need a stiff drink."

"I'll get it." She stood and stretched her arms, arching
her back.

In the kitchen she splashed a generous shot of bourbon
over some ice and took a sip herself. She felt its warmth
spread comfortingly in her stomach as she slowly climbed
upstairs. *I wonder if the baby could get drunk?* she wondered,
handing him the glass.

He drank quickly and turned to her with a strange
expression on his face. "I haven't told you the rest of the
story. I thought you might guess. . . ."

"Guess what?" She sat on the bed, watching him.

"*I'm* Lord Briarly now. I left England to escape that life,
and the title followed me here."

She frowned, staring at him, feeling the baby move in her stomach.

"Of course, I don't have to use the title," he reflected.

"Don't be silly," she said automatically. "Of course you'll use it. You think I'm not going to give birth to the child of a lord? Why, it's like some fairy tale! I'll be the Princess Grace of the Bronx. . . ."

They searched each other's faces. He couldn't help smiling at her words. "You still haven't put two and two together, have you, Mack?" he asked.

She shrugged. "You won't be quite a princess," he explained, "but if you marry me, you'd become Lady Briarly."

That was it! The excitement swept her body as it had when she'd won the *Divine* contest. The same half-scalding, half-freezing sensation at something fantastic coming true— something that would totally change her life. Lady Mackenzie Briarly! What girl alive could resist that?

"The first titled designer in the *schmatta* industry," she said dryly. "Not counting Comte Hubert de Givenchy. . . ."

Alistair gazed seriously at her, sipping his drink. "So? Will you marry me, Mack? Will you be Lady Briarly?"

"Lord and Lady Briarly!" Mackenzie said for the hundredth time. "My family will just pee in their pants!"

It was a week after the news about Lord Briarly's death had been announced. She had summoned Mia to the apartment. "I'm sorry—I can't really get that sad about a man I never met," she said. "I just keep picturing my parents' faces when they hear I'm Lady Mackenzie! And my brothers! Can you imagine? They think they're big shots because they stay near Beverly Hills when they visit L.A., and I'll be part of European nobility!"

Mia watched her. "Mackenzie," she said gently. "You shouldn't live your life trying to impress your family."

"Fuck *them!* I'm impressed! My child will be in society! It will be able to go anywhere. How can I deny my own child that opportunity?"

"You're listing every advantage to this marriage without mentioning one thing . . ."

"Like, do I love him?" Mackenzie asked angrily. "You're such a Pollyanna, Mia. What would you do if you were pregnant and walked in on your man screwing some

gorgeous model while a dozen creeps cheered them on like
it was a hundred-yard dash?"

"I—" Mia began.

"What would you do if that man became a lord and
asked you to marry him? What would you do if you knew
he was addicted to speed, dope, and just about every
controlled substance known to man? What if he—"

"Mackenzie!" Mia stopped her. "I'm sorry, but I just
don't understand you!"

"No...well...we're very different." Mackenzie popped
open a bottle of champagne and poured a tall thin flute
for each of them. "That's why you design elegant clothes
for classy ladies and I design stuff for crazy mixed-up
kooks like me. Our clothes reflect *us*, darling!" She held
the champagne glass up to clink against Mia's. "To...my
baby loving champagne! She's sure getting enough—I've
been drinking it all week."

"Why?" Mia took a sip. "Celebrating?"

"Oh..." Mackenzie looked searchingly into Mia's eyes,
then looked away. "I can't kid you—Mia, I'm in love with
another man. Have you ever heard anything so stupid?"

"That business manager who works for you?"

Mackenzie nodded. "Eddie...Oh, God, Mia...you're
so lucky to be cool. I wish I could be cool. I wish I'd never
laid eyes on him."

Mackenzie lay back on the sofa, her feet up. "I've
always wanted certain things. *This*"—she gestured at the
apartment—"is what my entire life was aimed at! And a
man—a loving, caring man—I certainly wasn't thinking of
a *titled* man! If I read about myself now in some magazine,
how I'd envy me!"

Mia continued to watch her, saying nothing.

"Oh, God!" Mackenzie raised her eyes to heaven. "Why
couldn't Ed Schreiber have been a lord? Would that have
been too perfect?"

"Is Alistair being a lord so important to you?" Mia
asked.

"Everything about Eddie is exciting to me," Mackenzie
chattered on, as if she hadn't heard. "I like a man who
looks sort of...chunky? Teddy bearish? And what does
he have to be? An accountant, adding up the money
everyone else makes! I can imagine dining out with Eddie:
He'd gulp down any wine they brought and say 'Fine!'

Alistair talks with the wine waiter for hours. When they finally bring some dusty old bottle from the cellars, he turns it into an Academy Award-winning performance...."

"So what?"

"I *like* a man who knows how to do that! That savvy! I was deprived of it in my childhood, Mia. You had your mother and her friends to watch. I had Abe Goldstein! You think he knew from Château Rothschild? He was happy if there was a can of *beer* in the fridge! Even when I was a kid I used to gag on Manischewitz! I've grown to appreciate the finer things in life—this champagne we're drinking is Dom Pérignon. Did ya see the label? And now this lord falls in my lap... why, I'd be out of my mind not to marry him!"

"Have you asked yourself whether he'd be marrying you if you weren't so successful?" Mia asked her. "It seems to me he enjoys the good life, too."

Mackenzie glared at her friend. "That's a lousy thing to say!"

"*Why?* You still haven't said you love him!"

"He loves *me!*" Mackenzie cried. "Get it? He loves *me!* Sometimes that's enough! Life isn't always a fairy-tale, dearie! *His* love will see us through. My child will have a father. And I'll get what *I* want out of it."

"That's treating marriage as if it's some kind of bargain basement."

"Better than treating life as if it's a convent!" Mackenzie shot back. "Have you been to a therapist yet?"

Mia's lip trembled. "What are you talking about?"

"For your frigidity problem? I don't know why I listen to you—you don't know what goes on between men and women. That's really why your clothes are so different: Yours are so ladylike and constipated while mine are so sexy and funky!"

There was a horrible silence. Mackenzie realized she'd been cruel, and sipped her champagne quietly, like a naughty child.

Mia got to her feet, staring at Mackenzie. "That's an unforgivable thing to throw in my face," she said. "I told you all that in confidence. But whatever I am, I'm more honest than you. I'd never marry some poor sap I didn't love for his stupid *title!* What's the good of everyone kowtowing to you as a lady if you're miserable with him and pining for Ed?"

She walked quickly to the front door.

"I *won't* be miserable!" Mackenzie yelled.

"Well, you *should* be!" Mia slammed the door behind her.

Twenty-one

Mia walked angrily out of Mackenzie's apartment building and down Madison to Fifty-seventh Street. Some friendship! She was furious with herself for ever having confided in Mackenzie. Mackenzie was simply not that interested in her life. She hadn't thought to ask how her meeting with David went, whether her clothes were selling well, or anything else. Everything revolved around Mackenzie's own life and problems.

Mia turned right on Fifty-seventh and crossed the street to peer in the Henri Bendel windows. Some Zandra Rhodes evening gowns were fluttering on tall, faceless mannequins. An enormous fan ruffled the layered, pastel-tinted chiffon. Mia stared, hypnotized by the ethereal clothing.

Could Mackenzie possibly have been right about her being frigid? People like Mackenzie had an instinct about these things. She had preferred to blame David for his lack of finesse. It had been more comfortable to believe that if Phillipe ever made love to her, it would be perfect. But being called frigid hurt so much that there might well be some truth to it.

She had not seen David since that evening in the Russian Tea Room. She could see then that he still wanted her. She would meet him again, get him to make love to her . . . gently, carefully. It was the only way. It was still early and she decided to call David now. First she had to call Mackenzie to get David's number, which was humiliating but she didn't care. David agreed to meet her at the coffee shop on West Fifty-seventh Street—the same one where she had first met Mackenzie. As she hung up, she felt a faint pang of shame that she could get him to drop everything at a moment's notice.

She was sipping hot chocolate, watching the street, when a cab pulled up and David's tall, athletic figure bounded out. She watched as he paid off the driver. He was so good-looking and strong, what girl wouldn't like him? He spotted her through the window and waved, smiling.

She stood to hug him. He felt solid, reliable, exactly what she needed at that moment.

"Hey!" He looked at her with surprise. "Did I suddenly get lucky or something?"

Embarrassed, she let him go, and he bent to kiss her forehead. "I'm sorry," she said. "I got a bit emotional tonight. I was with Mackenzie and we had a row. I walked out on her and was on my way home when I suddenly realized how much I'd like to see you."

He grinned, sitting down opposite her. "Well, here I am!"

"You never liked Mackenzie, did you?" she asked. "Tonight she was such a bitch!"

He shrugged. "I can take her or leave her. What were you fighting about?"

"She—" Mia looked away from his penetrating eyes. "We don't agree about anything. . . ."

After the waitress took his order, David asked, "Still missing Paris?"

"I'm assimilating," she smiled. "New York's okay. Before you know it, it starts feeling like home."

David hunched forward, his large frame crushed in the narrow booth. "Last time, you were going to tell me about Roux's technique. You said he used some kind of pad for making up clothes?"

"Yes. He holds it inside the shoulder or bodice as he steams it."

"Is that what gives his clothes that sculptured look?"

"Right—he *shrinks* the shape into the fabric. . . ."

"I *see!*" David clasped his hands on the table excitedly. "It's not a technique for ready-to-wear, but it could sure make the sample models look a lot better. I'm getting a small collection together. It's taking a long time but—" He sat back as the waitress brought his order. He shoved a paper napkin over to Mia. "Could you sketch the shape of the pad he uses?"

Mia frowned. "This is starting to be an interrogation."

He reached for the napkin and crumpled it. "You're right. I'm sorry. I just never know quite how to . . . to *be* with you, Mia. I guess I try to keep it impersonal, but . . ." He looked intently in her eyes. "You know, I'd rather be telling you how beautiful you are. . . ."

She returned his gaze. "Maybe that's what I need to hear tonight." She placed her hand on his. "The last time we met, you didn't even ask for my number. . . ."

"Mia, you know I've always been crazy for you. Don't be coy with me, okay? I'll lose my respect for you. I've tried to wipe you out of my life . . . I wish I could. I'm considering a lobotomy. . . ." He smiled. "It's just that—well, ever since the day I met you I've had this loony conviction that you and I . . . belong together. I don't know why I still believe that; you certainly haven't encouraged me."

"Until tonight . . ." she raised her eyebrows.

"And why is tonight so different? You quarreled with Mackenzie and found yourself at loose ends?"

She shook her head. "Don't!" she begged. "Please don't, David. Mackenzie really got me thinking tonight. She said some very cruel things, but there's often truth in a cruel remark."

"I see . . ." He looked at her interestedly. "Well, I won't probe any deeper. I should be grateful to Mackenzie for sending you my way. . . ."

Outside on the street he put his hands on her shoulders and she let him kiss her, gently, slower this time, feeling the tip of his tongue just graze her lips. "Take me home," she whispered.

David watched her, his blue eyes fragmented into chips of color. "Are you sure that's what you want?" he asked. "Remember what happened last time? I don't think I could take that again."

"It'll be different," she whispered, holding his arm. "You'll be very gentle. We have to try. Don't you think?"

"Oh, Mia . . ." He nuzzled her cheek with his nose. "If you knew how much I want you . . ."

In the taxi to his apartment she held his large hands tightly, willing the strength of him to flow into her. She

wanted to be enfolded in two strong, confident arms that
knew what they wanted. She recalled Mackenzie's words:
"He loves *me* . . . sometimes that's enough."

As soon as he unlocked the apartment, she remembered his style: white, straightforward, and spare. She
stood on tiptoe, her arms around his neck, pressing
against his body.

"Love me," she whispered. "Love me, David."

He covered her lips with his warm mouth and, without
interrupting the kiss, carried her into the bedroom. As
bare as the other room, it held a large white bed and a
pine dresser. He set her gently down on the bed, breaking
away to remove his jacket. As he knelt at her side, she
recognized the fresh clean smell of him. The hall light lit
his face as he brushed his lips against hers. Carefully, he
loosened her clothing and removed it, and she helped
him, realizing she felt no shyness. She was proud of her
body; Phillipe Roux had made love to it. David looked
down at her when she was naked, undressing hurriedly.

"You have the most beautiful body," he told her, tracing
his fingers down her side. "Your torso . . . the way your
breasts point so perfectly . . . that flat stomach . . ."

He was in his underwear but she could see that just
looking at her aroused him. She placed her hand on the
thick outline of his sex. Why did she find this hard muscle
so frightening? She felt it move under her fingers. She
knew if she dragged down the elastic waistband, it would
leap out at her.

"Please, turn out the lights," she asked.

He did, returning to kneel beside her on the bed, his
face hovering over her breasts. He was naked now, and
she saw his erect outline. She touched him there and he
groaned. Bending, he lapped gentle circles around her
breasts with his tongue.

"I can't believe this is happening, Mia," he whispered.
"I wanted you so much. It was starting to become an
obsession . . . you were all I could think about."

"Oh, God, be gentle with me, David." She trembled.
"Be as gentle as if I were a fragile porcelain doll."

"Yes. Oh, yes, my darling; I would never do anything
to hurt you. Do you like to be touched here?" He lightly
brushed her nipples, the gentle touch of his fingertips

making them hard. "And here?" he bent to nuzzle her thighs.

"I don't know!" she whispered urgently. "I don't *know!*"

It was true: His touch aroused and disturbed her, the pleasure drowned out by the dread and expectancy of what was to come. She tried to relax. She arched her back, giving her body over to him, letting his hand, his fingers, slide between her legs, caress her. She squeezed her legs together on his hand. She tried a dirty trick: substituting Phillipe for him. She let her hands roam over his naked, muscular back, his hard, square shoulders, pretending she was holding Phillipe. But she knew it was David's back she felt, broader than Phillipe's, and younger. Why had it been so much more exciting with Phillipe in Paris? She could not help comparing. Phillipe had wanted her, but he would never have made a move if she had not pressed him. She pushed to the back of her mind this quick glimpse into herself, this sudden insight into why it was exciting when she was the instigator. She concentrated instead on what David was doing—teasing the tips of her breasts, breathing on them with hot, moist breath and finally taking one into his mouth, gently sucking. It tickled. It connected with sensations she began to feel in her groin. As he kissed her now, probing her mouth with his tongue, she gently stroked the back of his head, feeling the width of his neck. His urgent hardness pressed against her body.

"Now, David, I want you to do it now," she whispered.

He hovered over her. "Are you sure you're ready?"

No! God, *no!* She would never be! She was like a child about to take its first frightening ride at the fairground, half-wanting, half terrified. Everyone else was loving the ride—everyone else was laughing and enjoying it: They wrote songs about it, saying it was the very best thing you could do in life—being in love, *making* love!

"Don't ask anymore!" she begged, almost sobbing. "Just do it! *Do* it!"

She felt hysterical, angry; she wanted to scream. Why was the most exciting thing in most women's lives an ordeal to her? Yes, she was a virgin and she was ashamed of it. It made her sick. She wanted to be like other women. She wanted to forget Phillipe. She wanted a real lover, even if it meant submitting to this—this bitter medicine wrapped in a sugarcoating of affection. . . .

But she did enjoy the affection. When David enfolded her, his arms around her and under her back, she liked the closeness. Then he held her so tightly she was afraid her ribs might crack. It felt as if he were scared she might buck from beneath him. His mouth was close to her ear, groaning into it, and she felt his body raise, his feet move to each side of her. She parted her legs. He jiggled his body into place, easing the tip of himself into her as she held her breath. Her instinct was to push him off her, out of her, but she lay still. He moved very gently, easing a little more into her, a fraction at a time, slowly, until he was fully inside her. She hardly dared breathe.

His "Aaahhh" told her how good it felt for him, and then he was pushing himself back and forth inside her as she held onto his shoulders and pushed back at him, her head to one side. She bit her lip, praying he would not prolong this and that he'd reach his pleasure quickly. Then they could dress and continue with their evening, talking and laughing as though this had not happened, as though people did not have to do this to become close, to become lovers.

"I'm not hurting you, darling, am I?" he whispered.

Mia shook her head violently, clenching her teeth to keep them from chattering. "Just come!" she urged. "Come as soon as you like."

"My poor baby . . ." He quivered inside her, grinding his hips to hers. He held on to her body like a man at sea, his body moving with the current, away from her, toward her, panting softly.

As his body began to tense, she knew he was near. He suddenly planted his mouth over hers, then broke away, upward, to cry "Oh, *God*! Oh, *Mia*!" His body made the convulsions and spasms she remembered so well from the first time. She felt his sex pulse inside her, his pleasure spasm, his long drawn-out cry of pleasure signaling his ecstasy. The tremor ran the length of his body, ending with a sigh of exhaustion and contentment. She felt a kind of pride at having submitted to this without screaming aloud. Through gritted teeth she had conquered one part of her fear.

In another moment he had kissed her fingers and

murmured, "Thank you." Then his breath became even, deeper. She wriggled her body away from his, until he was no longer inside her. Soon he was asleep. . . .

"I'll be a *lady*, mother," Mackenzie said. She sat hunched forward on a chair, facing her mother in the old family dining room. Her dream that Esther's life would be magically changed by their success had not come true. Her parents had resisted the idea of moving to a house or a more luxurious apartment. A fresh coat of cream paint had not much changed the look of the apartment. It smelled the same. Esther hung onto her old furniture as if her peace of mind was contained in it. It always gave Mackenzie a creepy, depressed feeling to visit.

"Lady Mackenzie Briarly," Mackenzie repeated, because Esther had not seemed to take it in. "Lord and Lady Briarly—"

"Stop saying the same thing to me as if I were an idiot!" Esther suddenly snapped. "I don't care if he makes you the Queen of Sheba—do you love him?"

Mackenzie laughed, breathless: "Would I live with a guy for so long if I didn't?"

"You see?" Esther pounced. "You're answering my question with another question. You won't come right out and say, 'Yes, Ma, I love him.' Let me hear you say that."

Mackenzie shook her head. "I'm not a ventriloquist's dummy, Ma. Don't tell me what to say." She looked away from her mother's gaze and stared at the tumbler of lemon tea her mother had pressed upon her, the homemade kugel nestling alongside. She bit into it. "You still make the best kugels, Ma," she said.

"Now she thinks I'll get off the subject if she flatters me!" Esther announced to the room. "I'll tell you what *I'd* like to know about, young lady. What about Ed?"

Mackenzie started, her eyes widening. "Who are you talking about? Our business manager? What does he have to do with anything?"

"Eddie's like a third son to me," Esther told her. "He confides in me. His mother died when he was just a kid. He can't compete with this Alistair. He won't be a lord. But he's a fine man, and he loves you, Mackenzie. I know he does."

"He had some nerve to tell you that!" Mackenzie said,

her eyes blazing. "Alistair loves me, too! And he at least tells *me* about it! God, Ma, a million girls would give anything to become a lady. Alistair's chosen *me*! Why can't you be happy for me, and proud?"

"I'll be proud if you've chosen your husband for the right reasons. Not because you'll be Lady somebody but because you love him as much as if he were a plain old nobody."

Mackenzie glared at her. "I couldn't love a nobody. Why should I? I've accomplished a hell of a lot in my life—I want my husband to have equal accomplishments."

Esther snorted. "He inherited a title? *That's* an accomplishment? Eddie put himself through college!"

Mackenzie bit back her retort. She shook her head and made herself sit there for another hour, under her mother's disapproving eyes.

In the taxi back to Manhattan, she had to admit that Esther was right. She glanced at her black-lacquered nails. This feeling of matricide swept over her only when her mother was right. Yes, she was probably marrying Alistair for all the wrong reasons, and everyone knew it. She twisted impatiently on the seat, biting her lower lip, then leaned forward to draw back the Perspex partition.

"I've changed my mind. Take me to Second Avenue and Seventy-ninth!"

She would confront Eddie, settle things with him once and for all. She'd forbid him to confide in her mother—she didn't need that kind of emotional blackmail. Automatically her fingers delved into her huge cheetah-patterned purse and she began to put on makeup. It was more professional to be well-groomed for Ed, she told herself. It would show she meant business.

Telling the driver to wait, she ran up the flight of stairs that led to the company offices. She had a million other things to do, but this came first. She would take no nonsense from him; would tell him to stay out of her life now; to never contact her mother; to—

"*Yes?*" asked a new receptionist, looking up from her desk as Mackenzie entered the office.

"Is Ed in?"

"Who should I say wishes—"

Mackenzie continued walking, calling back over her shoulder, "I know my way."

She pulled open the door to Ed's office, and walked in. He jumped up from behind his desk, a surprised look on his face. Slamming the door behind her, she leaned back on it, glaring at him, her eyes flashing. She'd hyped herself into such a state of anger that for a moment she forgot what she was angry about. Ed was in shirt-sleeves and old-fashioned suspenders, his hair falling in his eyes, his rolled-up sleeves revealing muscular arms. His eyes were at their darkest, most intense navy, questioning her unexpected appearance.

Mackenzie said, "I came to see you because—" and stopped as he took a step toward her.

They stared at each other for one frozen second, and then their mouths were pressed together, open, tongues exploring wetly, kissing, breathless with a lust that surprised both of them. *This is what we've wanted to do ever since we met*, she thought, sucking on his moving tongue. Every resolution in her dissolved at his touch: His mouth, his body were all that mattered. She felt him bear down on her, press her back to the door. Her hands groped behind her for the key and she turned it.

Gasping, her mouth bruised, she broke away. "This is *crazy!*" she whispered urgently.

But he'd already thrust both his hands up under her top, caressing her breasts, his touch causing her nipples to spring erect. He nuzzled her neck, her ear, making her moan. He dropped his hand to her mound, fondling her.

"You're out of your mind!" she whispered, but she pulled off her skirt with one hand, clutching his head to her, wanting him closer, harder, *inside* her.

Quietly, swiftly, they arranged his jacket and her sweater on the floor and dropped onto them, pulling off their remaining clothes. She could not believe the marvelous feel of Eddie's face nuzzling her naked breasts, kissing and nibbling them. She had never wanted any man this much.

"Oh, baby... baby," he moaned. "I must have wished you into coming here."

He put his hand between her legs, stroking her firmly with his thumb. She thrust her body against his as, naked and breathless with desire, they relished the first, wonderful feeling of their bodies against each other, his skin against hers. Then Ed—her wonderful Eddie, was inside

her, and it was so incredible, she could barely catch her
breath.

"I'll *die!*" she gasped. "It's too good!"

She pushed down on his thick hardness, getting him as
far inside her as she could. It felt both new and as if they
had done this many, many times before. Moving her
groin, she slid up and down on him, her mouth dry as
she gasped from the delicious pleasure. Opening her
eyes, she found his dark blue ones an inch away, heavy-
lidded, looking into hers. They stared into each other's
eyes as he continued to rhythmically move his body
against her, inside her.

"Kiss me, Eddie . . ."

She pursed her lips, and he lowered his mouth to cover
them, sucking gently on her tongue. As he pumped
against her body, he took each nipple between his thumb
and third finger and gently pinched.

"Oh, my God!" Her climax came so quickly she could
not help a cry escaping her, and he held a hand over her
mouth to quieten her. The waves of pleasure amazed her
with their keen intensity. She hooked her legs up behind
Ed's back, making herself hollow for him, wanting more
of him, wanting him deeper, deeper inside her. As he
moved faster, his bearlike body almost covered her face,
spattering her with droplets of his sweat. She pressed her
face up into his chest, relishing its maleness. Alistair was
white, hairless. This was animal-like, sexy, exciting.

Her pleasure came again and again until it was too
much to take. Great shattering rushes of sensation elevated her to another dimension. Tears flowed down each
side of her face as they clutched each other, rocking on
the floor. And now, as Ed moaned uncontrollably in her
ear and she felt his body tense for his release—felt his sex
expand and throb inside her—she suddenly understood
what it was that two lovers were intended to achieve. *This*
was making love—the full sensual and emotional impact
of it—the emotion that had always been missing from the
technically perfect lovemaking with Alistair.

She watched Ed's head jerk back as he came, biting his
lip in ecstasy, his eyes tightly shut. As he slowly stopped
moving, he let his head come to rest on her breast. She
put her arm around him and held him tenderly to her,
their sweat mingling, his brown hair tickling her collarbone.

"Oh God, Eddie," she gasped as the echoes of her pleasure softly ebbed. "I have *never*, *never*—" She shook her head, still breathless. "That was the real thing. There's no point in telling you that, but—"

"Why is there no point?" he demanded, raising his head. "Don't you think it was the real thing for me, too? Do you think *I've* ever felt like that before with a woman?"

"I don't know. I only know this must never happen again!"

"Oh, *please*!" He laughed, jerking his body back to look down at her. "You think something as good as us together stands a *chance* of not happening again? I'd just like to be in a *bed* the third time we make love."

"The *third* time? What about the second?"

"*This* was the second!"

"Really? So when was the first?" She looked into his eyes, which sparkled mischievously.

"You really don't remember?" he asked her. "You were all of sixteen, and you wanted a black leather jacket *so* bad you'd have screwed every kid on the block to get one. I just happened to be the last boy, remember? I can still feel that concrete floor! At least we progressed to a wood one today!"

"Oh, God . . . oh, wow!" Mackenzie cried. "I remember! You were the cute one at the end. And I had my first orgasm with you! Of course, I didn't realize it at the time!" She stared at him, her eyes wide with horror. "You knew all the time and you never said anything? You bastard!"

He laughed. "Oh? When your brothers introduced us, I should have said 'Hi! I'm the guy you screwed for a leather jacket'?"

He planted his mouth on hers, and she relaxed in his grip. He had the kind of mouth she could go on kissing forever. She could not get enough of him. But she made a supreme effort, and pushed him away, pulling herself to her feet by grasping the edge of his desk.

"I gotta go." She picked up her clothes and hurriedly dressed. "I only came to—" She frowned, tying a belt. ". . . to tell you that we mustn't see each other again. And I don't want you whining to my mother. I'm marrying Alistair."

"Don't give me that crap!" he said, dressing too. "You're

as crazy about me as I am about you. I can *feel* it—*here!*"
He placed his hand on her mound and squeezed gently.

She leaned against him, letting him touch her. Desire
leapt up in her again, and she moaned. "Oh, God, I could
do it all again with you right now, Eddie." She broke
away, looking for her shoes. "But I have to go—"

"I love you, Mackenzie," Ed said softly, watching her
pull on her shoes. His eyes brimmed with feeling. "I've
never said that to anyone before. . . ."

"That's great!" Mackenzie joked, keeping her back to
him. "And I guess you'd like to marry me and adopt our
little blond child when I have it?"

"I'd do that," he said, staring at her as she turned to
face him. "I told you, I love you."

She looked into his navy eyes and nodded. "Yeah," she
said. Inside, she answered: Oh, and I love you, too, my
Eddie. God, am I crazy about you. But I'm going to marry
Alistair. . . ."

She had no need to speak the words. She could see in
his face that he knew everything she was thinking. Her
silence said more than any muttered excuse and his expression became grim as he finished dressing. They said
nothing else; the situation was set. Not even their passionate time together could change it.

Just before she opened the door to leave, he pulled her
urgently to him. "Don't marry that guy," he said. "It'll be
a big mistake."

She gave him a steely-eyed look and unlocked the door,
blowing him a sad kiss.

She set the wedding date with Alistair that night.

Mia carefully eased out from under David's arm, which
had pinned her to the bed. He rolled over onto his side,
grunting. His bedside clock showed three a.m. Dressed,
she stood by him, watching his swimmer's body rise and
fall with his deep breathing. He was handsome, desirable;
his body would please any woman. Pulling down the
covers, she studied him. His sex hung limply now. What
made it so frightening when it was hard? She replaced the
covers, and he tugged them to his shoulders in his sleep.

She pressed her forehead to the cold glass of the bedroom window, staring into the harsh glow of a streetlight.
Could anywhere be bleaker, more lonely than a Manhat-

tan street at three A.M.? she wondered. A car or two
passed, a drunk, a taxi, a police car. *Phillipe, Phillipe . . . are*
you awake, somewhere in Paris, perhaps thinking of me now?
You could have helped me. . . .

Finding a notepad in the kitchen, she wrote: "David,
dear—you are a special person. I want to always be your
friend. Please forgive me—I could not sleep. Went home.
See you. Love, M."

Mia tiptoed back to the bedroom and left the note on
his pillow. She found her coat and was walking to the
door when a hand touching her shoulder made her cry
out, her whole body jolting in fright. Spinning around,
she faced David, naked in the dark.

"How could you just run away like this?" he asked
gruffly.

"I—I couldn't sleep," she stammered. "I left you a
note—"

"Are you trying to make me feel like a leper again?"

Mia heaved a great sigh. "No. No, you know it's
nothing like that. I just—" She shook her head helplessly.

"Mia . . ." He put his arm around her. "Are you going to
let me love you?"

She stood frozen still. "Maybe it's better if you don't. . . ."

"But I don't understand!" he cried. "This was *your* idea!
Remember?"

She broke away from him, sitting down on a chair near
the front door, her face in her hands.

He knelt by her side. "Was it so awful? Am I that
clumsy?"

She lifted her face from her hands and looked at him.
She could see the hurt in his eyes. In the dark, his
powerful body and broad shoulders reflected the glow
from the street and shone palely.

"I don't enjoy sex, David!" she blurted out. "I *want* to! I
wanted to so much! I thought tonight might be different. I
thought if *I* instigated it, it would seem less . . . I don't
know—threatening."

David shook his head disbelievingly. "Mia, I only want
to make you happy."

"I know. I *know*!" A tear began its slow trickle down her
cheek as she stared at him.

"Is it only me?" he asked. "Or is it any man?"

"I haven't tried that many men. . . ."

"Can't we find a way to deal with it?" He took her hand. "Mia, this is my life, too! If you have this problem, I'll help you with it." He watched her sad face for a moment, then smiled. "We can always practice a lot!"

She recoiled from him. "Yes, that would be fun for *you!*"

He stood as she did, his face changing. "You're really still in love with Phillipe Roux, aren't you? Isn't that what this is really all about?"

She leaned against the wall wearily. "No. You haven't heard anything I've said, David. What I wrote in that note was true. I want us to be friends. I think you're a special person. Okay? But now I want to go home...."

He seemed about to plead with her, but instead his expression became stony. Silently he opened the door for her.

Mia walked out without touching him. In the elevator her eyes filled with tears. No self-pity, she told herself. You have everything any girl could want, but there is something wrong with you. Something terribly wrong. No! she thought. She could not accept that. It's just that I'm still terribly in love with Phillipe.

She walked several blocks in the chilly night air. At least she was no longer a virgin, she thought bleakly. To make herself feel better, she vowed that no man would ever be allowed to enter her except Phillipe. She'd been put under some kind of spell by him, a spell that erected an invisible screen between her and other men. She almost managed to convince herself that it was not a problem at all, but simply a beautiful secret.

She found a cab and arrived home at three-thirty. Closing the front door softly behind her, she tiptoed into Wayland's apartment and heard noises coming from his bedroom: whoops, yells, and the sound of a breaking glass. Her eyes wide, she listened for a moment, and in her disturbed state imagined someone beating up Wayland. She knocked on his bedroom door. There was silence. Then Wayland finally said, "Yes?"

"It's me, Mia. Is everything all right?"

He opened the door and peeked out. He was naked, from what she could see. "The boys are a little noisy tonight," he whispered. "I'll get them to cool it. Sorry, pet!"

She felt nauseous when he closed the door. She ran to her bathroom and threw up in the sink. A feeling of déjà vu pervaded her. She took a long, hot shower, her mind whirling, and roughly toweled herself dry. Crazed thoughts raced through her brain: She wanted to phone her mother, to put through a call to Phillipe Roux just to hear his voice, to jump on a plane and go somewhere—anywhere that was neither Paris nor New York. To jump out of her skin!

She went to bed and tried to sleep, but her half dreams were nightmares of sexual images. She saw all the people she knew at an orgy—Wayland with an entourage of male hookers, Mackenzie hugely pregnant, Alistair cavorting with a faceless model, her mother trying to seduce Phillipe. David was cracking a huge whip, and she was naked and horribly ashamed, her hands tied to a ring in the wall. Suddenly, she sat up in bed, damp, tired, trembling; it was 6:45. She realized that there was only one person in New York who could give her advice.

At seven-thirty Mia walked slowly down Lexington Avenue toward Beaumont's apartment. Lack of sleep made her feel as if she were still in a dream. She didn't even know why she was doing this except that she had to talk to *someone*. She'd never gotten to know Colin well, but had heard so much about him, first from her mother, then from Wayland. She had always been intrigued when they met, wanting to know him better, wanting to ask him so many questions. She had heard that he advised people, and, perhaps because he was so tiny and talented, he had a mystique that attracted. It attracted her to him this morning.

It was a gusty morning, and most of the streets were deserted. New York looked like a foreign city to her. A coffee shop or two were open, and she looked in and saw people eating their breakfast, usually alone. The idea of food repulsed her. At a corner pay phone she dialed Colin's number.

Colin did not sound at all surprised to be hearing from her, out of the blue, so early in the morning. "There's a coffee shop on the corner of Lexington and Fifty-first," he instructed. "Would you mind meeting me there? I'll be fifteen minutes..."

She found the shop and waited, sipping coffee, wondering what she was going to say to him.

He bustled in after ten minutes, slipping into the booth opposite her, wearing his usual uniform of black corduroy pants and black turtleneck.

"What a lovely surprise!" He leaned over the table to kiss her cheek. "I've been worried about you: living with Wayland, cut off from your mother—"

"How is she?" Mia blurted out. "I have so many things to ask you...."

Colin regarded her seriously. The waitress came for his order, refilling Mia's cup. "You want the unvarnished truth?" he asked. "Are you ready for it? I know you're going through a very difficult time right now—"

"How do you know?"

He laughed softly. "Well, I'm not so vain that I think beautiful girls come by early in the morning merely for my company. You came because you're in some kind of trouble, right? Emotional turmoil, I'd say, from the look of you...."

Mia looked away from his kind, penetrating gaze. "I really needed... someone to talk to," she murmured. "I know we're not that close, but... you've always seemed such a level-headed, sympathetic person. I mean, from what I've heard of you...."

Colin smiled. "I do seem to have developed a reputation for sorting out people's problems. I can't think why. My own life is far from perfect...."

"It's because you're *good!*" Mia blurted out. He raised his eyebrows, then sat back as the waitress set a plate before him. He took a bite of his scrambled eggs, chewing slowly, before replying. "I've always felt somewhat of an observer of life. Maybe that gives me a clearer view?" He took a sip of coffee. "Now listen, Mia. I need *your* help, too. I need you to help me with someone who is slowly destroying herself. Someone I love and admire too much to just stand by and witness this... disintegration."

"Not my mother?"

He nodded. "She's in a pretty bad state. It's the drugs, of course: Those so-called vitamin shots from a quack Doctor Feelgood. It's affecting her work. If she keeps it up, I see her out of her job within a year or two, unemployable!"

"Oh, God..." Mia leaned her chin on her hands. "I had no idea. Wayland doesn't see her anymore, so I hadn't heard any of this from him."

"Since he dropped out of her life, she's gotten worse. But there's a ray of hope, Mia." He smiled at her. "She's absolutely bananas about a new young designer she feels she's discovered. One Anais Du Pasquier!"

"You know?" Mia asked.

"Don't worry—the secret is safe with me. Wayland showed me the clothes, and I guessed they were yours. You're an extremely talented designer, Mia. You've hit on a section of the market nobody was catering to, and you've kept it fashion."

"It's so funny that she likes them...." Mia smiled ruefully. "I always thought mother would love my clothes if she didn't know *I'd* designed them."

Colin leaned toward her: "Mia, will you do something for her?"

"What? She won't even *see* me!"

"Wayland told me you don't give interviews. You've ensured the mystery and anonymity of Anais. Why not give your mother a real fashion scoop? Allow Headquarters to set up an interview with her: When she arrives, she'll meet *you!*"

"And you think we'll fall into each other's arms, vowing eternal devotion?" Mia stared at him sadly. "Oh, Colin, she'd just turn around and walk off."

"Perhaps you're right," Colin acknowledged. "But we have to do something, try anything, to help her." He signaled for the check. "Would you like to see what a disheveled, untidy, shabby place an illustrator can turn his apartment into?"

When they got to his place, she glanced around at the sparsely furnished room and cleared a pile of magazines off a sofa. Colin's latest drawings hung on the walls: beautiful, colorful renditions of clothes from Bill Blass, Halston, and Geoffrey Beene.

"You've made them look so lush, so sculptural!" she congratulated him.

Colin drew up a chair opposite the sofa, his eyes concerned and grave. "Why did you want to see me?" he asked. She relaxed against the sofa cushions and took a deep breath. "I know I should find a shrink but I can't quite bring myself to do that. I figured you would be the next best thing—if you have the time." He leaned forward and concentrated on her. She told him her story. No one had ever listened to her the way Colin did now. He had a quality of listening that made what she said sound more intelligent than she could phrase it, made her feel interesting, valuable. Recounting her life was an enormous luxury. She was not even embarrassed by the sexual details which she described almost as if they were someone else's symptoms. Colin's interested expression put her life into perspective, into proportion. His presence, the lack of blame or criticism or shock, ironed out her panic, her hysteria.

When she came to the end, he put his hand over her clasped ones in a gesture of sympathy.

"I understand everything you've told me perfectly well," he said softly. "I'm *not* a shrink, Mia. Perhaps a shrink would help you dig down inside yourself to find the reason for your . . . fear. I'm not qualified to diagnose—"

"It doesn't matter!" Mia stood up and stretched her arms wide. "I feel a thousand times better already. Just telling it all to you has . . . well, relieved me of the pressure somehow. I may just learn to live with it, to not expect too much from that side of life."

"But why live your life as some sort of emotional cripple!" Colin suddenly burst out. "You're beautiful, you're talented . . ."

She looked at him, surprised. He shook his head. "Oh, don't mind me, dear. I have my own hang-ups. I always feel that beautiful, full-grown people *should* surely be one hundred percent happy. I don't see why you should miss out on *any* aspect of life—*especially* the loving or sexual part. But if life ever gets too painful, promise me you will find some therapist or see me again?"

Mia sat down again, thoughtfully rearranging her long, gathered skirt. "What if Phillipe and I are truly, truly in love?" she asked. "What if he *is* exactly the right man for me? Don't you believe in love?"

Colin smiled regretfully. "Oh, yes, I believe in love," he affirmed softly. "I've loved your mother for years. But I don't allow it to become an obsession. It's *easier* for you to believe your love for Phillipe is the obstacle between you and happiness—it's the perfect excuse!"

"But I *feel* Phillipe's love!" Mia protested. "Even now! I just know that one day we will be together!"

Colin shrugged. "Plenty of people live in hope, Mia. Personally, I feel that's a tragic way to live. It ignores the joy of *today*—while you live in hope, you're not really living *now!*"

"You said you loved my mother!" she said almost harshly. "Aren't *you* living in hope?"

"Oh, no." His eyes bored into hers. "I don't hope for or expect anything to come of my love for her. I've turned it into a loving friendship. And that's what it shall remain."

"My mother's lucky to have you for a friend," Mia said. She felt tears for her mother and herself roll down her cheeks. "Thank you for trying to help." She glanced at her watch. He stood with her and she bent down to kiss his cheek. "I always knew you were someone special," she told him.

Mia walked up Lexington Avenue toward her bank, to discuss her finances. The checks from Headquarters had accumulated in her account, and since Wayland provided board and wardrobe, she'd spent very little. Colin had made her realize one thing: It was time to start a new life—her *own* life.

A month later she moved into an apartment in an East Sixties brownstone. At first she worked out of her living room, installing a long trestle table and sitting in a high director's chair to sketch and cut her patterns. She tried to summon some excitement about designing a new, small collection of twelve garments. She thought of them as providing a wardrobe for a smart working woman and her different needs. Everything would be clean-cut, well-proportioned, and figure-flattering. She chose the most luxurious, soft, thick fabrics she could afford. Wayland guided her to new cutters and sample makers. By showing them methods of construction she had learned in Paris, she was able to produce sleek, beautifully made clothing at a fraction of the cost of French garments.

She enjoyed being involved in work again, and imagined Phillipe in his Avenue Marceau studio, selecting fabrics, supervising fittings, worrying about details like buttons and collars. Their lives were touching.

Meanwhile she kept everyone else at a distance. David had called her a few times, Mackenzie still owed her an apology, and Wayland seemed a little miffed that she had moved out. She ate dinner with him once a week, and saw Colin now and then for an evening. She became solitary, but not lonely. Speaking to Colin had released and calmed something within her; for the moment she was content to coast along. On some restless hot spring nights she would finger her body, explore it, touch her breasts as she lay on her bed, let her hand caress between her legs, as she pretended it was Phillipe's hand or David's. She wondered how sexual pleasure worked and why her body rejected it. It was too confusing, too charged. Better to plunge headfirst into work.

She decorated her apartment in her favorite blues and grays. It was very soft, very feminine. No visitor to her bedroom with its lacy pillows and snowy-white coverlet would have dreamed that this beautiful, willowy blonde had banished sex from her life.

Mackenzie Gold became Lady Briarly at a private ceremony in the chapel of New York's British Consulate. It was July and by then she was, in Wayland's words, "as big as Cleveland," so close to giving birth that a nearby clinic room was booked for her to check into immediately after the wedding. The short ceremony was attended only by her parents and brothers, and Alistair's sister Hilary, who flew in from Shropshire and wore the tweediest suit the Goldsteins had ever seen.

After many transatlantic calls and meetings with lawyers, it had gradually been revealed that all Alistair would bring to this marriage was his title and some death-duty taxes.

It didn't matter, Mackenzie thought—she'd make enough for all of them. Her designs would provide an endless income. Gold!'s sales were booming. The Los Angeles branch was doing incredible business, and already her pop-style wedding dress—perversely sexy, white lace with a laced bodice, making her look as if she'd been caught in her underwear—was in great demand by young, mod brides, thanks to Mackenzie having carefully leaked her design to the press two months before.

"The first designer-label maternity bridal gown!" *Labels* had crowed at the time. *WWD* had captioned a drawing of the dress: "Gold kills two birds with one stone: a bridal gown that can be worn nine months before the marriage!"

At the wedding the press had a field day, *Labels* leading the paparazzi, planting photographers at the front and back doors of the Park Avenue Maternity Clinic. It was unusual for a Jewish bride to marry into the aristocracy in a chapel, but influential friends of Alistair's father had managed to pull strings.

"The new Lord and Lady Briarly exchanged rings," deadpanned *Labels'* reporter, "and went straight from the small chapel to the chic Park Avenue Maternity Clinic, where a two-room suite provided the setting for a champagne reception...." As they ducked out of their limousine and into the clinic, they were snapped by a *Labels* photographer.

Her family joined them in her rooms, where Esther Goldstein wore a look that Mackenzie knew well and simply ignored. Her air of tragedy and great suffering had been assumed since Mackenzie had refused to invite Ed Schreiber to the wedding.

Champagne toasts were proposed by Alistair, and tears ran down Esther's face as she clinked glasses with her daughter, lying propped up on the bed. It was awkward when the family got together, especially now that Alistair was part of it.

"I'll have to call you Mum and Dad now," he tried to joke with Esther.

"And are we supposed to call you Lord Alistair?" she asked.

Abe Goldstein was bemused. He could not understand the clipped English words of Alistair's sister, and left her to Reggie and Max. The newlyweds sipped champagne, giggling and whispering.

The Honorable Jordan Aquarius Briarly, "the first Mod Aristo Rich-Hippie Fashion Baby," according to *Labels*, arrived two days later. Mackenzie begged the photographers not to report that Alistair was stoned at the moment his son was born.

"It's the shock of losing his father and brother," she whispered, and the photographer, high on the hash Alistair had shared, nodded. The family portrait, commissioned by *Divine*, appeared in the magazine two months later. There was a stand of white roses from Coral Stanton, flowers from all Gold!'s fabric manufacturers, bouquets from the staff at all the boutiques, and one pot of flowers from the Goldsteins, welcoming their first grandchild.

Mackenzie returned home after four days in the clinic, her son anointed with patchouli oil, wearing a tiny beaded headband sent by her Village friends. Up in her penthouse she withdrew her baby from the ribbon-embroidered carry cot sent by a fabric supplier, holding him up before the mirror. Alistair ran upstairs to the bedroom to find a secret horde of cocaine. A huge bouquet had been delivered to the house with a congratulatory card from Ed.

"Nice of him," Alistair sniffed, raising his eyebrows.

She glanced at him to see if he was being sarcastic, but he was busy setting up neat lines of coke on a glass table.

"I'm getting an Oriental butler," she announced to Alistair. She had already engaged a maid who would act as baby-sitter. "For God's sake, don't let the girl catch you doing that! Alistair, you said you were going to give up that stuff—you promised!"

He was leaning back on the couch, making faces at the baby. "I can play better with my son if I'm high," he said.

"Bullshit!"

He tossed her the latest issues of *WWD* and *Labels*. She idly leafed through the papers, finding the page that featured their marriage.

"I guess these are our wedding albums?" she said. "God, I was huge!" Holding Jordan up to the reflection in the mirror, she cooed, "That was *you*, baby! *You* were that big lump in my tummy! Oh, look, Alistair—his eyes are closed tight—he doesn't even know he's home."

Jordan gurgled and she nuzzled his head, covered with soft blond hair.

"Let me hold my son," Alistair said. He sat down next to her on the couch and took the tiny bundle. She was scared to give the baby to him: What if he dropped it?

She watched him closely as he cradled the baby in his lap, peering into its face.

"Do you think anyone will call him Aquarius?" He looked at Mackenzie and laughed.

The coke had made him high, sociable. Why couldn't he always be like this? she wondered.

"Are you proud of me, darling?" she asked him.

"Of course! You were very brave! But...I don't know ...this baby doesn't look much like you, or me—you don't think they gave us the wrong one, do you?"

She giggled, saying, "We'll soon find out. If he starts snorting coke, I'll know he's your son."

Alistair glanced at her, then abruptly put the baby back in her lap. "Here. I'd better start answering some of these calls. They might be about business, and we can't afford to lose money now, can we?"

She frowned at him. "Not if you keep spending it on dope."

Alistair strode whistling out of the room. She glanced at the beautiful flowers from Ed, a twinge of pain sounding in her.

"You are going to have a perfect life, my darling," she whispered to her child. "With taste, art, culture, money...all the stuff I didn't get."

She could hear Alistair on the phone in the next room. Lord Briarly, she thought. The reflection in the mirror showed her Lady Briarly, the woman who now had everything—a fortune, a title, a beautiful baby. Why, then, did she feel so sad? That wasn't difficult to figure out. Every time she thought of Eddie, she heard the answer ring loud and clear: She had married the wrong man. An ominous feeling in the pit of her stomach told her so. She suddenly felt very alone: She had alienated her parents, Mia, Eddie. She'd better start making up with everybody, she decided, because something told her this marriage was not going to work out and she'd need them in the coming years. Now that Alistair had given her the title, he felt he had a perfect right to do whatever he wanted, and what he wanted was to stay high.

The baby started to cry.

"Oh, *shit!*" the new Lady Briarly said.

Twenty-two

Lord and Lady Briarly were photographed, chronicled, and interviewed so relentlessly that a new term had to be invented for them: They were "raped by the media." Along with their "mod baby," they were in danger of overexposure. Depending on which paper you read, they were "the In Couple," "Couple of the Year," "the Titled Mods," or "the Trashocracy"—*Labels*' term for young people from good families, determined to trash their heritage.

Everyone wanted the Briarlys at their openings, first nights, and parties. They brought the stamp of success if they appeared together at an event. Mackenzie added a touch of the hippie lifestyle to the chic watering holes they visited, causing mouths to drop when she breastfed Jordan in public. Screens were quickly set up around their table at Rumors the moment she began unbuttoning her dress. At Saint Tropez she was asked to leave when she refused to feed her son in the powder room.

The resultant publicity built up Mackenzie as a rebel, a rule-breaker, and it prompted a run on the Manhattan stores. Gold!'s biggest problem was getting enough clothes manufactured. Everything pointed to increasing production in California as a solution. The Goldstein brothers flew out there to set up a deal. They signed an agreement with a factory to produce their entire output.

"But no sweatshops!" Mackenzie warned before she signed. "I'm Lady Briarly now—I have high visibility. I don't want to be associated with exploitation, or profiteering...."

"I'm not sure what profiteering *is*," Reggie replied, sneering. "If it's making a profit, I intend to do it."

"But not at the expense of the workers!" Mackenzie shouted. "I want them working in decent conditions, earning a fair salary."

"You leave that to us," Reggie said, and walked away from her.

Her biggest fear now was that her brothers would do something really crooked, giving the business and herself a bad name. Perhaps if she kept in contact with Eddie, she thought, she could prevent that from happening. But she wasn't ready for that.

For three weeks after the baby was born, Alistair played the doting father. He enjoyed posing with Mackenzie for all the publications clamoring for shots of America's first aristocratic rag traders. Once the excitement died down, however, he excused himself to "do the rounds," leaving Mackenzie alone in the evenings.

She dialed Mia's number the first night Alistair went out. "Will you ever forgive me?" she asked. "I know I was a bitch! I've missed you—"

"You betrayed my confidence," Mia said. "It's very hard to forgive that."

"*Try!*" Mackenzie pleaded. "I didn't mean anything I said! Women get into funny moods when they're pregnant, you know. Make some allowances!"

"I'm always making allowances for you, Mackenzie."

Mackenzie glanced at her sleeping son in his Porthault-lined crib. "Just come see my baby. He's so darling, and I have no one to show him off to!"

"Are you kidding? You're always being photographed with him!"

"Yeah, but I mean, my mother keeps her distance...I don't *have* a real family! Mia, what are you doing right now? I'm so *lonely!* Alistair's out on his rounds. You know what that means? He starts at Max's Kansas City, links up with cronies, and goes on to The Dome, or Arthur's, or The Scene...."

"Didn't you know all that when you married him?"

"I thought marriage and fatherhood would change him." Mackenzie sighed. "Oh, Mia, please come over—don't *you* ever get lonely? We could have so much fun together. I've said I'm sorry, what else do you want? Blood?"

Mia shook her head. It was hard to hold out against Mackenzie, and she did get lonely.

She visited the next night. They settled back into an uneasy kind of friendship, but Mia held back a little—she would never again feel able to totally confide.

Mackenzie told her everything. "Sex with Eddie ruined everything," she told Mia as they leaned over the crib. "I guess you never get everything at the same time, huh?" She looked longingly at Mia. "Eddie showed me what it could really be like. I've felt my body aching for him ever since. Can you imagine how that feels?"

"Yes . . . I feel it for Phillipe. Your skin *jumps*!"

"You *do* know!" Mackenzie quickly kissed her cheek, leading her back to the huge living room. "What about David? He's so gorgeous—isn't he a good substitute?"

Mia met Mackenzie's inquisitive gaze. "I tried to make him one, but it didn't work. I'm still in love with Phillipe."

Mackenzie grabbed her. "We're both in love with other men, and we're *both* doomed! Oh, God, Mia, it's tragic! And we'll both stay *terribly* successful and have *tons* of money but be *desperately* unhappy!"

"I can't explain it rationally," Mia said. "He just *feels* like the only man I'll ever love. We . . . fit! Do you know what I mean?"

Mackenzie, about to pop a champagne cork, leaned back against the wall, closing her eyes. "You *fit*! Oh, God, do *I* know what you mean!" She sighed, popped the cork, and it flew up, hitting the ceiling. "We may as well get drunk, we're doomed anyway!"

Mia smiled, sitting down next to Mackenzie on the giant sofa. "*I* don't feel doomed!" She took the crystal glass. "I know in my heart that Phillipe and I are fated to be together. It doesn't make sense, but it's what I believe. . . ."

Mackenzie held her glass aloft. "I wish I could believe that about Eddie and me, but . . . well, I'm a married lady now, right? Why the hell should he hang around for me? What can we drink to, Mia? I'm fresh out of toasts!"

They clinked glasses. Mia shrugged. "Let's just say to the end of the Vietnam war," Mackenzie proposed. "That's more important."

They drank solemnly.

"Do you still see Ed?" Mia asked.

"Not *see*: I speak to him on the phone. It's safer. But . . ." Mackenzie swallowed some wine and giggled. "Just hearing his *voice* turns me on! It kind of rumbles through my body, coming to rest in my crotch! By the time we hang up, I need a cold shower!"

Mia shook her head, laughing. "You're as Rabelaisian as ever."

"If that means horny, you're dead right, kid!"

"Did you ever ask Ed if he'd meet up with David and give him some business advice?" Mia asked. "You said Ed knows everything."

"Yeah, he understands this industry. God, better than I do. I just like to design and arrange the stores. He knows the dollars-and-cents part. Oh, God, I love that guy!"

"Will he see David?"

"Why not?" Mackenzie poured more champagne, saying, "Let's get our men together, Mia! Gives me a great excuse to call him."

David Winters and Ed Schreiber liked each other immediately, perhaps because each man had expected to meet someone quite different. David had envisaged a dour, ink-stained accountant-type with no knowledge of fashion. Ed expected an effeminate designer. They were both pleasantly surprised.

The meeting was as important to Ed as it was to David. For some time now he'd planned to leave the Gold! operation as soon as something presented itself. Since Mackenzie's marriage, he had soured on the company. Before that he'd seen her at meetings and nurtured the hope that she would change her mind about Alistair and marry him. What's more, the decision to move the manufacturing base to California, where cheap, sometimes illegal, labor would be used, convinced him his days at the company were numbered.

Ed's goal was to start a new firm backing a new designer, using everything he had learned at Gold!, where he'd studied the retail business from the bottom up. He knew how to merchandise, how to manufacture, how to deliver the products and sell them. He also had an instinctive understanding of fashion which neither Reggie nor Max ever acquired: Ed knew how important the right label was to the customer, and was convinced that the label would be the merchandising tool of the seventies. Developing a label meant one could tailor a line to a particular market—it was no longer simply a question of design, but of *image*.

They met at a deli in Manhattan's garment district, and sounded each other out over lunch. David described the clothes he was designing—a capsule collection, he called it, featuring prototypes of good quality dresses, suits, and coats for the fashion-conscious woman. Ed asked lots of questions.

"How do you know so much about it all?" David asked.

"Are you kidding me?" Ed asked. "Being around the Goldsteins? They have *schmatta* in their blood!"

"*Schmatta?*" David asked, stumbling over the pronunciation.

"*Schmattas*, rags, fashions!" Ed said. "Don'tcha know the terminology?"

"I'll have to learn it!"

"Listen!" Ed waved a pickle at him. "I never thought I'd know the difference between a pleated skirt and a gathered one, but it rubs off. Tell me, how do you know Mackenzie?"

"We were students together at MacMillans. Even then you could see she was different from everyone else there. I knew she'd either be a spectacular success or a big failure."

"She's parlayed her taste into a multimillion-dollar turnover," Ed said, "and it gets bigger and bigger. Fifteen-year-old kids come to her stores knowing they can afford to buy the latest dress. She's putting out instant, affordable fashion! What do *you* offer?"

David put down his sandwich and looked seriously at Ed. "The exact opposite," he said. "My ideal customer will not throw away the clothes she buys from me until they're falling apart. She's a twenty-five-year-old looking for clothes to work in and to dress up in. Stylish, classy, and *not* disposable!"

"Which stores do you see selling?"

"Every designer's dream—Bendel, Bloomingdale's, Bonwit Teller. . . ."

Ed nodded. "You're a good-looking guy, you know, you could have been a movie star."

"What does that have to do with anything?" David said, and laughed with embarrassment.

"I'm thinking. . ." Ed began, tapping the side of his head with his finger. "It all goes in here, the computer starts whirring, and I come up with a winning formula.

You see, I know the secret of marketing tomorrow's fashion, David." He paused as the waitress refilled their coffee cups, then continued. "Is Mackenzie's stuff brilliant? It's been copied—sometimes copied better! Couldn't a dozen others design it? It's just mix and match, right? A blue top with a yellow skirt and you add a few medallions? But *that* isn't what the kids are buying! They're buying the image, the *label*! The lighting, the decor, the music, the colored shopping bags—"

"But my stuff will be clothing, pure and simple, Ed," David pointed out. "Well-cut, elegant clothes. No music, no environment—"

"I have my own ideas about that," Ed said. "But first I'll have to see your clothes, to get to know what you're doing, what kind of image you'll be selling."

They made an appointment to meet at David's apartment the following Sunday. There, David showed the prototypes for the four dresses, suits, and coats that could form a first collection. The dresses were cut from tubular jersey; seamless and figure-hugging, they were a new kind of garment, soft, clinging, and versatile.

Ed gave a low whistle, leaning back in the cream-colored canvas armchair in the living room. "This makes Gold!'s stuff look like Woolworth's. Can you really translate this stuff into mass production?"

"I work with a great old tailor," David said, sitting opposite Ed, his eyes shining. "I could work it out with him. Then it's a matter of finding the good machinists, the sample makers, setting up a workroom. But I don't have the bread to finance all that—"

Ed waved his hands impatiently. "That's my job. What do these retail at?"

"Around a hundred, a hundred twenty-five for the coats—"

"Are you willing to work really hard, David? This is one tough business!"

David nodded. "If you had asked me that a few months ago, I wouldn't have known what to tell you. But I did all these garments in the last two months. I'd been living in a kind of dream; suddenly I got ambitious again."

Without meaning to, he glanced at a photograph of Mia he kept framed on his bookcase. Ed followed his gaze. "You're ambitious for her? She's beautiful!"

"I'm ambitious because I know now I'll never get her."

David stood, removed the picture and placed it behind some books. He fetched more coffee from the kitchen, pouring them each a cup. Ed stirred his, shaking his head to himself.

"What's wrong?" David asked.

Ed looked up at him. "I can't believe it could be so easy. You have the talent and I've been telling myself that all I needed was a good designer and I'd be on my way! Now I have no excuse to stay at Gold!"

"You really think you could find the money?"

"I sure do. The fashion industry is growing like a monster, and the people I deal with at the banks are itching to invest! I like your stuff, David. And I'd use *you* to sell it—your name, your face, make a media personality out of you."

"I warn you, I'm no extrovert."

"Even better! You'll be an intense, moody loner! We'll invest in your image. That's what fashion merchandising will be all about in the seventies. Women will really go for it, I promise you."

They shook hands, David uncertainly, Ed with great confidence. He knew a good thing when he saw it. Fashion history could repeat itself—upmarket this time. David Winters was going to be one of the big names in American fashion!

Ed made up his mind that Sunday afternoon, walking back to his apartment on the West Side. He debated with himself about how to leave Gold! He didn't want to formally hand in his notice; that would be a cold, officious way to end a long, friendly working relationship with the Goldsteins. He decided to try to see Mackenzie on her own.

"It's kind of important," he told her when they spoke that evening. "Is there any way I could see you tonight for half an hour?"

"You do realize I'm a married lady now, don't you?" She giggled, wanting to flirt with him.

"This is business," he said curtly.

"Oh? Too bad..." she sighed. "Well, okay. I'm home for the evening."

Mackenzie hung up the phone and went upstairs to

change her clothes. She had become tired of wearing her
own pop fashions. Since her brothers resolutely refused to
allow her to buy expensive, quality fabrics which would
upgrade Gold!, she was wearing—almost as a rebellion—
expensive couture clothes. Halstons lined her closet alongside English clothes from Jean Muir and Zandra Rhodes.
Not really her style, but she was Lady Mackenzie Briarly
and she could hardly continue to wear twenty-five-dollar
vinyl miniskirts. She chose a gray silk print number that
was refined and yet sexy at the same time. Her breasts
had remained full since Jordan's birth, and she noticed
they pushed against the thin silk as she entered the
nursery to make sure Jordan was sleeping soundly.

Sunday was the night both members of the staff were
off, and Alistair was out for the evening. The baby was six
months old and just starting to sleep through the night.
She stood looking down at him, wishing he would cry so
she could pick him up and cuddle him. He was a beautiful, bright, sweet child, and now the most important
person in her life.

Suddenly, she remembered that Ed was about to arrive
and her stomach began to flutter. She had tried to forget
that incredible scene at his office, but it had launched
fantasies and desires that she couldn't always control.

She returned to the living room and tidied it carefully,
so Ed wouldn't see any of Alistair's drug paraphernalia.
She and Alistair had enjoyed very little sex since the birth
of the baby. Alistair was either up, after snorting coke, or
down and waiting to score more. She was tired of figuring
out his moods, and now that Jordan was there, she simply
didn't care. The marriage was a sham, a facade for two
unsuited people living under the same roof. She no longer
loved him—if she ever had. Alistair went out every night,
but she had lost interest in that scene—the smoky clubs,
the popping flashbulbs, and the eyes watching her. An
evening with Jordan was more rewarding. An evening
with Ed would be even more rewarding. . . .

When the doorman called to announce Ed's arrival, she
quickly checked her hair in the mirror. She wore it longer
now, tied back from her face with a black bow. When she
opened the door and their eyes met, her heart jumped.
His slightly subdued air made him even more attractive to
her. He was wearing a dark, checked sports shirt and

navy slacks. A loose cardigan was tied around his shoulders. His position at Gold! had given him a successful air; he was starting to dress expensively too. She ushered him in and kissed his cheek quickly. Ed did not respond.

"How are you?" she asked, walking him to the large living room which had recently been redecorated in soothing plums and grays. "I never see you at meetings anymore." She fetched champagne from a little cart, and put two glasses alongside it. "My father has stopped coming. I think he's starting to feel his age. I'm glad he doesn't come."

"And me?" he questioned. He sat on a couch, watching her.

She looked at him. "I don't know if I'm happy or sad." She gave him the champagne.

"Open this, will you, Eddie?" He popped the cork and they looked at each other.

"What are we drinking to?"

"I don't know. To my son, I guess. He's the most important thing in my life right now." They gravely toasted, and then sipped the champagne, staring at each other.

"Ya miss me?" she asked, finally.

"What do you think?"

"Baby, have *I* missed *you*." She sighed. "You gotta help me convince my brothers to upgrade the firm, Eddie," she began. "I can't talk to them anymore. It's as though my marriage has erected a bigger barrier between us. If you could make them see—"

"I'm leaving the company," he said bluntly, his navy eyes boring into hers. "That's what I came to tell you tonight. I'm quitting Gold!"

She stared at him, shaking her head gently. "I knew you would... I just knew it."

"You don't sound too disappointed."

"Oh, Eddie..." She reached over and touched his arm. "I'd give anything in the world to get you to stay. You're the only person I trust in the entire group. Is there anything I can do to convince you?"

"No. It's better this way, Lady Mackenzie."

"*Don't!*" She grabbed his hand and felt the same electric shock. "You'll make me hate my title if *you* use it to me. I think I already hate it. If you saw how headwaiters bowed and scraped—"

"Isn't that why you married him?" he asked quietly.

She stared at him frankly, releasing his hand. "I told you at the time—I wanted to give Jordan his father. His *real* father. I really *do* have a conscience, Eddie, whatever you might think. I thought it was worth a damn good try, even though deep inside me I knew Alistair was not the best husband material. I did it for my son, you see? Everyone thinks I'm a crazy, selfish bitch, but if they took the trouble to know me, they'd find I really *do* care! About people, about this country, about trying to end this ridiculous war—"

"I believe you."

"Eddie," she began urgently, leaning forward, "to me, life is not just about making money and enjoying yourself. I attend sit-ins, I protest unfairness...and *Labels* and *Women's Wear* have fun ridiculing me, but I *do* it! I want to help stop this war, stop discrimination! There are so many things we can help *change!*"

"I admire that," Ed said. "And don't lose it. Don't let anyone talk you out of it."

"Alistair doesn't give a shit about anything, Eddie, as long as he has his coke, his booze, his cigarettes around ...and those shots to keep him up!" Mackenzie said, suddenly realizing she was saying too much. She was only proving what he had said almost a year ago.

"Well, he's not the only one." Ed sipped his wine. "They say Coral Stanton's a junkie, and about half the rest of the people in the fashion industry."

"That doesn't make me feel any better!" she said. She kept her eyes on him. She was so tempted to sit next to him, to touch him, to lay her head on his shoulder, but she knew she must not give in to those urges.

"Okay." She controlled herself, taking a sip of champagne. "Break it to me gently. Who's getting you? Some big name, I'll bet. Betsey Johnson? Halston?"

"What would you say to David Winters?"

"*David?*" She sat bolt upright. "Are you kidding? *He's* not a big name!"

"I'll make him big!"

"I don't *believe* this! Mia said he just wanted to talk to you! I do a favor for a friend and my top man is stolen from under my nose!"

"Nobody *stole* me!" Ed said, rising to his feet. "I'm my

own man! I was looking for a designer to go into business with—and David and I clicked. I had planned to leave Gold! the day you married your lord."

"I'll bet." Mackenzie also stood, striding up and down the room. She whirled around to face him. "Where's the money coming from?"

"I'll hustle it. That's my part of the deal."

"And *his* part?"

"Mack, he's designed a prototype dress that every woman will want in her wardrobe. It's...I don't know, seamless? From jersey tubing, or something..."

"Jersey *tubing*!" she shrieked. "I *begged* Reggie to let me use it two seasons ago, and he said it was too expensive. I could've made the most fabulous things out of it."

"It's not cheap," Ed agreed. He collapsed on the sofa again, weary. "David told me the price. But his clothes won't be cheap, either. We're going for quality."

"He's not a businessman," she warned.

"*I'm* the businessman," he told her. "David just has to design and look handsome."

"Handsome?" She frowned. "What does that have to do with it?"

"I happen to think women will go for buying clothes from a good-looking guy like David."

She shook her head. "How the hell will women know he's handsome? You're gonna put his picture on every label?"

"Not such a bad idea...something like that," he said, and smiled.

"Trade secrets already, huh? And you learned it all at Gold!"

She refilled their glasses and drank quickly. "Oh, Eddie...you won't forget *me*?" she said, catching his hand and holding it. In spite of her resolutions, she could not keep from touching him. "I know I've made a mess of everything, but I'd like to think that maybe one day—"

"*One day!*" he interrupted her. "You think I'm the kind of guy that hangs around for 'one day'? *I told* you before you married his lordship how much I wanted you. You chose the title—"

"I chose Jordan's father!" she cried. "How *could* you have married me knowing I was pregnant with another man's child?"

"Because I loved you," he said simply. "This conventional Jewish accountant would have done it for love."

"Don't say 'loved' in the past tense!" she begged, all of her resolve collapsing. "You *still* love me, I know you do! I can see it in your eyes, Eddie! And I love *you*! Please—"

He stood up again. "This is ridiculous. I have to go."

He headed for the door, Mackenzie behind him. She reached around him and put her hand on the doorknob, forcing him to turn and look at her. "Aren't you going to kiss me good-bye?" she asked softly.

He leaned toward her, his eyes impatient, angry, sparkling. She closed her eyes. This was an exquisite kind of torture. His lips brushed hers gently. He refused to linger.

"You've made up your mind!" she cried, staring at him. "You've resolved to live without me!"

"You're damn right I have!" he said. "Don't be so fucking unreasonable! What else could I do? I haven't seen you for months!"

"But I can find ways to see you now, Eddie! I have a thousand opportunities!"

"It's too late now, Mackenzie. It's too messy, and I'm leaving the company and—" He made a hopeless gesture. "I don't sneak around with other men's wives."

His eyes flashed fire at her now and she found him completely irresistible. She put her hand to the side of his face, stroking his fresh-shaved cheek.

"God, you're tough!" she tried to laugh. The softness of his cheek made him feel so vulnerable. Her eyes brimmed with feeling as she looked into his dark-lashed eyes that now showed such a mixture of emotions.

"Does this give you some kind of kick?" he asked bitterly. She saw him swallow with difficulty. "Because *I'm* not playing that game..." For a moment he placed his hand to her cheek, and she felt his warmth and desire as his eyes bored into hers. Then he opened the door and quickly walked out, without turning.

She turned back into the living room, empty and desolate, tears rolling down her cheeks. "You blew it, kid!" she said aloud. She glanced in the mirror at this woman who had just been denied what she finally admitted she so craved. "Lady fucking Mackenzie!" she taunted her reflection.

She finished off the rest of the champagne before picking up the phone. "Reggie?" she said when her brother answered. "Ed Schreiber just quit. Don't let him in his office tomorrow. Change the locks *tonight*. I don't care how—use an emergency service. Have someone clean out his drawers and give him anything personal. And pay him exactly what we owe him."

"You're absolutely sure about this?" Reggie barked.

"Absolutely. He just left my apartment—"

"What's going on between you two?"

She hesitated, then said, "Less than nothing... He's starting up his own firm with some new designer. I don't know whose money they'll be using, but they're not learning any more from us."

She hung up. She knew she was being unreasonable, but the emotion and frustration and champagne had built up in her until she had to blame someone. If Mia hadn't introduced Ed to David, she thought, this would never have happened.

She dialed Mia's number. The phone rang for a long time. Don't tell me that bitch is out having fun somewhere, Mackenzie thought, getting angrier. She let it ring one more time.

"Yes?" said a female voice.

"You fucking *bitch*!" Mackenzie exploded into the receiver. "Remember your brilliant idea—introducing Ed to David so he could advise him? If I wasn't alone with Jordan, I'd come right over and tear your fucking blond hair out by the roots!"

She paused for breath and the voice said, "This is Mia Stanton's answering service. Do you wish to leave a message?"

"Damned right I do!" Mackenzie growled. "This is Lady Mackenzie Briarly calling—"

"And the message is for?"

"For Mia Stanton. You *will* make sure she gets it, won't you, miss?"

"Of course. May I have the message?"

"Yeah. The message is"—Mackenzie raised her voice, *"go fuck yourself!* Did you get that, operator? Go fuck yourself!" She hung up grimly, feeling a little better.

Cracking open a fresh half-bottle of champagne for herself, she checked on the baby, then made herself stay awake until Alistair got home that morning.

He staggered into their bedroom at two-thirty, his eyes bright and hard. She was sitting up in bed with piles of fashion magazines on her knees. He looked surprised to see her still awake. "What's the matter? Couldn't sleep? Or waiting up for hubby?" He threw his jacket onto a chair and fell full-length over the end of the bed.

"I could sleep all right," she said. "But we have to talk."

"It'll have to wait," he mumbled. "I'm wiped out. Had a very tough night promoting Gold!..."

"Like hell you were!" she cried.

"Shhh!" He placed a finger to his lips, his eyes closed. "You'll wake Jordan."

"Don't worry about him—he's sleeping soundly. Why are *you* so wiped out? Been screwing models again, promising them contracts?"

He rolled onto his back, smiling. He seemed to be shivering. He hugged his knees. "Do you know what a speedball is, Mack?"

"Who cares? A cocktail?"

He laughed. "It's a cocktail all right, but you don't drink it. It's pure heroin in one arm, pure coke in the other...."

"Alistair, if you ever get into heroin, consider yourself fired *and* divorced!"

"Do the two go together?" he said sarcastically. "Does the job come with the marriage? You didn't think so when I was working my ass off launching that first tacky boutique."

"I'm not living with a heroin addict!"

"I haven't had a speedball...not yet," he murmured. "I'm saving it for a big treat...."

"Your son was supposed to be the big treat!" She paused, then asked, "Alistair, why did you marry me?"

"Seemed like a good idea at the time. The more interesting question is why you married me! You *are* Lady Briarly now, aren't you? What more do you want?"

"But I thought *we'd* be together. I thought we'd lead a full life—"

"Call Ed Schreiber—he makes a great stand-in."

"Has someone told you some bullshit about Ed and me?"

"Oh," he groaned, "I don't even care...."

"He was here tonight. He came to tell me he's leaving Gold!"

"Best news I've heard this year!"

"I was longing to go to bed with him, and I didn't...."

"I'll have the Lord Briarly blue-ball medal struck for you tomorrow, darling. Although women don't get blue balls, do they? Well...I'll think up something."

"Alistair! I'm trying to get through to you! The drugs are making you crazy, to say nothing of impotent."

"And Ed is so very potent, I'm sure...."

"Oh, just leave him out of it. He really has nothing to do with us."

He twisted around on the bed to look at her, his blond hair disheveled, his face pale. "I don't really understand why you married *me*. I mean, I know it was the title, because you only considered marriage when my father was killed...."

"I hoped we could make a success of marriage," she said. "We were called 'Couple of the Year' so often that even *I* started to believe it. I knew we weren't in love, but I thought we liked and respected each other. Now, I'm starting to lose my respect."

He eased his legs over the side of the bed, kicking off his shoes. He lay back on the bed with a sigh. "Mack...my life is so fucked up."

"Why?"

"I don't feel anything unless I'm high."

"So see a shrink, Alistair. We can afford the best. Get help! You're an intelligent person...."

He shrugged. "Yeah. Maybe I'll see a shrink. Some very old, very wise man. Help me find someone good, Mack."

"Oh, baby, of course I will!" She bent over him to kiss his forehead. She had got him to admit he needed help. That was one hurdle cleared. "Things will be all right, Alistair, I know they will. We have everything, darling. It would be too dumb to blow it!"

She pulled him up into bed, helped him take off his clothes. Soon his thin naked body was against hers. She pulled him into her embrace—she was naked, too, placing his body between her legs, rubbing against him. His limp sex merely teased her.

"Mack?" he said in the dark. "I didn't have a speedball tonight. I got pure coke. It's okay...it's not addictive. This was dealer's quality...before they dilute it—"

His words became mumbles, and he fell asleep in

mid-sentence. Suddenly he snored. She listened to his rasping breath, worried by the raucous sound of it, new for Alistair. A shrink would get him off drugs, find out *why* he was self-destructive. He would shape up. Their marriage could survive, if she fought for it. But Ed . . . she thought. *Are you finding it as difficult to sleep as I am? Are you thinking of me now? Or did you find someone else tonight? A sexy guy like you must have no trouble finding girls.* She felt painful jabs of jealousy as she pictured him making love to some girl, making love passionately, as he had to her, going a little crazy, losing control.

She drew the covers up over Alistair's shoulders, and he muttered something unintelligible in his sleep. She smoothed the Porthault sheets she had always dreamed of having, ever since reading that Jackie Kennedy and C.Z. Guest insisted on them. Had she ever imagined covering a drug-addict husband with them? The three-hundred-dollar cashmere throws piled neatly at the foot of the bed were another thing she'd always wanted. She pulled one over them and huddled next to Alistair, trying to impart some of her own warmth to him.

In the morning the alarm woke her and Jordan cried softly from the next room. He would need changing and the nurse would not arrive for an hour. During the night Alistair had moved into his usual position of holding her from behind. He was still cold, but at least the loud breathing had stopped. She began to wriggle carefully out of his embrace so as not to wake him, but he was holding her tighter then usual. It took her a minute or two of wriggling, Jordan's cries gradually getting louder, before the danger sign swept her body—that half freezing, half scalding sensation that engulfed her in its icy-hot grip whenever something momentous in her life had happened. When she'd won the *Divine* contest, when Alistair told her he was a lord, and now . . . now it was as if her body knew something terrible had happened before she did.

She suddenly realized she was being held fast in the stiffened embrace of a dead man.

As her mind took this in, her eyes opened wide, staring blindly. She froze in horror and her mouth opened. Without thinking about it, she began to scream. Fighting to release herself from Alistair's last cold embrace, she screamed over and over again until her throat was raw, her cries first matching, then drowning, the cries of her son from his crib. It was 1968, but for her it was the end of the sixties. . . .

Book Three

Twenty-three

"He'd have been a lot better off if the coke *hadn't* been so pure. Cocaine that pure can stop the heart. . . ."

"I think he's better off dead anyway—the guy was a nonevent."

"He left her nothing—just his title and lots of debts. Every coke dealer in Manhattan claims he owed money. . . ."

"She only wanted his title, you know: They were both carrying on with other people."

"She won't leave her apartment—she blames herself for his death."

The gossip had flown thick and fast. Colin, bemused, overheard it all. Now he was on his way to meet Wayland for dinner. He would fill Wayland in on Coral's latest tantrum, pulling the hair of a model and slapping her face, which would doubtless be in the next week's issue of *Labels*, anyway. Worse, he would confide his fears that a systematic plan to ruin Coral had surely been devised by Howard Austin and someone at *Divine*, probably Donna Brooks. The worst feeling of all was this premonition that Alistair Briarly's death was not only a death knell for the sixties—two years before they were over—but just the first of many tragedies about to hit the fashion world.

Colin's premonition proved to be right.

The easy money and overnight success of the mid-1960s began to evaporate in a cloud of pot and a shower of coke. The disposable clothing of the sixties began, overnight, to look tawdry, skimpy, and cheap. Vinyl did not wear well. Nothing cheap wore well—it was not designed to do so. Status, a new word in fashion, reared its head as women began to want quality clothing that looked expensive.

"Cheap is *out!*" Wayland crowed.

371

Halston was one of the first American designers to provide this new conservative, quality look. He was watched carefully by Ed Schreiber, who had his own plans for saturating the new upcoming market. Fashion was about to turn full circle, and Coral, for one, was ready for it, had predicted it. Through the ups and downs of her addiction, her eccentric behavior, and her feuds and shenanigans, she still kept an eagle eye on the future, still understood the evolution of fashion as no other individual did.

"You have to hand her that!" Wayland admitted. "She's still got the antennae. They're built-in."

Coral welcomed the return to elegance. Beautifully-cut clothing in quality fabrics would, once again, be hanging from her chrome selection frames. And she would rule, as always, supreme!

High on a supershot from Dr. Robbins, she left her office for the first interview granted by Anais Du Pasquier. The limousine whisked her to Headquarters. As a surprise, Wayland Garrity was waiting for her at the store's main entrance. They had not spoken since their fight over his support of Mia. Now, as the limousine drew up, he stepped forward and opened the door.

"Coral!" He held out his hand: "You look *marvelous!*"

"Wayland . . ." She smiled coolly. "What a surprise."

Coral stepped out of the limousine. She did not look marvelous at all. She looked like a very sick woman fighting to stay normal. The strain on her face, the expression in her eyes, the tiny twitches of her red mouth, all gave her away. He took her arm—she was frail. He led her up the steps to Headquarters' massive front doors, into the special elevator for VIP's, up to the fourth-floor showrooms.

"What sort of person is she?" Coral asked. "I've imagined a rather winsome beauty—rather Bardotesque. . . ."

"Well, she's beautiful—you got that part right," Wayland agreed. They stepped out and he guided her along the corridor toward the showroom.

"How've you been, Coral darling?" he asked her kindly.

She squeezed his arm. "Couldn't have been better! Fashion is about to reenter a new age of elegance. It's going to be a very exciting time! I can *love* fashion again, Wayland!"

Mia had been awaiting her mother in the showroom for the last half hour, arranging her new collection on the portable show rails. When she heard Coral's voice, the cold ball of fear in her stomach churned, even though she'd been the one to finally decide she was ready for this meeting. She had dressed very carefully today, wearing one of her sample dresses in a soft white wool. Her life was now so centered around her designing that her mother's approval and potential friendship meant a lot to her. She stood to face them as they entered the room.

"And here she is!" Wayland made a flourish and presented Mia.

Coral stared at her daughter. "I don't understand. Where is Anais?"

"I *am* Anais, Mother," Mia said. "I'm so happy you like my designs. I'm the designer of this line. It's *me!*"

Coral's eyes bulged. She gazed around the room, glancing at the new samples hanging on the rail, moving away from her daughter.

"Isn't it wonderful!" Wayland beamed. "She's had such a success!"

"You mean, I was *tricked*?" Coral cried. "There *is* no Anais?"

"There is—she's *me!*" Mia moved forward to hug her. "Mother, you love the clothes, and *I* did them! You were admiring something *I* did! Let's forgive each other everying! Please, let's be friends!"

Tears ran down her face as she hugged her mother's frail body. She had had no idea this reunion would affect her so much. Now, finally, she could see the scar, and it was not as bad as she'd feared.

Wayland put his arms around both of them. "Let's all bury the hatchet! Let's make it like old times again!" he urged.

Coral wriggled out of their embraces. "I'm afraid it's too late for that."

"Mother, please—"

"I suppose you both think you've been terribly clever, fooling me this way?" Coral cried. "Well, you *have* made a fool of me—I was taken in by you. And I'm furious with both of you." But almost unconsciously, she reached out to finger a particularly beautiful coat. Removing her own shawl, Coral slipped into the coat, admiring it on herself in the mirror.

"I have to pop out," Wayland said. "I'll leave you two alone."

Coral, continuing to look at the coat in the mirror, turning this way and that, didn't even notice that he'd left.

Mia watched her mother. Obviously it was not going to be a lovey-dovey reconciliation. But she felt she had to take some responsibility for this frail creature.

"Mother," she began, "you don't look well—"

"I feel *marvelous!*" Coral snapped. She removed the coat and looked at the dress hanging near it.

"You're far too thin. . . ."

"The Duchess of Windsor said a woman couldn't be too thin." She held the dress up against herself in the glass.

"Mother," Mia said, putting her hands on Coral's shoulders. "Look at me!" Coral's slightly wild eyes moved to her daughter's face. "How do you think *I* look?"

Coral's eyes flickered. "You're a beautiful woman, Mia," she said. "I could almost be jealous of you . . . jealous of your youth, your beauty. . ."

Mia shook her mother a little, still holding her shoulders. "So why can't you stop this . . . animosity? I could use your interest, your friendship. Why do you make it so difficult for me?"

Coral stepped away. She pushed back one side of her hair with a dramatic sweep of her hand. "*This* is why!" she announced, revealing the scar. "First you tried to kill me. Now you want to be chums. I don't know if I can forgive—" She suddenly stumbled, and Mia quickly placed a chair near her. Coral sank into it, shaking her head.

"You see? You aren't well. I could help you, take care of you. Mother, please, I beg of you. . . ." Mia knelt down beside the chair, her hand on her mother's arm. "Stop taking those shots. That stuff is killing you. You'll need more and more, and one day—"

Coral pushed away Mia's hand. She stood unsteadily, resisting Mia's attempt to help, and laughed weakly. "*You* help *me*? I think it's positively absurd when a child thinks it can tell its parent what to do." She looked around for her wrap, found it, and threw it over one shoulder. "Goodbye, Mia."

Mia watched helplessly as she walked out of the showroom.

* * *

Coral stopped off for a booster, keeping the car waiting. Back in her office, energetic and buzzing, she set about rearranging the July issue. She could not possibly feature Anais Du Pasquier now, which left her with six empty pages.

Virginia buzzed her intercom: "Donna Brooks to see you."

"Send her in." The back of Coral's coiffed neck pricked as Donna, smiling her outdoorsy, fresh smile, walked in.

"Did you meet her?" Donna asked eagerly.

"Who?"

"Anais Du Pasquier. Lloyd told me you snagged the first interview with her. What a coup! Congratulations. What was she like? I adore her clothes!"

"That's too bad, Donna, because we're not featuring them." Coral pointed dramatically to the July schedule pinned to the wall behind her, indicating six large X's across the center spread. She beamed at Donna. "How's my favorite fashion editor?" she asked. "Some Perrier, darling?"

Donna shook her head, watching while Coral poured herself a glass, curling one leg beneath her as she sat on the long couch.

"Why have you blanked those pages? Anais Du Pasquier is a hot designer. Was her collection that bad?"

Coral sipped her Perrier slowly, maddeningly. She replaced the glass and looked innocently at Donna. "It was *stunning*," she stated. "I tried on a coat that was a *dream*. The dresses are to die for. But *we're* not going to feature one button!"

"*Why?*"

"Because Anais Du Pasquier happens to be my daughter," Coral stated flatly.

"Your daughter? Mia? Are you sure?"

"I met her this morning, didn't I? Wayland Garrity set it up. Don't you see? She hid behind that name because she knew I would never feature her otherwise. I'm livid that we showed so many of her things last February—we undoubtedly helped her to achieve success!"

"But she deserves success, whether she's your daughter or some stranger! She's still a very good designer. Didn't she design for Phillipe Roux?"

"Exactly, and that's what this is—ersatz Phillipe Roux!"

Donna shook her head, standing up. "Oh, no, Coral, Anais Du Pasquier is beyond Roux. I shall just have to go see the new collection for myself—"

"I said we're not featuring it, Donna," Coral insisted. "Not as long as I'm editor-in-chief!"

Donna stared piercingly at her, allowing Coral's words to hang in the air just long enough to take on a new meaning. "And just how long do you think *that* will be if you keep up these ridiculous embargoes?" Donna questioned. "I suppose you have some long-standing grudge against your own daughter?"

"She tried to murder me!" Coral swept back her hair, displaying the scar.

Donna walked quickly to the door and closed it, coming back to sit in the chair adjacent to Coral's desk. "If you had been *my* mother," she said, and leaned toward Coral, "I'd have murdered you long ago!"

Coral bristled, her eyes widening. "How *dare* you say that to me! Get out of my office!"

Donna remained seated, very calm, very controlled. "Coral, I'm not going to bullshit you. I have worked around you for a few years, and this confrontation has been looming. Do you really think we're going to base *Divine*'s fashion philosophy on who *you* get on with? We'd be featuring nothing but Colin Beaumont's portraits of society ladies if we did that. That is not the way *Divine* will be run. It's time *I* had a lot more say about our direction."

"I can't believe what I'm hearing," Coral murmured. She poured more Perrier, her hand shaking, spilling water over her desk.

"You're still seeing that doctor, aren't you?" Donna asked. "One of our models told me she saw you there, trembling in the waiting room because you needed a shot so badly. You're letting us down, Coral! Did you slap Marcie Phillips's face the other day? She's suing us for a broken tooth cap and two days' work. *Did* you set fire to the hem of a Bill Blass ballgown?"

"We ran out of dry ice!" Coral cried. "I wanted a smoky effect!"

"They've billed us for two thousand dollars!" Donna told her. "I spend half my time on the phone defending

your... 'offbeat' behavior. Last year I urged Lloyd to renew your contract because I respect your work. But I did
think you'd start cleaning up your act once *Labels* started
dropping hints about you."

"*Labels*?" Coral cried. "It's libelous, all untrue—"

Donna raised her eyebrows but said nothing.

"And when *did* Lloyd last renew my contract?" Coral
asked.

Donna shrugged. "Last September, I believe."

Coral glanced at her calendar: "That means I am editor-
in-chief until next September. It's March now. By my
calculations, that gives me five more issues to edit. Start
crossing off the days on your calendar, Donna, because I
intend to work out my year to the last *minute*!"

"I'd never expect Lloyd to fire you," Donna said gently.
"You'd be elevated. To chief consultant editor. You'd keep
this office—"

"I *know* that one, Donna!" Coral snapped. "I presented
it to Maynard Cowles in exactly the same way! And you
know, as well as I knew, neither she nor I would stay
under those conditions. I'd rather defect to the enemy,
Vogue or *Bazaar*...."

"I think they're perfectly happy with their current editors," Donna said sweetly. "Diana Vreeland is particularly
revered...."

They were silent for a moment, Coral glancing around
the domain where, for the last years, she had ruled
supreme. The fashion kingdom of Manhattan—millions of
square feet of selling space, boutiques, stores, designers'
studios, showrooms, photographers' studios—it was such
a glamorous kingdom to relinquish! She glanced out at the
familiar sills and parapets of the nearby buildings, at the
beautiful green-toned copper detailing of a roof.

She looked back at Donna, realized she was being
closely watched, and laughed aloud. "The windows? Frightened I might take a running jump like poor Maynard?"

Donna raised her eyebrows. "I know how much *Divine*
means to you."

"Almost as much as it means to you, Donna," Coral
agreed, "But not quite enough to be able to bring myself
to marry its owner. Or let him touch me with his moist
little hands."

Donna's smile did not leave her face. "Lloyd's a real

man, Coral, whatever his appeal to you. In my book that's a hell of a lot better than those misfits *you* run around with. . . ."

Coral took a deep breath. "I *do* have some very dear friends amongst the talents that keep *Divine* way ahead of the competition. If you think sports jocks are the clue to creativity, it doesn't reflect too well on your fashion sense."

They stared at each other until Donna finally asked, "So you won't accept consulting editorship?"

"You can stick it up your tight little Nantucket ass," Coral said.

Donna shook her head. "You fool. You can't afford to speak to me like that."

Coral picked up a magnifier and began to inspect a fresh pile of proofs. "I have five months of contract to go," she said. "I'll leave September the first. Don't set foot in here before that date if you value your eyesight, Donna."

Donna got to her feet, her mouth tight. "You've been unnecessarily and *bloody* rude," she told Coral. "I could get Lloyd to fire you *today* for what you've said to me, but I sympathize with your problems. I'm genuinely sorry for you, Coral."

When she'd left the office, Coral fished in her desk drawer for a joint, lighting two Rigaud candles to mask the smell.

"I suppose I'm lucky she didn't expect the editorship on her return from their honeymoon," Coral told Colin that night in her apartment. He had been summoned to comfort her. A bottle of champagne was on ice, and caviar on crackers surrounded a mound of sour cream. She watched him nibble. "And all this ambition is masked in a kind of Nantucket mock sincerity that drives me *bananas*! A concern for my *health*! Ha!" She clinked her glass to his. "We'd better drink to a generous pension from *Divine*!"

"Are you kidding?" Colin said, leaning forward to kiss her cheek. "The other magazines will be fighting over who gets you!"

"You really think so?" she asked. A note of doubt had crept into her voice. "I wish I had enough money to retire!"

They finished the bottle during the evening, and Colin told her his news. "I'm planning *my* retirement from the fashion world," he said. "Nobody seems to want that many drawings these days. The art directors are all turning to photography."

Coral placed a hand on his arm sympathetically. "How shortsighted of them, darling. What a stupid world it is out there. Well, I suppose the sixties are about over. What will you *do*, Colin?"

He looked into her strained, tired face. "The last time I was in Paris, I took a trip to Provence and scouted around. I'm sinking my savings into the sweetest house you ever saw, with accompanying garden. I'll commune with nature, I suppose...."

"I'll visit!" she promised him. "Often! Just let me get over this trauma. *God*, what a day! On top of the dreaded Donna, I had the nightmare of Wayland and Mia playing a very silly trick on me. Did you have any idea that Mia designed the Anais Du Pasquier collections, Colin?"

He took her hands and looked seriously at her: "Yes, I did. And I'm afraid I am responsible for this morning's meeting. Wayland called me and told me it had backfired. I'm sorry...."

"Why did you get involved?"

"I thought you should be friends. With Wayland as well as Mia. Why keep enemies? If you're really going to be out of a job, you'll need all your friends, Coral. And your daughter needs you."

"She seems on top of the world!"

"Oh, Coral, you know Mia's a very unhappy girl...."

"Are you trying to say it's my fault? On the contrary, I've gone out of my way to help her, to be supportive . . . and what did I ever get back for it? She's either done shifty deals behind my back, almost costing me my position, or she's thrown heavy glass objects at my head."

Colin stood. "You've had a long day, and I think you should sleep," he said.

She saw him out, feeling drained and tired.

In bed that night she could not stop thinking about Donna Brooks. That woman would have to be dealt with somehow. Later, when she had nothing else to lose. She must first get some fabulous position on another prestige publication, then spit in her eye! In a stylish, chic way of course!

Coral drifted off to sleep with a half-hatched plot forming in her tired brain. . . .

* * *

The new firm of David Winters Inc. became a legend during its first wildly successful year. David always credited Ed Schreiber for the incredible Cinderella story.

The tale of their wheeling a rack of the first sample dresses and coats all the way up Eighth Avenue and crosstown to Bloomingdale's, Bendel, and Saks, getting orders from all three stores, had soon passed into fashion myth.

The clothes were acknowledged as brilliant designs, timely, quality fashion for a market satiated with novelties and fads. The fabrics they used were not cheap, nor were the clothes, yet they had gone from zero to an annual turnover of a million in their first year.

The publicity campaign started a new trend: twelve-page advertisements in the top magazines, showing sexy, moody photographs of David, sometimes shirtless on the beach, a female model wearing his dress in the background.

The unusual photo campaign established an image for the firm and made the point to admiring females that this very attractive male designer liked women and wanted them to wear his clothes. They responded, mobbing him at his personal showings in department stores, asking for autographs, advice, and even dates. David took a trunk tour across America, presenting a tightly choreographed fashion show in most of the major cities, making a short speech afterward, selling clothes to customers who became loyal fans and clients.

Ed and David were seen with the most beautiful models in New York. They were photographed with their latest dates, always gorgeous, by *Labels* and *WWD* at all the big openings, first nights, and private views. Yet both men considered their playboy images a joke; each was waiting for a sign from the woman he loved and could not replace or forget.

David continued to call Mia from time to time. Their conversations were awkward, punctuated with gaps when neither of them could think of anything to say. They spoke about Mackenzie and her new reputation as a recluse: She would not see them and had not appeared in public seen Alistair's funeral.

Mia's world, too, had shrunk. She had few friends and

too much time to sit at home and read the latest items in *Labels*. One in particular concerned her:

Is trouble brewing in the volatile Roux household? Married less than two years, Phillipe Roux yesterday denied rumors that his marriage to Josephine was nearing an early finale. Observers say the couple do not seem to get on that well. In New York, Headquarters' Wayland Garrity, early champion of the Roux style, cheerfully reported good sales of Roux's ready-to-wear, exclusive to that store....

Mia devoured the rumors, hardly daring to think what might happen if Phillipe were suddenly free.

Wayland was urging her to undertake a cross-country trunk-show promotion for her clothes, to be arranged by him. She refused to do it; the public exposure scared her. She wanted to stay anonymous. Despite this reluctance, *Labels* wrote: "Anais Du Pasquier is nudging Mackenzie Gold and David Winters for the designer name best known to the public," even though they had been unable to unmask the designer's identity, since Mia would not pose for a picture or give an interview.

"You're the Garbo of the fashion industry," Wayland said, chucking her under the chin. "What do *you* care, as long as it sells?"

But the success of her firm had not brought Mia the happiness or peace she sought. On the hot New York nights when her body seemed to know something her mind could not fathom, she felt herself aching for a caress, a tender touch, some interest in her as a woman. Manhattan trapped her, yet she did not want to leave it.

She read every word printed about Phillipe. He had never again gained the critical plaudits that "their" collection had received, but his name was so well-established that he was able to coast along by repeating her designs in different fabrics and combinations. Meanwhile, Phillipe cologne was proving popular, and advertised widely across America, using Phillipe's face. Unfortunately, that face seemed to confront her at every street corner, from buses and billboards.

* * *

During the weeks following that horrifying morning when she had awakened in bed with a dead husband, Mackenzie nearly ceased to function. Friends, family, and even some employees tried in their different ways to comfort and console her, but only her son seemed to hold any meaning for her. She remained reclusive, could not bring herself to respond to the hundreds of letters she received or to call back the many people who left messages with her answering service.

She was visiting a therapist to relieve her of the trauma that horror had brought. Ed Schreiber was the only person she both longed and feared to see. "But it's like, if I see Eddie, I'll feel I practically murdered Alistair," she explained to her friends, Luke and Loretta. They still lived in the Village and Mackenzie sent a car to bring them to see her. They were the friends who brought her the most comfort now. "Do you understand?" she asked them, and they nodded. "I want to see Eddie so much that I don't dare see him."

She left all Gold! business to her brothers, signing whatever they asked her to sign now that nothing really mattered much any more. She only enjoyed the time she spent with Jordan, playing with him, teaching him little things. Being with Jordan was the only escape from her self-imprisonment, though taking him to the park or the zoo was one long chase from photographers.

The worst feeling was that she might have saved Alistair's life. This guilt spilled over into all aspects of her life, especially into what was most on her mind—continuing her affair with Ed. That would really brand her as wicked now.

Ed refused to understand. He would call many times during the day, but they only spoke for a few minutes before he had to hang up.

"It's like she's grieving for a guy she didn't even really love!" he reported to David. "As if she felt obliged to grieve just to make herself feel better."

Soon Ed rationed himself to a phone call each week. But he never said good-bye without asking Mackenzie when they could meet.

"Oh Eddie . . ." she burst into tears the last time he had asked her that. "How can I see you? Right now I feel like it was *our* love that killed Alistair!"

"Oh no!" Ed protested. "That guy was on a self-destruction course long before I even laid eyes on you. You didn't kill him, and neither did I. He overdosed, it's as simple as that!"

"Baby—" Her voice cracked. It was husky at best, now that she wept daily, it was hoarse. "I wanna hold you and be held by you more than anything in the world. But it just wouldn't feel right now."

Ed shook his head, holding tightly on to the receiver. "Oh, Mack! I didn't want the guy dead, I swear to God. But now that's he's died, why shouldn't *we* be happy?"

"Because I can't be happy," she said glumly. "Not yet. . . ." After hanging up, she continued to sit, the telephone cradled in her lap, staring sightlessly out of the window.

In May, Colin Beaumont was commissioned by *Divine* to draw portraits of the top four American designers, as chosen by Coral for an Americana issue. He was one of Mackenzie's first visitors from the fashion world since her widowhood and he sketched her sitting on her huge Italian couch in the window of the living room.

"I could so easily sink into a long depression," Mackenzie told him. "But for Jordan's sake, I have to pull myself out of it. And for the company, too, of course."

"Your brothers won't be happy until they have Gold! stores in every major U.S. city," Colin joked, busily sketching Mackenzie's mane of dark hair.

When he'd finished, they sipped coffee together.

"I know what it's like to see someone you love slowly destroy themselves," he told her. "Why don't you do something helpful for young people hooked on something? Form some kind of committee to fight drug-peddling or something?"

She stared, mesmerized by this little man dressed in black sitting on her couch. "How do you fight drug-peddling?" she asked. "Isn't that the fuzz's job?"

Colin shrugged and sipped his coffee. "It was just an idea. Support some kind of fund-raising—with your glamour and visibility, you'd rake in the money. . . ."

"Money for what, though?" she asked dispiritedly. They sat in silence for a moment. Suddenly she answered her own question: "Money to open a drug-abuse center!" she cried. Then she added, "The Alistair Briarly Drug Abuse Center! Oh, Colin!" Her eyes lit up with sudden energy.

"I could help to ensure that no one has to suffer from this stuff—I could help them finance new ways to wean addicts off drugs. I've read about synthetic drugs that can help...."

After Colin's visit, Mackenzie began to return to normal. She resumed designing, and once more took an interest in the empire she headed. With Jordan, she took trips to Paris and London to look at the sites for the proposed first two European Gold! stores. And she devoured the stacks of magazines and papers she'd been unable to even open before, catching up on all the news. Her self-imposed exile had cleansed and refreshed her. The world looked different. Fashion looked different, too: There had been a subtle, but definite change, and she felt it.

She called a meeting with her brothers, cloistering them in their office boardroom for two hours, watching them carefully to see if there was any glimmer of understanding or interest in her proposals. Reggie sat with a self-satisfied smirk on his face, overweight, defensive. Max, balding at thirty, let his eyes roam around the room, impatient to be on the move.

"Do either of you care at all about what I'm saying?" she asked them.

"Sure!" Reggie nodded, and Max sat up attentively.

"I've done my market research! I'm *back*! I checked out all our competition and looked over our last quarter's sales. We can do better, boys. We *have* to take Gold! up-market now. We have the perfect opportunity by opening in London and Paris. Maybe we could be manufactured in France—"

"We have perfectly good workrooms in L.A.!" Max said hotly.

"Well, at least we can go for better fabrics, higher-priced clothes. I am *not* going to use vinyl anymore, *or* acrylic, *or* rayon. I have to trust *my* instinct, which is: Girls are going to want better stuff. Everyone else is starting to do it—look at David Winters. His clothes are double, triple the price of my stuff, and they're selling like hotcakes."

"Mack!" Reggie interrupted, raising a protesting hand. "How many times do I have to tell you: One of the first principles of business is that you don't fool around with a winning formula...."

"There *is* no formula for fashion, Reggie!" she said

impatiently. "Fashion changes constantly—that's *why* it's *fashion*! We're going to swing back to conventional styles. I've been crazy long enough, but there's a time for everything. Look at what Ed Schreiber's done for David Winters. And look at the success of Anais Du Pasquier. It's no coincidence that they're *all* up-market! That's what women want now."

"They're selling hundred-dollar dresses, Mack," Reggie replied. "Yours are forty-five bucks, for Christ's sake!"

"I *want* that market!" Mackenzie said. "I wanna get my hands into some silk and cashmere!"

"That isn't your image, Mack—"

"My image is whatever I *want* it to be!" she yelled. "I'm not *stuck* with anything! It's our company, for God's sake—we can do anything we like!"

"Not exactly..." Max squirmed uncomfortably, looking at Reggie. "Why don'tcha tell her about it, Reg. You're gonna have to, sooner or later."

"Look, Mack..." Reggie twisted in his chair to face her. "Since Ed left the company, we've been trying to manage our own financing—"

"You never replaced him?" she shouted.

"Wait a minute—I'm trying to tell you..." He waved his hand impatiently. "Every time we open a new store, we need big backing. The stores cost up to a million, you know? We've accepted financing from various backers, and *they* want us to stick with what you're best at—the young market, reasonably priced clothing, all that...."

Dismayed, she stared at them. "Didn't you clowns know that we needed someone to take Ed's place? Did you replace Alistair?"

"Don't get so excited—we're doing just fine. The press comes to *us* now, we don't need to pay someone to court them...."

"But who *deals* with them? The shop assistants? Oh, Reggie, don't let everything slide because you're too cheap to hire new people. I want you to put ads in *Women's Wear* tomorrow for a press person—"

"We're making more money than ever!" Reggie told her angrily. "We don't need to change anything too drastically right now. Gold! was built on the idea of providing low-priced fashion to young kids. It's done fine on that level. No one can touch us for cheapo fashion!"

"*Reggie ... Max,*" she said slowly, exaggerating her patience. "I am trying to explain to you that we need to be *ahead* of the game; that we can do even better if we anticipate what is *going* to happen—in a year's time, in two years...."

They argued for an hour. They were as tight-fisted about letting her spend more money on better quality fabrics as they had always been about the stores' locations and decor. They still did not trust her, she realized. And the idea that there were anonymous backers telling them what to do was too horrible even to contemplate. Finally they agreed to let her begin work on an experimental range of better clothing to be tried out in the Madison Avenue store to see how it sold. Afterward they produced documents for her to sign. She signed forms without reading them, and finally pushed the last one away: exhausted. "I now declare this meeting over!" she cried. "God! It's past eleven...."

As they stood outside the office, waiting for the elevator, she told them, "I'm giving my first interview in months. Howard Austin finally talked his way into my apartment. He promised *he'll* write the interview and it won't be bitchy. I'm only doing it to plug a foundation in Alistair's name—a drug-abuse center."

Reggie and Max exchanged glances. "Drug abuse?" Reggie echoed. "Great publicity, huh? Great for your image? Are you going to be one royal pain in the ass again, Mack?"

She turned on him furiously. "What does this have to do with you? I'm doing this for Alistair. So his son can be proud of him..."

"But it's not very tactful!" Reggie said. The elevator arrived and they stepped in. "*Drugs! Abuse!* People hear those words and they think—"

"Who cares what they think?" Mackenzie shouted.

They reached the ground floor and stood in an uneasy group in the lobby as Max fumbled for keys. "You want a lift home?" he asked Mackenzie.

"I'll walk—it's only a few blocks."

"It's night, and you're gonna walk alone?"

She turned around to face them both, her eyes blazing. "I'm not *afraid*! Do you understand that? My husband died in my arms! After that, what do I have to be afraid of? If someone wants to mug me, let him! I don't give a shit! The way I feel now, *I'm* ready to mug them right back!"

She strode off down Madison as her brothers looked darkly at each other. Max grunted as he knelt down to lock the heavy plate-glass door. "It was going so smoothly with those four designers she'd hired," he said. "They did what they were told. She's always found something to bitch about, and it'll always be something we have to cough up more dough for. Now it's cashmere and silk!"

Reggie made a resigned face. They walked toward his car.

"Reggie?" Max turned to him. "Do we really need her? Are the designs so good, or would they sell anyway?"

Reggie shrugged. "One day we'll find out." He ripped open a fresh pack of cigarettes and stuck one in his mouth. "We'll have to find out because my guts can't take all this aggravation. I got too many other problems, like production and delivery, and right now they're more on my mind than Lady Mackenzie and her fucking drugs and silk and cashmere. . . ."

"It would kill Ma if we ever tried to fire her," Max remarked.

"It was gonna kill Ma if she had a *goyishe* baby, but Ma survived," Reggie said, chuckling. "If she starts seeing Ed Schreiber again—and those two always had the hots for each other—we'll be in more trouble. He'll fill her head with quality and upgrading ideas. That's the time we'll find out whether Gold! needs Lady Mackenzie or vice versa."

Twenty-four

Coral was persuaded to stay at *Divine* until mid-September, although her name would remain on the masthead until the end of the year.

"For continuity's sake," Donna Brooks argued.

But the fashion world began to buzz with the news. *Labels* wrote:

> Which top editor at one of the most prestigious fashion mags has been told her days at the desk are numbered? The news is being kept top-secret so as not to scare off advertisers, but the publishing world is wondering. . . .

Wayland stared puzzled at the item. Could the fall come so soon? So finally? He felt a pang of regret for the good days with Coral. Donna Brooks would not be nearly as much fun. As he thought that, the phone on his desk rang, startling him.

"Wayland? It's Donna here . . . Donna Brooks."

"I was just thinking of you!" he replied. "I must have conjured you up. That item in *Labels* . . . it's—"

"It's Coral, yes. You'll have to know, because I want to organize the next *Divine* Fashion Awards with you. I intend to keep the collaboration between Headquarters and us alive as ever! I hope you agree!"

"Why, of course, Donna! I was just thinking how much fun you and I will have together when you take over! I've always loved the work you did on *Divine*—you have marvelous taste!"

"Why, thank you, Wayland. Please keep all this to yourself, won't you? Poor Coral will have a hard enough time without all Seventh Avenue knowing about it. I guess the awards will be a little late this year, but I'm determined to hold them...."

"Who's choosing the winner?"

"*I* am, of course!"

"Any hints as to who it is? I have a hunch you'll pick Mackenzie Gold...."

"Well, since you're so curious, I'll tell you: I'm giving the award to Anais Du Pasquier. You'll have to get her out of hiding, Wayland. She *will* accept it in person, won't she?" She hung up, leaving Wayland staring wide-eyed into space.

"I feel like a new woman," Mackenzie told Ed on the phone, the day after her *Labels* interview appeared.

The interview changed everything. Seeing herself written about respectfully alongside a flattering photograph of herself with Jordan, seemed to put her life into perspective for her. The public announcement of a drug-abuse center named for Alistair made her plans official.

"People have been calling me all week," she said. "Congratulating me because it's the first *un*-bitchy long piece *Labels* has ever run! The gamble paid off, Eddie. It's the first bit of respect I've ever gotten from the trade press. It allows me to think of the future...."

"The future?" Ed grunted.

"We're going to start fresh," she told him. "I don't want to talk about anything that happened before today. I want to think and talk about the future."

"Meaning me, too?"

"Of course meaning you, too, baby," she murmured. "God, if you knew how my entire body's been aching for you, darling. It always has, you know. Will you stop by tonight? Sevenish? We'll have the reunion of all time, Eddie. It'll go down in history as—"

"Just like that?" he asked. He sounded resentful, snappy.

"What d'you mean?" she said, surprised. "I've been looking forward to—"

"You think you can keep me waiting for months and then just snap your fingers? What am I, a trained dog?"

"Oh, Eddie..." She sighed. "Oh, baby, you're bigger than that, aren't you? You're not going to give me this hurt male pride bit, are you? I've been grieving for a dead

husband, for Christ's sake—I haven't been playing around
with other men. There's only been you!"

"Well, I know I'm supposed to jump for joy, but my
pride *has* been hurt. I would have liked to help you
through your grief. I would have liked to have been there
for you—"

"You *were* there!"

"At the end of a phone!"

"More than that. Knowing you cared helped me get
through this. Oh, darling, don't make me beg you. Just
come at seven—we'll talk here. I want to see you so
much." She hung up before he could say no. God, men
were touchy, she thought.

At five that afternoon Mackenzie soaked in a long,
warm bubble bath. She emptied half a bottle of Chanel
into the tub, to be perfect for Eddie. After patting herself
dry with a thick, soft bath towel, she dabbed more perfume on her body. Was it possible? she wondered. *Could*
you actually get it all? She was suddenly so happy it
scared her. She tried to stop counting all the good things—
her son, her career, her firm . . . and tonight, her lover.
Nobody got everything, did they?

When Ed knocked gently on the front door, after being
announced by the doorman, she dimmed the lights and
started a Sly album from the first track. She had imagined
they would fall into each other's arms, but when she
opened the door there was a strange, shy silence. She was
wearing a long, black slinky dress. Ed wore a suit and tie
and was immaculately groomed. Only his uncontrollably
floppy hair fell in his eyes; it was longer, fuller, and his
navy eyes gleamed as intensely as ever. He took her hand,
looking at her very seriously.

She did not want to talk. She had lit dozens of candles
throughout the large living room, and they flickered
invitingly as they walked through to the couch by the
window, where two bottles of champagne in ice awaited
them on a chrome cart.

She guided him to the windows to look out at the view.
Standing in front of him, she pulled his hand over her
shoulder and leaned back on him. He stood up close
behind her. The electricity was there—*God*, was it there! It
was the last day of August, and Manhattan shimmered in
a haze of heat, but the soft purr of her air-conditioning

insulated them against the humidity and noise outside. She could feel his warm breath at the back of her neck.

With a groan, because it was more than she could stand, she turned, pulling him close to her. They stood like that, unmoving, for a long time, just holding. She drank in the warm, clean smell of him—the cologne she remembered, the smell of his hair, of his breath. He turned slowly and pressed his lips over hers; softly at first, then his tongue broke through her lips and they were kissing hard, as hard as anyone could kiss, and groaning the low, murmured sighs of pleasure—a surprised, involuntary sound that only lovers, only two people whose bodies are totally in accord, can make.

He slipped a hand under her loose black sleeves, his touch surprising her. Very gently and tenderly he touched unexpected parts of her—under her arms, the small of her back, up under the hair at the nape of her neck. These light touches, as he refamiliarized himself with her, combined with his intense stare to awaken her body, set it on fire. His touches were so gentle, they made her want more, her body pushing against his hand. When he reached her breasts, he caressed underneath and around them, making her nipples long to be touched, to be crushed, to be nibbled!

She moaned, turning limp in his arms. "I want this to last forever!" she whispered.

She felt the broad thighs that tensed beneath the fine cotton fabric of his pants, squeezed the hard cheeks of his clenched buttocks, slipped her hand between his legs to feel how much he wanted her. Her other hand found its way through a shirt opening to touch his chest. She could feel his readiness. His sex was rock-hard. He gasped as she quickly unzipped his pants and grasped him in her hand, relishing the feel of him. She held his stiff muscle in her fist, looking down at the pink head as she moved her hand slowly up and down. He had wriggled two fingers into her and was massaging gently inside her. Her eyes closed against the intense pleasure. He freed her breasts from the top of the dress and began to suck on the tip of one.

"Wait!" She jerked back. "Eddie," she whispered, "let's make our fantasies come true tonight. Let's do everything to each other we've ever dreamed of doing to someone!

I've never had a man lick me all over. I've never done that to a man! I want to do it to you tonight—!"

He groaned hoarsely into her ear, "Whatever you do to me, I'll be doing to you. . . ."

She forced herself to break away from him, adjusting her dress. Wheeling the champagne over to them, she bunched some cushions on the sofa and pushed him down. "Oh, baby, I just want you to hold me and love me all night . . ." she told him.

He opened the champagne and they stared at each other with unashamed lust and love. She greedily drank a whole glass after saying "To us!" He was looking at her with a serious expression, almost hypnotized, and she found it unbearably sexy. She refilled their glasses.

He allowed her to undress him. His body was as chunky, tanned, and hairy as she remembered it, reliving that afternoon in his office. He undressed her and she flinched as he examined her body. She still had stretch marks from Jordan's birth and she was older, but as he covered her body with little kisses she relaxed in the wonderful knowledge that the magic, the magnetism, was still there between them.

She leaned over him, her tongue finding his soft places, the smooth silky planes at the sides of his body. There was nothing about him that displeased her. She knew the taste of him, the smell of him, the touch of him. His tongue was as busy as hers. He licked across her shoulders and into her ears, her neck, under her chin. She licked his arms, his back, his thighs. And whatever she did, his tongue echoed on her body. The feel of his gentle lapping caused such a yearning pleasure in her that she almost came from that sensation. His body aroused her in an almost primal way. When she finally planted her mouth on the essence of him, tonguing his proud male stiffness, he parted her legs and buried his face between them. She felt his tongue probing up inside her, his nose rubbing against her mound, and she wanted to scream with the feeling. A thrilling, melting fulfillment coursed through her, making her arch her body, offering more of herself to him. Then she felt too far from him, and reversed their positions to get back into his arms again, her mouth pressed against his.

"I forgot how good it is just to be kissing you," she told him. "I can never get enough of that. . . ."

He laughed, holding her close, their naked bodies smooth and warm against each other. His hands were behind her, under her thighs, his fingertips curving into her crevice, exciting her. His fingers inside her now, he bent his head to nibble on that part of her which was so sensitive, spreading a glow of sexual pleasure through her. She had her first drenching orgasm from that. She held him in her hand, caressing him with her fingers, his pulsing sex growing to its full length. She licked her fingers and rubbed a slippery, slow massage over the tip making him tremble. He held a nipple gently in his teeth and every time he nuzzled it softly, she felt him tense with desire in her hand. That made her desire grow, until she urged him to lie full-length upon her.

"Eddie, I'll go crazy if you don't come inside me now. . . oh, my darling, enter me . . . please enter me."

She bit gently on his earlobe as he slid into her and slowly thrust deep. Then she closed her legs on him and pumped him to pleasure, to satiation. He had been so hard, so excited, for so long, that he could not hold out. Her squeezing, in spite of himself, forced a gasp of surprise, then a long drawn-out cry of impending pleasure. He felt a tickle of sensation begin at the back of his groin, then quickly explode up through his body until his entire person seemed about to burst into pleasure. The seed rushed up his sex like a volcano erupting, an unbelievable gush of sexual feeling accompanying it. He clutched her shoulders, buried his face in her neck, then jerked back to look at her. Mackenzie, sensing it happen inside her, felt another, greater wave of passion break, like a volatile sea, upon the previous one. It swept her, drowning her in sensation as Ed pulsed and rocked on her, crying out in her ear with overwhelming pleasure. The sensation was so great that she felt it literally turn to love. *Become* love! For him!

"Do you love me? Do you *love* me?" she cried, thrusting her hands through his thick hair, pulling it hard.

He squinted, his face almost agonized, brow furrowed, as he stared at her, nodding.

"Yes! I *love* you! I *love* you! Damn it! I also hate you, but *love* me!"

She laughed and cried because she knew what he meant. She wanted to be close to every inch of him, for their bodies to meld, for them to become one person. She wrapped her legs behind his, her feet under his, her lips between his, their breaths intermingling. She was now one with her Eddie. They were a couple.

The December issue of *Divine* was put to bed in late August. It was Coral's last issue. She had summed up the 1960s with a ten-page retrospective of the decade's fashion. It would be another collectors' issue.

A few days later Coral stripped her office of its personal possessions. The zebra skin was unpinned from the large desk chair she had always used. Several old colleagues had sent bouquets of flowers. No future plans had been announced. Donna had tactfully gone out for the day on a location shooting in Chinatown. Coral put on a cheerful face, almost whistling as she packed toiletries and gloves into wicker hampers to be transported to her apartment. Virginia sat in her adjacent office, sniffling.

"*Please* don't, Virginia," Coral said, placing her hands on her shoulders. "The second I take a fabulous new job, I'll insist that you're part of the package. We'll soon be working together again."

Virginia looked up at her, her tearstained face grimacing. "*Will* we? Will you send for me? It won't feel right working for Mrs. Brooks. I feel so terrible today, I can hardly work. Would you like a cup of sweet tea?"

"I don't think so, dear," Coral replied, and turned away, her mouth suddenly trembling.

She sought Lloyd in his office that afternoon. "Adieu," she said, and kissed his cheek quickly. "Good-byes can be so tacky...."

"Coral..." He tried to swallow. "I...I don't feel good about this at all. You won't let me take you out for lunch? I'll happily pay for a stay in a sanitarium, Coral, if it would help?"

"I'll be much too busy for that!" she replied, waving aside his offer. "Bless you, Lloyd dear," she said, pressing his hand. "Au revoir! We're bound to bump into each other! Often, I hope!" Her eyes were dry and hard, but she hurried out of his office as if afraid she would break down.

The art staff filed into her room during the afternoon, kissing and hugging her good-bye, and she found it very hard to keep from crying.

When Donna Brooks returned to the office that afternoon, she found her husband sitting pensively behind his desk. "She looked so sad, so vulnerable!" he told Donna. "Are you sure you can't talk her into staying on as associate editor or something?"

"She told me to stick it up my ass!" she said, nuzzling his cheek. "Don't cry for Coral, darling. She's a survivor!"

Donna left early, to prepare for a gala dinner party at their town house that night to celebrate her fashion editorship ending with this brilliant promotion. She had invited Howard Austin and a few others from the trade press. Everyone would be there. And Coral would be celebrating her freedom, sharing a bottle with Colin Beaumont. Trying not to scream.

Coral sent Virginia home early; her sniffs were getting on her nerves. At five she walked calmly out of the building and took a cab to Gilles's salon for a two-hour total treatment. She would be dining out with Colin and wanted to look her best—there were bound to be photographers around, stalking her. She would not let a bright smile be absent from her face for a second!

It had taken Coral weeks to manipulate her time so that she could be absolutely certain Donna had the following appointment with Gilles.

"*Et voilà!*" Gilles said as they both scrutinized her face in the mirror. "You have never looked more beautiful, Coral." They stared at her ravaged face, trying to ignore the nervous little twitches of her mouth due, they both knew, to her need for a booster shot. She would get it on her way home, she decided. She squinted at her reflection.

"You don't think it's a little *too* red, Gilles, darling?" she asked. "I'll have dozens of meetings next week regarding new jobs and—"

"It is perfect for you," he assured her, his handsome face beaming.

She turned to kiss him, and handed him a hundred-dollar bill to change for her. When he left the private cubicle, it took just fifteen seconds for her to refill his hair-conditioner bottle with a phial of hydrochloric acid she had secreted in her quilted Chanel purse.

It was her last piece of work as editor-in-chief of *Divine*. Now she could relax. Donna's hair might regrow. But it would take forever. Coral raised her eyes thankfully to heaven: Thank you for wigs, she prayed. Donna will be so grateful.

Labels' Tittle-Tattle column on Monday, September 2nd, included:

A fire engine, an ambulance, and two paramedics were rushed to Gilles's—a hair and beauty salon that caters to a jet set and celebrity clientele—on East Sixtieth Street Friday night, when *Divine*'s brand-new editor-in-chief, Donna Brooks, was involved in an accident with hydrochloric acid. She was treated for shock and released later that night in time for the party celebrating her editorship at the Brooks's town house on Park Avenue. Mrs. Brooks termed the whole thing "an accident—just that. I'm sure no one meant to do it," and announced that she would not be pressing charges against Gilles Huppert, owner of the salon. Sources indicate that someone with a grudge against Donna Brooks may be behind this "accident." The party, at which Mrs. Brooks covered her baldness with a beautiful Pucci turban uncharacteristic of the sporty editor, was a great success.

"Of course I know Coral did it," Donna said, watching as Howard Austin poured her a glass of wine in the tiny darkened bar of an unknown hotel halfway down Madison. It was late afternoon, the day after her party.

"To the new editor-in-chief," Howard toasted her. "I still think you should let me run the full story *and* press charges. The woman's out of her mind. She could have killed you. . . ."

Donna nodded, then shrugged. "I'm rather sorry for her, Howard. I never thought I could be, but there's something pitiful about a woman who self-destructs. She was all set to be the longest-reigning editor in fashion history—I'd have been honored to work with her. . . ."

"No one told her to get hooked on speed," Howard shrugged. "Our story has probably finished off any career she might still have left."

"She'll be more or less banished from the fashion world, I'd think," Donna agreed. "Only Wayland Garrity, Colin Beaumont, and her daughter will have anything to do with her."

"And you're definitely giving her daughter the fashion award? Just to spite Coral?"

"No, I really think she deserves it. Anais Du Pasquier is showing the best clothes I've seen in years. David Winters isn't far behind. . . ."

"The Queen is dead, long live the Queen," he said, and clinked his glass against hers. He eyed the silk scarves she had wound around her head: "Does it hurt?" he asked.

"Not much . . ."

The smiles left their faces as they stared at each other. "Go up," she whispered. "I'll join you in five minutes."

She watched as he strode to the tiny reception desk, confidently asking for the room under an assumed name. They had to be very careful. Donna stretched her body, her arms high above her head, and glanced at her watch, imagining Howard undressing and lying on the bed, awaiting her. Her stomach lurched with a barely contained jump of lust. She would let him make love to her very slowly, pretend she needed a lot of time to get in the mood. As editor-in-chief of *Divine*, she felt a new sense of power, of control. Slowly she stood and made her way to the elevator.

Coral seemed to disappear off the face of Manhattan for several weeks. She did not answer Colin's calls. In an attempt to bury the hatchet, Wayland wrote her, dangling front-row seats for Nureyev at the Met. Coral did not respond.

Colin called her every day. Sometimes Coral picked up the phone and told him brusquely, "I'm busy!" Many times she did not answer the phone at all. Finally Colin received a summons to visit.

"Don't expect dinner," she warned over the phone. "I'll crack open a can of nuts—*if* I feel up to it."

He called Wayland with the news. "Whatever you do, don't mention that Mia's getting the *Divine* Fashion Award," Wayland cautioned. "That would probably send her over the edge."

Colin was there just after seven, a bouquet of the prettiest flowers he could find in his hand.

"Darling, how *sweet!*" she said, opening the door, bending to kiss him and ushering him in.

He was shocked at her appearance. She had not done her hair nor even slashed any color on her lips. He'd never seen her this careless. Her thin legs were encased in tight black pants, and a white silk shirt emphasized the ivory pallor of her skin. She looked very old.

Coral fetched an ashtray, nervously fussing around. "I hope you aren't ravenous, Colin, because I cannot bear the sight or smell of food!"

"I can see that!" He caught hold of her hand and swung her around to face him. "Coral, you're positively *skeletal!* Honestly, you must try to—"

"Now don't be all motherly, Colin. . . ." She went into the kitchen to fetch a chrome cart on which stood champagne, deep in an ice bucket, and wheeled it across the room.

Colin could not take his eyes off her. She saw him scrutinizing her and snapped, "Don't look at my hair! I'm suddenly persona non grata at the hair salons. Gilles has forbidden me to set foot in his place—I can't for the life of me think why!"

"Oh, Coral," Colin said, and shook his head sadly. "I'm sure you can if you try!"

She indicated the champagne glasses on the cart and collapsed on one of the oversized couches. Colin opened the champagne and poured a glass each, handing her one.

"What shall we drink to?" he asked, trying to be cheerful.

Coral held up her glass expectantly, but suddenly let out a piteous wail. The sound tore through him, freezing his blood. He set down his glass and put his arm around her.

"Coral, what is it?"

Her eyes filled with tears, and she took a long sip of her drink. "They don't *want* me, Colin!" She quickly drank the rest of her wine.

"*Who* doesn't?" he asked gently.

"*Any*body!" She gulped, and held out her glass for more, like a deprived child.

"Okay. Let's define 'anybody,'" he said, and refilled her glass.

Coral lit a cigarette and sat back, puffing on it in jerky little gasps. Her eyes grew large and they fixed on his. "I fixed eight *clever* little luncheons in this very room," she told him. "A Japanese restaurant catered them. I never want to lay *eyes* on sushi again! They were perfect luncheons! I even had a goddamn pianist cart his baby grand up here to entertain! I must have been totally crazy but I wanted style—I wanted to dazzle them! Well, obviously I dazzled them into total speechlessness! I started with *Vogue*, then *Bazaar*, and so on through all the rest. I concentrated on a publisher at a time—made up little groups: publisher, owner, editors—it was all very civilized ... and when it was over, I was offered a shopping column for *Mademoiselle* and some vague ideas for freelance articles! I balked at talking to *Women's Wear*, and of course I couldn't possibly have called *Labels* after what Howard Austin's printed about me. No one is interested. Nobody wants me. My worst nightmare has come true!"

Her lower lip was trembling, her facade down. He was seeing a pitiful, aging, lonely lady.

"What shall I *do*?" she asked him. "I *can't* retire!"

"What about retailing?" he asked. "Did you consult with any department stores? Headquarters could surely use you?"

"Work with Wayland?" she snorted. "He's betrayed me too many times."

"I'm sure he would want to help you—"

"I won't accept charity, Colin!"

"Don't think of it like that...."

"Not a word of this to anyone, Colin! Promise?" she said urgently. "If it leaks out in *Labels*, I'm finished. Oh, God, maybe Maynard was right to jump? Maybe there *is* no life after *Divine*?"

"Let me talk to Wayland. I'm sure he'll come up with something. And it wouldn't be charity," he assured her.

"I have printing ink in my veins, Colin—you know that!"

They sat in silence for several seconds, then Colin said sadly, "Mia's doing so well—you should have forgiven and forgotten and become friends again.... You two could really use each other."

Coral sighed. "Oh, I don't know. I felt a bit guilty about it. I mean, her stuff is wonderful, and perhaps I should have settled our feud, but I was too taken aback, too surprised when I realized she was behind Anais Du Pasquier. I expected a French woman, and suddenly I saw Mia. I felt as if they had played a trick on me. She looked so beautiful, so lovely. I *have* missed her these last weeks...."

Colin watched her carefully. If he could bring his mediating talents to patch up this broken, bitter family, he would really feel he had achieved something.

"Coral, I've just had a marvelous idea!" he said. His heart had begun to beat fast, because an incredible scenario had suddenly hatched in his brain. "I'm going to tell you something I was told not to tell you, but I think it's important that you know. Mia is going to get this year's *Divine* Fashion Award."

Coral's face showed a mixture of emotion: pride, envy, joy, and anger. He watched them pass over her wretched face, fascinated. Whatever Coral was, she was never someone you could take your eyes from for a moment.

"*Donna!*" she said. "Donna Brooks chose her, to spite *me!*"

Colin groaned with exasperation and grasped her arm. "Forget about people doing things to spite *you*! The world doesn't revolve around *you*, Coral. She would have won the award anyway—don't you see? She's really good! She deserves it!"

Coral slumped back against the couch. "So what?" she asked dully. "What does any of this have to do with *me?*"

"Your name will still be on the masthead of the magazine until the January issue hits the newsstands," he pointed out. "To many people, you're still the editor-in-chief of *Divine*. If I pull enough strings—perhaps I could arrange things for *you* to present your own daughter with the award? It would be fabulous publicity for you, and generate a lot of goodwill! You could make up with Mia, everyone in the fashion industry would see you—and you could get yourself in shape and look fabulous by then! But you have to lay off the booze, the pot, and the shots!"

Coral made a face. "I don't know what you mean—I only drink a little—" pouring more champagne.

"Coral! Darling!" Colin put his arm around her emaciated shoulder. "Did it ever occur to you that this is *why* people don't want you? Everyone knows that junkies are the *worst*! Why, there was an article in the *Times*—"

"Is that *really* what you think I am?" she interrupted. "A junkie?" She turned to look him in the eyes, and hers were suddenly clear and blue.

"I'm sorry to be so blunt, Coral, but... that acid on poor Donna's head! Don't tell me you were thinking rationally? It *is* the kind of thing people on speed do—and everyone knows it was you. That's why the salons won't let you in. You're lucky not to be in jail...."

Coral stared at him for a moment, then suddenly burst out in a cackle of laughter. "Revenge is sweet, Colin!"

"Coral," he said, sitting back on the couch and watching her, "if I can get Donna Brooks to allow you to present the award, you won't let me down, will you? You'll be the elegant, poised Coral Stanton I've always known...."

She sighed. "Oh, I suppose so. I know you're right. I *would* like to be friends with Mia now, but I am terribly proud. You know, I had my tarot read by that Jimmy Palazza last week—everyone uses him. Every question I asked turned up that damned woman with her head in a noose! He tried to gloss it over but I know that card means doom and death, Colin..."

"You need to spend a week or two in Provence with me, Coral. The change will be marvelous for you. We'll go after the awards... *if* I can arrange things—and I'll have to pull a lot of strings."

Twenty-five

"That was the best *ever*, Eddie! Ever ever, *ever!*" Mackenzie told him. She lay beneath him on her wide bed, his head under her chin, her hands lightly smoothing his shoulders as their breathing returned to normal and their bodies cooled.

Ed laughed. "You say that every time!"

"It's *better* every time! *Really* it is! Don't *you* think so?"

He laughed his low, rumbling laugh. "Sure I do!"

Each time they were together she marveled at their chemistry, at two people experiencing such intense sexual attraction. It did not lessen in any way—it grew.

Before Ed's visits, she enjoyed the ritual of preparing for him, of taking a long, warm bath and then spraying perfume on the parts of her body she knew he would kiss or nuzzle up against. She kept their meetings secret; she wanted no one to know. Jordan had to be taken care of, the maid and butler dismissed. Ed would arrive. They would kiss, and then without speaking, he would carry her up the twisting stairs to the bedroom. She had changed the position of the bed, covered it in black satin sheets. In the haven of her bed, she undressed Ed, then herself, and as their skins touched, she stared into his dark blue eyes which stared back so intently into hers. He loved her body so thoroughly, investigating every corner with his tongue, his lips, raising her to a point of expectation that was almost unbearable, then thoroughly satisfying her. The enjoyment felt almost immoral, forbidden, and this gave a keener edge to her pleasure.

As she held him in her arms, opening her eyes to glance into his now and then, she thought: *I love you so much!* Since that first night she had not said it again.

Saying it might break the spell. No one but she must know of this love . . . but surely he could tell from the way she held him that she loved him?

"So when do we marry?" he asked.

She sighed. "You ask that every time . . . and it's still not the right time."

"Mack, you think people are going to line up on Madison Avenue to stone you because you remarry?"

"I never give a shit what 'people' think—you know that. It's what *I* think that counts, and *I* don't feel right about it yet."

"*You* don't feel right about not being Lady Briarly," he said bitterly. "You don't feel like losing your precious title." He moved away from her, swinging his legs over the bed to pull on his slacks.

"Don't get dressed so soon!" she cried, touching his arm. "You know I love lying here with you, feeling your skin. . . ."

"You hate the idea of being plain old 'Mrs. Ed Schreiber,' face it," he said, and continued to dress.

"Eddie—" she plumped two pillows behind her back and sat up, watching him. "I'll be absolutely honest with you," she said. "Look at me, please!"

He turned to her, and they stared intently at each other.

"The *Divine* Fashion Awards are just about due to be announced. I think I have a good chance of getting one this year. If I win, it would mean a lot to me to accept it in Alistair's name—he was my first encouragement. Do you understand?"

Ed went back to dressing. "Did you ever wonder how I feel? Maybe I'd like to take Jordan to the zoo, be seen in public with the woman I love—like ordinary people. . . ."

"Well, I'm not ordinary people, Eddie. I've done so many talk shows and ads that I'm a household face, like Lucille Ball!"

"Well, *I'm* ordinary!" he said, and shrugged into his jacket.

Mackenzie reached out and pulled him to her, kissing his lips. "Please, baby," she crooned. "Don't sulk. You're the only man for me." She kissed him with all her feelings, her passion expressing itself through her lips and tongue. She persuaded him to stay.

Later, they sent out for Japanese food, and dined on

salmon teriyaki and sake, their bare feet touching under the table.

"So, how's it going with David? Still Mister Success?" she asked.

Ed nodded. "It's phenomenal. He should be walking on air, but the guy's such a grouch. I call him 'the doomed romantic.' Those moody, glowering portraits we take of him aren't so far from the truth, you know. He dates the most gorgeous models in the business. Actresses pursue him. But no one really gets through. He's so hung up on one screwy girl. . . ."

"Mia?" Mackenzie speared a tempura carrot. "She lives like a nun. He'll never get her. I'm not speaking to her at the moment—can't even remember why. She sent a nice letter when Alistair died. I should have answered but . . . there's something ice cold there. I'm crazy about her clothes, though. *So* classy! David's stuff is pure class, too. Where do you find those incredible fabrics?"

"They're around," Ed told her. "Your brothers just don't let you go near that price range."

"Eddie, they're trying to control me—" she began, but he gently hushed her with his fingers on her lips.

"I don't work there anymore," he reminded her. "Even if I did, I wouldn't get between you and your brothers."

"You don't like them, do you?"

He shrugged. "Now that I run my own company, I see there are other ways to operate, without exploiting people."

"*Who* do they exploit? *Me?*"

"Are you kidding?" He laughed. "You own a quarter of the firm, you get a quarter of the profits. I'm talking about those poor machinists in L.A."

"What about them?" she demanded hotly. "Reggie and Max are operators, aren't they? Don't they haggle everyone down to a rock-bottom price?"

"And you know what *that* means in California? I thought you were so politically aware?"

"I *am*, goddamn it!" she said indignantly. "Christ, I was nearly arrested for picketing against buying lettuce at Gristede's last month. I haven't eaten grapes in months—"

"Let's just forget it," Ed muttered.

"You promised you'd always tell me if there was anything wrong," she demanded. "Do we underpay our workers?"

He shook his head. "I'm not getting involved. I have enough problems with you already," he said, looking around for his jacket.

Mackenzie placed her hand on his arm as he tried to put it on. "Won't you stay the night, baby?" She looked up into his face, pleading. "I could get Jordan's nanny to take him out very early, and pretend you came for brunch—"

"I told you, Mack, I'm not going to keep sneaking around here. You know how I feel but if you don't want to get married, let's call it a day. I've waited long enough for you. Christ, I'm nearly thirty—*I* want a family, too!"

He kissed her quickly at the front door and entered the elevator without his usual wave.

Mrs. Ed Schreiber, she thought to herself as she walked back into her living room. Could she possibly allow herself to become that? She shuddered, picking up a magazine. It was too impossible a decision to make right now, and it was not her first priority. Her first task was to find out how her workers were being treated in California.

"Fresh carnations!" Wayland said over the phone. "*Scads* of them! White! Nothing but white! We'll make them up into garlands and they'll signpost the way to the elevators! Maybe they'll disguise some of the three thousand security people!" He was in his element, arranging decor and lighting for the awards presentation at Headquarters.

"Keep Coral's name out of the program," he warned Donna Brooks in another phone call. "Just in case Colin is unable to deliver... She can be a wonderful *surprise* for everyone."

Mia had been thrilled when she heard she was getting the prestigious award, given in October this year. Some of the excitement had vanished when she heard Coral would be presenting it.

Donna Brooks, meanwhile, was drumming up as much publicity and glamour as she could to inaugurate her reign as new editor-in-chief of *Divine*. Since Coral had originated the event, the night of the *Divine* Fashion Awards had quickly become the most important night of the year for the fashion world—it was their Academy Awards evening. This year Lloyd Brooks had used his considerable clout to find the biggest celebrities. By donating the evening's proceeds to charity, they had attracted socialites and fashion groupies, many of whom were flying in from Europe to attend. Stars like Liza Minelli, Lauren Bacall, and Catherine Deneuve had also promised to appear. *WWD* and *Labels* each planned an entire issue dedicated to the event.

"It will be *the* fashion freakout of the year!" Wayland happily promised Colin. "After Coral, Donna Brooks is a breeze to work with. We see eye-to-eye on most things, and she has all that *marvelous* influence with her husband. What's Coral wearing?"

"She chose a long, black, sequined sheath," Colin replied. "Balenciaga?"

"Of *course*! She says he's the *only* designer. . . ."

"Then it's just as well she's quitting the fashion industry—he isn't designing anymore!"

Wayland gave a wicked laugh. Colin eyed him, annoyed. They were at their favorite restaurant, Divertimenti, on one of Colin's few nights off from baby-sitting Coral. The awards were in two days' time, and both men were exhausted from all the work.

"How will she look?" Wayland asked, twisting angel's-hair pasta on his fork. "I used *all* my influence with Elizabeth Arden to get her in. I booked a hairstylist *and* a special makeup by Pablo. He's especially skilled at disguising up ravaged faces, you know."

Colin nodded glumly. "She'll be okay, I think. She promised me that she stopped the speed shots, and I believe her. I have to trust her, I guess. She says she's 'resting' for the event."

"Has she found a job?" Wayland asked.

Colin grimaced. "No one wants to take the risk and hire her... afraid they might wake up with hydrochloric acid in their hair, I suppose, and who can blame them? If I get her through this awards ceremony, I'm insisting she come with me to Provence for a few weeks—just for some peace and quiet. The trouble is, she's spent so much on her drugs, I don't think she can even rake up the fare."

Wayland ate his last forkful of pasta, sighed, and said, "*I'll* pay for the trip, Colin. I owe her so much, and I'm just as sorry for her."

"I have to beg her to eat!" Colin complained. "I take her all the things she used to love, but she just drinks now. If she continues to deteriorate like this, she'll be as odd-looking as me soon! Maybe then I'll get the guts to ask her to marry me!"

"You're *kidding*!" Wayland's eyes bulged as the waiter set down a plate of petit fours.

"No. I'm absolutely serious," Colin said. "And I could save her life, too."

Wayland signaled their waiter. "Bring us espresso and the check." He held up his glass of Cointreau and proposed a toast. "To you saving Coral's life and, meanwhile, to her *not* falling flat on her face at the awards presentation."

"I don't see why I should attend the awards if I didn't win one..." Mackenzie said sulkily on the phone.

"Do you want to win one next year?" Ed asked.

"Of course. You think I want to be the only designer out of David, Mia, and me, who didn't get one?"

"Then you're going next week," he told her. "You're going, Mack, no ifs or buts about it."

"*Eddie!*" she marveled. Alistair had never tried to lay down the law to her like this. It felt incredibly sexy! "Okay," she said, pretending to give in. "But I'm not sitting near Mia. You better call Wayland Garrity or Donna Brooks or whoever's in charge of seating and tell 'em that from me!"

She hung up and dialed a new number, a direct line to Gold!'s new accountant, Jim Leopold, who professed total ignorance of Californian conditions.

"But surely you know the hourly wage we pay machinists?" she persisted.

"I think you'd better ask Mr. Reggie or Mr. Max, Mrs.... er, Lady Briarly," he stammered.

"They're the last people who'd tell me," she muttered, hanging up.

She invited her mother for lunch that week, thinking she might be able to discover something. Esther Goldstein had kept her distance somewhat—miffed that Mackenzie had not leaped into marriage with Ed. The next day Mackenzie's heart dropped when she saw her mother in her doorway—accompanied by Reggie.

"Hello, honey!" Esther kissed her warmly, handing her the candy and flowers she always brought.

"Reggie!" she said to her brother.

He was wearing a navy suit whose shininess reminded her of her father's clothes. He had added a wide kipper tie and, unbelievably, a Peace and Love medallion swung around his neck. "What a lovely surprise!" she said sarcastically. "To what do I owe this honor?" She tried to smile at him, but his presence unnerved her. He ambled into the living room. He had a habit of looking very closely at everything, a furrowed, critical expression on his face.

"Jordan will be back from playschool soon," she told them. "Sit down, Ma." She turned to her brother. "Would this visit have anything to do with a phone call I made to Jim Leopold yesterday?"

"I think it's lovely that he wants to see his nephew," Esther chattered. Then, unable to stop herself, she added, "Please don't make trouble, Mackenzie. Leave the business side to your brothers."

Mackenzie felt her face flushing. "What kind of trouble am I supposed to be making, exactly?" she asked.

"We don't have any secrets," Reggie said with annoyance. "But what we pay our machinists in L.A. has nothing to do with you. Your job is designing!"

Mackenzie stared at him, hating his condescending manner. "You know damn well how much I care about the exploitation of workers!" she snapped.

He turned to her angrily. "Don't you get your way with locations? Decor? Clothing?"

"You *bet* I do, because that *is* the business!"

"Manufacturing is the business, too! Your ideas would be chickenshit without us making things run smoothly!"

"Reggie! Mackenzie! Don't raise your voices!" Esther clucked. "Why can't you be nice together, like you used to be?"

"We were never nice together," Mackenzie corrected her. "We were forced to tolerate each other, but they never respected me—then or now."

Reggie glowered at her. "Just don't make waves!" he warned. "Then I'll respect you."

She sank down on a couch, staring up at him. "So, it's true?" she asked quietly. "It must be or you wouldn't take it so hard."

"What does she mean, Reggie?" Esther asked. "What's she talking about?"

Reggie shook his head. "I don't believe her, Ma," he said. "I thought they made up that stuff in the papers about you radical chic phonies. I know it's 'in' to have a conscience about the workers, but don't *you* enjoy living up here in this ivory tower? Don't you love being called Lady Briarly? People like you can afford to be radical...."

Mackenzie stood up, placing her hands on Reggie's shoulders. She searched his face for some sign of emotion she could respond to. "Reggie... if we're profiteering off the lousy circumstances of our workers, I'd rather give the whole thing up and live in a crummy apartment in the Village. I did it before and I can't say I wasn't as happy."

"Nobody is profiteering," Reggie said, pushing her hands away. "We make *profits*—isn't that why people run businesses? We're not doing anything that dozens of other firms aren't doing. Everyone makes up in California using the exact same kind of labor—"

"You bastard!" She lunged for his jacket but he swatted her away effortlessly.

"*Reggie! Mackenzie!*" Esther stood to separate them, clutching her breast. "You're giving me a heart attack!"

"Have you *seen* the workrooms?" Mackenzie asked, her eyes staring. "*Are* they sweatshops? What are they like?"

Reggie grinned. "California's a warm-weather state—what can I tell you? You think we import French seamstresses and run air-conditioned offices in Beverly Hills? You have to go for economical overheads—"

"I'll go see for myself!" She turned away from him and took her mother's arm. "That's the only way I'll know," she stated.

"You're not going anywhere, Mack!" Reggie shouted.

"Why? What are you going to do?" She laughed. "Put me under house arrest? You think you can restrict my movements?" She picked up a telephone and dialed information. "American Airlines, please..." She eyed her mother and brother as she dialed the number. "I'd like to make a reservation for one adult and one child, round trip to Los Angeles, first class, leaving Friday at—"

"*Gimme that!*" Reggie snatched the receiver from her, slamming it down as she gave a cry of rage. They wrestled for control of the telephone, Reggie holding it down grimly, effortlessly, with one strong hand.

"Is this what I brought you up for?" Esther cried. "To see you fighting each other? Why can't you enjoy your success? You've all worked so hard—"

"You *asshole!*" Mackenzie kicked Reggie's shin, breaking away from him.

"You're acting like savages!" Esther screamed.

The front door suddenly opened and the butler entered, holding Jordan by the hand. They stood in the small entrance, sensing the violence they had missed seeing.

"You want we should come back later, Lady Briarly?" the elegant Japanese man asked.

"Mommy!" Jordan ran to Mackenzie for a kiss, then to his grandmother.

"That's all right, Iko. Just make a sandwich for Jordan, will you, please?" Mackenzie said. "Get him out of my house," she told her mother. Reggie reached out to pat his nephew but Mackenzie quickly yanked Jordan away.

"Oh?" Reggie sneered. "I'm not good enough to touch his lordship? C'mon, Ma..." He held out his hand to Esther, helping her up from the couch.

Esther peered worriedly at her daughter. "I just don't understand why you two have to antagonize each other. What about our lunch?"

"I'll take you to lunch," Reggie assured her, guiding her to the door. "I'll give you a better lunch."

"Mackenzie, darling?" Esther twisted around, her eyes brimming. "*I* don't want you should go to California on your own, like that. Listen to Reggie. Let him and Max take care of it. They've done very well for you. You're all millionaires—what else do you want? The clothes make a good profit, and that's all that matters...."

Mackenzie shook her head despairingly. "Ma! It's *not* all that matters! Exploitation matters more! Why can't you ever respect *my* opinion?"

Reggie pushed his mother out through the front door, turning to hurl a final threat: "Go to L.A. and you're out of the firm! I *mean* it! You'll be out on your titled ass!"

Mackenzie laughed. "That could be the best thing that ever happened to me, 'cause if I find what I think I'll find out there, I'll make damn sure that the publicity will wipe out Gold! No one will want the clothes—you'll be left holding a big empty bag. Ma, I'm sorry about lunch...."

Reggie slammed the door on her mother's sad expression.

Mackenzie picked up Jordan and kissed him. "We're going to California!" she told him.

* * *

Mia stretched luxuriantly in bed, extending her arms and legs to their limit, rolling over in the lacy, fresh sheets. It was seven-thirty, and there was a small hard ball of dread in her stomach. Then she remembered! Tonight was the *Divine* presentation, tonight she would stand before the entire fashion industry and reveal not only that she was the designer behind the firm of Anais Du Pasquier, but also that she was Coral's daughter. They would embrace for the audience and the cameras. What would happen afterward? She did not trust Coral, even though Colin had reported that her mother was improving.

Reluctantly, Mia slithered out of bed and stood, her white cotton nightgown falling around her like a cruel parody of a bridal gown. She had drenched herself in Chanel after her bath last night, and the perfume clung to her, making her feel expensive, womanly. She glanced at her tousled reflection in the deco dressing-table mirror Wayland had given her. *Womanly!* She laughed bitterly to herself. How womanly could she ever be? She was wasting her life loving a man who was unavailable, ignoring all others, including David Winters. David had called to ask her if she would like him to escort her to the awards that night. She knew Wayland and Colin would be backstage, looking after Coral, so she'd agreed. It would be great publicity for David and her to arrive together—Mr. and Mrs. Fashion. Sometimes she thought of the way she pined for Phillipe and the way David pined for her as representing a long ladder of unrequited love in which everyone stood despairingly on a rung, gazing up at the unavailable love object one rung higher.

"What about Mackenzie?" David had asked. "She'll be there with Ed. . . ."

"The last I heard from her was a message saying 'Fuck you!' with my answering service," she told him. "I sent her a letter of condolence when Alistair died, but I've heard nothing from her. I really think the next move must come from her."

Wayland had arranged for the two couples to sit on opposite sides of the auditorium for the presentation.

In the shower Mia's brain came alive and started to plan the day. She had bought the most expensive dress of her life—a two-thousand-dollar Zandra Rhodes, covered in the quirky, loopy embroidery and dangling spangles that

were her signature. I might as well look my very best for
tonight, she told herself. It was an ordeal to get through,
that was all. She toweled her body dry and threw on a
robe to enjoy her breakfast ritual. She usually read *Labels*
and *WWD*, delivered to her door early. She sat in the
window seat, sipping herbal tea and slicing an apple.

Turning immediately to the Tittle-Tattle column, she
nearly dropped her teacup.

> After much speculation, Phillipe Roux last night
> admitted to our Paris office that his marriage has
> collapsed. Josephine Roux is staying at their St. Tropez
> villa while he occupies the *hôtel particuliere* in the
> Champ de Mars area of Paris. The often stormy
> relationship has been a curiosity in fashion circles.
> Observers often noted that the pair seemed mis-
> matched. Suave, urbane Roux, one of the very few
> *couturiers* with a married life, has been dressing celeb-
> rities like Jackie Kennedy, the Duchess of Windsor,
> and Catherine Deneuve. Mme. Roux had no com-
> ment for *Labels* on the separation. It was announced
> that she would no longer be Roux's design partner.

Mia read the item twice, although she knew it by heart
after the first reading. Something within her leaped alive
as she stared down at the tree-lined street below. Why
today? The very day she was to receive the identical award
Phillipe had won two years ago? A conviction sprang up
inside her that Phillipe was now, at last, *hers*! Ridiculous,
she knew, but this feeling refused to disappear even when
she laughed at it.

She had planned to spend the morning working in her
office-studio, but now she knew she'd be unable to keep
her mind on anything. She called her secretary and told
her she would not be coming in.

She made-up lightly, humming. Now she could at last
admit to herself that there had always been an excited
little corner of her soul awaiting some word from him.

The phone rang shrilly, making her heart almost stop.
She looked at it, fearful to pick it up. Then she made
herself lift the receiver. Cautiously, she said "Hello?"

"Did you read it?" Mackenzie's gruff voice asked. "I'll
die if we don't discuss this, Mia. Can we be friends—

please! Did you read *Labels* yet? About Phillipe Roux? What are you doing about it?"

Mia shook her head to herself. Mackenzie was talking as if their friendship had never been interrupted. She laughed nervously. "Why nothing," she replied. "Nothing at all!"

"Then you're the dumbest, stupidest person in the world!" Mackenzie shouted. "If *I* were that much in love with a guy, I'd catch the first plane to Paris and *grab* him! For Christ's sake, Mia, men don't chase women anymore."

"Well, *I* don't chase men. . . ."

"But you always said he was the one guy in the world to turn you on!" Mackenzie cried. "You've been living like a goddamn nun because of him. It's gotta be worth a fuckin' plane fare?"

Mia was silent for a moment, thinking. "He *is* the only man in the world for me, Mackenzie," she finally said. "But he knows how I feel. And now it's for him to contact me if he—"

"Mia Stanton!" Mackenzie yelled. "If you don't get your little ass over to Paris today, I don't think I'll ever sympathize with you again! This is the love story of all time: *I* wanna know what happens!"

"I do have an engagement tonight, Mackenzie," Mia said softly. "Remember?"

"Oh, yeah," Mackenzie said gruffly. "Congratulations, I guess. Nice that your mother managed to squeeze you in there before she quit the magazine."

Mia smiled. She had forgotten how bitchy a rival designer could be. "It had nothing to do with her, actually," she informed Mackenzie. "Donna Brooks gave me the award. My mother's merely presenting it to me. It's all Colin Beaumont's idea. He thinks it will rehabilitate Mother in the eyes of the fashion industry."

"She needs it," Mackenzie agreed. "I hear the weirdest stories about her. . . ."

"We're all praying she'll be all right tonight."

"Well," Mackenzie muttered awkwardly, "I guess I'll see you tonight. You'll probably be looking super-gorgeous, right? I'll be my usual tacky self. Put in a good word with the top girls tonight—I'd like an award, too! Next year, maybe . . ."

She hung up before Mia could think of the right thing

to say. She did some chores, trying not to pick up *Labels* to read that paragraph again. How could a few lines of print change your head so quickly? she wondered. What if Mackenzie was right? What if she *should* do something dramatic to show Phillipe how much she still cared? She wondered if he was already involved with someone else? A beautiful French actress? But something inside her just knew *she* was the reason for the separation. Phillipe had never stopped loving her, just as she had never stopped loving him.

She paced her apartment, tidying up, becoming more and more nervous. When she finally knocked over a vase of flowers, she cursed herself aloud. "I've got to get out of here!" she cried. "I'll go crazy if I stay here."

She had never acted like this before, but today nothing about herself would surprise her. Grabbing a blazer, she hurried downstairs. She wanted simply to walk, to distract herself watching peoples' faces and shop windows. Walking restlessly down Lexington, she came to a corner drugstore and pulled up short. A large display of Phillipe cologne featured a blown-up black-and-white Avedon portrait of Phillipe. His laughing face, four feet high, froze her before the window. She stared at the photograph— knowing every millimeter of that forehead, those cheekbones, the expressions that shone out of those eyes. She knew the touch of him, too, could smell the delicious cologne he used that mingled so enticingly with his own natural smell. She wrenched herself away from the window and forced herself to continue her walk.

What if he's trying to call you at this very moment? she asked herself. Are you kidding? she answered sternly. He hasn't seen you in over two years—do you really expect him to pick up the phone and call you now? He could get my number from Wayland, she thought. This internal argument annoyed her, but she made herself walk many more blocks, just to show herself how disciplined she could be and how ridiculous the idea that he was trying to reach her. He was making clothes for the most beautiful women in the world—the most glamorous, the richest, the most powerful—why would he bother with her?

Slowly she walked back to her apartment, putting her key in the lock of her front door and hearing the shrill bell of the kitchen wall phone. Her body tingled as if a magician who had once locked her soul in a bottle had just now set it free. The lock took an eternity to open. The bell continued to shrill. When she ran in and grabbed the receiver, she heard the delay and crackling over the line, and she knew it was him, as she had always known that one day this call would come, that their love was not over, would never be over. . . .

"Mia? *Mia?*" He was calling her name across the Atlantic, halfway across the world.

To know that the man she loved was at that moment in Paris calling her name, after the hundreds of times she had prayed and wished that he was thinking of her, made her light-headed. She could not swallow nor speak. . . .

"*Mia?*" Phillipe called. "Mia . . . you are there?"

Finally she managed to croak out: "Yes . . . yes . . ."

"This is Phillipe! Are you all right? Did you hear my news? I am *free!*"

"I read it this morning. What happened?"

"Oh, Mia, what happened is that I cleared my conscience. Completely! I know now that I can never satisfy her, never make her happy. Instead, we would make each other miserable. She knew from the first day I met you that I loved you, Mia. Even as we undertook this charade of a marriage, she knew that deep inside me I loved you. But I was obligated. Josephine, my village, our friends, even myself—all thought the right thing to do was to marry! Now she realizes that this is not so . . . and I—I realized it always. Ever since that night we were together. So . . . come to me! Come to me now, Mia!"

"Oh, God," she murmured.

She felt as if she had entered another dimension. Her body, her life, her brain had undergone some kind of transformation in the last few minutes. Dizzily she gripped the top of the counter to help her stay upright. What do you do when your whole body is screaming, your spirit soaring, your brain in a turmoil because you finally hear in real life what you always dreamed of hearing?

"I send you the plane ticket, Mia. Will you come tonight?"

She leaned back against the familiar, cool, tiled wall of the kitchen, her eyes closed against the tears that forced themselves through her lashes. She had to steel herself not to sob aloud.

"We have already waited too long. You do not have someone else? You still love me, Mia?"

"No! *Yes!*" she cried. "Oh, Phillipe you *do* take a lot for granted, don't you? But you *know* I could only love you! I'll be with you as soon as I can, my darling," she told him, imagining what his lips, his mouth, would taste like, and how it would feel to be held in those strong, all-enveloping arms, this time without restraint or guilt. "I'll be with you very soon. . . ."

At six o'clock that night anyone in Manhattan with social or fashion pretensions was getting ready. The rich summoned hairdressers to their bedrooms. The less rich made pilgrimages to their favorite salon. The poverty-stricken few carefully heated their hair rollers.

Mackenzie poured her voluptuous body into a tight black cashmere sheath she had designed that week; it was the new longer length—miniskirts were passé. The sparkling diamanté buttons shimmered under the makeup lights in her black marble bathroom. She turned this way and that, squinting at her reflection.

"Not bad . . ." she decided.

Not far away, Mia, her breath and heartbeat almost failing her, packed a small suitcase with jeans, sweaters, and nightgown, then carefully stepped into the new Zandra Rhodes gown. Her long hair had been piled high, ribbons and flowers dangling from the back of her head, matching the pastel embroidered dress. She put her passport in her sequined evening purse, called Pan American to confirm her reservation, and eyed a bottle of champagne in the refrigerator, wondering if it would calm her down or excite her even more. She was already in a dreamlike trance where nothing seemed quite real. But the ordeal of accepting her award in public had shrunk to manageable proportion compared to what lay in wait for her after the awards—a flight to Paris, and Phillipe!

Meanwhile, Colin arrived at Coral's apartment, wearing a tuxedo that had been specially altered for his small size.

"My *God*! How *elegant*!" Coral's eyes lit up when she opened the door to him. She bent to kiss him. "You should *always* dress like this, Colin! It *does* something for you!"

He eyed her warily; she seemed almost like the Coral of old. She had been beautifully madeup, coiffed, and the

Balenciaga black sequined sheath hugged her body perfectly. He gazed at her in wonder; fashion was indeed magical.

"Have you been behaving yourself?" he asked, entering the living room and sniffing the air.

"Just one small joint... to relax me," she said, and led the way into the room. "Don't treat me like a naughty child, Colin. How do you think I look?" She twirled in the center of the gray carpet and he nodded approvingly.

"Absolutely super!" he said. "I'm so proud of you!"

"Good!" She clapped her hands and handed him a glass of champagne. "There's life in the old girl yet, then?"

"To a successful evening!" Colin proposed. "You'll walk onstage and you'll be holding the award," he told her. "All you have to say is this..." He fished out of his pocket the typed paper Wayland had given him.

Coral took it and read. He watched her carefully. She was definitely up, but whether that meant she had had a shot of speed or not, he wasn't sure. It was impossible to watch her twenty-four hours a day.

"Got it!" Coral said, and folded the speech neatly.

"Let me hear you say it," Colin insisted.

"Oh, really!" She shook her head at him, unfolding the speech. "'The Divine Fashion Award this year goes to the firm of Anais Du Pasquier, who, as few people realize, is my daughter, Mia Stanton. To avoid charges of nepotism, this brilliant designer has been using her company name as a fashion pseudonym. I'm happy to announce that the award was decided by Divine's new editor-in-chief, Donna Brooks, before she knew who Mia was!' Do I have to say all that, Colin? I might choke on Donna's name...."

"Absolutely! You can read it, if you prefer."

"I'll ad-lib." She stuffed the speech in her purse. "I have done it before, you know! Several times, starting with one Phillipe Roux, remember?"

The limousine arrived for them at seven-thirty. Chattering, laughing, Colin got Coral out of the apartment and into the car, two fingers firmly crossed behind his back.

The line of stretch limos waited outside Headquarters at eight. A huge light at the main entrance pointed up, moving its wide, bright beam slowly through the navy sky. The car in front of theirs disgorged Halston and Liza

Minelli. Andy Warhol walked slowly along the sidewalk, surrounded by a gaggle of his superstars.

Colin saw David and Mia ahead of them, waiting for an elevator. He spotted Donna Brooks and Lloyd; Howard Austin appeared to be on his own. Stylists, photographers, editors, and assistants were following the white-carnation-strewn path through the front door of Headquarters to the bank of elevators. There were Seventh Avenue designers dressed in ther finest, hoping to outglitter their rivals. Colin tried to shield Coral from the mob; she looked straight ahead, unwilling to recognize friends or enemies.

A cordon of security guards checked names and invitations against a list, while rock music blared from loudspeakers to welcome guests.

Coral stood in line, regally erect, her cut-out neckline showing the sculpted bones of her neck. Large, glittering Kenneth Lane earrings and flecked black stockings with diamantés scattered over them gave her a festive air. Her arms were heavy with silver bangles. The crowd seemed aware of her in some uncanny way: Passing the guards, people seemed to open up, allowing Coral and Colin to pass to the head of the line, murmuring and indicating the proud, charismatic redheaded woman. She certainly had an aura about her, Colin noted, guiding her into the elevator and whizzing her straight up to the top floor.

They emerged amidst another throng of chattering, perfumed, craning people, and he led Coral through the mob, to the backstage area. People tapped him on the back to say hello. He kissed and was kissed by several models. Coral appeared calm and composed, smiling graciously at the faces pressing around them, most of whom she knew.

Award presenters were led to a special corner table where they were plied with drinks and advice. Wayland was there, and he greeted them both, kissing Coral, finding a chair for her.

"Don't let her drink too much," he whispered in Colin's ear. "And don't even let her go to the Ladies unescorted. If she *has* to pee, stand guard outside."

"Where's Mia?" Coral asked, gazing around the room, squinting at people.

"She's going to be seated in the audience at the end of a

row," Wayland told her. "We're handling it just like the Hollywood Oscars—the winners will get up from their seats and go onstage to receive their award. Oh, God, I hope it *works!*"

Out in front a chattering, kissing, scented, screaming commotion of people attempted to settle in their seats. They craned their necks to spot celebrities, waved at each other, tried to act naturally when a photographer focused his camera three feet from their faces.

The names of the sixties—Betsey Johnson, Joel Schumacher, Mary Quant, Zandra Rhodes, Jean Muir—were all in the front rows. Models, familiar faces from hundreds of glossy magazine pages and covers, shone like stars from their seats. Twenty-five models had been booked to show the clothes of the winners, in a specially choreographed go-go showing. Dionne Warwick was scheduled to sing, and a small orchestra had set up on one side of the stage. A suave male master of ceremonies was on hand to orchestrate the proceedings.

Mia was sitting on the opposite side of the audience from Mackenzie, next to David, as cameras flashed at them. He was wearing a perfectly cut French dinner jacket and black tie; he looked worried and elegant. Mackenzie was holding court to various visitors, shaking hands and kissing, Ed at her side, nervous and hyper in his tuxedo.

At eight-thirty the lights dimmed and a medley of tunes that mentioned clothes in the titles was struck up by the band. When that was over, Wayland Garrity took the stage.

There were interminable speeches. People fidgeted impatiently as first Wayland, then Lloyd Brooks, then Donna Brooks welcomed them, thanked them, plugged their store or magazine, respectively, and asked them to join in the appreciation and applause for the many fashion awards to be made that evening, culminating in the most coveted: Designer of the Year.

There was a fashion showing of one outfit from every designer's collection, the finale being a full showing of all the outfits from Anais Du Pasquier's fall line. Mia's coats and dresses looked clean-cut and hard-edged, wonderfully fashionable and right under the spotlights on a bare white stage.

The show reached its end to a roar of applause from the

thousand-strong gathering, then the stage was cleared
and a rumble of drums announced the actual award
presentations.

Mia clutched David's hand until he winced. She was in
a kind of dreamlike agony. She kept thinking of the
suitcase stashed backstage and the faces of the organizers
when they saw her make her getaway before the big party
planned for after the show. This waiting was like drowning
slowly, she thought, watching your past life flash before
you. *Phillipe!* she called silently. *I'll be with you very soon,
my darling. Very soon . . .*

Backstage, Coral was feeling no pain. She had surrepti-
tiously swallowed two tranquilizers since arriving at Headquarters, washing them down with two glasses of champagne. She reached out now for a third glass, but Colin
tactfully waved the waiter off.

"No more now, darling—it'll soon be your turn."

He felt her trembling under the hand he had placed on
her arm. She had shrouded her pitifully thin shoulders
and arms with a black net stole.

Wayland signaled to him from the wings of the stage.
Colin held out his hand to Coral, pulling her gently to her
feet and guiding her through the crush of backstage
people clustered in the hospitality room.

They stood in the wings together, peering out. A designer who had won in the sportswear category was
fervently thanking his parents for all they had done for
him.

Finally the commentator said: "And now for the final
award of the evening—Designer of the Year! And to present it, Mrs. Coral Stanton . . ."

There was a gasp and a cheer from the audience. Eyes
peered, heads shook, lips whispered comments as Wayland
gave Coral a gentle push, propelling her out onto the
stage. The spotlights dazzled her. She saw hundreds of
lights, all focused upon her. She was back in the spotlight
where she belonged. The applause—from people in the
fashion industry who knew little of the inside power
struggle at *Divine*—warmed her heart. Coral walked with
her head high, regally, like the queen of fashion she once
was.

Mia, sitting on the edge of her seat, grabbed David's
hand. "God, she looks totally out of it!"

The brilliant makeup so artfully applied at Elizabeth Arden did indeed form a kind of painted mask on a strained, stretched face. The famous brilliant smile was almost a grimace. Coral concentrated hard on completing the seemingly interminable walk to the podium in the center of the stage.

The crowd hushed as she reached the microphone. Her slender, black-clad, sparkling figure looked like an exclamation point in the middle of a vast white expanse. The speech she had been instructed to read was forgotten, folded in the purse she had left with Colin. She would have to ad-lib.

"I'm so happy to be here tonight," she said. "I've been away for a few weeks and I've missed you all so much...."

A few people clapped weakly. In the wings Wayland and Colin almost clutched each other with tension. Mia, sitting on the edge of her seat, sank her nails into David's palm, and he grimaced.

"Fashion is..." Coral began, and faltered, her eyes going out of focus. A few people murmured. Someone laughed. "Fashion is..." Coral repeated. She suddenly pulled herself together with a start. "Well... it's my whole *life*! It truly *is* the only thing that matters to me." She beamed. "That's why I am so very proud to present the *Divine* award to... to a great talent who designs under the name of Anais Du Pasquier... and I'm even more proud that she happens to be my daughter, Mia Stanton!"

There was a burst of applause, and Wayland and Colin nearly passed out with relief. David nudged Mia, and she jumped to her feet and hurried down to the side of the stage. She walked up four steps and onto the stage, her arms open to her mother.

Coral held both arms out to her, one clutching the *Divine* statuette. They embraced, and the crowd went wild. Coral handed the statuette to Mia and Mia smiled at the applause, acknowledging it. When it died down, she leaned toward the microphone, still holding Coral's hand.

"I want to thank *Divine* magazine for awarding me this great honor. I want to thank my mother and Wayland Garrity for encouraging me—and my wonderful co-workers at Anais Du Pasquier for their support and hard work..."

She smiled at the new burst of applause, and took Coral's arm to lead her offstage. Coral resisted Mia's support. She shaded her eyes with her hand, peering into the crowd as if to see if there was anyone out there she recognized.

Suddenly, she grabbed at the mike: "All of you out there," she cried. "I need a job! Did you hear me? I said, I need a job!"

"Oh, my God," Wayland groaned, covering his face. "Draw the curtains, somebody. . . ."

The audience tittered, then froze, mesmerized by this stark, thin, tragic figure. There was a hushed silence.

"I was very good to most of you!" Coral continued. "I gave many of you your first breaks. Now some of you are in a position to help *me*! You all know my qualifications. I've had damn good experience! I've been on the job! I know how to—"

Mia had been pulling at her gently since she'd begun to speak. Abruptly Coral gave way and allowed Mia to guide her offstage, blowing kisses at the audience. The curtains swung closed. A few people applauded, but mostly there was a stunned, silent reaction to the spectacle of Mia Stanton, a successful, vibrant young designer, leading her wasted, pitiful mother off the stage.

In the walk to the wings Mia suddenly felt an overwhelming resentment. The tension and nervousness built up, as it sank in that Coral had ruined the most important moment in her career, and humiliated them both. They almost fell into the arms of Wayland and Colin in the wings.

She turned to Coral, her anger out of control. "Why did you *do* that?" she demanded.

Coral laughed. "Because I *do* need a job! You're successful now, Mia, perhaps *you* could give me one?"

"You selfish, selfish—" She broke off. "I wouldn't give you a job if my life depended on it."

Coral's mouth fell open, her eyes glazed.

"You *had* to ruin it for me—just as you always do. No one wanted you here tonight! Certainly not *me*!" Mia cried. "Colin begged everyone to allow you to do this—"

Colin tugged at Mia's arm: "*No!* Don't say that! Coral's still a big name in fashion! Many people think—"

Coral hushed him: "*Let* her get it out. *Let* her spill the bile she's kept inside her!"

"Tonight finishes you, Mother!" Mia spat. "You're through!"

Coral's eyes changed. They showed hurt, incomprehension, and then even a strange kind of triumph. She turned to Colin, saying proudly, "You see how cruel my daughter can be?" She turned back to Mia. "We've been locked in competition ever since you were born. Maybe I was the worst mother in history, I don't know. Now I'm on my knees, Mia—I'm humble—you've *won*! I'm begging you for a job. There must be *some*thing I could do for you? Give me a job, Mia! I can't exist without one. I shall simply—" She broke off, her mouth soundlessly moving, staring at Mia piteously.

They all looked at Mia.

"*No!*" Mia cried. "*No*, Mother! I've finally learned to say no to you! I don't need you. I don't owe you a thing!"

Coral's eyes widened. For a second they overflowed with pain. Then she reached out and slapped Mia's face hard.

Mia didn't hesitate: She slapped her mother back, even harder. The stinging blow sent Coral reeling into the arms of Wayland. Colin leaped forward to restrain Mia, but she was suddenly whirled around from behind by a new, stronger arm and she felt a powerful palm slap into her cheek, hard. She stumbled, dazed, a cry of shock coming from her. When her vision cleared and Colin had steadied her, she saw who had hit her: Mackenzie.

"What the hell?" She reached out for Mackenzie's shoulders.

The girls stared into each other's eyes with a mixture of bravado, hate, and surprise. Then Mackenzie nimbly kicked a leg from under Mia, and before anyone realized what was happening, both women were rolling on the floor, tearing at each other's dresses and hair.

Colin shooed onlookers from the scene as Wayland held onto Coral and shouted: "*Help!* Will *someone* get some help!"

David and Ed came running backstage, stared down at the scuffling women then pulled them apart, holding them as they stood up, faces flushed and panting, glaring at each other. Mia's flowers had been ripped from her hair, her gown ripped, a panel dangling.

Mackenzie was trying to catch her breath. "I won't let you abuse your mother, I just won't!" she screamed.

"What the hell does this have to do with *you*?" Mia demanded.

"She started me off in this industry," Mackenzie told her, rubbing her arm. "I owe her a lot. I'm not going to let anyone hit her when she's down, least of all *you*! What makes you think you're any better than your mother? At least she's *lived*! What have *you* done except hide away from the world and mope?"

Mia shook her head, looking down at the tatters of her gown. "This was a new Zandra Rhodes!" she suddenly said.

Mackenzie's eyes flashed as she glanced at the torn panels. "It looks better this way..." she said. David watched Mia holding her arm. He had never seen her looking so beautiful, her face flushed, her disheveled hair adding a kind of provocative sexiness to her usual demure state. Meanwhile Wayland quickly and quietly led Coral away.

"What this is really about is that *you* wanted this award!" Mia said in the sudden silence. "You can't live with your jealousy...."

"That's not true!" Mackenzie yelled. "I came back here to congratulate you! I thought we could be friends again. I didn't expect to see you beating up a poor, defenseless—"

"Oh, that poor defenseless woman is a *killer*!" Mia snapped. "She could have injured Donna Brooks for life. She's emotionally crippled me! She's caused more trouble and heartbreak than she's worth! And as for the award—*here*!" She picked up the bronze statuette from the floor and thrust it at Mackenzie. "I don't even *want* it! It means nothing to me! It's *yours*—congratulations!"

Mackenzie held the award, speechless, and Ed moved toward Mia to say something. Mia wrenched her arm out of David's grasp and pushed past them all, through the wings, walking quickly down the brightly lit corridors to the small offices that had been turned into dressing rooms for that night.

"*Mia!*" David shouted after her.

"I'm late!" she called over her shoulder. "I just have to get out of here."

She reached the dressing room and closed the door quickly, bolting it. There was no time to change into the jeans, shirt, and jacket she had planned to wear on her flight. Her body ached from the tussle on the floor and her face very clearly showed an outline in red of a hand and four fingers. She quickly splashed some cold water on that cheek, threw a coat over her torn dress, and grabbed her suitcase.

David and Wayland were standing outside the door when she unlocked it. "Do you feel okay?" Wayland asked. "Do you need a doctor? My, such goings-on. I never—"

"Mia?" David questioned, his face strained with concern. "Is there anything I can do?"

She shook her head at both of them, smiling, walking past them toward the elevator. They both noticed her suitcase.

"Where are you going?"

"What about the party?"

She turned back. "Listen, I'm sorry to do this to you, but I'm flying to Paris tonight. Phillipe is waiting for me. We're going to be together forever!" David's face crumpled. "Don't look at me like that!" she cried as the elevator arrived. "I never promised you anything, David. You *knew* I loved him. I *always* did!"

"Mia, are you sure—"

Wayland said, "I can't believe you're actually going to—"

She stepped inside the elevator and turned to face them, her eyes sparkling and happy. "I've never been so sure of anything in my life!" she said, as the doors slid closed, cutting off their anxious expressions. "Good-bye!" she called.

Outside, the limousine she had rented for the evening was waiting as arranged, at the corner of Thirty-fourth Street. It took her straight to Kennedy Airport. She just had time to call Phillipe, and she just made the Paris flight.

Twenty-six

"God, what an anticlimax!" Mackenzie kicked off her shoes in the backseat of the limousine as it eased its way across Thirty-fourth Street. The awards party had fizzled out at eleven o'clock. She looked at Ed and sighed. "Somehow, once I'd pulled that stupid headdress off her head, slapped her around, and rolled on the floor with her, the evening just seemed to go downhill," she said, and widened her eyes innocently at him.

Ed stared at her regretfully, shaking his head. "Lady Briarly?" he asked. "You should be a lady *wrestler*! That poor kid! When David and I ran in—*Well*, we couldn't believe our eyes! The two top female designers in America slugging it out!"

"She had it coming to her," Mackenzie mused. She stuck her feet up into his lap, wriggling her toes. "I can't stand those prissy holier-than-thou types! She's running off to 'the love of her life' in Paris. *Ha!* All she needs is a good fuck! That would scare the life out of her, of course, and God knows what will happen in Paris! She didn't even thank me for persuading her to go!"

Ed leaned back as the car turned up Madison, his eyes closed. She traced a line down his forehead and nose, coming to rest on his lips. He opened his mouth and gently bit her fingers.

"That poor Coral Stanton," she continued. "I guess *I* should give her a job at Gold!, but it's not up to her couture standards. Maybe if I get this cashmere line to work—"

He leaned toward her and kissed her, stopping her words. "Gonna offer me a nightcap?" he asked.

Mackenzie thought of the suitcase she was packing,

open by her bed. She did not want Ed to know she was going to Los Angeles the next day: He might try to stop her.

"I have a breakfast at eight!" she hedged. "I have to impress some out-of-town buyers. I'll need to be fresh for that. I'll call you later, baby."

She dropped him off at his apartment and gave him a deep, loving kiss good-bye. He didn't know it, but that kiss would have to last awhile.

"I assure you I'm all right, Colin." Coral held his hand at the door to her apartment.

"And you'll come to Provence with me this week? I have a ticket for you, compliments of Wayland."

She smiled wearily. The events of the evening had taken their toll on her. Even though he had whisked her away from the party early, she looked haggard. "How very sweet and dear of him," she said. "I'll call and thank him tomorrow. Everyone's suddenly being so kind, Colin. I don't even hold a grudge against Mia. In a way, I admire her for growing up. . . . I do wish she'd have said she had a job for me, though."

He watched her, as fascinated as ever. She had miraculously regained her dignity. She was sober, lucid, regal; as if the confrontation with her daughter had released something, sorted something out. Before he left, kissing her cheek, he said, "I'm proud of you. I'll call you tomorrow. . . ."

"Colin?" she called as he walked down the corridor. "Do you think *Labels* will be merciless in their report?"

"I'll try Howard Austin tonight and see what I can do. Maybe if I offer a few free drawings, he won't dwell on tonight's grislier aspects?"

The apartment somehow looked different when she let herself in, stretching emptily before her, unwelcoming and strange. She dropped the regal pose as she closed the door. She had expected more from tonight—*much* more!

She turned on the lights and made straight for her bedroom. There was one LSD capsule in an evening purse somewhere. Reality was a little too hard to take tonight; she would transform it, take a trip. She found the purse, found the capsule and swallowed it, then went to the living room to light the newspapers under the log in the grate. She wanted the comfort of a fire, the warmth and

sound of it. Soon the newspapers were blazing, the crack-
le of flames leaping toward wood. She lay full-length on
the floor before it, stretched out in the Balenciaga she was
too tired to remove, watching the colors....

"Lady Briarly?" The nasal voice sounded slightly familiar. Mackenzie squinted at the clock radio: eight a.m. "It's
Jim Leopold—remember, we spoke last week? You wanted
to know the salary of the machinists in California? Your
brothers have fired me, Lady Briarly. They said I should
have told you it was the basic minimum wage. Since I'm
out of a job, I may as well tell you they're paid fifty cents
an hour—way below the minimum. Your brothers take
advantage of the fact that most of the machinists are in
the country illegally. They're happy to get fifty cents."

Mackenzie sat up in her bed, reaching for a pad and
paper. "Thank you for calling me, Jim," she said. "You've
been a real help. Could you give me your phone number
or address so I—"

"I think it's better if I don't. Good luck, Lady Briarly."

She called American Airlines, confirming passage on
that afternoon's flight to Los Angeles. The rest of the
morning was filled with packing, arranging Jordan's clothes,
and calls to the design studio to alert her designers to
stockpile designs for her to approve when she returned.

"When will that be, Mack?" her head designer asked.

"God, I don't know!" she replied.

Ed called at noon. "How was your breakfast?" he
asked.

She raised her eyebrows, shrugging. "Same as usual.
Two pieces of rye toast. Jordan had his cereal—"

"You didn't go to your breakfast meeting? You said it
was at eight!"

She held the phone close to her mouth and murmured,
"Eddie, you're gonna hate me for this, but we leave for
Los Angeles this afternoon. I didn't wanna tell you before
because I was afraid you'd try to talk me out of it..."

"Who's we?"

"Jordan and I."

"Is this that cockamamie scheme to meet your workers?
What do you think you're gonna *do*, Mack? Change the
facts of life?"

"*I* don't know! Give them all a bonus? Show them

there's someone at Gold! who does care about their welfare! Find an agency to keep an eye on them . . . *whatever* I do will be better than sitting in New York doing nothing."

"I'm coming over right now, Mack!" he told her. "Hold everything."

"There's nothing to hold," she yelled, "we leave here at three!" But he had already hung up.

He was there in twenty minutes. "I had to drop two business meetings to do this!" he told her as she let him in.

She hugged him quickly, and he followed her up the twisting stairs to her bedroom, where a large Louis Vuitton suitcase lay open on the floor. He sat on the bed, watching her fold sweaters. "How long you packing for?" he asked. "A year?"

"I'd like to go for *ten* years!" she replied, and sat down next to him. "Come with me, Eddie?"

"I can't just walk out on David. We're about to show our mid-season collection."

He leaned toward her and they kissed. Reaching out, he touched her breasts, sliding his fingers over the nipples, which pressed against the silk of her blouse. His tongue entered her mouth. After a few days of not seeing him, everything he did felt fresh to Mackenzie, exciting her as it always did. She made a great effort and broke away, saying, "Not now, Eddie. I'd get the spooky feeling you were trying to seduce me so I'd miss my plane."

"Call and cancel it!" he told her, holding her arm. "This is a dumb thing to do. *You* won't be able to change anything! It might even be dangerous for you and the kid."

"Come with me, then," she said again. "If you love me, if you *really* want me—come *with* me! We'll start a better firm together! A firm that won't treat people like shit!"

"I can't just walk out on David, and you know it. The fashion world doesn't revolve around you, Mack. We all engage in a few borderline ethics—every business does. I don't know the setup your brothers have out there, but *we* have to manufacture David's stuff at realistic prices, too."

"How do *you* do it?" she asked.

He shook his head. "I keep costs down in different ways."

"I bet you don't use illegal labor?"

Ed gave a great sigh, his eyes burning into hers. "Look, Mack," he said, "I'm just an ordinary guy raised to earn a living and keep on the right side of the law. Reggie and Max aren't doing anything illegal. Maybe it's immoral, but that's for God to judge...."

"*When?*" she scoffed. "On Judgment Day? If people like Reggie and Max aren't stopped, we won't be around for that."

He pulled her to him, caressing her, his hand between her legs. "Don't put me on the spot right now, Mack. I don't have all the answers. I just want a peaceful life." He lifted the skirt of her dress and knelt, burying his face between her legs. "Right now, I just *want* you. Oh, God, I want you so much!"

"Be careful—Jordan," she murmured.

"I've got to make love to you, baby." He groaned. "I'll come in my goddamn pants if I don't...."

Wanting him just as much, she hurried over to the door and quickly locked it. She'd tell the cab to drive extra fast to the airport: This would be worth it.

He pulled her to him, pushing up her skirt, dropping his pants. Their bodies pressed together and the frenzy of his hurry excited her. She fell back across the bed, her back arched, letting Ed straddle her. It had been a week since they'd last made love, and she needed him. He tongued her face like an eager puppy as their lower halves touched, rubbed together, and then he found his way easily into her. He buried his mouth in her neck, nuzzling around her ear. Twisting her head toward him, she wanted his tongue deeper in her mouth, his sex deeper inside her, wanted to be totally invaded by him. He moved inside her, pumping quickly, groaning with pleasure, and her own pleasure began unbelievably quickly.

"Oh, baby..." She gasped, holding onto his head, burying her fingers in the thick hair at the back of his neck. "Oh... *baby!*"

They came exactly together, holding onto each other, breathing hotly in each other's faces, the short, sharp, sweet pleasure exploding quickly inside them. He hovered over her, his eyes sleepy and dazed with pleasure, but there was little time to enjoy the comfort of being held afterward in his warm arms, as she liked.

"This is so crazy, Mack!" he said. "Why are we doing

this to each other? Why don't you marry me and put an end to it?"

Mackenzie gave a hoot of laughter. Pushing him gently off her, she sat on the edge of the bed and began to dress. "Put an end to what?" she asked. "I'd still be going to L.A. even if I were married to you. You think little Mrs. Eddie Schreiber would be more obedient?"

His eyes flashed with hurt. "Don't keep saying that name as if it's the biggest put-down you can think of," he said, and padded to the bathroom.

He returned with a warm, moist facecloth. Tenderly he wiped her with it. "Baby, you're worth a few million, right? Why invent worries for yourself?"

She grabbed the washcloth from him and angrily tossed it to the floor. Jumping to her feet, she brushed down her clothes, adjusted her dress. "You know, *I* used to think like that before my consciousness was raised by my Village friends—"

"Those hippies?"

"They're humane, decent people. They don't think like you and my mother—'as long as you have a million, keep quiet, don't rock the boat!' It's *because* I can afford it that I should do some good, help others less fortunate—and these people are working for *me*! They're helping make me rich!"

"Radical chic?" Ed sneered. He buttoned his pants, looked for his shoes.

"No, Eddie!" She caught his shoulders and forced him to face her. "I'm not doing it because it's chic! I really *believe* this!"

He stared quietly into her earnest eyes. "Yeah..." He nodded. "You believe it. I can see you do!"

He found his other shoe and turned away from her, descending the twisting staircase to the front door below. She looked after him, feeling torn by two great needs.

"Wait!" she called after him. "Don't go like this!" She ran down behind him.

At the front door he turned and faced her. "You know what I really think this is about, Mack?" he said. "Guilt. You *never* loved that guy! You're laying your guilt on everyone. Alistair was a jerk! Just because he died doesn't turn him into some saint, you know. But *you* can't accept that! You have to make something fancy out of it! The Alistair Briarly Drug Abuse Center—"

"We're helping young addicts!" Mackenzie said. "I'm relieving some suffering—what's wrong with *that*? And maybe I can relieve a little poverty in Los Angeles—I only want to see it! You should admire me . . . respect me for it. . . ."

Ed had opened the door. They stood frozen, staring at each other.

"*So?*" she asked him. "I'd hate to keep you! *Go!* Go back to making a few more bucks on Seventh Avenue."

"Mack, don't go to L.A.," he said softly. "It's crazy! You're misguided, you're blowing up this whole—"

"That's right!" She gave him a little push. "Misguided Mackenzie, that's me! A heart of gold and a hippie-liberal conscience, and it's too bad if I have a multimillion-dollar business and my baby's a lord—I sure as hell didn't plan it that way. . . ."

He moved toward the elevator. As she closed the door on him, he said, "Call if you need me!"

Through the door she yelled, "I won't need you!"

After that there was just time to grab Jordan, call the doorman to get a cab, and pay the driver fifty dollars to fetch her bags and drive as fast as he could through the Manhattan traffic and to the airport. For some reason, she could not stop crying. They just made the plane.

It was five A.M. and Coral had run out of logs. She fetched a pile of *WWD*'s, *Labels*, and the *New York Times*, and fed them to the fire, which gratefully devoured them.

This trip had been quite different. The visual effects were not so vulgar. Her mind was seeing everything in a new way. She watched the flames streak up in orange, yellow, red—not this season's colors. She frowned. In the fire she saw characters, faces, fashion people she knew, both dead and alive. The newspaper supply ran out and she casually fed an expensive lacquered box to the fire. Fire could destroy, and from the ashes something new might be reborn. She wished she could destroy her old life and create something utterly new. Fashion had always been her entire life: Maybe it shouldn't have been? She threw her black shawl into the flames. She'd once said Paris is dead: Maybe fashion was dead, too? She hurried to her closets, bringing back armfuls of clothes to feed the fire. Out of the ashes would arise a new phoenix, she thought. One by one she threw Chanel, Dior, Norell, Galanos, and Halston dresses into the flames. Ultrasuede proved delightfully inflammable! In the flames she relived the history of fashion. Collections were modeled by haughty mannequins stalking down the runways into infinity: Givenchy, Ungaro, Phillipe Roux. The clothes mingled in her acid-doused brain, exploding into luminous color. She frowned, watching them: It was all wrong! Mods from the sixties wore 1930s' *tailleurs*, shingled twenties' flappers wore Mary Quant and Courreges!

The fire became a hungry animal demanding more food. On no account could it be allowed to fizzle out. It commanded her to burn her old life. It ate up the clothes hungrily; the fire loved fashion as much as *she* had! Suddenly she spoke aloud, as if lecturing a class.

"Even if a style does return, it has a different look to it! It's not a copy of a style, it's a reference to it! It's fashion's subtext!"

Fashion must move forward, never backward, so...goodbye to the old life, she thought. When there were no clothes left to feed the monster, she dragged the rug toward the fire and fed just the corner to the mouth of flame. At first the fire merely licked at the rubber underlay as if tasting it. Then it burst into a glorious green blaze which spread into the room.

Coral clapped her hands. "Emerald green!" she cried. The entire living room would soon be wall-to-wall emerald! She would feature nothing but emerald in a spring issue of *Divine*! It could be a reference to the Kay Thompson 'Think Pink' scene in *Funny Face*. Then she remembered she no longer directed *Divine* and gave out a piteous wail. As the floor blazed, she looked around the apartment, her wide eyes trying to take in what was happening. The hem of her dress was melting.

If she had to die, she wanted to die with the choicest name of all on her lips "Balenciaga!" she cried. Down in the lobby the smoke indicators for that floor were soon triggered, giving off their high-pitched scream.

* * *

The front page of *Labels*, October 18th, 1968, read:

Coral Stanton, Fashion Priestess whose antennae
kept her ahead of everyone in the industry, is missing, presumed dead, after a fire yesterday gutted the
luxury condominium in which she lived on West
Fifty-seventh Street. Although Mrs. Stanton's body
has not yet been recovered from the wreckage, she
had been seen entering the lobby some six hours
prior to the blaze, returning from the *Divine* Fashion
Awards presentation at Headquarters. Inhabitants of
the building were led to safety by doormen and
firemen.

Since 1964, the controversial editor-in-chief was the
mastermind behind *Divine*, the most influential fashion publication in the world. Coral Stanton was responsible for bringing the Mod Revolution to the
attention of the New York fashion industry in the
mid-sixties, for discovering designer Phillipe Roux,
who received the first *Divine* Fashion Award in 1966,
and for maintaining a high standard of quality and
design in her pages. Perhaps what she most stood for
was fantasy—that coming-together of fashion and
fun and inspiration that made her magazine so stimu-
lating and inspiring.

Lloyd Brooks, owner-publisher of *Divine*, joined
the staff for a two-minute silence in tribute: "We'll
miss Coral terribly. She inspired us with her far-
reaching and erudite taste. She was a very special
woman."

Headquarters director and close friend, Wayland
Garrity, said: "They don't make 'em like Coral anymore. She was a fashion great."

Colin Beaumont, fashion artist and best friend,
could not be reached. Friends said he was en route to
his Provence, France retreat.

Coral Stanton is survived by her daughter Mia
Stanton, who designs under the name Anais Du
Pasquier. She was not available for comment.

California dazzled Mackenzie with its light. When they
landed, the sun streamed into the plane, waking Jordan.
"Disneyland, Mommy?" he asked sleepily.

Mackenzie glanced out the TV-shaped window. "Absolutely!" she told him.

She had decided to fly economy class as a sop to her liberal conscience. I'll need all the money I can save, she told herself.

A taxi driver in a Stetson took over her baggage cart, wheeling it to his car. "Which is the best hotel in town?" she asked him. He was a grizzled, handsome man—a central-casting cowboy reject? she thought.

"Beverly Hills Hotel," he said, steering them through the slow-moving late-afternoon traffic. "Took Racquel Welch there last week. . . ."

"Take us there!" Mackenzie commanded.

Jordan fell asleep again in her arms as she stared out at the wide boulevards. "Where is everybody?" she asked the driver. It was unsettling to see the streets so empty.

"In their cars."

The only girls she saw looked like Sandra Dee in *Gidget*, or ravaged hippies. My God, they're ten years behind out here, she thought. We should send the L.A. branch all our old stock! They were still wearing minis and bell-bottoms. She struggled out of her long black coat.

When they reached the hotel, she gave a twenty-dollar bill to the driver, and the bellhops quickly wheeled her luggage to the desk. At the reception they acted as if an eccentric, titled English lady with a Bronx accent often stopped by.

"A suite!" Mackenzie decided.

"And how will you be paying for this, Lady Briarly?" She flashed her American Express card at the manager. "Thank you." He waved to the bellhop to accompany her to her rooms.

"Oh, Jordan darling, you'll love it here! You can learn to swim," she crooned to him as the bellhop showed her the bathroom, the refrigerator, the closets.

Gold! had a wholesale showroom at the downtown California Mart, but it was closed for the evening when she called. She left a message for them to call her the moment they opened the next morning. Exhausted, she ordered a club sandwich from room service and put Jordan to bed. She fell asleep before finishing the sandwich.

Jordan woke her very early the next morning. After

breakfast and her shower, it was eight-thirty. The Mart office called at nine.

"This is Mackenzie Briarly!" she said. "I want the address of the factory that makes up our garments."

"I'm not sure if I know that, Mrs., er, Lady Briarly," a young girl replied. "Can you hold?"

Another voice came on the line, more confident. "Lady Briarly? This is Brad Powell, manager of the showroom: What can I do for you?"

"I want you to pick me up at the Beverly Hills Hotel and take me to our workrooms. . . ."

"I'm afraid that won't be possible, ma'am. They're way out of the city, and it means a one-hour drive each way. My agenda is full of selling presentations today."

Mackenzie rolled her eyes. "Then find someone to take me or I'll go myself. This is urgent!"

They sent a driver in a shabby pickup to fetch her. She left Jordan in the hotel nursery, kissing him and promising not to be long. The driver stared at her clothes as she walked out of the hotel. Her black lacy tights looked ridiculously sexy in the Californian sun.

"Where are we going?" she asked the driver, climbing in next to him. He was Mexican. A good sign, she thought.

"We go to East L.A., lady," he said, starting up. She wondered if he knew her title or if he was just saying "lady." He reached across her to press the door lock. "It's not a very good part of town."

"I'll bet," she muttered.

They drove for what seemed like dozens of miles down hot boulevards and dusty streets, passing "Do-Nut" shacks, used-car lots, and fast-food outlets. Every corner seemed to boast a gas station. Her makeup was melting off her face, and the sun's rays through the window made her hotter. The sky was a bright cerulean blue. The only people she saw were old or poor, sitting helplessly at bus stops, on benches advertising funeral homes.

By the time they reached the workrooms, she was almost fainting from the heat. There was no sign that the workrooms belonged to Gold. The exterior of the building was rundown and shabby—it looked like a large, anonymous warehouse. She was ushered inside, into a hot, untidy little office belonging to the manager.

"Welcome to Los Angeles!" he greeted her, standing and smiling, his hand outstretched. His name, Angel Flores, was taped to the office door.

"Hi!" Mackenzie shook hands. "Got any water?" she croaked, eyeing a container. He gave her a paper cup and she downed it, requesting another, then another.

"Oh, God, I needed that!" she gasped.

She touched his arm and he winced. He was very formal and nervous, a small, dark-haired Mexican man with a wary look in his eye. He dismissed the driver with a quick muttered word. "Please take a seat!" he said, indicating a dusty typing chair, and Mackenzie collapsed into it. "We are honored by this visit!"

"Oh, *please*..." She waved the honor aside. "I shoulda come months ago. To check it out, I mean. I feel guilty I didn't—did you know I was coming today?"

He nodded. "Mr. Reggie...he call me last night. To my home. Very late. To tell me you are coming. Welcome to Los Angeles!"

"Thank you," she replied.

Her mother must have told her brother. She stared at him, trying to recover from the heat. He stared back, at a loss.

"How many workers you got here?" she finally asked.

"One hundred twenty," he said.

She stood up. "Let's go..."

Angel Flores proudly led the way to the workrooms. As they traipsed the dusty corridors toward the back of the building, Mackenzie could hear the sound of babies crying. The door to the workrooms, humming with the sound of machines clattering, was flung open. Mackenzie gazed in; the humidity of the pressed bodies and hot machinery was overpowering. She forced herself to enter. The hundred and twenty workers were predominantly women, crushed into a room full of sewing machines and cutting tables. In a corner a playpen of babies and tiny children, most of them screaming, their noses running, kept the noise level high. Mexican girls at table after table turned their heads to regard the visitor, their dark eyes inquisitive, foreheads shiny with sweat. From the playpen a distinct odor of urine and shit made its way to Mackenzie's nostrils, and she did her best not to react. She took a few steps down a gangway, gasping; she could hardly breathe.

She glanced at the windows which, although open, hardly allowed any air into the room. She turned to Flores and demanded, "Don't you have any fans?"

Flores shrugged helplessly. "It is hot, very hot, yes?" He grinned.

"It's unbearable!" Mackenzie shouted.

She made a gesture indicating that she wanted to walk around the room, and Flores pushed through a group of staring women, leading her up and down the aisles, where she smiled at the machinists. Some smiled back, some looked afraid or shy, some simply stared. The clatter of the machines was so intense that it set up vibrations and noise that reached a crescendo almost too loud for the human ear to bear.

She walked down a few more aisles before tottering and looking around for a chair. A smiling, older woman got up and gave her wooden stool to Mackenzie.

Mackenzie gasped, fanning herself with her hand. "Is there any water?" she asked.

They brought her someone's flask with some Coke in it, and she swallowed the liquid gratefully. She noticed that the woman who had given her the stool now stood and continued to machine a pair of pants, standing. The clothes being made were all familiar to Mackenzie; she had designed them.

"What are these people getting paid?" she asked the manager.

"The usual."

"And what's that?"

"Fifty cents an hour."

"That's *terrible*! How many hours a week do they work? Listen, can they just stop for a minute so I can talk to them?"

"They have a quota to get out, lady. If you stop them, they lose money."

"Okay, I'll talk to them while they work. Help me up." She held onto his arm, climbing atop the stool, waving to everyone. "Do they know who I am?" she looked down at him.

In Spanish he announced that the lady who designed the clothes had come to visit them.

"Hallo!" Mackenzie shouted. "Listen, everybody! *Ola!* I'm Mackenzie Briarly. I used to be Mackenzie Gold. I design these clothes. I'm from New York. I came all this way to visit you. To show you that someone in the management cares about you!"

Someone shouted "Nueva York!" and a few women applauded. They watched Mackenzie wearily, most of them continuing with their machining, so she had to shout.

"I've come all the way from Nueva York to see you!" she said again. "I wanted you to know how much I appreciate your work!" A young girl came to stand by her, and she fingered Mackenzie's shoes wonderingly.

"I just heard the kind of salary you get, and frankly, I'm shocked! I never wanted Gold! to be the kind of company that profited from its workers—these conditions are pretty appalling. I want to share our profits with you. Obviously you need more money, and we could put some money into improving this place. I want to try to make it up to you. I'll reorganize things somehow, I promise. Meanwhile, I want to give each one of you *something* to keep you going—how does two hundred dollars each sound to you?"

Somebody—probably the only one who understood her—cheered and whistled. *"Dos cien dollars,"* was whispered around the room, and they stared at her with renewed interest. A baby cried and was hushed. The clatterings of the machines slowly ceased as they stared up at her, amazement on their faces.

"I want you to line up here in front of me . . . I'll write you each a check," Mackenzie said, climbed down off the stool and rummaged in her purse for her checkbook.

Flores cleared his throat nervously. "Er . . . Miss Mackenzie, please . . . a check won't be so good for most of these people. They would find it very difficult to cash. May I suggest, if you are determined to do this, a cash payment?"

"Sure. Count everyone here."

"There are one hundred twenty-one today. . . ."

She made a quick sum on the back of the book. "That's $24,200. I'll make this out to you, Mr. Flores, and I shall trust you to distribute the cash among them—two hundred dollars each, okay?"

She waved good-bye to the smiling women, shaking hands with some of the girls who stuck out their hands as she passed, walking back into the office. Behind his desk

Flores stared at her curiously. "Your brothers—*they* know of this? This plan has their approval?"

"My plans don't need their approval," she said, writing out the check.

"But you realize that some of these girls—if they get two hundred dollars, just like that—they will not come in to work. We have big orders to fill—you must realize?"

"Oh, yeah..." Mackenzie frowned and bit the end of her pen. "Let me speak to them again."

She left him in his office and walked back toward the workroom as Flores quickly reached for his phone and dialed New York.

She flung open the door to the workroom, now bustling with chattering women discussing that morning's strange event. "Everybody?" Mackenzie called. They stopped work and looked at her. "Your work is *very* important to me! Without your work, my designing cannot go on. Nor could the stores *or* the wholesale business. We count on you so much! I want your assurance that you will continue to come in to work, even when you get the extra money. I will try my hardest to improve conditions here. Don't let me down, okay? You *will* all come in, won't you? We have a lot of orders to fill, and we'll make the firm the biggest ready-to-wear firm in the country if we can work well together...."

They smiled at her and waved, and by then she was so hot that all she wanted to do was get back to the Beverly Hills Hotel and an iced drink.

She dragged herself back to the stuffy office just as Flores hung up the phone. He stared at her strangely. "Your brothers—they do *not* know about this bonus," he told her. "You do this without their permission...."

Mackenzie laughed at him. "I don't *need* their permission! This is *my* money I'm using, not theirs. If I choose to reward the workers who've helped me earn my money, that's my business, isn't it? You see, Mr. Flores, my brothers don't care about the conditions of your people. And I *do*! That's the big difference between us. I'm so happy I can help them in some way."

Flores stared at her, expressionless. She signed the check and handed it to him. "I know I can trust you with this. You'll give everyone who works here two hundred dollars cash, won't you?"

He took the check and read it, frowning, his lips moving. Suddenly he grinned. "This is the biggest check I ever saw," he marveled. Then he became grave again.

"And that's just the beginning," Mackenzie told him. "I'm gonna find out about getting this place redecorated, putting a sign up, and giving them some pride and some identity."

"Miss Mackenzie," Flores interrupted her. "Do you have a credit card number I can put on the back of this check? They demand it at the bank sometimes...."

"Oh? Sure..." She rummaged in her wallet and held out the American Express card to him. He took it, read it carefully, then picked up a large pair of dressmaker's shears that were lying on his desk and snipped through the card.

"What the hell did you do that for?" Mackenzie screamed, picking up the pieces of the card, "Are you *crazy*?"

"I am not crazy, Miss Mackenzie," Flores said. "I did this because your brothers tell me to do it. Just now when I phoned their offices in New York. They told me you no longer work for Gold. When I tell them you intend to pay each worker two hundred dollars, they said to destroy your credit card—they said they think *you* are crazy!"

"But that was my only card—how could you *do* that!" she raged. "And I own twenty-five percent of Gold!—there's no way they can take that away from me. I won't be able to pay for anything out here now. What'll I *do*?"

He shrugged. "I must ask you to leave, that's all I know. Please..."

She looked at him, hurt and suddenly afraid. He took her arm and tried to guide her out of his office. She pulled her arm away.

"I'll be back here with the police!" she promised. "That card was my property. You had no right to destroy it—no right!"

Outside, the factory door closed behind her. The midday sun was cruel and seemed to bleach the colorless street of all identity. She had no idea where she was. Her driver was lounging against his pickup, talking to another man.

Mackenzie tapped his shoulder. "Take me back to the Beverly Hills Hotel."

He shook his head. "I stay here now, lady. Sorry..."

"This is ridiculous! Here..." She fumbled in her purse. "It has to be worth twenty dollars to you." But she realized as she went through her wallet that she did not have twenty dollars. She had intended to cash a check at the hotel that afternoon. She had no credit card and no cash.

"Here!" she waved her checkbook at him. "I'll write a check. It won't bounce—it'll be fine...."

He shook his head and went back to talking to his friend. A wave of horror passed over her. Had Reggie and Max really cut her out of the company? But how? And how the hell was she going to get back to civilization? As she stared, squinting in the bright sun, at her ex-driver, Flores reappeared at the door, yelled a command in Spanish to the driver and the driver hurried into the building.

Mackenzie walked listlessly down the street, the sun knocking all resistance and thought out of her. She shaded her eyes to see if there was a taxi stand anywhere. She was definitely in the Mexican part of town—every sign was in Spanish. The clothes in the tawdry, flyblown windows she passed were garish, cheap. The fast-food stands reeked of stale frying oil. She passed a storefront that was the saddest one of all, a big tattered sign reading SALA DE FIESTA. People stared at her black clothing as she stumbled, sweating, past them. At one corner, a group of children laughed at her, two of them dancing around her.

She stopped at a store doorway and fumbled in her purse to see exactly how much money she had. It amounted to a handful of loose change. This can't be happening to me, she thought. I must not panic—that'll get me even hotter. Across another wide stretch of road she saw a gas station and a pay phone. Clutching her loose change, she waited for the light to change. The sun continued to dazzle her, even through her dark glasses. She was gasping by the time she reached the phone. She longed for a Diet Pepsi, but it was a drink or a call—she did not have enough for both. She got the number of the Beverly Hills Hotel through Information, then inserted a dime for the call. "Forty-five cents, please," came a recorded voice. She just had enough. "Thank you," said a recording. The phone rang and a voice answered, "Beverly Hills Hotel, good afternoon!" Civilization at last! she thought.

"Oh, God, am *I* happy to get *you*," Mackenzie began.

But then a click and a buzz suddenly disconnected her and the line went dead. She pressed the Coin Return button, but no coins were returned.

"Oh, *no!*" she screamed, and pressed the button again and again, hitting the machine with the flat of her palm. A little boy ran up to the booth and pressed the button several times, on tiptoe. Then he shrugged at her and ran off.

Hot tears ran down her face, melting the makeup even further. *I'm Lady Mackenzie Briarly,* she reminded herself, *and I am not going to lose control!* As she stumbled back to the sidewalk and looked up and down, a car came to a slow crawl alongside. The two men inside it looked her over.

"Need a ride, lady?" one called out.

"Lost?" asked the other.

She stumbled on in her high heels, not answering, the sun beating down on her head, making her nauseous.

After several more blocks, each resembling the other, she realized she did not know where she was going, so why get hotter from walking? Seeing a bench on a side street, she sat down. Gasping with thirst, wondering what would happen if night fell and she couldn't get back to Jordan, she burst into fresh tears. This is what you get for trying to help people, she thought. By that time, a group of curious women and children stood around Mackenzie, staring at her. Now and then someone addressed her in Spanish, but all Mackenzie could cry was "Beverly Hills Hotel" before she began weeping again.

Her head swam with dizziness: She felt she was going to faint. She just managed to lie down full-length on the bench before passing out.

Twenty-seven

Phillipe waited at De Gaulle Airport, an enormous bunch of white roses in one arm, his dark eyes darting from one passenger's face to another, until he saw Mia. He caught her gaze and held it, the intensity of his expression deepening, his unselfconscious eyes still those of a child. He gave her one of his marvelous smiles, and she felt the way she had felt in Paris whenever he'd entered the room: blessed, as if just being around him was a special treat. She began to run toward him, but he inclined his head slightly, and she noticed the photographers watching him and slowed down, directing the porter to follow the man with the flowers. Outside in the dark car park the photographers gave chase when they realized what was happening, the camera flashes a sudden lightning storm in the crisp French air.

He did not touch her until they were safely inside the limousine. Then, as a driver with a peaked cap steered them smoothly onto the highway, Phillipe took her in his arms. The roses filled the car with their perfume. He kissed her throat, her face, her lips, and she was swept back to the night when they had first kissed. But how much more she knew now, now that beyond all doubt he was the only man in the world for her. She leaned back in the seat as their hands clasped, giving herself up to him, feeling the first excited stirrings as he lightly touched her legs, her breasts, her stomach, his fingers lingering gently between her legs, caressing her. She felt a sudden intense longing, wanting him.

He did not make love to her in the car as it swept toward Paris, but they came very close. She breathed in the aroma of him as they kissed, and she held his tongue

444

in her mouth for long moments, pressing her body up against his.

As they entered the city, he broke away. "I am a little embarrassed about this house we are going to," he confessed. "I was advised to buy property. I have become a capitalist, Mia. . . ."

He might just as well have told her he was a swindler or a murderer—it didn't matter, none of it mattered but the feel of his mouth upon hers, his breath against her lips, and the knowledge that they would be together forever.

"It is so large," he said, as if apologizing, "and so empty. There has been no time to choose furnishings." He laughed, touching her cheek affectionately.

"I'll love it, Phillipe," she kissed his cheek. "I'd love it if it were a hole in a wall."

When they reached *Etoile*, the driver was dismissed and they climbed into the front seat as Phillipe drove them the rest of the way. She kept her hand on his hard thigh to make herself believe this was real.

The house and its setting were unbelievably romantic. The street was lined with a well-groomed facade of nineteenth-century buildings, proud behind perfectly shaped dark green bushes and shrubs. The house itself was the most spectacular private dwelling Mia had ever seen: a whole courtyard of cobbled stones for the car to park in, twenty windows, and each one framing a candle Phillipe had lit in her honor. They overlooked the square central court planted with boxwoods and bushes cut in pyramid shapes. A small fountain trickled a musical stream of water. A full moon, as if ordered, bathed the scene in a soft white glow.

When the car stopped, the night became silent, shrouded. Phillipe got out. He scooped Mia off the seat and into his arms, carrying her up the stone steps. She pushed her face against his, kissing his smooth cheek over and over again, trying to convince herself she wasn't dreaming.

He paused in the hallway. "You are hungry?" he asked her. "We go to the kitchen first?"

"No! *No!*" she cried.

Phillipe laughed delightedly and continued to walk up the long, curved stone staircase. The candles set on the windowsills made fantastic flickering shadows on the wall as they passed. They finally came to a large room with a beautiful canopied bed in the center.

"This is our room," he said, setting her gently down on the bed. He stretched out full-length beside her. "All the time I thought of you, my Mia. Did you feel me?"

"But you never wrote," she replied, touching his temple, his eyebrows. "You never called...."

"Because of my stubborn sense of honor," he smoothed back her blond hair. "I owed it to her to try to forget you. But I couldn't...."

"And I thought of you every minute, darling, every second."

He pressed his mouth down on hers, and she was lost in the kiss, lost in him. She ran her hands over his back, feeling its breadth, its warmth, its power.

"I tried so hard to please her but she was—"

"No!" She touched his full lips with her finger. "Don't talk about her now, darling. I want this evening to be something I remember forever. I don't want to spoil it. Just us, Phillipe...just you kissing me."

He kissed around her face, nibbled gently on her lips. "But it is only fair to tell you that she has no intention of letting go," he warned. "*I* have escaped. *I* have announced our marriage is over. But for her it is not over. She plagues me, she calls me in the middle of the night, she comes here—"

"She won't come tonight, will she?" Mia asked, alarmed.

"I pray to God, no!"

"As long as we're together."

She kissed over his smooth forehead, pressing his black silky eyebrows with her fingers. He laughed, kissing her ear. Her body was coming alive, as if awakening from its long, long sleep. As his fingers touched her in gentle, exploring caresses, he started tremors, urges, currents in her. Suddenly her teeth began to chatter.

"You are cold?"

"No. Phillipe...please don't laugh at me—I'm...not experienced. I've always been so frightened of love...of sex...of what men do—"

"No...no..." he hushed her, nibbling on her lower lip, slipping his hands between the buttoned front of her shirt and caressing her breasts so gently that she seemed to swell toward him, wanting more of his touch. "We will approach our love gradually. It is like preparing a fine meal. You do not gobble up the ingredients. We will be gentle, careful, slow. I am not like most men, you will see. . . ."

"I trust you, darling. I know it's stupid, but I'm just so afraid."

He freed her breasts and began to nibble on the tips. At the same time his hand slipped under her skirt and onto her sex, fondling it gently, making a fire leap up within her. She let out a low groan of desire mixed with fear.

He took her hand and placed it gently on the shape of his aroused sex through his clothing. "You can feel?" he asked. "I am impatient. Impatient to be joined with you. But I have discipline . . . only when *you* are ready, not before."

"Yes. You'll wait until I'm ready," she repeated. "Thank you, darling. . . ."

His hand became more insistent. She thrust up toward it, his fingers finding their way into her, then stroking, probing, softly, giving her that pleasure she remembered so well from the first time. She left her hand over his hard sex, trying to quell the flutter of fear that touching him awoke in her. He felt so big, so hard.

"I want to enjoy this so much, my darling," she whispered. His fingers inside her now excited a whole new host of conflicting feelings. She withdrew from him. "Please . . . be slow. Be very slow," she begged.

He sat up and removed all his clothes, then hers. She looked at him in the moonlight that bathed their bodies in white light while he ran his hands over her smooth body, over the sides, the back, the breasts. He was like a sculptor testing a new piece of marble, deciding what to do with it. His body was bronzed, spare, shaped like an Egyptian statue with broad shoulders and flat tapering chest. She put her hands up to it; it was burnished, smooth, hard. He groaned, leaning his head to her groin and resting his face between her legs. She felt his tongue flick out over her mound, and closed her eyes to give herself up to his exploration, gently opening her legs to him. The pleasure was beginning. Her teeth had stopped chattering. She felt a thrill of elation—it was going to be all right. . . .

He guided his sex so that it just nudged her, the tip just

grazing her crevice. He stroked her gently, as one would calm a frightened animal. And for long minutes they stayed still. Then he removed his hand and flexed his sex against her. She felt it move, as if it were another limb. It pushed against the lips of her sex. She held her breath, not daring to breathe. Everything in her life had led to this moment. If there was going to be a forever with Phillipe, it would begin *now*! Gently he inserted the thick head. Oh, God, let it be all right! She wanted the stiff muscle inside her, yet she dreaded it. If she could, she would have pushed him away, brought him closer, pushed him away—teetering on the very edge of this moment for eternity. Yes! *No!* Yes! *No!* her body cried. *Let* him! *Don't* let him! *Let* him! Her teeth began to chatter again, and she clenched her mouth closed. She felt herself shrink against him. He was going to be too big for her! He stroked her face with his hand, guiding himself into her with the other, pushing the hardness up inside her. A spasm of fear sounded in her.

"*Phillipe!*" she cried. "I—"

The candles in the room suddenly flickered, and a bell sounded, shrillingly loud, shattering their solitude. They both jumped. It sounded again.

"*Merde!*" Phillipe cried, startling her. He eased himself off the bed and pressed his face to the window, trying to see who was outside.

The bell sounded again, in short piercing bursts.

"I shall not answer," he murmured. She joined him at the window, standing behind him, touching the soft back of his head, fondling his strong neck where the hair grew in straggling tufts. Her stomach was against his buttocks and she pressed to him, loving the touch of their skins together.

The bell sounded a few more times, as if it had no intention of letting up.

"It's her, isn't it?" she asked.

The bell was pressed more quickly, its blasts shattering the night.

"She is going to ruin everything," Phillipe muttered, and they listened, pressed together, hardly breathing.

She felt around to the front of his body. His sex was less upright, but it was still heavy, swollen with his desire for her. She allowed herself to feel the pendulous, weighty sac hanging beneath it. He groaned as she touched him, the delicious smell of him coming to her. The bell was now being held for long periods of thirty seconds. As though the sound didn't exist, he turned and put his teeth gently around her nipple, teasing it. She wanted him to suck hard on her, and as if reading her thoughts, he did. The sucking seemed to connect and relax her down there, and she felt herself opening up to him. His hand was there, on her, the fingers curving tenderly inside her, rubbing her into life again.

Another long burst of the shrill bell and he broke away from her, peering out the window.

"I must answer. She is capable of waking the entire neighborhood!" he said. "How can we make love to that accompaniment? She is so crazy, so demanding..." He found a silk robe and threw it on, returning to the bed to kiss her, as she lay down.

"You will just get rid of her, won't you, Phillipe? It's six in the morning for me—"

"I'll tell her to leave me alone," he promised. "We are finished. She must stop this. I'll be back as soon as I convince her, Mia." He bent over her and they shared a long kiss, his tongue moving deeply in her mouth. Then he broke away and moved out of the room, padding down the staircase.

Mia heard the bell ring a few more times and the sound of the front door opening, then voices. Although she fought to stay awake, she could not do it—she sank into a stupor, a half-asleep, half-wakeful state in which she was almost conscious of her strange surroundings. Maybe the entire event had been a dream, she thought, drifting off. Maybe she would wake and find herself in her apartment, the victim of a cruel self-deception or fantasy. This sort of adventure did not happen in real life, surely? In her dream she tried to pinch herself, and she could not feel the pain.

Then other things began to happen. Phillipe was shouting, there was a crash of glass, a door slamming. A woman screamed and her screams turned into the sounds of begging. Phillipe pacified this woman with soothing sounds, with a glass of wine, with murmured vows never to leave her side. Mia tossed on the bed, twisting in the bedclothes, frowning in her sleep, a terrible anxiety pervading her dream.

The dream changed. They were in a shadowy château where lanterns and candles sent caricatured silhouettes leaping on the rocklike walls. Phillipe was making love in the dark to someone very familiar, someone who had been crying so much that her eyes were like slits. Someone who was now gasping with desire as Phillipe fucked her. *Yes—fucked!* That was the word she thought in her dream. There was strange accompanying clanking music, in an Eastern rhythm, which became louder and louder and suddenly stopped—

Mia sat bolt upright in the strange bed, wide awake. Her throat was dry. The bed was empty and no sound came from the large house. She had no idea how long she had slept, but it was still dark, the night lit only by the moon. Phillipe surely should have returned by now? The white, silent moonlight cast the eeriest light she had ever seen. It accentuated the strangeness of this night, this day in her life. She got out of bed, stumbling over her suitcase, stubbing a toe. The candles were smoldering, their red wicks filling the rooms with an acrid smoke. She found a light switch and turned it on, but there was no bulb in the socket. Her eyes became accustomed to the darkness, and touching the walls with her hands, she walked out into the corridor. There were many rooms, and she peered into them all; most were empty or held a simple chest or a piece of furniture covered with a sheet.

She retraced their steps down the wide flight of stairs to the ground floor. There, she thought she heard a rustle. A few seconds later she thought she heard another sound—a gasp. Her dream returned vividly to her—the French voices shouting, the shatter of glass. Maybe it had not been a dream, but real sounds infiltrating her subconscious? Maybe thugs had entered the house and fought with Phillipe? She shivered. There were more sounds coming from a downstairs room; perhaps Phillipe was lying on the floor somewhere, gasping for breath? Her eyes bulged with fear as she heard another long, rasping sigh from a room to the right of the wide staircase. If only there were some light! She could just see a candelabra on the windowsill holding melted-down candles, but there were no matches.

She followed the sounds, her feet reluctant to move, half frozen in fear, as she forced herself to approach the room from which the sounds came. She tiptoed to the door, staying very silent in case the intruders lingered, waiting for her. Very gently she pushed the door, and it swung slowly open onto a living room bathed in moon-light. There were two people in the room making strange, thirsty sounds together. Something about the rhythm of these sounds awoke memories stored within her from long ago. Somewhere, once, in some other house, she had tiptoed to the door of a room and looked inside, staying as quiet as she was now, witnessing a similar scene.

"Ohhhh . . ." she heard a voice moan, and another, deeper voice echo it, alongside it. She stifled a quick, painful intake of breath for she already had a premonition of what she was about to see. She approached the large couch in the center of the room and closed her eyes tightly, knowing that when she opened them, she would be able to see more clearly. When she did, she saw their bodies—Phillipe and Josephine. Saw the lean, brown back of the man she loved moving, causing Josephine's moans, as she held him to her by crossing her legs over his, sliding under him then up against him, hollowing herself for him as if she could never get him deep enough inside her to satisfy herself. And with each thrust, Phillipe let out a resigned grunt that somehow signified to Mia how pitiful humans were, how like puppets or animals in this sexual display, this game which, if one were merely ob-serving, seemed so ridiculous and yet so hypnotic. She watched Josephine's face bathed in moonlight as it gri-maced, eyes shut, mouth hungrily open, in a kind of cruel parody of Mia's own love.

And in a sickening flash, Mia suddenly remembered. She remembered standing at the door of her parents' bedroom watching that inexplicable game, the sound of it, the sucking and fucking . . . and suddenly she became that little girl again, the seven-year-old Mia.

"*Mommy!*" she cried in a childish voice, and the lovers jumped in fright. "*Mommy!*" she cried, "don't let him do that!"

She felt a wrenching gasp, a breath she was forced to take, and it shook her body with shudders. Hardly knowing what she was doing, she fell on Phillipe, pummeling his back with her fists.

He cried out in surprise, and Josephine screamed, her eyes flashing open, glazed in confusion.

Mia pulled at Phillipe with superhuman strength. "Daddy!" she screamed. "Don't do that to her!" She gripped Phillipe's neck and dragged his head back, then his body. Then she lunged at Josephine, scratching her face, shouting, "Don't let him do that! Don't let him!"

Eyes wide with horror, Josephine shielded her face with her hands. She slid from under Phillipe, grabbing a shirt and hurriedly covering herself. Together they held Mia off as she screamed, fought, kicked. Finally, in the wooden-floored, cold, half-empty room, they watched in amazement as Mia ran, like a sulky child throwing a fit, to a corner of the room where she crumpled to the floor, sobbing as if her heart was broken, taking shuddering great gasps of air as if being reborn.

David stood at the Arrivals gate at Kennedy Airport at six-thirty in the morning. You must be the biggest chump in the world, he told himself for the twentieth time. What other man, having taken all he had taken from Mia, would agree to meet her returning from her Paris lover? Yet there had been something so urgent and different in her voice when she woke him at three in the morning and asked him to be there, that he had felt impelled to agree.

"I need you, David," she had said.

He could hardly believe she had not yet heard the tragic news about her mother, and after listening to her nearly incoherent call, he did not want to break it to her over the phone. She'd said something about discovering herself, about exorcising a ghost from her past, which she wanted to share with him.

Her flight was announced as thirty minutes late, and he bought a cup of coffee to fill the time. The headline of the *Daily News* read: FASHION ED BURNS CONDO, SELF. He decided he would steer her away from the newsstand, straight into a taxi, and tell her gently, in private. A giant billboard inside the terminal advertised David Winters Jeans, and he was soon spotted by a young girl who asked him adoringly for his autograph. He put on some dark glasses, watching the Arrivals board.

When the plane landed, he expected a long wait as Mia passed through Customs, but he was roused by a loud cry of *"David!"* and when he turned, he saw Mia running down the slippery, tiled passageway from Customs, holding just an overnight bag. Her face was radiant, her blond hair flying out behind her, and her eyes seemed alive for the first time in a long while. He cursed his role as bearer of bad news. The next moment she was in his arms, her mouth on his, and she was kissing him in a way she had never kissed him before.

"I see. Thank you for calling me, Wayland."

Colin replaced the telephone receiver and gazed blankly out of his living room window, not seeing the pretty Provençal scene outside. He stood, shakily, and went next door to fetch the neighbor's dog, a healthy Collie who enjoyed the extra walks. Keeping the dog on a long leash, he walked the hedgerow-lined path toward the town. His mind worked mechanically; he must buy the papers, a loaf of bread, perhaps some of the white, fresh butter that they cut from a huge lump at the local store. Coral dead? It was much too soon to start thinking about that in any detail. Or even to commiserate with Wayland on their loss. It must be a mistake. When he returned home there would be another call, surely, saying it was all a mistake. His heart felt as heavy as lead. He could hardly drag his feet along the dry, mud-caked walk. The tall trees loomed up on either side of them and the dog ran ahead eagerly, looking back as if asking "Why are you dawdling?"

And I had such plans for her, Colin thought. I thought we might work on a book together—Coral doing the writing, me the illustrations. Perhaps a history of fashion. I even thought we might perhaps one day—Suddenly he sat down on a stump, burying his face in his hands. The dog ran back to lick at the salty tears that leaked through Colin's fingers.

David carried Mia gently into his bedroom. She was exhausted, yet conscious enough to wryly reflect that this was the second time in forty-eight hours that a man had carried her to his bed. David had insisted that she come back to his apartment with him, not be alone. In the taxi from the airport she had tried to explain the confusing encounter with Phillipe Roux—as much for herself as for him.

"One day I'll try to tell you the whole story," she promised him. "But you can see I'm a different person, can't you, David? I don't feel frightened anymore. I've suddenly grown up. I've been carrying a terrified little child of seven inside me all my life and suddenly she's vanished."

He nodded, holding her hand, trying to be understanding when he really didn't understand at all. But she sounded so happy, so lucid and so calm, that he believed something good had happened to her in Paris. He placed her very carefully on the bed and she slept immediately. Later he came in and covered her with a white comforter. And later still, he decided to lie down next to her, snuggling up to her.

Mia slept through an entire day. When she finally awoke, it was dark outside and David was snoring softly next to her. She stretched, disturbing him, and half-conscious, he held her. She eased her body next to his and their mouths sought each other's and kissed. Half-asleep, they removed their clothes, rearranged their naked limbs against each other and embraced. Everything happened without her thinking, without planning. David was suddenly, gently, inside her. There was no fear, no panic. She enjoyed the feeling of him being inside her. As he moved gently in her, she felt her body begin to answer his. He nuzzled his face in her neck, near her ear, then lovingly lowered his lips to rest on hers, barely brushing her mouth. She felt his breath against her face. She continued to move her body in answer to his, pushing gently back at him as he plunged slowly, deeply into her, rotating her hips to give him pleasure. She could tell that the ecstasy would not sweep her tonight, but she came very near to a new kind of pleasure. Her body-murmurs, and the new flutterings inside her, showed her she would be able to respond, that her body was as capable of pleasure as any woman's. When she felt him reach his climax, she urged him on, holding him lovingly, covering his face with tiny kisses, grateful that he could still love her after all she'd put him through. David had waited for her. He had proved to be solid, decent, not a fantasy, not an idealization. It was the way a man treated you that counted, not the words, not the flowers, not the candles in the windows. She knew now that Phillipe and she could never have been a couple. Not for very long.

She remembered the first attraction she had felt toward David—the natural urges of a young woman before she had allowed her fantasies to rule her. David was everything she had ever needed in a man. And he had been in her own backyard, she thought, smiling. She held onto him as he drifted back to sleep, feeling proud, fulfilled, and optimistic for the first time in her life. Her new life would be one in which she explored herself, her feelings, and David. She would learn how to accept happiness. It would be a beautiful thing to learn. She was smiling as she allowed herself to become drowsy again, to sink back into a peaceful sleep. But life does not aways allow things to be quite so simple, or so easy. Just as she was about to fall asleep, David moved away from her and sat up abruptly in the bed. He flicked on the light and his eyes were wide with concern, as hers squinted against the sudden brightness.

"Mia, darling," he took her hand. "I can't believe I forgot to tell you. Something terrible has happened to your mother...."

"You are the first guest to arrive at the Beverly Hills Hotel with police escort since...since Elizabeth Taylor," the Mexican maid said adoringly, bringing Mackenzie an armful of fluffy towels..

Mackenzie lay full-length, submerged in her bubble bath, with Jordan sitting by her side in the water. She giggled. "Yeah? That was nothing! Next time I'm going for the U.S. Navy rescue team."

"More champagne, Lady Briarly?"

"Why not?" Mackenzie shrugged, holding up her empty crystal glass. "I'll probably need it, by the way that phone's ringing...."

There were a dozen phone messages to be answered, and the phone seemed to ring every few minutes. She would deal with the callers later. Right now she wanted to revel in the feeling of relief at being with Jordan again. Thank God, the Mexicans who had surrounded her as she lay passed out on the bench had called the police. They, in turn, had finally been convinced by her that she was Lady

Briarly and belonged in the Beverly Hills Hotel and not on
a public bench in East L.A.

An hour later, when she was in her robe, her hair piled
up in a turban, she began to answer calls. A reporter from
the *Los Angeles Times* asked, "Is it true you visited the
workshops and wrote out a twenty-four-thousand-dollar
check?"

"I'd prefer you didn't write about that," she told him.
"It's a private matter."

The reporter laughed and said, "Lady Briarly, I just got
off the phone with three of your Mexican employees,
telling me how they plan to spend their bonuses. It's a
great human-interest story. If *they're* talking about it, surely you can give me a comment. Why did you do it?"

Mackenzie thought a moment, then finally replied, "Just
say I wanted to share my appreciation of their work and
set an example to the garment industry. We *must* share
profits with our workers—especially when they work in
conditions like I saw today. I aim to change that...."

"In spite of being ousted from your company?"

"Who *said* I'm ousted?" Mackenzie snapped.

"Your brothers. Reggie Goldstein said—"

"I can't comment on that now. I'm sorry—good-bye."
She hung up the phone and looked at her watch. It was
eight-thirty. That meant it was eleven-thirty in New York.
She dialed Reggie's number.

He answered the phone with a grunted "Yeah?"

"What makes you think you can oust me from the
company?" she yelled, cradling the phone to her ear,
lighting a cigarette.

"What makes me think it?" Reggie sounded cockier
than usual. "I'll *tell* you—it's because you *are* out! I told
you I'd kick you out on your titled ass if you stuck your
nose into our business."

"You fat, ignorant bastard—I'm gonna sue you for every penny you have!" she screamed. "But first I'm gonna
find the best lawyer in the country and see whether you
have the right to *do* this!"

"Save yourself the fees," Reggie said, laughing. "We
talked Dad into selling us his shares. We now own seventy-
five percent of the company between us, and *we* voted
you *out*, Mack! We never have to deal with your shit

again! Thanks for training the design team for us. We'll
give 'em a raise!"

"They won't stay with you!" she screamed. "They'll
come with me."

"With *you*?" he sneered. "To *where*? You think after the
press gets hold of the story of you giving away money,
any firm will want you? You think it'll be so easy to start a
new firm? You're a kook, a *nut*, and tomorrow *everyone*
will know it!"

She slammed the phone down and burst into angry,
helpless tears. She felt utterly alone. Hugging Jordan to
her, she could not stop crying. The phone rang and she
picked it up, gulping. It was Ed.

"I said to call me if you needed me, and you said you
wouldn't need me!" he told her.

"I *need* you!" Mackenzie wailed. "Oh, Eddie, if you
knew all I've been through today! Someone cut up my
American Express card, and now I'm in debt to the tune
of thousands at this hotel. I'm out on my ass, no job, no
company. My brothers have booted me out."

"I just got tomorrow's *New York Times*," he told her.
"Did you really give away all the profits to the machinists?"

She burst out laughing, then gave him a full account of
her day. "Baby, I'm *liberal*, but I'm not *dumb*!" she ended.
"All I did was give each one two hundred dollars. It
makes *me* feel good, that's all. It salves my conscience. If
you saw the conditions they work under, if you saw what
I looked like after one *hour* down there . . . then I didn't
have a penny, Eddie! I had to call the police to bring me
back here. My phone is ringing off the hook, Jordan was
alone all day, I have twenty messages from—"

"Do you want me there? We could give a press confer-
ence tomorrow, once I've bailed you out."

"Oh, Eddie, *could* you?"

"Will you be Mrs. Ed Schreiber?"

"I'll be Mrs. Golda Meir if you come get me out of this.
I *hate* California! I hate the sun! I just wanna go home!"

"Not before our Beverly Hills honeymoon, Mack! And I
want a singing rabbi at the wedding, okay?"

"Sounds *wonderful* to me! I'll order some chopped chick-
en liver from Nate 'n' Al's in Beverly Hills. It's time I
discovered my roots."

"And our new firm? What'll we call it?"

"How about *Schmatta Modes*?"

"Think we could get it together?"

"Eddie, if you just came out here and held me in your arms, I could do *anything*! I learned today just how much good a fucking title does you when you're down and out in East L.A."

"Have you seen a newspaper since you left?" he asked. "Did you hear about Coral Stanton?"

"No—*what*?"

"She died in a fire in her apartment."

"Oh, my God, oh, *Eddie* . . ." She held onto the couch as she shook uncontrollably. "Oh, that's *terrible*! And I had to go and beat up Mia the last time I saw her! What should I *do*?"

". . . so Eddie rushed out on the next plane. We got married two days later! Do you know what a *chuppa* is, Colin? It's a Jewish canopy, and you get married under it! Kinda dumb, huh? I guess the first Jewish bride was some princess—terrified it would rain on her hairdo . . . anyway, we had one set up at the Beverly Hills Hotel pool! This singing rabbi strumming a guitar walked down the aisle ahead of us—you should have seen my parents' faces!"

"Were your brothers there?" Colin asked.

"Are you *kidding*?" Mackenzie cried. "I just slapped a twenty-five-million-dollar lawsuit on them. . . ."

She paused to take a big gulp of Evian water. They were sitting on the bed of the second guest room. It was noon in Provence. Mackenzie had talked for two and a half hours.

"David was best man," she continued. "I wanted so much to have Mia there, too, but she was still in a state of shock. David said she was dying of guilt. There was no body, you see, Colin! Nothing to bury or take flowers to, and the police made Mia identify bits and pieces of burnt *junk* they found in the apartment. The whole thing was so damn *spooky*! I got to feeling worse and worse about Mia. I kept telling Eddie—'I gotta see her. I gotta make up with that girl. . . .' Once I was plain old Mrs. Ed Schreiber, I felt different about *every*thing! When I heard she'd come here to see you, I decided to kill two birds with one stone. Have a great honeymoon and—"

Mackenzie interrupted herself with a loud yawn. Colin had never seen a mouth open so wide. She began to talk again, and to his amazement, fell fast asleep in mid-sentence. Colin covered her with a quilt, gently removing the fine suede boots. He peeked into Mia's room and saw she was sleeping soundly, her beautiful hair spread out on the *broderie-anglaise* pillow.

"What stories!" he said, and chuckled to himself. He now had the ending to his novel—real life always provides better endings than any work of fiction, he thought happily. And he had yet to provide the twist to the ending. That would come tonight, once his secret was out in the open. . . .

He worked all afternoon, scribbling down the ideas that raced through his mind, patching some holes in the story that Mackenzie had filled. At six he carefully dialed a number.

"They're here," he said softly into the phone. "Not only Mia, but the ex-Lady Mackenzie, too. I didn't expect quite such a full house, but no matter . . . when they wake up I'll make them a light supper. I'll call you while they're eating and hang up. That will mean you should come over. Oh, I can't *wait*!"

At seven-thirty he heard a door open, a tap running water, the sounds of movement. Mia found him first, as he set the table with bowls of salad, raw vegetables, dips, and fresh fruit, wine, bread, and a large pot of coffee.

Mia leaned to kiss his forehead, her face sparkling and calm. "It's so beautiful here," she told him. "I've felt better since arriving." She sat down on a floral-chintz armchair, gazing around the room. "I can't believe how much I miss her, Colin. It's as though her death has released all this love in me that I never knew what to do with at the time. I see us both so clearly, now—the way we fought. You know how they say 'love is very close to hate'? That's another thing I've been thinking about. . . ."

"What about you and David?" Colin asked, and poured her some coffee. "Is that finally going to happen? And Phillipe Roux—is that really over?"

She smiled calmly, looking into his eyes. "That was an enchantment. Now that I've faced something in myself, I have years of my own behavior to shuck off—years of hating my mother . . . so much to undo. And I know now that Phillipe must stay with Josephine. Those two are fated to be together. Besides, she'll never let go. She'd make life miserable for any woman who loved Phillipe . . . so in a way, I'm quite grateful to her! I'll tell you everything—it's very melodramatic."

" 'Hell is other people,' " Colin quoted. "That's what Sartre said."

"They do tend to complicate life. Things would have been perfect if my mother hadn't died. If I could only have had the chance to talk things out with her. I can't stop replaying in my mind the last scene we had together. When she asked me for a job at the awards—remember?"

"How could I ever forget?" Colin muttered.

"Did she kill herself because of that?" Mia asked, turning an agonized face toward him. "I can't help feeling she did! And I'll never ever forgive myself for it. . . ."

"Don't be so hard on yourself. Remember the dreadful condition she was in—but you're going to learn a lot about your mother while you're here. I promise you you'll have nothing to reproach yourself for."

"I want to hear everything, of course, but I'll *still* never forgive myself. I just wish I'd been big enough that night to say, 'Okay, mother—I'll *give* you a job. Anything you like!' It would have been the one thing in my life *I* could have done for *her!*"

Tears trembled on her eyelashes. Colin leaned forward to pat her arm. "She hadn't been the kindest mother. . . ."

"Why couldn't *I* have been the kind one? The more generous one? Who said the child has to keep revenging the parents' mistakes? Maybe a daughter can be wiser than her mother, sometimes? That didn't occur to me at the time because I was always a child with her. Now I'm an adult, at last!"

"Yes . . ." He peered at her interestedly. "I can see that. You've grown up, Mia."

They silently drank some wine, enjoying the evening peace of the house.

"No wonder you're so content here," Mia said, looking out of the window at the fairy-tale garden. "Do you have friends in the village?"

Colin grinned mischievously. "Oh, yes, including one very special one I want you to meet. You'd better try to eat something, my dear, and prepare yourself a little, because I have a couple of surprises for you."

She raised her eyebrows. "I hope you haven't lined up a hectic social program? I really want to be quiet—"

A door slammed above them, and Colin cleared his throat. "Not much chance of *that*, I'm afraid. You see, you were followed from New York...."

Mia frowned, glancing up at the sound of footsteps clattering down the stairs. "By who?"

"Is she awake?" Mackenzie called, followed by a frantic rat-tat-tat of high-heeled mules down the wooden stairs.

She half-fell into the living room, grabbing the banister to steady herself. She was wearing a terry robe in deepest fuchsia, her face puffy from sleep, her makeup smeared, eyes bleary. Only half awake, she stopped at the foot of the stairs and stared at Mia. "You *would* have to see me like this!" she finally said. "And *you* looking like Grace Kelly."

There was a silence in the room, and Mackenzie took a deep breath. "I'm sorry!" she said simply. "I'm just ... *sorry*! About *everything*! I'm sorry I slapped you, I'm sorry your mother died, I'm sorry I haven't been the kind of friend who could—" She broke off, shaking her head, tears filling her eyes. She took a step into the room. "Listen, Mia, I know what it's like to lose someone close to you. When Alistair died I got all these letters—including yours—and you know something? They didn't mean a thing to me. I needed *people* around me—*friends*! And I shut them all out! Don't shut *me* out, Mia! I've come five thousand miles to comfort you—five thousand and ten, including the taxi ride! I just want to be with you and try to make you feel better. Will you let me, Mia?"

Mia stared at her for long, silent seconds, then rose and held out her arms. Mackenzie opened her arms wide, and the two stepped toward each other. They hugged for a long time.

Finally Mia broke away and looked at her friend. "This is the kindest thing you've ever done, Mackenzie...."

Mackenzie blushed, and muttered, "Aw, shucks..."

"You, too, Colin..." Mia turned to him, holding out her hand to him. He joined them, his arms around both.

"Come off it, you two, or you'll make *me* cry!"

Mackenzie broke away, walked back to the table laden with food, and jabbed a celery stalk into a wedge of soft cheese. "God, that's yummy!" She chewed sensuously, rolling her eyes in pleasure. Then she sat down at the table and began to fill her plate.

"Ed and I are married, Mia!" she chattered as she dished out salad for herself. "No more Lady Mackenzie: You may now call me Mrs. Schreiber. I mean, who was I kidding? I never *felt* like aristocracy! My brothers kicked me out of the firm, you know? Best thing that ever happened to me! God, I miss my husband! He'll be out to join me in a couple days. We're going to Cannes, wanna come? What's with you and David? How did it go with Phillipe? *Not* too great, I presume? I'm starting up my own new firm—called *Schmatta*—do you think people will understand? What kind of cheese *is* this, Colin?"

"Goat!" Colin said promptly.

"You mean they milk *goats* here?" Mackenzie clapped her hand over her mouth. "Oh, my God, I think I'm gonna throw up...." She made a run for the stairs and clattered up them.

Colin and Mia exchanged looks and burst out laughing. "I think she's given me *my* appetite back," Mia said.

Colin picked up the phone as Mia served herself bread and cheese. He let it ring twice, then hung up.

By the time Colin and Mia had finished eating, Mackenzie rejoined them, her hair carefully pulled into shape, make-up repaired and emphasizing her exotic look and dark, passionate eyes.

"Okay," she said, settled in an armchair with a plate of cookies and a cup of coffee. "Start from when you left that fucking awards party with the imprint of my hand on your cheek...."

Mia shook her head. "I've told the whole story to Colin, and I'm sure he doesn't want to sit through it again. Tomorrow we'll take a long walk and I'll tell you everything."

"Including the sexy bits?" Mackenzie asked anxiously.

Mia smiled thoughtfully, glancing from Colin to Mackenzie. "Well, it's no secret. I confided in both of you. You both knew there was something very wrong with me. *I* did, too, but I couldn't face it. In Paris...something happened that *made* me face it! I feel completely different now. I fell out of love with Phillipe *instantly*! I'm not in love with David, but...well, it's wonderful to know he's there. He waited so patiently for me—*he* believed in his dream, you see. Sometimes they do come true...."

They all stared off into space, thinking about their dreams and whether they'd come true or not, or were about to.

Mia thought of David introducing her lovingly now to her body, gently and sweetly showing her the delights of sex and love, without the undercurrents of fear that had always spoiled everything for her. The last few nights with him had been revelations to her. She was allowing herself pleasure after all those years of fearing it, denying it. She remembered his caresses and attentions, and she stirred restlessly on the couch.

Mackenzie was thinking of Eddie and the way *he* made love: how it was always fresh, different, and exciting. How she loved simply lying next to him, tracing her hand down his body. How it felt when he touched her....

And Colin was dreaming, too. He had long nurtured a dream which he'd never dared to share with anyone for fear of being laughed at. He was a kind, loving man trapped in the wrong body. It was very much like a fairy tale: If the right woman would only love him, he could indeed be magically transformed into a prince. And now... and *now*... his alert eyes saw the shadow of a figure walking up his front path. Everyone's dream could come true, he thought quickly, if they wanted it badly enough, if they were prepared to go with some of the odd curves fate threw them.

The doorbell sounded softly.

Mackenzie's eyes widened at the sound. "If that's my husband—" she cried.

Mia jumped. Could David have followed her here?

Colin left the living room to answer the door. He said something softly to his visitor that the two girls couldn't hear, and he returned to the living room, looking kindly at Mia. "I don't want you to get too much of a shock," he told her, touching her arm gently, "but be prepared for a very big surprise, my dear."

Mia's eyes lit up. "David?" she asked.

Colin shook his head. He went to the table, poured her a glass of wine and handed it to her. "Just take this out to the garden, would you? And take a deep breath...." He opened the front door for Mia, and she stepped out while

Mackenzie giggled nervously. "This is like a goddamn Hitchcock movie, I swear to God!"

Mia walked across the grass, breathing the sweet-smelling night air. It was chilly, and she shivered slightly. Balancing her coffee and the wine, she walked carefully around the side of the house. There was a lot of land with the small house, and a long, narrow strip of orchard at the back. There, a figure stood under a plum tree, just visible.

Mia frowned as she approached, trying to see better in the dark. It wasn't David, that was for sure. The figure was feminine, small, with white hair that glowed as it caught the light from the moon. As she got nearer, the defiant set of the shoulders and stance seemed familiar to her. "Hello?" she called softly. Then, *"Bonsoir?"*

She was nearer the woman now, and she bent to place the coffee and wine on a small wrought-iron garden table. The woman turned to face her and as she did, the blue eyes caught the moonlight—

"Mother?" The word spilled from her lips before she could rationalize it. But it *couldn't* be! Without the fiery red hair and with little makeup, it could have been Coral's older sister. A long-lost aunt?

"Let me see you!"

Mia wobbled with shock at the sound of Coral's voice, and she held the small table for support. "I don't *believe* this! Everyone thinks you're *dead!*"

"I *was* dead!" Coral said. "I *had* to destroy my life in order to start a new one. Evidently, I succeeded!"

"But Mother, how could you cause such suffering?" Mia cried. "I've been crying for a week! I couldn't forgive myself for not giving you a job, for not being more loving, for not—But I don't understand how you got here!"

"I set fire to the apartment and walked out onto the next plane to Paris!" Coral said simply. "I wasn't exactly responsible for my actions, you see. I was a drug addict, Mia. I still am, but I'm slowly getting off the stuff. I'm just so terribly lucky that nobody was killed or hurt."

"Do you realize the papers have run obituaries on you?"

"Yes, Wayland mailed them to Colin!" Coral said, and laughed. "Not bad, some of them!" Her eyes still had their glint of fire, and she steadily held Mia's gaze.

"Oh...Mother!" Mia stepped forward and embraced

her. "I'm so glad you're alive! This is the greatest gift Colin could have given me."

"*Is* it, darling?" Coral hugged her tighter.

The skinny, insubstantial figure in Mia's arms did not feel like her mother anymore. It was a fragile, tender stranger to whom she felt protective. They broke away to look at each other, tears in their eyes.

"I'll take care of you now, Mother," Mia said. "I'm so grateful for this! I couldn't have lived with that guilt...."

"I've been guilty, too, darling," Coral replied. "I've had time to think about my life, and I see how out of balance it was. And you won't have to take care of me, Mia darling— although I do thank you for the offer. Colin is doing that supremely well. It's better if I never set foot in New York again—not to mention the arson charges that could keep me behind bars for the rest of my life! You see, I truly burnt my bridges! I don't own *one* Balenciaga, darling— although Colin knows this little *antiquaire* who deals in used couture clothing..." Holding Mia's hand, she sat down at the little table and sipped some wine. "I want you to give me the luxury of forgiving you, Mia," she said, touching the scar on her face.

"I didn't mean to hurt you," Mia whispered.

"The last I heard of you, you'd been sent for by Phillipe. Did you join him? Is it working out?"

"There's a lot to tell you," Mia said. "Phillipe has—"

"Colin says that just having me to look after is his reward," Coral interrupted. "He says I've always been some kind of shining idol to him. You see, he loves fashion as much as I do. *Did!* He has all his magazine collection here, you know. Forty-year runs of *Vogue*, *Divine*, *Bazaar*. We look through them and reminisce. We'll write a massive history of fashion together—he'll do the drawings, I'll write it. He's nursing me back to health. I'll soon be as right as rain."

Coral linked her arm through Mia's and led her slowly across the grass, toward the cottage. "I always adored Colin, but I never realized what a saint he is. He must have been sent from heaven as my guardian angel. He never says a bad word about anyone. He just listens and cares. He adores me, of course, and now that I've started to get to know him, I can quite truthfully say that it's mutual. I don't know that we'll ever be a *real* couple, darling—*you* know what I mean. But he gets more attractive to me each day—just by being such a kind, dear friend. And even if we always remain very good, very close friends, well, *that's* not so bad either, is it?"

"No . . ." Mia pressed her hand gently. "Not at all."

"And now I want to hear *everything*, every tiny little detail about *you!*" Coral said. "I want to know what reaction the trade had to your award—did it bring in lots of orders? And your designing? What plans do you have for your company? Are you still friends with David Winters or did he just escort you to the awards that night?" She pressed Mia's hand with each question.

Mia returned the pressure, laughing. "Wait a minute, Mother—remember, I've spent the last week talking to the police about you, identifying the most grisly remains of your personal effects. There's been no time to design—"

"Colin plans to start inviting P.G.'s from England and America soon," Coral told her. "Paying guests, you know. We'll prepare simple little meals for them, cosset them, and if it takes off, we may start up a small hotel—*very* chic and exclusive—we won't take just anyone. It *could* catch on. He'll invite some fashion people, so eventually they'll all know I'm alive or resurrected . . . you know how gossipy the fashion industry is. . . ."

Mia smiled to herself as Coral continued to chatter. She will never really listen to me or be too interested in what I do, Mia thought. But it didn't matter to her now, no longer hurt. Coral could remain center-stage star in this setting, with the adoring Colin to wait on her. In one person's eyes, at least, she would always be the chic, elegant, powerful fashion editor, Coral Stanton—able to make Seventh Avenue leap trembling to her bidding.

Mia walked with Coral into the house. Mackenzie's shriek was heard throughout the village. Then the air was filled with screams, cries, and kisses as everyone hugged one another. A champagne cork popped gustily. Colin filled their glasses, then, taking his charcoal pencil, did portraits of all three of them, as, in turn, they each called New York to tell David, Ed, and Wayland that all three Queens of Fashion were very much alive.

Afterword

Colin
Provence, France, 1972

I like the way my story ends because more or less everyone gets a happy ending. Mine was happiest. Coral and I opened the Auberge Divine a year after our collaboration on *Figleaf—a Definitive History of Fashion*, which as you all know was a nonfiction best-seller. A few months ago Coral became Mrs. Colin Beaumont, the proudest moment in my life. Perhaps we make a strange couple, but I have always liked to believe that real love, great love, conquers everything—even a face and body like mine!

Fashion will continue without us, of course. There will be long skirts, then minis, gathered skirts, then pencil-slim ones. Women will always want the latest style, and it will change, cycle, constantly. Today, fashion has aligned with status—to the detriment of both. It sells by label. Whatever is designed by Mia, David, Mackenzie (her new line—Schmatta—is, perversely, very expensive cashmere, linen, and silk!) will sell on their names. One day all that will change, too, and clothes will again sell on their own merits. My friends will be ready for that because they all have talent.

The fashion world will probably disown Coral and myself when they read my book, so please, if you do recognize anyone in it, keep it to yourself. I never intended to stir up trouble, and I'm truly not malicious. I just tried to "tell it like it was" (a delicious sixties' phrase!), and I think I did. And if you ever need a quiet, restful, reasonable, exclusive place to stay during a trip to Provence, don't forget us!

ABOUT THE AUTHOR

After studying fashion design in London, Harold Carlton worked in Paris, designing for Nina Ricci and André Courreges. Later he illustrated for the French magazine *Elle*, and for several years drew the Paris collection reports for the *London Sunday Times* and the Associated Press. In New York he illustrated for *Mademoiselle* magazine and later switched to journalism, writing on fashion and the arts for the American Broadcasting Company, *The Village Voice*, the *Los Angeles Times*, and many other publications. His previous four novels were published under the pseudonym Simon Cooper. Born in London, Harold Carlton currently divides his time between Manhattan and Europe, working on his new novel.

BANTAM BOOKS
GRAND SLAM SWEEPSTAKES

Win a new Chevrolet Cavalier . . .
It's easy . . . It's fun . . . Here's how to enter:

OFFICIAL ENTRY FORM

Three Bantam book titles on sale this month are hidden in this word puzzle. Identify the books by circling each of these titles in the puzzle. Titles may appear within the puzzle horizontally, vertically, or diagonally . . .

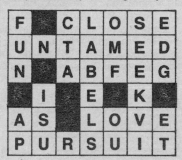

This month's Bantam Books titles are:

LABELS

CLOSE PURSUIT*

UNTAMED

In each of the books listed above there is another entry blank and puzzle . . . another chance to win!

In Canada, be on the lookout for these Bantam paperback books: PAST CARING, SLEEP WHILE I SING. In each of them, you'll find a new puzzle, entry blank and GRAND SLAM Sweepstakes rules . . . and yet another chance to win another brand-new Chevrolet automobile!

MAIL TO: GRAND SLAM SWEEPSTAKES
Post Office Box 18
New York, New York 10046

Please Print

NAME _____

ADDRESS _____

CITY _____ STATE _____ ZIP _____

*U.S. Only

OFFICIAL RULES

NO PURCHASE NECESSARY.

To enter, identify this month's Bantam Book titles by placing a circle around each word forming each title. There are three titles shown above to be found in this month's puzzle. Mail your entry to: Grand Slam Sweepstakes, P.O. Box 18, New York, N.Y. 10046.

This is a monthly sweepstakes starting February 1, 1988 and ending January 31, 1989. During this sweepstakes period, one automobile winner will be selected each month from all entries that have correctly solved the puzzle. To participate in a particular month's drawing, your entry must be received by the last day of that month. The Grand Slam prize drawing will be held on February 14, 1989 from all entries received during all twelve months of the sweepstakes.

To obtain a free entry blank/puzzle/rules, send a self-addressed stamped envelope to: Winning Titles, P.O. Box 650, Sayreville, N.J. 08872. Residents of Vermont and Washington need not include return postage.

PRIZES: Each month for twelve months a Chevrolet automobile will be awarded with an approximate retail value of $12,000 each.

The Grand Slam Prize Winner will receive 2 Chevrolet automobiles plus $10,000 cash (ARV $34,000).

Winners will be selected under the supervision of Marden-Kane Inc., an independent judging organization. By entering this sweepstakes each entrant accepts and agrees to be bound by these rules and the decisions of the judges which shall be final and binding. Winners may be required to sign an affidavit of eligibility and release which must be returned within 14 days of receipt. All prizes will be awarded. No substitution or transfer of prizes permitted. Winners will be notified by mail. Odds of winning depend on the total number of eligible entries received.

Sweepstakes open to residents of the U.S. and Canada except employees of Bantam Books, its affiliates, subsidiaries, advertising agencies, and Marden-Kane, Inc. Void in the Province of Quebec and wherever else prohibited or restricted by law. Not responsible for lost or misdirected mail or printing errors. Taxes and licensing fees are the sole responsibility of the winners. All cars are standard equipped. Canadian winners will be required to answer a skill testing question.

For a list of winners, send a self-addressed, stamped envelope to: Bantam Winners, P.O. Box 711, Sayreville, N.J. 08872.

Experience all the passion and adventure life has to offer in these bestselling novels by and about women.

Bantam offers you these exciting titles:

Titles by Jean Auel:

☐ 25042	CLAN OF THE CAVE BEAR	$4.95
☐ 25053	THE VALLEY OF HORSES	$4.95
☐ 26096	MAMMOTH HUNTERS	$4.95

Titles by Cynthia Freeman:

☐ 26161	DAYS OF WINTER	$4.50
☐ 26090	COME POUR THE WINE	$4.50
☐ 25433	FAIRYTALES	$4.50
☐ 26092	NO TIME FOR TEARS	$4.50
☐ 24790	PORTRAITS	$4.50
☐ 25088	WORLD FULL OF STRANGERS	$4.50

Titles by Barbara Taylor Bradford:

☐ 26534	A WOMAN OF SUBSTANCE	$4.50
☐ 25621	HOLD THE DREAM	$4.95
☐ 26253	VOICE OF THE HEART	$4.95
☐ 26541	ACT OF WILL	$4.95

Titles by Judith Krantz:

☐ 25917	MISTRAL'S DAUGHTER	$4.95
☐ 25609	PRINCESS DAISY	$4.95
☐ 26407	I'LL TAKE MANHATTAN	$4.95

Bantam Books, Dept. FBS2, 414 East Golf Road, Des Plaines, IL 60016

Please send me the books I have checked above. I am enclosing $_____ (please add $1.50 to cover postage and handling). Send check or money order—no cash or C.O.D.s please.

Mr/Ms _____

Address _____

City/State _____ Zip _____

FBS2—2/88

Please allow four to six weeks for delivery. This offer expires 8/88. Prices and availability subject to change without notice.

Special Offer
Buy a Bantam Book
for only 50¢.

Now you can have Bantam's catalog filled with hundreds of titles plus take advantage of our unique and exciting bonus book offer. A special offer which gives you the opportunity to purchase a Bantam book for only 50¢. Here's how!

By ordering any five books at the regular price per order, you can also choose any other single book listed (up to a $5.95 value) for just 50¢. Some restrictions do apply, but for further details why not send for Bantam's catalog of titles today!

Just send us your name and address and we will send you a catalog!